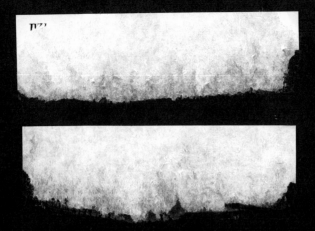

When the Enemy Is Tired

ALSO BY RUSSELL BRADDON

Fiction

THE PROUD AMERICAN BOY

COMMITTAL CHAMBER

Nonfiction

THE NAKED ISLAND

CHESHIRE V.C.

JOAN SUTHERLAND

LORD THOMSON OF FLEET STREET

When the Enemy Is Tired

RUSSELL BRADDON

THE VIKING PRESS / NEW YORK

When the
Enemy
Is Tired

For the fifth time — at your insistence — I start writing.

My first attempt, you said, was too short. Well, perhaps seven lines was over-concise. Athough it brought back most of twenty years to me.

Enough, anyway, to enable me on my second attempt to produce a heroic and most evocative nine pages. But instead of being gratified by this profusion you were vexed. And when you are vexed I find you most inhospitable and suspicious.

You suspected me, you said, of "evasiveness and arrogance": and when I replied that, not knowing what it was I had to avoid, I could not be guilty of evasiveness, and that, being neither brave nor power-ful, I was incapable of arrogance, you became more vexed than ever.

My third attempt covered nearly forty pages, an effort I consid-ered mammoth: but one which only increased your dissatisfaction. And my fourth, all of ninety-two pages, to my astonishment, left you vexed in the extreme.

In fact — and I recall it vividly, because previously I had only witnessed it in infants — you screamed with rage until your eyes literally bulged. You were beside yourself, as they say: though what they mean when they say it has always escaped me. And what you screamed, as your eyes bulged, was:

"You will write it again! At length, colonel. Do you understand? And in depth, colonel — or you will be very sorry."

So now I know what I must avoid — shortness and shallowness. Otherwise, metaphorically amoeba-like, you will get beside yourself again; and I shall be sorry. So be it. I am not pressed for time and I find words most amiable companions: I shall pass the one and exploit the other to provide you with what you require — a portrait, at length and in depth, of myself as a child. Much good may it do you.

As I have said four times before (an ungracious preface: I promise not to resort to it again), my earliest memory is of biting my mother's thumb. What I have not said before, however — because, until now, I had not really bent my mind to it — is that I see myself do it. As a bystander, I mean — or rather, a backstander, since I watch myself and my mother from about ten feet behind.

They were walking along a pavement. Camphor-laurel trees flanked it. The sun was shining on their backs. The boy was about two and a half years old, dressed in white shirt and pants, and white socks and shoes. His hair was very fair, and he was holding the hand of the woman. She was tall, wearing a short, fawn, sleeveless dress, its skirt above her knees, with long, good legs.

She walked easily, and he trotted, two paces to her one, his small right hand clutching the long, loose fingers of her left hand. In his left hand he carried a short stick. Ahead of the boy and his mother moved their shadows.

(Yet I, who watch, and see them so clearly from only ten feet behind, cast no shadow. Why is that?)

Suddenly, as she walked and he trotted, the boy halted, dragging at her arm. When she looked down at him inquiringly, he threw away his stick.

"Don't you want it any more?" she asked (so that, even from behind them, one realizes immediately that this has been a much-loved stick).

"No."

"Are you sure?"

"Yes."

"Because if you do . . ."

"I don't."

". . . you'd better get it. We're not going back for it."

"Don't want it."

"All right," she said, "come on." And on they walked.

Ten paces later (her paces, or mine: not his) he stopped.

"I want my stick," he announced, and she laughed.

"I *want* my *stick!*" he shouted.

"Should have thought of that before," she told him, dragging him forward, "shouldn't you?"

"*I want my stick!*" he shrieked, pulling her to a halt.

"Now look," she said good-humouredly but with a touch of menace, "I asked you did you want it, and you said no. I told you we weren't going back for it, and you said you didn't want it." Loosely she shook her left arm, whose fingers were angrily clutched in his right hand, as if seeking, by a gesture so relaxed, to relax him too. "So come on."

Then, as she looked down at him, brown eyes meeting brown eyes, his expression changed from mere contorted rage to sheer animal savagery and, dragging her loose left arm towards him, fastening his sharp baby teeth onto her long, adult thumb, he bit: and joyously tasted blood.

(By now I am standing immediately behind them, so that I can see the mixture of pain, incredulity, and suppressed mirth on her face; and the gloating, puppy wickedness on his. But the instant her free right hand flashes to his jaw, prising it open so that she can retrieve her mangled thumb, I cease to see her, and instead hear and feel her.)

"Beast!" she hissed and, bending down, snatched my hand to her mouth and quite deliberately bit *my* thumb.

Shocked and incredulous, I looked up at her, imploring her to take back that bite: and she looked down at me, grinning her rueful authority. Then, demanding unstinted maternal care, I howled.

At which moment an old man tottered furiously across the road.

"How dare you?" he demanded of my mother, panting and incoherent. "Wicked thing to do. Saw it with my own eyes. Couldn't believe . . . Should *report* you. Poor kid. Woman like you . . ."

My mother became instantly unsmiling.

"Mind your own business, you bloody old fool," she advised, "or I'll bite *your* thumb too." Then she turned to me. "As for you, my boy, I'm taking you home, giving you a hiding, and putting you to bed." Which, coldly and silently, both of us hating the old man, she did.

Some time later I resumed my role as observer.

The pyjamaed child was in his cot, which stood near the parental bed. He was awake, flushed, lonely, and contrite. Tentatively he called for company.

"Mum?"

No answer.

"Mu-um!" — louder.

She came to the door. "What?"

He held up his thumb. "Kiss it better."

"What about mine?" she demanded, crossing to him.

He took it and kissed it. "All better?" he asked, holding up his own, which she kissed in her turn.

"Yes," she told him, "all better. But promise you'll never bite again. Not anyone."

"I promise," he agreed. "Do you promise?"

"I won't have to if you stop, will I?" she countered, and stroked his hair until he went to sleep.

I spent three hours writing those first few pages — and once again succeeded only in vexing you.

I have never known pain like that before. Curious how one reacts. One curls up, like a porcupine. Lacking quills, of course, it's useless, and the infliction of pain continues: but it is rained down only upon soft external flesh. One's real self contracts into a tiny foetus deep inside the soft flesh and lies suspended there in a sea of swooning helplessness.

At the moment of the worst pain, in fact, I suddenly stopped being frightened — absolving myself of all adult responsibility — and waited confidently, like a baby, for someone to come and pick me up. Love me. Your men must have realized that something of the kind had happened: because they stopped what they were doing and quite carefuly brought me back here.

Thinking of how fear first shrank all my awareness into a dried pea inside my gut, and then transported it, swooning, into a protective womb, reminds me of something that may interest you. My first memory, I am suddenly aware (though not quite certain that I really do remember it), is not of biting my mother's thumb but of lying wrapped in a shawl beside a tennis court.

It was long before I could walk — and once again it is something I see vividly as an onlooker.

From one side of the court I look across to a four-foot-high bank that runs parallel to the opposite sideline. On top of that bank, swaddled in a small grassy hollow, lies the infant me. However, although I hear the rhythmic *ping* of long baseline rallies, I do not see any players — presumably because the baby does not see them. In support of which presumption, I offer the corroborative evidence that, in my nostrils, the sweet, felty scent of the nap of a new tennis ball is as strong as the humid tang of long grass — and the baby I look at lies in long grass and clutches to its mouth a new tennis ball.

It is a fact, by the way, that my mother resumed competitive tennis very soon after I was born and that she used to take me with her and plant me somewhere in the sun while she played. But do I really remember it? Or do I merely reconstruct from the evidence? On the other hand, if I reconstruct, how subtle of my subconscious to add those two corroborative touches of my hearing (but not seeing) rallies and of my smelling both tennis balls *and* long grass.

Grown-ups were always strongly associated in my mind with tennis. Not only did my mother play it competitively during the week, but she and my father, with all their friends, played it socially every week-end.

Also they played music. All of them.

And between times the men talked of the Somme and Passchendaele, and the women about people who, if they hadn't been killed in the War, had died of the Spanish flu just after it.

I suppose all I really remember from the time when I bit my mother's thumb, in 1923, and the time when my sister was born, in 1925, is this confusion of grown-ups who were all—except for our neighbours Mr and Mrs Barker, who were old, and Mr and Mrs Schmelling, who were Huns but all right, unlike any other Huns — known to me either as aunty or uncle. There were dozens of them, and they all played tennis and they all played the piano, or the violin, or the flute, and they all talked either about the Somme and Passchendaele or the Spanish flu. I neither liked them nor disliked them — except on those nights when, after their tennis, they played progressive pingpong on the verandah and shrieked with excitement. Then, because they seemed so animal and savage, they frightened me, and I hated them.

I had learned, however, not to howl when I was frightened. My father flatly forbade howling.

As well as the uncles and aunts, there were two old people whom my father called mater and pater, but whom I was required to call Gar and Gan. Names, in fact, seem to have been things treated with less than tender respect in my family. My mother's father was known to my father as Prof, but I was brought up to call him Doc. My mother's name was Doris, but everyone called her Liz. My father's name was Edward, but everyone called him Mitt. And my name was Anthony, but everyone called me Tige.

One of my uncles (of whom I saw comparatively little because he played bad tennis) was also, I was told in 1925, my godfather, which I did not understand. Nor, I gathered, when I asked him about it, did he; which left us with very little in common and was awkward because my father had just abandoned us to spend an evening together. It was the first occasion in my life upon which I was socially embarrassed.

Uncle Gordon (that was his name) was also embarrassed and suggested that we should go for a walk — which is not the kind of suggestion that endears a four-year-old to his godfather. Walking, to four-year-olds, is simply a form of locomotion, a boring one at that, and why grown-ups derive such pleasure from it is one of the great mysteries of infancy.

Although I agreed to go for a walk (my father also forbade disagreement with grown-ups) Uncle Gordon perceived that I did so with less than abandon and therefore offered an incentive.

"I'll show you the man in the moon," he promised — and extinguished thereby the last faint flicker of my respect for him. Now I knew what godfathers were. They were grey people: people who played bad tennis and had not gone to the War: people who never sat at a piano or shrieked frighteningly at progressive pingpong: silly people who said there was a man in the moon. Because if there had been a man in the moon, my mother or father would have told me.

But Uncle Gordon *was* a grown-up and *had* said that he would show me the man in the moon: he must, therefore, show me something. Curiously I walked up the front drive with him, out through the front gate and on to the pavement's grass verge, which my father, every Sunday morning, as the Schmellings went to church, weeded and mowed, muttering to himself, "bloody paspalum." Now, though, it was night time, and silly Uncle Gordon was pointing at the sky (which was very black and very high, with very bright stars and a very round whitish moon in it) and asking "See the man?"

I looked where his finger pointed. I saw the round whitish moon and on it some greyish shapeless blotches: I did not see a man.

"No," I said.

"Up there," he insisted.

"There isn't any man," I told him.

"You're a funny kid," he observed. "What if I told you the moon was made of cheese?"

"Where've mum and dad gone?" I asked, ignoring this last idiocy.

"To buy you a baby brother. You'd like a baby brother, wouldn't you?"

"No," I contradicted, wickedly perverse, "I'd like a baby sister."

"All right," he said, sighing, "a baby sister."

"But you said a baby brother."

"If it's a sister you want, they'll get you a sister."

"How will they know?"

"Didn't you tell them?"

"No," I said. All I'd ever asked for was a giraffe, which, being grown-ups, they had refused.

"Well," he reassured, "God will tell them."

"Who'll tell God?" I demanded: and for some time he stood looking at the moon, saying quietly to himself, "Jesus!"

Which seemed a perfect answer to me.

But he spoiled it by looking suddenly back at me, down at me, smiling, and patting my head with a hand that was hot, and saying, "*I'll* tell Him."

I knew he couldn't. Or *could* godfathers?

"Ask him for a giraffe," I instructed, in case he could.

"A flaming orangutang, if that's what you want," he offered thickly, as if he had a sore throat.

"No," I told him, "a giraffe."

In spite of which, the next morning, I was advised that my father and my mother had acquired for me a baby sister.

It had black hair like my father, and it howled all the time. I waited for my father to roar "Stop that" and wallop it, the way he did to me, but instead he just smiled. And I knew then that I was going to have trouble with this sister.

"Been a good boy?" my mother asked me.

"Yes. Why are you in bed?"

"Because the doctor said so. But I'll be home soon. Did you enjoy being with Uncle Gordon?"

"No" — not looking at anyone, least of all at Uncle Gordon.

"Tige!"

"Uncle Gordon," I told her as I looked at my shrieking, black-haired, non-giraffe of a sister, "is a fibber."

I was at once made to apologize, then walloped and taken home by my father: at which significant moment I learned that the opposite sex is overprivileged and that grown-ups believe in Might rather than Right.

This lesson was confirmed the day my mother came home. She was standing at the kitchen stove and I was standing beside her: and abruptly there came to me a blinding revelation — that the world was populated entirely by children who grew up and by grown-ups who grew down. It *had* to be so. Why else did grown-ups comment so endlessly, "Last time I saw you, you were only *so* big." Why else, except that I was getting bigger and they smaller.

"Mum," I advised, looking up at her so tall above me, "when I get big and you get little, if you don't do what I say, I'll give you a bloody good hiding."

Not even looking away from her saucepan, she clouted me. "Don't ever say 'bloody' again."

"Dad does."

"Your father," she explained, "is a grown-up man. You're just a little boy."

"From what I've read so far, colonel," the Chinese officer remarked, smiling, "my predecessor in the matter of your two months of . . . um . . ."

"Interrogation?"

"Yes. My predecessor was not sympathetic?"

"Not conspicuously." The final syllable faded ironically.

"You mustn't blame him if your peculiarly Australian mentality defeated him," the younger man chided. "He was Chinese, you know."

"And you aren't?"

"Yes, but born and educated here in Singapore, and later I studied at Sydney University. So I've known Australians all my life. My predecessor, on the other hand, was undiluted Peking."

"Then God forbid I ever go there," the colonel grunted. "He was — and if you've known Australians all your life, you'll understand the term — a bastard! By the way, what do I call you?"

"Just call me major. We can dispense with the formality of names. We'll be seeing quite a lot of each other."

"Why?"

"Because it is my job to get to understand you — and then to break you."

"Physically or mentally?"

"Politically."

"You haven't a chance."

"On the contrary."

"More of those electric shocks and things your predecessor specialized in?"

"No. They weren't successful. Not because you're brave . . ."

"Oh, I'm not brave."

"Agreed . . . but because, as you wrote here" — the major scuffled back among the grubby pages of manuscript — "ah yes. You wrote that whenever you were badly hurt you became a tiny foetus, back in the womb, insulated against external brutality by 'a sea of swooning helplessness.' In other words, colonel, whenever you are hurt you faint!"

"To be frank with you," the colonel replied, "after a while, I faint as soon as I'm *going* to be hurt."

"Which, just as it made you unsuitable for the particular techniques of my predecessor, makes you a perfect subject for mine. 'At the moment of the worst pain, in fact,' you wrote, 'I suddenly stopped being frightened — absolving myself of all adult responsibility — and waited confidently, like a baby, for someone to come and pick me up.' What I must do, colonel, in the weeks that follow, is find your moment of worst pain — not in the hands of my predecessor, but during your childhood — and make you relive it. Then, when you absolve yourself of all adult responsibilities, I shall pick you up."

"Sounds fun."

"It will mean hard work for both of us. For you, lots more writing . . ."

"Oh no."

". . . and drugs on occasion. Quite painless, though. For me, lots of reading and questions."

"What if I refuse to write any more?"

"You won't. For one thing, having started four times already, you'll have no particular scruples about carrying on. For another, if you do refuse, you will be tried with your colleagues as a war criminal and executed. You can't win either way: my way, though, you can always delude yourself that you will."

Thoughtfully the colonel stared at the major, noticing the heavy crop of tough, black hair, the bland, youthful skin, the smiling white teeth and the unsmiling Chinese eyes. The lad was fit, confident, fanatical. Did a prisoner of fifty-four, somewhat battered and easygoing, stand a chance against him? A better chance than against a firing squad, that was for sure.

"You could be right," he announced, so laconically that the Asian looked up sharply, suspecting insolence: but saw only a lined, wry face and speculative eyes. A sudden chatter of machine-gun fire, very close, made the Australian jump.

"More executions?" he asked sarcastically.

"Liquidations," the major corrected. "Dissident elements."

"Malays, you mean?"

"I mean people guilty of crimes against State security, for which the punishment is death. Talking of which . . . I have some preliminary questions. Just for the record." He opened a dossier. "What were you doing at Bukit Langkap where we caught you?"

"I've already told your predecessor that at least twenty-five times."

"Then tell me once."

"When Thailand agreed to accept Chinese 'protection,' on December the sixth," the colonel recited wearily, "and the governments of Malaysia and Singapore announced that the Australian and American garrisons out here were no longer welcome, Computer Command, Canberra . . ."

"Computer Command?" the major interrupted.

"Look, you know more about that than I do," the colonel said.

"Tell me what *you* know."

The colonel shrugged. His knowledge of the subject was not expert: to confess it could do no harm.

"Most of our logistics and troop movements are now handled by computers in Canberra. They've been programmed with all the available data. Among other things, they churn out movement orders for any given situation. Prevents human error."

"So?"

"So, the Malayan Government in the meantime having gone Communist and joined the Peking-Tokyo Axis, my orders were to set up four radio posts on the east coast and to look out for and report the arrival of any troop transports from China or Japan. We were to man these posts until two days before the expiration of the withdrawal period, when we would get further orders as to a rendezvous from which we could be flown home. My own post was at Mersing. And the last order I got was to proceed upriver by Hovercraft — one had been left there for me — to a certain map reference, which turned out to be the disused tin mine at Bukit Langkap. I was to hide out there till one of our aircraft picked me up."

"But it didn't pick you up?"

"No."

"Why?"

"Because the computer gave me the wrong map reference! Not only that, it gave everyone else on the east coast the wrong map reference. They *all* came to Bukit Langkap. Not that we knew it was the wrong place. All we knew was that Bukit Langkap was crawling with us. All waiting to be lifted off. And all ordered to maintain absolute radio silence. We only broke it when your blokes — thousands of 'em — attacked at dawn on . . . on . . ."

"February second."

"That's it. And the answer we got then was that we couldn't be

Australians if we were congregated at Bukit Langkap, because no airlift from there had ever been planned. And that was the moment your blokes chose to throw hand grenades all over us, blow up our set, and take the eight of us who survived, four officers and four corporals, prisoners."

"Colonel, we did not take eight prisoners: we captured eight bandits who, by clandestine radio, were directing the operations of the main bandit group in the Batu Caves area. You and your seven colleagues are therefore guilty of war crimes."

"You're crazy."

"The bandits in the Batu Caves area have already ambushed eleven of our convoys."

"The bandits, as you call them, are a few Malays who know their number's up because they used to be pro-Western, so they're having a go now before you murder them. And far from our directing their operations, I happen to know they were advised by both Canberra and Washington not to start anything because they hadn't an earthly and they'd get no help from us."

"Well, the People's Court will decide that. But I wouldn't care to be one of your seven colleagues."

"Execute us and you'll start World War Three."

"So your people told us before we executed other war criminals in North Vietnam, Cambodia, Laos, and Thailand! However, let's talk about something more agreeable than executions."

"I don't feel agreeable."

"Think of your seven colleagues, then perhaps you will."

"Have you notified anyone that you're holding us?"

"Why should we? Surely, since *they* sent you here as spies and saboteurs, the onus is on your government to claim you? When your government claims you, we'll admit we've caught you. But if your government doesn't claim you, the first it'll hear of you will be the trial and execution of seven war criminals."

"There are eight of us."

"I doubt we'll be saying anything about you."

"I demand the right of all prisoners of war . . ."

"You are *not* a prisoner of war, colonel. You are a spy and a saboteur."

"Then I request permission to write a letter to my family."

"Permission denied. You no longer have a family. Nor a country, nor friends. You are in our hands and you live by our grace. Your past will end at whatever point we shall want it to end; and your future will take you in whatever direction we shall decide it should take you. Remember that and you'll live quite comfortably: but any attempt to cling to the identity you brought with you into this jail will be regarded as a further act of sabotage for which you may be summarily executed."

"So that's why you took away my letters and photographs?"

"It is."

"What do you think you're going to do with me?"

"We're going to make a new man of you. One of *our* men. Now, tell me about the street you walked up with your mother, just before you bit her."

The colonel blinked at the suddenness of the switch and then, frowning, spoke slowly.

"It was quite an old street—for Sydney, that is. Old houses . . . well, bungalows. Red bricks. Red tiles. Sensible brown and black paint. Asphalt pavement. And instead of the strip of grass with hibiscus bushes on it that you had beside the pavement at our end of the street, there were trees — camphor laurels — every twenty feet or so."

"But you said it was sunny on the pavement?"

"Well?"

"Through these trees?"

"The sun struck obliquely across the gardens of the houses on the right of the pavement."

"Cars?"

"Where?"

"Parked or on the road?"

"Never parked in those days, and rarely on the road. This was 1923, remember. You could walk all the way to the shops and back and not see a car."

"Describe your mother."

"I did."

"In more detail. Hair?"

"Brown and long. She wore it in plaits, either knotted into a bun or pinned round her head. She used to brush it with a hard-bristled brush, with a black back and the bristles set in a sort of blister of pink rubber. She had a silver-backed brush, I remember, with fine white bristles in it, but she always used her battered old black one."

"What age was she?"

"You know, one's parents never actually looked *young*, did they?"

"I wouldn't know. My parents vanished when I was an infant. They were killed some time later by British servicemen on a rubber estate near Batu Orang."

"Bandits, were they?" The colonel's inflection was so wry that the major merely smiled. "Who brought you up then?"

"Relatives."

"And did *they* look young, or old, to you?"

"They looked," the major acknowledged, " as old in 1949, when they took me in, as they do today, twenty-six years later. I accept your point. But, in retrospect, what *must* your mother have looked like?"

"A girl of twenty-three. Tall. Long legs. Good figure but not much chest. That was the flapper period, remember?"

"No."

"Chests were out of fashion."

"With my people, they always have been."

"We catch up on you only occasionally. It was the twenties that time; the sixties last time; and the next should be about two thousand and four or five."

"You won't see it," the younger man observed curtly. "Obviously you hated your mother."

"Don't you jump about?"

"Well, didn't you?"

"Passionately at times; the rest of the time I was devoted to her."

"And your father?"

"Oh, I hated him too. On occasion. And my sister. On occasion. In fact the only relative I never occasionally hated was my grandmother. She used to give me money. But I was devoted to all of them."

"You mean you respected them?"

"I've only learned to respect them since they died. You don't know much about people, do you?"

"Perhaps not. But I intend knowing all about you, so you may now go back to your cell and write me some more about growing up with the family to which you were so devoted."

Sentries appeared as the major spoke. Escorted by them along prison corridors, only half aware that he was passing cell after cell packed with listless Malays and guarded by contemptuous Chinese, the colonel went back over the conversation that had just concluded.

Not even frightening.

The other bloke — the first one — had been terrifying.

But one mustn't sell any of them short. If one of them was less terrifying than another, he was probably cleverer. At what though? What did they want with his written life story? Surely not the story? The handwriting itself? Well, they were out of luck if that was it: from the beginning he had added a most uncharacteristic and vulgar squiggle to the tail of his g's and y's. If they were to forge anything in *this* handwriting, any one of his family, or of his friends, or of the brighter Intelligence boys, would pick it up at once. No one, he was fastidiously certain, would ever associate Colonel Anthony Russell with a g or y whose tail was squiggled.

His cell door slammed behind him, and he sat on the edge of his bed. Nothing to do. Each day nothing to do. Except attend those ridiculous morning indoctrination classes and write a few words for whoever it might be was going to read them. Nothing to do.

"Here, take a pull at yourself," he ordered aloud. He must find something to do.

"All right," he declared, "If that's what you buggers want." And took up one of the three ball-point pens with which his captors had supplied him. From now on, until he was so tired he could only sleep, he would engross himself in his own past and the careful reconstruction of it. He gazed at the top sheet of blank paper.

"Yes," he murmured, "so that was the beginning — now what came next?"

My mother, after the arrival of my sister, was for some time (though I cannot remember how long) rather unwell (though I then had no idea why). Fortunately, however, my father's barristering so prospered that we acquired not only a high-backed, canvas-hooded Fiat motorcar but a cook-housemaid-nanny called Agatha as well. Now my mother could drive to the "village" to do her daily shopping, and Agatha could help in the house.

Agatha was a tall stringy woman, with ginger hair, red hands and the temperament of a sergeant-major. My mother tolerated but disliked her, referring to her as Ag the Nag, and I loathed her: mainly because she compelled me to accompany her for mile after interminable mile as she took my howling new sister in a black pram on a daily walk.

Reciprocally, Agatha loathed me — loathed all children — and cooking and housework as well, which is why, each day, towards all and sundry, she generated so constant a voltage of aggression.

What Agatha liked, I discovered, was sailors and potato chips and tattoos and lying on her bed in a black petticoat that made her arms look more stringy and her chest more freckled than ever. She sublimated all four of these passions in the person of Gus, an English cook from Manchester serving in the Merchant Navy.

Gus visited Agatha one day when his ship was in port, my father in court, and my mother playing a tennis match at Strathfield. He at once took off his shirt and shoes and socks and strode importantly round our kitchen in his vest and pants, which were pulled in tight round his waist with a thick black leather belt. His arms were white and hairless — a thing I had never seen in a man before — and tattooed with serpents and belly dancers and a cross on top of a tombstone below which were words.

"What's it say?" I asked Agatha, who sat at the kitchen table in her black petticoat, propping up her ginger head with red fists under her bony chin.

" 'In Loving Memory of Mum and Dad,' " she read: and terrified me.

"What's wrong with mum and dad?" I demanded.

"Not your mum and dad," she snapped. "Gus's."

"But he's grown up."

"Well?"

"Grown-ups have maters and paters."

"Frigging little snob," Gus observed.

"What's a frigging little snob?" I asked Agatha.

"Never mind," she told me — and the conversation languished.

Bustling and humming, Gus lit the stove (*our* stove) and put a pan of dripping over the flame, and then peeled and sliced about ten potatoes. The oil swirled and spat and fumed a bluish smoke; Gus bustled, his bare feet sluff-sluffing on the linoleum, his muscles rippling under the hairless white skin and the blue and red tattoos; and Agatha, glumly propped, sweated.

"There y'are," Gus announced finally, thrusting at me a saucer with half a dozen sallow chips on it. "Take these with you."

"Where?"

"Outside."

"But what'll I do?"

"Eat 'em," he said, handing Agatha a huge plateful of his slimy confection.

"Play," Agatha advised, beginning to eat greedily. "Go on. Outside."

Outside, I tried one of Gus's chips and gave the rest to the cat. I then consciously played all the games I could think of. Twenty minutes later I was back in the kitchen, looking for company. But Agatha and Gus had gone.

I looked for them in the dining-room (thinking that, being grown-ups, they had perhaps gone there to eat their chips) and in the drawing-room (where grown-ups sat and talked after eating) and in the front garden (where grown-ups were taken to see the gladioli). Agatha and Gus were in none of them.

So then, being a logical, lonely child, I opened the door of Agatha's bedroom. On her bed, in her black petticoat, looking very flushed, lay Agatha; and beside her, in nothing but his tattoos, and white all over, lay Gus.

"Fookoff," he shouted, frightening me — so I left and talked for a while with my sister in her pram and forgot Agatha and her sailor.

Agatha did not stay much longer as our housemaid-cook-nanny, because, quite soon after that, my mother having told me to be a good boy and go outside and play, I said, "All right, I'll fookoff."

I had been saving it up for her, savouring it and practising it privately for her, for weeks, and I was hurt, now that I had offered her this jewel, that she looked so unentranced. Very faintly amused, perhaps; severe and thoughtful, certainly; but emphatically unentranced.

"Who said that to you, Tige?" she asked.

"Gus," I told her. "Agatha's friend."

"I see," she said. "Well, don't say it again, darling, because nice people don't. Understand?"

"Yes, mum," I said. And soon after that Agatha, without even saying good-bye to me, left our house and was succeeded by a "nice" young woman called Anne. She was Irish, and my mother told me I must be good with her because she wasn't used to work, which she had never had to do before.

"Why's she have to work now?" I asked.

"Her mother and father died a little while ago, in Ireland, and now she hasn't any money or anywhere to live. But you mustn't ever ask her questions about it, see?"

I said yes, I saw; and as soon as my mother went out in the new car to play tennis, I went into the kitchen.

"Anne?"

"Yes."

"Are your mother and father dead?"

"Yes."

"What made them dead?"

"It was the Troubles."

"What's the Troubles?"

I remember her looking at me then, her eyes very blue in a face whose skin was clear and fresh in a way that I had never noticed before on any grown-up. Also, her hair was very black and her teeth very small and white. (Queen Victoria, it will doubtless interest you to know, commenting on her visit to Dublin, frequently noted in her diary how white were the teeth of Irish girls.)

"The Troubles were people killing people. My mother and father were killed, and our house was burned down."

"Our house was burned down too," I told her. "But it was at Cronulla, and I was only little then, so I don't remember."

"I'm glad you don't," she said. "It's not a good thing to remember. Now why don't you go outside and play? I've got a lot of work to do, you know. I can't stand around talking all day."

And so I discovered chivalry, because my mother had said that Anne was not used to work.

"I'll help you if you like," I offered.

"Thank you," she said, "but don't you bother yourself. There's plenty of time in life to work. It's not for little boys like you. You go out now and play."

My sister never for a second relaxed her demands for attention: nor failed in them. Sensitive always, in the era of Anita Loos, to anything that influenced men, she abandoned raven hair almost at birth and became a ravishing blonde before she was three months old. She also made such prolonged and dramatic attempts to die that the uncles and aunts even forgot to talk about the War and the Spanish flu and became completely preoccupied with her and how much, or little, each day she had managed to swallow and retain.

In her interests, we went so far as to depart, for a few weeks, from our house in Lindfield, which is a suburb of Sydney, and drive to Bowral, which is in the mountains, where everyone said the air would be good for her. But she, ignoring them, weakened dramatically, and an anxious hush enveloped the big wooden house that belonged to Gar and Gan. It had verandahs right round it, and enormous rooms, one of which was full of brass that Gar (who, because of bronchitis and her "heart," had to flee Australia each winter) had brought back with her from the Far East.

I used to examine this exotic brass while everyone else attended to my sister. I was always alone: but I didn't mind, so long as I could examine the big brass trays and bowls, and the candlesticks fashioned like snakes, whose little red eyes were made of jewels which Gar said were precious. After I had looked at them for a while and felt them with my finger, I used to be able to imagine the Far East. Then I would crouch beneath a small round table by a big window that the sun came through. Over this table hung a silk cloth of bright colours with, all round it, a long fringe of tiny beads in blue and green and red. Hiding alone under this table, the secret air around me stained luminously green and pink as sunlight shafted through my tawdry canopy of silk, the skin on my hands and arms and legs magically dappled with intangible spangles of blue and red refracted from the fringe of beads, I was regularly transported to a world of hallucinogenic privacy.

One day, though, as I emerged furtively from this marvellous secret place, my grandmother saw me.

"Darling," she gasped, with that extravagantly unreal assumption of astonishment at the cleverness, or strangeness, or surprisingness of children which only grandmothers can assume, "where *have* you been? We've been looking for you *every*where."

And even though I knew that no one had been looking for me anywhere — that in fact she had just tripped over me and now was making the best of it — I felt safe with her.

"I've been in there," I told her, as I would have told no one else, including my parents.

"Ah, of course, the colours," she said, instantly comprehending. "The lovely, lovely colours. Gar brought that cloth back from the Far East, you know."

"Yes, I know."

"But little boys shouldn't spend all their day sitting inside, should they?"

I looked at her fearfully. Surely, having understood about the colours, she wasn't now going to become an ordinary grown-up and tell me to go outside and play. (What with? I always wanted to ask, specially at Bowral, but I never did, because I would only have been walloped.)

"I know," she cried. "We must get you a horse."

"A real horse?" I asked incredulously.

"Of course, darling," she told me: and next morning hired a real horse — which my grandfather, having no soul, called a pony.

But life is full of bitter disillusionments. Horses, I quickly learned, were vile quadrupeds, steeped in cunning and riddled with a hatred of small boys. This particular horse, in the next three days, would only walk crabwise, would put its head down to eat and keep it down till it had demolished twenty to thirty square feet of rank grass, and then would fart uproariously and prance wilfully off in the wrong direction, scraping my bare legs against tree trunks and gateposts and fences. In three days this vicious animal twice galloped me southwards back to its stables, though I had its head pointed northwards to Gar's house; twice threw me and bolted; once threw me and stamped on me; and finally, knowing exactly what it was doing, swerved abruptly under a clothesline and left me, legs flailing, swinging by my chin.

Thereupon the brute was returned to its owners, and I was not required to ride any more.

That very night, though, I was awakened in my room by a rumbling that was all round me and under me. The brass knobs of the bed rattled, and the picture of a sailing clipper on the wall fell to the floor, its glass breaking, and the jerry under the bed clumped up and down. And I knew at once that this was no mere physical phenomenon: this was God, come to get my sister.

Whom suddenly, passionately and protectively, I loved: so I struggled upright in my shuddering bed and swung my legs over its edge, determined to save her. Even from God.

At that very instant, to my joy, my mother appeared in the door with my sister in her arms and my father beside her. He turned on the light.

"All right, son?"

"Yes, dad."

They all sat on my shuddering bed; my mother (and, in her arms, my sister) on one side of me, my father on the other.

"It's an earthquake," my father explained. I had never heard of such a thing.

"I was coming to save Pat," I told him.

"We're all right here," he said. "It's only a little earthquake."

"It's stopping," my mother commented and looked at my sister, who (typically) had slept through the entire upheaval. "Lie down now and go to sleep." I lay back, and my father gave me his hand to hold — a thing I never remembered him doing before — and his other hand held my mother's, which picture of myself, framed by my entire family, I found immensely gratifying; but before I could weep with the sentimental joy that suffused me, I fell asleep.

"You must be brave," Gan said to me, apropos of nothing, the next day. I wasn't sure whether he referred to the near garrotting I had endured on the clothesline from the horse or the tumultuous tumbling I'd received in bed from the earthquake, so I looked up at him and waited for him to elaborate. He had short, wiry grey hair, a short, wiry grey moustache, high cheekbones, and flaring nostrils, and he was — I knew — famous. I knew it because all the uncles and aunts endlessly told me so and referred to him, always, as Sir David:

as if, by merely uttering his title, they momentarily elevated themselves from the professional middle class into which, since the War, they had either graduated or married. "How's Sir David?" they would ask my father. "The pater?" he would reply. "Busy as ever. He's on the Board of the Ferries now." "Good God," they would say, "how many boards is he on, then?" "Don't really know," my father would say. "Must be a dozen or so."

I used to wonder where my grandfather kept all these boards, but Gar said they were in Sydney.

"Very brave," he repeated, his greenish eyes looking down at me over his flaring nostrils. "Your sister Pat may die."

Uncertain what this meant and bored by solitude, I went into the big drawing-room where the brass trays and bowls and snakes were, and the table with the silk cloth, but my grandmother was there, wearing the big straw hat she always wore in the morning, indoors and out, and gloves as well. She was rubbing the brass trays with the acid green face of a sliced lemon and then drying them with a soft, clean cloth.

"To get the cleaning powder out of the cracks, where the patterns are engraved," she explained. But she was not warm, as she usually was, and seemed unable to sound excited at seeing me, as she usually did. I waited for her to sound excited.

"Don't bite your fingernails, Anthony," she instructed. "Be a good boy and play outside."

Most perturbed, I went outside and, putting each fingernail in turn between my teeth, tried to bite it. But they were all too tough. I had never tried it before; I wasn't trying it when my grandmother told me to stop it, and I never tried it again.

I now know that what my grandmother really meant was: "You must be brave; your sister may die," because that was the day Pat should have died. Of course she didn't, and I could have told them that she wouldn't, but for the grown-ups at Bowral that day was an agonizing one.

The years that followed, on the other hand, were largely — if in an occasionally macabre kind of way — idyllic.

Having languished at death's door almost a year, my sister now determined to live spectacularly. Not for a second, though, did she relax that grip on her adult audience which she had first seized by transforming herself from brunette to blonde and then consolidated by one death-bed scene after another.

She rarely, for example, condescended to talk. Not for her the fascination of acquiring a vocabulary of emotive words like mummy and daddy. Not even of useful words. If she wanted someone she wailed — so terrifyingly that everyone came running. If she wanted something she pointed, mutely but imperiously.

Unless I had it.

Then, knowing that I habitually ignored her imperiously pointing finger, she would utter.

"Gimme," she would snap. And if, instantly, I did not give, she would open her mouth and emit such a long, shrill, and indescribably penetrating scream that, within seconds, every civic-minded adult in the parish had rushed to her side. Then, whatever it was I had was taken from me and given to her. And I was walloped.

Admittedly she coveted nothing unless she considered it either edible or potable: but she would eat and drink anything. Not just dirt from the garden and the dregs of grown-ups' alcohol (like normal children), but the cat's dinner, lipsticks, eau de cologne, coins, lavatory disinfectant, petrol, screws, ammonia, and old sump oil as well. She wouldn't talk, but she could certainly read, and anything marked POISON was instantly consumed. Her wantonness, in fact, was only equalled by the stoicism with which she endured both the agonies consequent to her strange appetites and the doctor's antidotes.

Because her name was Patricia, my father — blind to all her wilfulnesses — lovingly called her "Littly." Sensing some advantages in this, she decided to add it to "gimme" and double her vocabulary. But, contrary as ever, pronounced it "Ittly."

It was as Ittly, therefore, that my parents subsequently knew her, just as they knew me as Tige. She and I, however, recognizing these as loving names — doting, tender, cuddly names: which our relationship was not — were less sentimental. I became Tony to her, and she became Pat to me.

In the three years that followed I was spared much of her company because I had started going to school, where I met children older and less primitive than she. But it is incredible how little I remember of those years — or of anything else — until she was four and able to inflict her company on me again, simply by always being there and refusing to go away.

I remember the song "Who Killed Cock Robin?" because I found it so passionately sad, especially the lines:

All the birds of the air
fell a'sighing and a'sobbing,
when they heard of the death
of poor Cock Robbing:
When they heard
of the death
o'of
poor
Cock
Robbing

I remember practising the basic exercises in cursive handwriting — pothooks, they were called — and I inscribed them in my copy book by the hundred with a joy the intellectual intensity of which has never since been equalled.

I remember a big girl called Beth, who one day said to me, "Give me the lolly you're sucking and I'll suck it a bit and then give it back to you."

Politely I gave it to her. She put it in her mouth, sucked it energetically, and then, having extracted it wetly, attempted (prising at my lips with her sticky fingers) to return it to me.

To this day I am perplexed that I surrendered it to her, because I did not like her and I loved lollies, and I knew that once this one had been in her mouth I would throw it away.

Certainly it was not gallantry that prompted me to compliance: I fought girls as ruthlessly as I did boys. Nor was it physical fear: I could have kicked Beth to a pulp any day and would cheerfully have done so, given good cause. It may, though, have been moral cowardice, my father having so confused me as to the distinction between doing pleasantly what you are asked to do, whether you want to or not, and not doing what you don't want to, when there's no reason why you should.

I remember a little girl called Helen, in a school play. I had to kiss her. We were five years old, and we kissed square on, like budgerigars: yet that kiss tingled as sweetly in my groin as if I were an adolescent.

I remember the same sensation exactly — sharp and sexual, plucking at the very core of me, so that I shivered — when I sang "Oh, Rose Marie, I love you" with the rest of my class of six-year-olds.

Finally, I remember learning to draw very good maps of Australia; maps with no blots on them and, all round their bold, bumpy shoreline, a fringe of fine horizontal lines in ink, each fine line about a quarter of an inch long, to indicate the sea.

But that's all I remember — which doesn't seem much. I recollect no friends, no teachers, and no lessons — only Pat, at home, endlessly screaming and being taken away for the stomach pump.

I lie: I remember one lesson. From a clergyman, about God and Jesus and how children should go to Sunday school. So we all, the following Sunday, went. And after a while we had to stand up and sing: by which time I had transported myself into the same kind of private ecstasy as I had occasionally known at Bowral, when I had hidden under the small round table and canopied myself in silk, except that there it had been a flight of the mind into an intoxicating nothingness of colour, whilst here it was a flight of the mind into an intoxicating nothingness of Jesus-song. Nothing existed but Jesus-song.

Which, being passionately involved, I made up as I went along.

My contemporaries, unfortunately, sang a less impromptu tune with more formal words, neither so loudly nor so purely as I, nor with anything like my fanaticism, so I was taken out of that Sunday-school class and told gently to go home: which was the end of being Church of England for me.

I must also have learned to read and write, and add and subtract, because I can remember asking questions about words and numbers at home. Naturally I asked them of my mother, because my father came home from being a barrister too late each day for questions, and my sister, though she had at last begun to talk, was conversationally as useless as ever because she elided the first letter from all words beginning with y or l, as well as from many beginning with b, and treated all words of more than one syllable in a fashion that can only be described as cavalier.

"I'm a ittle ellow undlebug of miffish," she was in the habit of advising the unwary (this being her version of "I'm a little yellow bundle of mischief," which Gar had once foolishly called her). But the unwary didn't know that. They only knew that she had a funny look in her eye and talked gobbledegook. Most of them thought her insane.

She wasn't, of course: but equally she was not the sort of girl with whom one discoursed, of whom one asked questions.

So: "Mum," I would ask, "how do you spell sugar?" And: "Mum, do you write forty-seven 47 or 74?"

And: "Mum, how do you spell fuchsia? . . . and Betty? . . . and tongue? . . . and shoe?"

I don't believe I asked for the spelling of anything but sugar, fuchsia, Betty, tongue, and shoe, but I do vividly remember asking for each of those.

Of them all, sugar was the one I could never grasp. Each time my mother told me, my mind boggled at the stark improbability of *sug* being *shoog*. *Shug* I could have accepted: and would have, because I was an amiable and undemanding child. *Chsug* I was positively prepared to welcome, because even then I had a weakness for anything exotic. But at the bleak, take-it-or-leave-it arrogance of *sug* I boggled. "Mum," I kept asking, "*how* did you say you spelled sugar?"

Finally she said, "Tige, I'll tell you just once more, and then, if you forget it again, you'll write it out a hundred times." Then she told me: *s-u-g-a-r.*

And the next day, having boggled as usual, I felt compelled to ask her again.

I was at once despatched to the room in which Pat and I kept our clothes (our beds were on the verandah) with a pencil and several sheets of paper and told to write *sugar* one hundred times.

Obediently I wrote five columns of twenty *sugars;* then, as a gesture, I wrote five columns of twenty *soes.*

My mother opened the door and looked in. "Finished?"

I nodded.

"Let me see."

I handed her the sheets of paper.

"What's this?" she asked, pointing at the hundred *soes*.

"Shoes," I told her.

"Come here," she ordered. And walloped me.

Yet when Pat was sent to our room and told to stay there till she had printed TONY a hundred times, things went quite differently.

It happened because she always copied what I did: so when I asked how words were spelled, she had to ask too. Of course she never listened to the answers, because she was only three and couldn't write: but even at three, sensing that *yellow* did not spell *ellow*, and that *mischief* was a terrible corruption of *miffish*, she contrived an air of impatient contempt at the orthodoxies of written English.

Only two words ever really interested her. The first was PAT (the printing of which she mastered almost at once — though PATRICIA she rejected as coldly as if it had required a knowledge of Sanskrit) and the second was TONY. But the latter she could not master. Constantly she demanded that my mother show her how to write TONY.

Until one day she forgot how to do it, and asked how it was done, once too often, and (to my joy) was shut up in our room to print it a hundred times.

There ensued a great silence.

Never since the day she was born had there been such a silence. My mother smiled at the thought of Ittly's concentration; and I gloated at her confinement. But the great silence prolonged itself and became an eerie silence; and my mother, remembering that Pat's silences had always meant inspired wickedness, began to lose her nerve.

"Hurry up," she ordered from our side of the closed door. "How many have you done now?"

The eerie silence, remaining unbroken, became evil.

"Pat!" — very sharply.

"What?" — insolently.

"You heard me. How many?"

"I don't know. I can only count to twenty."

My mother's lips twitched with that mirth that Pat's reckless insolence so often evoked.

"Well, hurry up," she advised.

Silence again.

After five minutes of which, my mother, unable to contain herself and her curiosity any longer, flung open the door.

Over every inch that she could reach of the wall, Pat had printed TONY. Into every drawer (full of my clothes) that she could straddle, she had widdled. And into each of them that she couldn't widdle she had spat. At this very moment, like a berserk llama, she was spitting into the top one. Balefully her purple face turned to meet my mother's, and then, so that there could be no mistaking what she had been doing, she turned back to the drawer and, hawking lustily, spat again.

This, I knew, could only mean for Pat the direst punishment in the parental repertoire. For this, I knew, she would get not a tanning, not a walloping, and not a belting, but a bloody good hiding. Gleefully I waited for it to start.

But instead, my mother's lips were twitching again. And when she dragged *them* straight, her nostrils started. And they seemed even harder to control than her lips, because suddenly her whole face went pink and her eyes began to water; and then, with a terrible snorting noise, she whirled around and ran to her room at the end of the hall where she slammed the door.

Listening at that door, I heard hoot after hoot of mad laughter. I returned to Pat.

"You've made mum cry," I accused.

"Mummy's laughing," she retorted coldly — and then, casting a last glance round the scene of her anarchic triumph, favoured me with a small, sour smile.

The major, addressing the two guards who had escorted the prisoner from his cell to the interrogation room, uttered curt monosyllables, at which they withdrew, closing the door behind them.

Smiling then, he said, "Sit down, colonel. Cigarette?"

"I don't smoke, thank you."

"You used to."

"Lately I haven't had the opportunity."

"You have it now."

"No. It's been a month . . ."

"And you've kicked the habit?"

"Yes."

"Or you don't want any favours? To be under an obligation?"

"That too."

"But, colonel" — and the major smiled patronizingly, revealing gold fillings in his back teeth — "you are obligated already."

"Whatever else I am, major, I am not obligated."

"Your seven colleagues, since their capture, have lost an average of six kilos in weight. You haven't lost a milligram. For that you must thank me."

"Then I am obliged to you. Obligated is an appalling word."

"Excuse my poor English," the major murmured dangerously, his eyes sliding from those of his prisoner to the wodge of manuscript that lay under his left hand, and then to a neat stack of buff cards beside the manuscript.

"It's because your English is excellent," the grey-haired Australian explained, "that I bother to correct it."

"I am obliged to you," the younger man replied sarcastically, picking up the first of the buff cards and reading the few words printed on it. "Now, perhaps we could abandon these tiresome semantics. I see that, in the five days since last we met, you've written only twenty-one quarto pages."

"Of *small* writing," the colonel demurred.

"Don't be flip, colonel."

"The word is flippant, major."

"Your Mr Fowler always said that usage made words acceptable. When I was at Sydney University, in 1966, *everyone* said flip. They've said it ever since. Ten years' usage, I suggest, makes my word acceptable, yours obsolete. And why, in any case, this sudden pedantry?"

"Last week you said you'd take my words and destroy me with them. I've decided that even if they're going to be one of your weapons against me . . ."

"They are."

". . . they're still my only weapon against you."

For a moment their eyes met, thoughtfully and with hostility; then the major shook a pack of cigarettes, extracted one with his teeth, and lit it with a table lighter of green onyx.

"From the American PX," he advised, indicating both the cigarettes and the table lighter. "They left in such a hurry they forgot all about their PX. Such luxuries make a change for socialist soldiers."

"Only for socialist *officer* soldiers, it would appear," the colonel suggested. "I don't notice your men smoking Chesterfields and lighting 'em with Ronsons."

"Talking of distinctions of rank, I see here" — the major jabbed at one of the pencilled sheets (and the colonel tried to read his own upside-down writing across the desk) — "that you make a point of mentioning a servant. A woman called Agatha."

"Agatha could never in one's wildest dreams have been described as a servant. She was simply one of that class in Australia at that time who were employed domestically and lived in."

"Yet you mention her patronizingly."

"I mention her with distaste. I am attempting to show that children can be sensitive to coarseness even though they don't understand it."

"I suggest that you mention her as a symbol not of coarseness but of the bourgeois privileges to which you are accustomed — like the car your family acquired at the same time."

"Balls!" observed the colonel.

"Then why mention either of them?"

"The one was a rearguard, the other a forerunner."

"Colonel, I do not care for allusion."

The colonel raised an eyebrow — not far, but slightly — and explained. "Agatha represented a domestic type soon to vanish; our Fiat was the first privately owned car in our street. Can you imagine a street with only one car in it, major?"

"My friend, in China I have seen a whole province with only one car in it."

"Probably only one Ronson lighter too."

Unexpectedly the major flung himself back in his chair and laughed. His chest, in the V of his crisply starched, open-neck shirt, was smooth-skinned, like his arms in their short sleeves. And his hands were small, like a boy's.

"Why really did you dislike Agatha?" he asked and seemed genuinely interested.

"She was ginger and scraggy."

"A purely physical prejudice?"

"Aren't almost all initial prejudices — for or against — purely physical?"

"Even in the family, colonel?"

"Family affections are entirely umbilical and chromosomatic. In retrospect one may be able to justify them; but they're there because they were physically implanted."

"Can you justify yours on any grounds other than physical implantation?"

"I'll leave you to decide that."

"So I may expect some further instalments, may I? A week ago you didn't want to write at all."

"If I must write . . ."

"You must."

"But what good's it do you?"

"It's part of our technique, and it works."

"I could write lies."

"You undoubtedly will."

"So?"

"So next time you write the same story . . ."

"What do you mean 'next time'?"

"When you finish, you start again. And after that, again. And again. And when you have lied about something, or omitted it, or glossed over it, you will write differently each time, because you won't be able to remember exactly how you got round it the last time. And these are the areas that interest me. The areas of inconsistency, of vulnerability. We need to find those; and in order to find them we'll use any method at all to make you write."

"That being the case," commented the colonel lightly, "I'll write and enjoy it!" He was confident not only that he would not be guilty of inconsistencies but that he had no areas of vulnerability. Areas of vulnerability he regarded as so much trick cyclist's claptrap.

"But *only* your childhood and youth," the major insisted. "Nothing else. Write about anything later than your twentieth year — or talk about it — and we'll punish you very severely."

"Okay by me." The colonel shrugged. "But why?"

"Because it suits our book," the major replied, smiling. "An apt metaphor, used deliberately, to impress upon you the fact that I am alert to all the nuances of your somewhat inadequate language. Now, about Agatha. When you saw her with Gus, what did you think?"

"Gus naked, you mean?"

The major nodded.

"I didn't think anything. Never thought about Agatha and Gus again till you made me continue what your predecessor made me start. Only thought about Agatha when I saw scraggy ginger-heads pushing prams. Afraid we can't extract any fearful sexual traumas out of Gus and Agatha, major. Just a lifelong dislike of potato chips."

"What else did you dislike as a child?"

"Questions not being answered."

"Explain."

"I used to hate the dialogue that ran: 'Mum, can I do such and such?' . . . 'No.' . . . 'Why?' . . . 'You're too little.' . . . 'When will I be big?' . . . 'Soon.' . . . 'When's soon?' . . . 'Not long.' . . . 'Today?' . . . 'No.' . . . 'Tomorrow?' . . . 'No.' . . . 'When, well?' . . . 'Don't say when well.' . . . 'Well, when?' . . . 'That's enough, Tige.' . . . 'Why?' . . . 'Because!' . . .

"I think parents should be forbidden to perpetrate dialogues of this kind on their children. They frustrate the child and stultify his capacity to reason."

"And you resented this?"

"Certainly. On the other hand, children need frustrating, and their quicksilver minds need occasional stultifying, so it's also a good thing." And in the colonel's mind the conviction grew that he could play this wordy game for ever.

"About your kiss, when you were only five, with the little girl . . . ?"

"Helen?"

"Yes, Helen." Quizzically the major picked up the next buff card and read, " 'That kiss tingled as sweetly in my groin as if I were an adolescent.' "

"Did too."

"When you were *five?*"

"Almost orgasmic it was. As sweet as that. Even now, thinking about it, I can feel it. But if I think about sex, which one tends to in jail, you know, I feel nothing. I was five, and that's how it was. Maybe I was a dirty little boy."

"No need to get angry."

"I'm not angry, I'm vehement: with the clarity of my recollection."

"Yet you felt exactly the same thing, you claim, when you sang 'Oh, Rose Marie'?"

"Exactly the same. So maybe the groin is the seat of all sensuality. Or sex is musical. Or music is sexy. I don't know. But I'm glad I remembered that kiss — and that singing. Since my voice broke, about a million years ago, I've had a range of three notes and not been able to sing at all. Even the national anthem defeats me. That mightn't worry you — do you people have a national anthem? Or just that 'The master class will rue the day' thing? — but it's often worried me. How did I get on the national anthem?"

"It was a logical train of thought," the major murmured, writing in his dossier. "You're an atheist, of course?"

"Am I?"

The major looked up from his writing. "Well, I gathered from the tone of your anecdote about Sunday school that you were."

"One of my best friends had a son expelled from his boarding school," the colonel replied obliquely.

"And?"

"The boy got a First Class Honours in his Law Finals five years later. He did not, upon expulsion, you see, cease to believe in education."

"You're saying you still believe in God?"

"I'm saying you mustn't interpret my words too optimistically. They're not there to help you: they're there to help me! I told you that when we started."

"So you did," the major agreed, stacking neatly together the buff-coloured cards to which he had referred throughout his interrogation and, as he lit another cigarette, enjoying a twitch of craving on his prisoner's lips.

"What're those cards?" the colonel asked abruptly.

"You imperialists are not the only ones to use computers," he was told.

"You're using a computer on *me?*"

"Naturally. It's programmed with all the findings of every expert in the fields of psychoanalysis and psychology on the case histories of every prisoner handled by our Special Branch for the last ten years. After each of our interviews, I feed into it your answers and what you have written, and it makes suggestions and observations. I work on these and then submit to it your responses to them. Gradually we come to focus on an area of weakness; and, after that, you crack. Fast."

"Computers can make mistakes," the colonel observed wryly, "as I found out at Bukit Langkap."

"This one doesn't," the major retorted, "as you'll find out right here." Exhaling arrows of Virginia scented smoke, he pressed a button. Immediately the door behind the colonel opened, and the two stolid sentries reappeared. "You'll find plenty of paper and ball-point pens in your cell," the major promised as the colonel stood. "Oh, by the way, your Australian press has started a furious campaign against your Minister of Defence."

"What about?"

"About what it calls 'The Missing Eight Men,'" the major answered. "The press claims that eight of the seventeen thousand Australian soldiers recently stationed in Malaysia did not return at the time of the Withdrawal. The press claims they're still here. Know what your Minister of Defence has said in reply?"

"No idea."

"He's denied it! Rather than admit the simple truth — that your absurd computer made a mistake — he has denied that you and your friends are missing. You see what that means, colonel? It means that you don't exist. Except in *our* minds, you no longer exist."

I suppose this was the time (when I was a little more than seven, and Pat about three) that the ramifications of family ties and the landscape of the suburb and the city in which I lived first began to impinge on my consciousness.

We lived, as I have said, at Lindfield. We lived about a quarter of a mile from the railway station, where you could catch the new electric train some ten miles to Milson's Point, on the north side of Sydney Harbour, then run down a long ramp (everyone always ran) and jump (everyone always jumped) onto a ferry that took you across to Circular Quay — the city's unpretentious front door ever since Governor Philip had rowed ashore there with his English convicts in 1788.

As well as the passenger ferry, there was a car ferry for those who were rich and drove into town. As you sat in your car, waiting for the ferry to arrive, you could survey the huge granite pylon which my father said would (with its twin on the far side of the harbour) one day support a bridge.

I used to look at the sky and space between the two pylons and try to imagine a bridge connecting them, but I couldn't.

"What sort of bridge, dad?" I asked.

"An arch," he said.

"Will we drive over when it's finished, instead of using the fairy?"

"Ferry," he corrected. He was always correcting me. "Yes."

I tried to imagine the Fiat climbing from the near pylon to the top of an arch in mid-harbour and then sliding down to the far pylon. Again I couldn't.

"When will the bridge be there?" I asked.

"God knows," he told me gloomily. And with good cause, since it went on not being there till I was eleven years old, which, my father observed — with more prescience than perhaps he realized — would increase its cost so astronomically that we'd never pay the damn thing off.

When you drove onto the ferry at night you had to get out of the car and turn the tail-light off. You had to get out because, in those more Spartan times, the switch was at the rear of the car, and you had to turn it off because otherwise, it was felt, some myopic captain in command of a huge liner, seeing ahead of him a car's red tail-light on the *starboard* side of a comparatively small, flat vessel, might mistake it for a port light (thereby misreading the vessel's course) and run it down.

If I remember rightly, there had in fact been such a case. Anyway, whether there had or not, on the car ferry, at night, in the darkness that was relieved only by a crimson light to port and a green light to starboard, in the silence that was broken only by the chugging of marine engines and the murmur of encapsulated conversations, I was always excitedly aware of the encircling gloom, and that out of it, at any moment, a vast liner might charge upon us.

But I still preferred the passenger ferry to the car ferry. Not just because of the jumping on and off, ignoring the gangplank, holding a grown-up's hand and swinging over the narrow, watery abyss and onto the floating jetty, but because the ferry skidded flat-bottomed across the harbour, so that, as you travelled, you stood only a few feet above the water and, looking down, watched the sunlight send slanted shafts of speckled gold plunging into the blue-green depths; and felt them dragging your consciousness down and down and down, remorselessly.

Much later in life, when I was twenty, I nearly drowned. I was swimming underwater one day when I suddenly realized that I had broken through all the accepted physical barriers imposed by the need to breathe: I could go on forever. Deliriously, then, I swam on; and I will never again know such insane power. There was no price to pay. No abrupt and frightful onset of pain. No fear. Just this dream-like, maniacal, exquisite sense of power.

Friends on the rocks above watched me, first with anxiety and then terror, as I swam on and on, from deep to too deep, to much too deep. And then saw a huge bubble erupt from my mouth and, after it, a few feeble pearls from my nostrils. Whilst I, totally oblivious, lay deeply submerged, limp and about to drown.

They dived down and hauled me up and out, and I woke up, still feeling exhilarated, but lying on my back on a rock, looking at the high, dry, blue sky, instead of sharking my tireless way through the depths.

Looking down from the ferry into the slanted gold-flecked rays of sun in water induced the same sensation — of becoming disembodied. Perhaps colour, like water, denies you oxygen, and when you get too deep in it, you swoon.

Travelling by night on the ferry was quite different, and even better, because then the blue-green harbour became an oiled sibilant blackness against which the inelegant hulls and superstructures of other ferries disappeared, leaving visible only hundreds of squares of light — their windows — flitting busy firefly courses from the Quay to Manly and Mosman and Clifton and Lane Cove and Kirribilli and Milson's Point. And if you looked down at your waterline you saw the rich blackness peeling away in long, low sighs, each soft exhalation brilliant with opal sparkles of phosphorescence.

Serried tiers of fireflies, magic phosphorescence, and the plangent silence of a deep, languid harbour combined at night to produce magic. At night, indisputably, ferries were fairies.

In which I believed implicitly — and not just because, as I lost my baby teeth, it was to my financial advantage to do so. We now had a new maid-cook-nanny — a Miss White, whom Pat promptly dubbed Ite — and Ite, having recently left an orphanage, knowing better than most how necessary to children fairies are, saw to it that the fairies, whenever they collected a baby tooth from under my pillow, rewarded me with a silver sixpence.

Ite made the bush that reached from the creek right up to our back fence — virgin Australian bush, of eucalyptus, begonia, and bracken — habitable for fairies; and I knew she was right when she said that this was where they lived. It was natural for anything winged to live there. Kookaburras lived there: and laughed at us every day. Sparrows and starlings and doves and magpies and butcher birds lived there: and made their nests neatly in the shorter flowering gums. Locusts (as we called them, though I think they were cicadas), from the moment they split their chrysalis — emerging all powdery and softly vulnerable — through to their glorious days of vibrant song and skimming flight on cellophane wings, lived there. Butterflies, in feckless clouds, lived there. Of course the fairies lived there — and the alarming goanna, with his suspicious little eyes and flickering blue tongue, was their guardian.

They lived, Ite convinced us, in a small circle of flat ground just up from the creek. It was fringed with ferns and, because the sun never quite reached it through the gum leaves, was always cool, but not cold; and shaded, but not shadowy. Dappled, rather. And instead of grass on the earth there was moss: which could only have stayed so green and soft (in spite of having been trampled so very flat) if the feet that had trampled it belonged to fairies.

In fact that round patch of moss surrounded by ferns, filter-lit and sweetened by clear creek water running busily over ancient sandstone, was a fairy ring.

Unluckily, although we knew the fairies were there, the bush was so thick that we never actually saw them. And anyway, as Gar explained, they only came out at night when we were in bed.

"Have you ever seen them?" I asked.

"No," she said. "Fairies are for little boys and girls, not for grown-ups."

I was glad of that. It was the first nice thing I had heard of that was not for grown-ups rather than children.

To go and see my grandparents we had to drive all the way to the ferry and then cross the harbour and drive some more to Edgecliff. Admittedly, when we got there it was worth it, because Gar always gave me money (which I put into the flat lid of a big cardboard box when I got home; and kept on top of the wardrobe where Pat couldn't steal it), and Gan carved a joint. This he did standing (as my father did) and hacking (which usually my father did not) and finally tearing with his fingers and flinging tattered hunks of meat onto each plate (which my father never did).

I could see, on these occasions, that my father and two uncles (Dudley, who was known as Jim, and Henry who, having been a frail child, was known as Herc, which was short for Hercules) strongly disapproved of this eccentricity, but they never actually said anything. Gar, though, loved it, laughing that laugh of hers that was all sunny and liquid — like the creek — until my father and uncles frowned at her. But, grey eyes sparkling against the darkness of her eyelids — the bruised darkness of physical pain — she used to take no notice of them. She adored my grandfather and was happy to spend all her life agreeing with everything he did and darning his old socks, her heavily jewelled hands — five or six rings on each — deftly stitching and stitching. She darned, in fact, as much as my mother knitted. But my mother could read a book at the same time, which Gar couldn't.

Once I asked her, "Is Gan poor?"

"*No*, darling. Gan's rich. If Gan were poor I wouldn't be able to travel every winter, would I? Why do you ask is he poor?"

"He has such old socks."

"He *likes* old socks," Gar told me. "And *cold* tea." It was a strange streak of frugality I was in the future to encounter often in my family. "Sit here at my feet and I'll scratch your head."

So, with my head being scratched, I used to sit on the floor (they used the wide neck of a T-shaped hall as an informal living-room), looking at the big mirror on the far wall. This reflected a similar mirror on the wall behind us — as well as *its* reflection of the far mirror's reflection — so that mirrors apparently receded for miles.

Below the mirror was a gong, which was struck by a maid in a starched white uniform half an hour before dinner. That told us to dress. Not that anyone except Gar ever took any notice. She always put on an elaborate gown and changed all her jewellery; the men just washed their hands, brushed their hair, and put on a tie and jacket.

Then the starched white maid would give the gong another drubbing and everyone — infinitely reflected — would proceed down towards the far mirror and descend two steps and turn left into the dining-room, where huge, black, elaborately carved chairs, shaped like thrones and immensely uncomfortable, were drawn up against a monumentally black and elaborately carved table. The furniture, of course, was the by-product of one of the grandmaternal voyages to the Far East (as were the two great wheels of beaten gold and silver that decorated the walls of the dining-room), but the dinner service was richly and uncompromisingly Royal Doulton, and the cutlery was heaviest Victorian silver.

After soup, Gan carved, and each helping was carried round by the white starched maid to a recipient designated by the point of his carving knife.

The maid next brought vegetables in big china dishes with heavy tablespoons sticking out of them; and while you dug out what you wanted, she breathed, and her stays creaked — in, out: in, out. Peas were very difficult to get onto your plate with her standing beside you, stiff, starched, white, not nearly as servile as she seemed, and creaking in and out.

I could never have imagined Agatha serving us vegetables like that. Nor creaking. Agatha had nothing to put stays round. And I would have hated it if Ite had done it. But there was no question of that. Ite had become part of the family.

Another part of the family was my mother's brother, who was

different from my father and his friends in so many ways that he sounded almost alarming.

My father and all his friends had "been on the Western Front": Uncle Dick had "gone to Gallipoli." My father and all his friends had either been gassed or blown up, or both, by Huns: Uncle Dick had been bayoneted — in the leg, many times — by the Turks. My father and all his friends were professional men who played tennis and were now adopting hobbies like bridge and fishing and flying: Uncle Dick was a farmer whose leg no longer permitted tennis and who lived alone on an allotment of brutally timbered land which would one day become his if he slaved on it unremittingly for enough years without going mad. My father and all his friends had married girls they met at dances or tennis parties: Uncle Dick had married his first cousin.

Whilst he laboured to make that uncleared allotment of land his own, he had sent his wife and two baby daughters to stay with her family in America, which, I knew from my father, was a terrible place full of terrible people, except for Charles Lindbergh, who was probably Swedish anyway. Americans made cars that my father refused to buy; and Americans said they had won the war — which even I could see was nonsense, because quite clearly it had been won by my father, his two brothers, and all my uncles except Uncle Dick, who had *lost* to the Turks because he had been wounded in the leg at Gallipoli.

Another part of my family was Aunty Ock's (short for Octavia). Aunty Ock was my mother's first cousin and was very good at golf, for which my family forgave her because she was nice and had married a pre-war Davis Cup tennis player. He was a quiet, clever, kindly man, and she was a lively, pretty, amusing woman with corn-coloured hair, very blue eyes, and very white teeth. They had two sons and a daughter (all, apparently, my cousins) and they lived on the other side of the hill from the creek.

To get to their place from ours, you walked to the corner, where there was a vacant plot of bush, turned right down the hill past Billy Hughes' house (he had been something called a P.M. during the War) to where the creek ran under the road, then up the hill again. At the point where the road, as if to get back its breath, turned left, along the flank of the hill, Uncle Al and Aunty Ock and my three cousins lived: and they moved to a bigger house — with a tennis court — just over the crest of the hill. There, playing almost the same role to their family as Ite played to ours, was a girl called Jean.

Probably Jean was more strict than Ite because Aunty Ock and Uncle Al were so much less brutal than my parents. Anyway, the big difference between the cousins' house and ours was that at our house you always got your walloping from mum or dad, at theirs you usually got it from Jean.

And the wallopings themselves differed. At home, for minor offences, you got the flat of my mother's hand (delivered with plenty of follow through) across the head; and for serious offences, her hard, black-bristled hair brush, or my father's razor strop, over the backside. At Aunty Ock's and Uncle Al's, for everything, it was Jean slashing at your bare legs with a riding crop; but when she slashed, you were allowed to run away and, if cornered, to jump.

Thus Jean, armed with the crop, would rush out and we would at once flee, each in a different direction, which meant always that two escaped entirely, whilst the third — eventually trapped — leaped high in the air as Jean slashed. It taught us to judge distances; it made us marvellously athletic; and it was much more sporting than the system at my home where one had to stand still and take whatever was coming. One's only chance at my home was to cast an agonized eye at my mother's upraised hand and, if her engagement ring (as occasionally happened) had slipped, so that its diamonds had become part of the striking surface, to scream, "Mum, your ring!"

This used to make her look up and then, giggling, relent — unless she found, on looking up, that her ring had not slipped. When that happened she went straight to her hard-bristled hair brush.

The result of all this was that when Peter and Bill, my cousins, came to my place to play, we spent our time either under the house or in the bush, in neither of which places the grown-ups could see us and therefore feel impelled to punish us: but when I went to their place, we played either in the garden or on the gravel tennis court, feeling tolerably safe even when we knew we were being naughty.

Wherever we played, of course, it was always in bare feet, shorts, and a shirt. At my place, in the bush, we built cubby houses, made dams in the creek, caught tadpoles, explored, and made believe we were jungle children: at theirs, in the garden, we played doctors.

shopkeepers, and hidings and made believe we were civilized grown-ups. For the next ten years our lives were largely spent together.

We began, then, to live on two levels: as part of an infant tribe, admission to which was difficult, escape from which almost unheard of; and as the children of our parents, where we hardly recognized one another.

My father, for example, as he came home from work each evening, when he reached the vacant lot on the corner, about seventy-five yards from our house, would put two fingers in his mouth and whistle. For a barrister, it was a not very dignified signal, but he did it because he liked to be welcomed at his own front gate — and because he enjoyed producing the most ear-splitting whistle in Lindfield.

Uncle Al would never have whistled to Aunty Ock and his children as he approached his house. Not that he couldn't have, he just wouldn't have. Nor would he ever have been guilty (assuming that he did go mad and whistle) of doing what once my father did, which was to fling himself down, in full view of all the neighbours, behind a hibiscus bush on the grass verge.

"Are you all *right?*" Mrs Barker asked him as my mother and Pat and I arrived at the front gate and peered up the road, looking for him.

"Shush!" he told her. "I'm hiding from my wife. She's bigger than me and she beats me."

Uncle Al would never have done that to Aunty Ock. But equally, my father, had he once played on Australia's Davis Cup Team and had been known as the Prince of Volleyers, would never, as Uncle Al did, virtually have concealed the fact. My family were never immodest, but somehow we always contrived to let our achievements be known.

What most distinguished our family life from my cousins', though, was my father's passion at this time (when I was eight, and Pat was three and a half) for cars and fishing. Uncle Al never even bothered to own a car, let alone become obsessed by one, and never showed the faintest inclination to fish. At holiday time he took his family eleven miles by taxi to a Sydney beach called Dee Why, where he owned a cottage on the headland: whilst my father, piling all of us, and Ite, into a new 1928 Austin, drove us three hundred and forty excruciating miles of boredom and carsickness to an ex-convict settlement called Port Macquarie, which offered jewfish off the beach and the breakwater, whiting on the sandbanks, mullet among the weedy shallows, and flathead up round the bend of Limeburner's Creek.

My parents quickly became friends with the other grown-ups in the boarding house and I became friends with their sons, whilst Pat, who had lately given up poisons and embarked on a back-to-nature jag, ignored everyone and spent her entire day exploring the salty agapanthus of the boarding-house garden and the black rocks of the breakwater.

The boarding house was somewhere to sleep and to have breakfast and dinner. Between breakfast and dinner, the males fished while the females swam. Male children, being literally in the same boat as their fathers, were required to fish properly and patiently.

I had to bait my hook and throw in my line and wait in utter silence for that faint pressure on the finger which means that a fish is nibbling: and then time exactly the moment when the fish would strike.

I had to lift my catch smoothly into the drifting boat; and, if it was bream or mullet, grasp it firmly and twist the hook out of its mouth; if it was a flathead, drop it onto the floorboards and pierce its bony skull, exactly between the eyes, with a bone-handled hunting knife, waiting, as its eyes bulged and squinted, till it was quite dead before removing the hook, because a flathead's gills and spikes are dangerous.

Only if I hooked a shovel-nosed shark or a stingray could I ask — quietly — for help. Then, as I pulled the head over the edge of the boat, my father would batter it senseless with the butt of an oar and, having removed my hook, allow it to drop back into the river.

But all the time we fished with a silent, obsessed skill, baiting the barbed hooks, replacing both sinker and hook when necessary, tying our fine neat knots in the catgut; each man — or boy — utterly self-sufficient and withdrawn into himself. As the boat drifted slowly sideways, four taut lines dragged slowly with it, each line held over an absorbed first finger through which was passed a steady stream of fascinating information. Through that finger one read whether the river bottom was sandy or rocky, weedy or clean; whether the fish that nibbled was a wary bream, a stupid mullet, a timid whiting, or a cavalier flathead; whether one's hook had been sucked bare of bait by a veteran too clever to snap; whether, as one struck, the barb had bitten into, or merely torn through, the tough tissue of a fish's jaw.

In the evening, as the men rowed back across the rough shallows, the boat's bow rearing up and walloping hollowly down again, I used to sit with my father's bone-handled knife slitting open the white-bellied flathead, the silver bream and whiting, and the sandy, Picasso-eyed flounder; de-gutting, with bloody fingers, the day's catch.

When the winds, or the tides, were wrong for fishing, we children would explore the relics of Port Macquarie's convict past. The massive breakwater. The graves, on the grassy headland, of one-time garrison officers. The old underground dungeons, stone-walled, dimlit, echoing and dankly fascinating. The large church, with graves inside it housing, rumour claimed, the bones of officers murdered in long-ago riots.

Port Macquarie, in 1929 — except for the crew of the pilot launch and the few farmers who, on its outskirts, grew pineapples in the dark red soil — seemed sleepy, almost moribund: but ghosts of violence haunted it and it never quite lost its air of belonging to another, rougher, and more exciting age, for all that it now boasted a talking-picture house.

Cows were frequently herded down the main residential road; and whenever they were, the doctor's dog attacked them until they bolted, and then swung joyously by his teeth from the tail of the fastest-moving beast, his terrier body deliriously airborne.

A half-naked woman, brandishing a carving knife, pursued a blood-drenched man from the lane by the wharf into the main street, where palm trees grew in the middle of the road. It required three policemen to disarm and drag her off.

"The local whore," my father advised my mother.

"What's a whore?" I asked.

"Never you mind," my mother instructed.

So I didn't. It was the blood I was interested in anyway.

At low tide, when the shallow dam created by the breakwater was dry, a barnstorming Tiger Moth landed on the bare, corrugated sand. In the next four hours, repeatedly snatching itself into the air, just clearing the jagged black rocks, soaring and banking over the church, and then plumping itself down again, it took us all, parents and children, one at a time, on a joy ride at ten shillings a head.

At high tide the pilot launch would race out to waiting coasters: and the pilot would bring 600-ton vessels in through the heavy seas that boiled at the bar and sometimes swooped down the channel as well.

All of it seemed perfectly natural at Port Macquarie.

Even Pat being carried almost unconscious by my father to the doctor seemed natural. Following her lifelong and cussed practice of doing what no sane person did, she had just stuck her forefinger down a hole in the ground. Holes in the ground in Australia are notoriously full of things that bite, and Pat not only knew this but had repeatedly been bitten: on this occasion she had been bitten by a small venomous trap-door spider.

The doctor at once gave her chloroform and lanced her finger deeply. Half an hour later my father, green in the face and staggering, carried her back into the boarding house, peacefully asleep. She stayed asleep, whilst he was repeatedly sick, until the following morning. Then, waking early, she went at once into the garden: where shortly she was discovered with another finger down another hole.

Christmas came and Santa Claus gave me a small electric torch over whose bulb one could slide either a red or a green or a colourless glass — which conjured up marvellous fantasies of pirate signals and high adventure. It was exactly what I wanted. Unfortunately it was also exactly what Pat wanted.

"Gimme," she ordered. Very properly I ignored her. "Gimme," she threatened, "or I cream." Which also I ignored. Whereupon, earsplittingly, her bandaged, spider-bitten finger held treacherously aloft, she screamed.

My father appeared instantly, his alert lawyer's mind swiftly interpreting the scene. I, he decided, as Pat had meant him to, had been bullying my sister and had not even respected her deeply lanced finger as I did so.

"Come here," he ordered. I came. "Put that down." I put down the torch. Then he walloped me — and Pat grabbed the torch.

But already my mother had appeared, her alert woman's mind working equally swift. Pat, she decided, as I had prayed she would, was blackmailing me.

"Come here," she ordered. Pat came. "Put that down." Pat dropped my torch. Then mum walloped her. "And in future," she added, "whenever your father belts Tige because you've screamed, I'll belt you."

Which is exactly what happened: but if anyone thinks that that ever deterred my sister, then I have failed lamentably in my description of the stuff of which she was made. Equally, however, if anyone thinks that we were incompatible or unhappy children, then again I have failed.

We were very close to each other, and to each of our Spartan parents. Admittedly our lives were rigorous and regimented; but we knew exactly where we stood. When a parent shouted, "Tige, what are you doing?" and you shouted back, "Nothing," you knew that the answer would be, "Well, stop it."

When a parent watched you doing anything, you knew that before long you would be admonished: "Look where you're going," or "Use both hands," or "Put it back where you found it," or all of them together.

These were daily dialogues designed not to intimidate but merely to maintain contact. As grown-ups there was little our parents could say to us that would interest us: we needed only to know that they were there and interested in us.

Apart from that, the rules of living were clear. We were at all times to do what we were told, to eat what was in front of us, to pass the pepper, salt, and sugar to grown-ups, to be seen and not heard (except when spoken to: then we must use the right word and pronounce it properly), to surrender our seats to grown-ups, to let them go first through doors, to go to bed when we were told, to spend all our time out of doors, to refrain from telling tales, to clean our teeth twice and go to the lavatory once a day, and to enjoy ourselves. If we wanted anything, we were to ask for it (when the answer would be no), and if anything worried us, we were to say so (when the problem would be solved). Ours were active, violent, disciplined, and most satisfying lives.

Not that I always thought so at the time; and certainly not that I thought so when, at the end of our Port Macquarie holiday, I learned that, instead of returning with Pat and my parents to Sydney, I was to be banished for several months to a country town called Inverell.

My mother, I was advised, needed a complete rest and was going on a sea voyage to somewhere called Fiji; and while she was away, I was to stay with Uncle Vere and Aunty Estelle at Inverell. I can't remember where Pat was sent — to a reform school probably — but I do remember howling my head off as I was driven in Uncle Vere's car away from Port Macquarie and Pat and the prickly bosom of my family.

To what must have been the acute discomfort of my hostess, her husband, and her two sons, I howled for about a hundred miles. Then, realizing that I had been irretrievably abandoned, I settled down to make the best of it.

At Inverell there was Aunty Estelle's son Vernon to play with, the loft of the barn to play in, eggs to collect from the chook yard, icy water to drink from the canvas bag that hung dripping in the shade by the back verandah door, sticky pepper trees to climb, rabbit warrens in the harshly eroded gullies to dig out and set with traps, milk to churn in the centrifugal separator, and, later, ice on the puddles in the road to crunch on the way, in the early morning, to school.

The school part, however, I did not enjoy. It began with a teacher making me stand up and asking me, "What is your father?"

"My father," I told her, and answered the same thing each time she repeated the question.

"Anthony," she demanded — and she sounded unfriendly — "is he a butcher, a baker, or a candlestick maker?"

"No," I told her.

"Anthony! What *is* he?"

"My father!" I insisted.

"He's a barrister," Vernon hissed. "She means what work does he do."

"He's a barrister," I shouted, enlightened at last: but it was too late. Already she had decided that I was mutinous, and my classmates that I was loony. There was no recovering from it.

That first day went from bad to worse. At play time, behind the lavatories, I was required, by some of Inverell's more criminal nine-year-olds, to smoke; the sandwiches Aunty Estelle had so kindly cut for my lunch were of peanut butter, which I detested, but ate because of my upbringing; and after lunch I was joined in the boys' lavatory by a ten-year-old girl with ideas about co-education that were decades ahead of her time.

The months passed slowly, but apart from having to smoke, and suffer the bitter cold of early morning frost, and eat peanut butter sandwiches, and fight off that sex-mad girl, I can't pretend that I found them any slower or less enjoyable than life at home. In fact, certain things — like the secret games Vernon and I played in the hayloft, and churning the milk separator, and hunting rabbits — I even missed when eventually I was collected by my mother and taken back to Sydney by train.

"How was school?" my mother asked as the train started.

"Not bad."

"Was the teacher nice?"

"No."

"Why?"

"She was a whore."

"That'll do, Tige." And a great silence befell us.

Until then I had always imagined trains to be thundering and exciting: the reality I found insufferably tedious and uncomfortable, relieved only by a few seconds of explosive activity each time we passed a gang of rail workers. Then, as they stood aside from the track, in the middle of nowhere, and we clumped past them, they would shout *"Py-ers"* — and instantly, from every window, a barrage of rolled newspapers would descend upon them. Passengers even had their papers rolled ready to fling.

Because, they said, it was a tradition in the outback.

It was more probably, I felt, with the cynicism of my age, the one opportunity passengers had of *doing* something.

Everyone said my mother looked marvellous after her voyage, but she looked exactly the same to me, in spite of the horrifying stories she told of mountainous seas and the ship being battened down and tables in the dining saloon having the fiddles up.

I had no idea what being battened down meant, still less how tables could have fiddles up, but I seized upon both these exotic new phrases and hurled them at my cousins as conditions that had been inflicted on me at Inverell, which must have been confusing for them at the very least. My father, however, as he listened to my mother, obviously understood everything because he groaned, "Liz, no more! I can't stand it. Big waves and little ships shouldn't be allowed."

"Your father's a coward," my mother explained.

Pat at once flew to his support. "Not! !" she asserted with her customary verbal economy.

"Littly," he told her, "don't contradict your mother. Because about big waves and little ships, I am."

"You're not a coward when we cross the rough bit over the sandbanks at Port Macquarie," I pointed out.

"No," he agreed, with the kind of grown-up logic that sows fearful neuroses in the subconsciousness of innocent children, "but that's different!"

At this time a series of dramatic changes took place.

First, Ite left us to become a nurse in a hospital — on which occasion Pat, usually so tough, bellowed with grief and wrecked the ceremony where my father presented Ite with one of those big watches that nurses wear, and Ite said she would never forget us.

Next, after she left, I was given her room (the one Agatha had had when Gus came visiting) because my mother said I was getting a big boy now — which vaguely I connected with the sex-mad girl in the boys' lavatory at Inverell, so that I wondered if somehow Aunty Estelle had found out and told on me.

Third, my father went away to the country on what he called the Circuit, leaving my mother with instructions that she was to build me a wardrobe, using empty butter boxes that she was to screw together and a few planks of wood that were to be attached to the butter boxes. There was a niche, about four feet wide, in the wall at the foot of my bed, and the cupboard was to fit in that, and be covered with a curtain. There was, as I have said, this strange streak of frugality in my family.

So, as soon as he had gone, my mother and I collected screws and screwdrivers, hammers and nails, saws and spirit levels, a brace and bit and a hand-operated drill, planes and trestles, planks and butter boxes, and carried the whole lot up to the verandah that ran from my parents' bedroom down the side and round the back of the house. My bedroom was on the back corner.

My mother's carpentry I found refreshing after the niggling orthodoxy of my father. He measured, planed, bevelled, dovetailed and sawed everything with a deliberate and maddening precision: she extemporized gloriously.

The first plank to be cut she placed across the trestles and (having marked it with a casual pencil slash) sawed at lustily till it was about two-thirds severed. Then, moving the plank along so that the cut lay between the two trestles, she said, "Get me the sledgehammer, Tige. This is too ruddy slow."

I sped to the workshop and back, and, incredulous but hopeful, handed her the sledgehammer: with which, right on the cut, she delivered a full-blooded smash. And, in one hundredth of a second, achieved what otherwise would have taken minutes. I was ecstatic.

Thereafter, length after length of semi-sawn, one-inch planking was bashed off with the sledgehammer. We then proceeded to the more sophisticated task of assembling the butter boxes, which, following my father's explicit instructions, had to be placed one on top of the other and attached, the one to the other, with screws.

"But Eddy," my mother had protested, "nails would be miles easier."

"Nails are useless, Liz," he had contradicted. "It must be screws. And sink the heads."

So obediently, with the brace and bit, we gouged out shallow holes the size of the screw heads; but then, on my mother's wicked initiative, using a drill one gauge smaller than the screws, I bored holes with the hand drill through the bottom of each box and into the top of the next and inserted a screw into each hole, which screws my mother, using a shameless hammer, drove swiftly home.

We finished the entire wardrobe in about an hour (an operation that would have taken my father a week) and, carrying it sideways through the verandah door into my new room, past my new bed, swung it round and pushed it back against the niche.

But it didn't fit.

"Blast," said my mother, surveying corners that protruded beyond the wall by a sixteenth of an inch here and a thirty-second there. Then, "Get me the sledgehammer again."

I got it.

"Stand back."

I stood back.

And swinging purposefully, she drove the too big wardrobe back into the too small niche. One last tap and it was home, perfectly flush, both perpendicularly and horizontally.

"There you are, Tige," she said, puffing slightly and pushing back into place a loose strand of hair. "Move your things into it straight away."

I started running to collect my clothes and my treasures.

"Tige!" she called after me.

"Yes, mum?"

"Don't you *ever* tell your father."

"No, mum."

As soon as my father came home he inspected the wardrobe, testing it with his strong brown hand. "Now you know why I insisted on screws," he told us. "That's as firm as a rock. I'll make carpenters of you two yet."

Fixing me with a compelling eye, my mother changed the subject, asking my father, "Did you win?" My father spent his life fighting what were called cases, and he liked to win.

"Yes," he said, and as he talked legalities, carpentry was forgotten.

The final innovation at this time was the construction, on the back verandah of another room, and the arrival, to live in it, of our new maid-cook-nanny, a girl called Ruth.

Ruth genuinely loved children and we genuinely loved Ruth loving us. Often, when my parents were out at a party and a friend visited Ruth, she would bring this friend out onto the verandah to look at us asleep.

"Aren't they beautiful?" she would insist. "Look at Tony. Isn't he angelic?" And I, who was wide awake, would deliberately assume the aspect of a sleeping angel, relishing every word of the maudlin muck uttered by two lonely girls admiring me. I woud even turn restlessly on to my back and sigh prettily if they sounded like departing too soon, so that, fearful lest they had wakened me, they would linger, making sure that I went properly to sleep again, whispering betimes how sweet I was. I never had too much of it.

Pat, on the other hand, was so indifferent to all flattery that she actively killed it. Ribbons and bows irritated her. Bloomers she discarded as soon as she was out of sight of the accursed grown-up. Her favourite stance was legs apart, hands twined behind her back, and stomach pushed out as far as it would go. And lest anyone should think her beautiful nevertheless, she took to cutting off clumps of her hair with my mother's dressmaking shears. She resembled a famine child with the mange.

Strangely enough, this had its advantage, because something called The Depression had begun now, and one of the side effects of The Depression was a steady of stream of men coming to the front door, trying to sell things. Bootlaces, rag dolls, Turkish Delight, mops, matches — anything on which they could make a few pence profit, anything they, or their desperate wives, could manufacture at home, to be hawked round Sydney's suburban streets.

Even as a child one could sense how these young but grey and despairing men, wearing their Returned Soldiers' badges, had consciously to sink their pride as they opened one's front gate and walked down the path to the front door, hoping to sell something useless to someone who did not want it, trying not to admit the fact that every purchase made from them was an act of charity — because a household can use only so many mops, matches, rag dolls, and bootlaces; can consume only so much Turkish Delight, so many camphor balls and lavender bags.

Yet my father insisted that we buy from all these men: that I, even, must retrieve Gar's threepences and pennies from my cardboard box and buy something. So that my lid was now full of safety pins and celluloid combs and collar studs (I wasn't allowed the Turkish Delight: "It'll spoil your dinner," my mother used to say, "and anyway it's bad for your teeth"), and I grew more and more miserly.

Only Pat stemmed this constant drain on my dwindling gold reserves: because if she was on the lawn when a hawker opened the front gate, more often than not he took one look at her and left.

"What's she got?" one of them asked me as I sat outside on the grass verge, trying, by looking as if I didn't belong to our house, to save the last of my money. "The bloody plague?"

"Yes," I said, having no idea what the bloody plague was but grateful to it for protecting my fortune: and just as they left secret marks that this house was a good one for sales, so also they must have left marks that it had the bloody plague, because, after each sighting of Pat, the stream of callers would dry up for days.

Unfortunately Pat was not sighted so often as she should have been because, having abandoned poison-drinking and spider holes, she felt that hair cutting alone was not enough. As well as that, this weird child experienced a strange urge, normally found only in the bosoms of adult Australian aborigines, periodically to go walkabout.

Naturally she confided in no one at home and (having been returned to us by the postman on her first jaunt because she had confided in him) quickly learned not to confide in strangers either. Indeed she went farther than that: once embarked on a walkabout, she refused to talk at all.

Instead, she simply mounted the first strange cart or stationary vehicle she came across and then, when its driver returned, pointed pathetically. Invariably he assumed that she was pointing in the direction of her home and was begging to be taken back to it. Invariably, of course, she was not. Invariably she was driven miles from Lindfield.

Quick to sense the onset of suspicion, she always demanded to be let down before her bluff was called and then, entering the nearest front gate, would wave good-bye charmingly. And get another lift.

In her time she was handed over to the police by a milkman at Gordon, a baker at Roseville, a railway porter at Artarmon, and a steam-roller driver at Turramurra.

Little wonder, then, that one of the great terrors of my childhood was the plaintive call of crows from the wild and uninhabited gullies that stretched for miles beyond the outskirts of Lindfield. To me — even though I had been told, time after time, that it was not so — these calls sounded like Pat screaming in the distance because she was lost, possibly even drowning in some deep rock pool, eels snaking out of black crevices to snap at her and drag her down. And so, at the age of eight, I grew fiercely and devotedly protective of her. She was a pest, but rather than abandon her to the crows (which peck out the eyes of newborn lambs) and the eels, I would keep her with me.

Interrogator and prisoner faced each other for the third time. An electric fan, hanging above them, chopped listlessly at the humid air: but the major looked fresh, and his shirt, as always, was crisp and immaculate. Like his thick black hair.

"Anything you want?" he inquired, lighting a cigarette.

"I wouldn't mind some news of the outside world," the colonel replied, fighting an almost irresistible impulse to lean across the desk, snatch the cigarette, and draw deeply on it just once before passing it back. "Like who won Wimbledon?"

"That, I'm afraid, I can't tell you. But I can tell you that as of last week there are no United States servicemen stationed anywhere in the world outside of America. As a result, Indonesia yesterday abandoned her policy of the last ten years and formally applied for membership in the Greater Southeast Asian Co-Prosperity Bloc. Her President said she was prepared to sign the 1970 Treaty of Tokyo unreservedly, and has invited Chinese troops and the Japanese Navy to help her defend Irian against the Australian imperialist armies in Papua-New Guinea."

"That's ridiculous. In all of New Guinea we've got only one battalion of infantry and a battery of artillery."

"Well, you may know that, but fortunately our allies in Africa and the Middle East don't."

Surveying the unlined features of the man across the desk, the Australian saw nothing but arrogance.

"How far do you people think you can go?" he asked.

"All the way," the Asian assured him.

"You know the States and Britain'll fight for Australia, don't you?"

"We'll see, colonel. Tell me, why did your family use so many ridiculous names? Mitt, Liz, Gar, Gan, Herc, Littly, Tige. They're all ridiculous."

"Unlike Chaste Daughter of the Sighing Monsoonal Winds and Sweet Petal of the Lotus that Floats on the old Mill Stream, which is what the womenfolk in your family are probably called."

"We're discussing your background, not mine."

"In that case, you should remember, from your days at Sydney University, that Australians can't stand names of more than one syllable. They may christen their kids with polysyllabic names — but they'll call 'em Les or Des or Snow or Blue or Marge or Bett. We're a very terse race."

"A very plebeian race, surely?"

"If you like."

"But with such affectations. *Sir* David. Maids. Speech training. The right schools . . ."

"Everyone has his affectations, major."

"What I'm getting at, colonel, is that you and your sister were grossly over-privileged children."

"Of course."

"You don't dispute it?"

"Why should I? To be as happy as we were, at that time, we almost had to be over-privileged. I'm very grateful we were."

"How did your less-privileged compatriots react to you?"

"Didn't meet any as a kid."

"As an adult?"

"First time I ever encountered what you call less-privileged adults was in the army in 1940. They called me a bloody old-school-tie type."

"They resented you?"

"You didn't get to know us at all, did you? They patronized me! Until I was put on a charge for not saluting an officer: then they accepted me."

"Was that why you didn't salute your officer: to make yourself acceptable?"

"I didn't salute him because I'd been at school with him. He'd been an idiot then, and he hadn't changed."

"So even in the ranks of the army you were aware of your innate superiority?"

"I was aware of everyone's innate superiority to this bloke I'd been at school with."

"But you *were* an old school-tie type?"

"Oh yes."

"And it doesn't, in retrospect, bother you?"

"Nothing, in retrospect, bothers me."

"Your life's been so blameless?"

"Look — I am what I am. I accept *me*. I am reconciled to my many failings. That's why you're going to make a balls-up of this job. There's nothing you can tell me about me that's worse than I already know: and I've already accepted all I know."

"That sounds complacent."

"Don't be such a prig. Until a man's prepared to admit what a wicked bastard he's been — and probably still is — he's not fit to judge anyone. That applies to you as much as me."

"Prig or not, I can still see that Australia, in the late twenties and early thirties, was strongly anti-American."

"As she has been in the late sixties and early seventies. As you Chinese have been since the year dot. Being anti is the one thing all races are good at. Australians are specially good at it."

"Strange. You sit there, exuding honesty, yet as a child you were obviously a terrible liar."

"Yes, wasn't I?" The colonel looked complacent and sounded pleased.

"Why, do you think?"

"I think really I wasn't lying so much as trying to bridge the gap between our childish world, which we knew off by heart, and the fabulous world of grown-ups, from which we were excluded. So I used to take grown-up words like battened down, with no idea what they meant, and try to weave them into the fabric of my own experience. Result: fantasy."

"Showing off?"

"Yes."

"Which your father forbade?"

"Quite so."

"Is that why your games in the hayloft, with Vernon, were secret?"

"Is what why?"

"Because you did something forbidden?"

"No, I don't remember it being that."

"Then what *were* your secret games?"

"An endless killing. We were snipers shooting Huns at Passchendaele. We were goodies fighting baddies. We were settlers attacked by Red Indians. Altogether we must have killed about ten thousand mixed Huns, villains, and Blackfoots. But we always shot them. No stabbing. No buckets of blood."

"Why?"

"Vernon's father owned a station — farm — outside Inverell. We used to go there occasionally, to ride, God help me . . ."

"You still hated it?"

"Horses still hated me. And I hated sheep. Their stupidity, and the appalling resignation of them. Anyway, it was seeing a sheep killed that gave me this thing about knives. The cook said we needed more meat — chops for breakfast and mutton for dinner: you know how it is in the bush — so before we went out to mend fences, one of the hands collared a sheep, sat it up on its backside, between his knees, yanked its head back, and then *sawed* his way, with a knife, through the short wool into the poor brute's throat. It twitched a bit, but that's all. Didn't fight. As if it knew it was done for. And while this bloke slit right round its throat — a leathery noise it made on the blade — which was all red and wet — it just stared up at him with a sort of reproachful look in its stupid, yellow eyes. Shocking eyes, they were. Agonized but thoughtless. Anyway, a last slash and a last yank, and it was dead, spouting blood, and its neck broken.

"It only took about five seconds altogether. But I lived all of them. On behalf of the stupid bloody sheep. And I've hated knives ever since. Even killing flatheads, I hated after that. The crunching between the squinted eyes.

"It's the time factor bothers me. The time of pain before death. To think about how much worse it can get.

"Shooting, though, was different. I mean, they shot a bull the day after the sheep was killed, and we watched from another paddock about half a mile away, and first the bull collapsed on his belly, as if his legs had been cut from under him, and then we heard the *crack* of the rifle. Instantaneous, that was. And no gore at all. We rode down to the paddock to see what they did with him, and do you know what the first thing was?"

"No."

"They slit open his genitals and cut out the whole of his penis. Bound with plaited leather, they said, it made a marvellous stockwhip handle. But the atmosphere was completely sexual. Not smutty, and not clinical, but sexual. They were all joking and laughing, but they were excited by what they cut out of the bull."

"Were you?"

"I was curious."

"Are you saying you already knew the facts of . . . ?"

"No. But a curiosity was developing."

"You were an unusually self-centred child, weren't you?"

"If you say so."

"How else explain the exhibition you provided so regularly for Ruth and her visitor as you lay in bed?"

The colonel looked indignant. "I did it to please Ruth."

"To make Ruth like you more than ever?"

"That's not true. In those days I'd been so strictly brought up I found it impossible to do anything other people would dislike. For example, I could never openly *disagree* with anyone because no one had taught me how to disagree politely."

"Are you saying you never did anything you were told not to?"

"Christ, no. But if ever I went against the will of a grown-up, I wrapped it up in words that were either ambiguous or untrue. I got very good at it. It was a difficult habit to break."

"But you feel you *have* broken it?" the major probed.

"Oh yes," the colonel told him quietly. "As I said, I'm now reconciled to me. I don't have to be devious any longer. In fact, after words, that's my best defence against you and your methods."

"So you're not afraid of my methods?"

"Not what I've seen of them."

"Well, perhaps, as you continue your writing," the major snapped, closing his dossier, "you will give some slight thought to the fact that so far you've seen very little."

The uncles and aunts — though I have mentioned them little lately — were always with us. The War seemed to have created a harsh bond between the uncles that grew tighter with the years; even though, nowadays, they talked less about the Front than they did about Kingsford Smith, unemployment, and someone called That Bugger Lang.

Working bees were part of the bond. Thus, my father wanted thirty feet of hill excavated from under the back of our house, to make a garage: a working bee of all the uncles dug it.

Uncle Roy wanted a ruinous patch of sloping weed turned into a lawn-tennis court: a working bee of all the uncles levelled and turfed and made the court.

Uncle Phil wanted a septic tank sunk in his back garden: a working bee of all the uncles dug the deep hole, and erected tripods and pulleys, and lowered the heavy concrete tank deep into the red, gas-smelling clay. Similarly, they worked on one another's cars, helped one another move house, felled one another's unwanted trees.

They worked in bare feet, khaki shorts and shirts — the week-end uniform of the young family man. Not that I thought them young: I just thought them grown-up. They were provided by the aunts with beer at regular intervals, and with tea and hot buttered scones and fresh sponge cakes at four o'clock. They formed a circle of friends, which seemed never to expand and which could be diminished only by death.

Perhaps that is why, the day he collapsed in court, first clutching his head in his hands and then becoming unconscious, three of the uncles drove my father home and carried him from the back seat of the car so tenderly and with such evident distress.

I watched two of them carry him, lifting him, limp, off that back seat, handling him carefully, up the verandah steps, manœuvring him through the verandah door into his bedroom; whilst a third uncle followed, carrying the long, narrow-folded document, bound with pink tape, which was the brief my father had been pleading when he collapsed; whilst my mother stood aside, jaws clenched, forcing herself to say nothing, to leave them to it.

I watched them come out of the bedroom and return to the car, frowning and shaking their heads, as if to say, "This can't happen to one of us, not after we survived the Somme and Passchendaele and the Spanish flu": but I knew really they were thinking, "If it can happen to Mitt, it can happen to any of us."

But when they had gone, leaving me, their hidden witness, acutely infected with their anxiety, my mother came out and dispelled my fears.

"Your father's very tired," she explained. "He's been working too hard. Do you think you and Pat could be good and play quietly?"

Pat rose to the occasion gallantly. "Tell daddy," she said, "I won't scream till he's better."

"*Dear* Littly," mum said and hugged her. But I knew better. Pat only screamed to get my father to wallop me even though my mother, at the first shrill, still walloped her. With my father incapacitated, the only walloper would be my mother: so naturally, for the moment, dear Littly would abstain.

Uncle Dick's wife, Aunty Helen, returned from America with my two cousins, Betty Lou and Molly Jane. Both girls had acquired strong Texan accents, which confirmed in my bosom all those prejudices against the United States aroused by cars my father wouldn't buy and claims to have won the War that were palpably false.

"I can't understand a word they say," my father declared. "They've got worse voices even than Clara Bow. If either of you children ever sound like that, I shall disown and disinherit you."

"What's disown and disinherit?" I asked.

"Cut you off without a penny and forbid you ever to darken my doorstep again," he told me ominously, so that for a while I became very wary of our guests.

However, prejudice soon died when confronted with the tomboyish vitality of both girls (Betty Lou, my contemporary, half killed me in our first fight) and with the presents they brought me from America.

These were two books about Doctor Dolittle which I found entrancing: I read them twice each; then turned to the books my father had had as a child, which now stood on the shelves of the wardrobe my mother had built me. Mainly these were *The Children's Encyclopædia* and a series about a magnificent Red Indian called Deerfoot. If I had been entranced by Doctor Dolittle, I became obsessed by Deerfoot.

In the encyclopædia what I liked best was the heroic series entitled "Golden Deeds" — of which I now seem unable to remember any, except Grace Darling rowing to rescue someone from somewhere in a fearsome gale; and a fanatical Greek (or was he a Roman?), for some splendid cause that now escapes me, plunging his hand into a fire and allowing it to be burned off.

Having been thus introduced by my girl cousins to literature, I never again had to whine, "Mum, what can I do?" (to which, in the past, callously, she had always replied, "Go for a run round the block"). Henceforth I could read. Any book whetted my appetite and, noticing the absorption with which my parents were reading *All Quiet on the Western Front* and *Anthony Adverse*, I even started them.

And would have abandoned them at chapter one had not my father, suddenly aware of what I was reading, exclaimed, "Christ Almighty," and, snatching them from me, hidden them. The following day I found them — on top of a high wardrobe — and for weeks after that I made regular excursions into my parents' bedroom (when my father was at work and my mother busy at her sewing machine or playing tennis), climbed up on a chair, retrieved both novels, and flogged my way through chapter after chapter. Until at last I came to the irreversible decision that grown-up books were boring. So I returned them to the top of the wardrobe and forgot them.

A parental acquisition that could not be forgotten, however, was a large and splendid dog called Peter, purchased to protect our household from burglaries — of which, lately, we had suffered two.

Unfortunately, Peter never properly understood the role he was expected to play, thinking that it was merely to please us, and attempting to do so by regularly bringing us dead chickens from our neighbours' chook yards, which embarrassed us and infuriated our neighbours.

So we put a long lead on his collar and attached it to the back-yard clothesline, which left him considerable room for manœuvre but none for chicken-foraging.

Taking this as a slur on his character, Peter used the room for manœuvre to station himself constantly at the foot of the steep steps leading up to the back verandah. Up these steps, daily, went the milkman (with his shining pail, from which, with pint or half-pint measure, he poured one's order, frothing and creamy, into the family jug) and the baker (whose warm, crisp loaves lay in a wire basket). Daily Peter bit them both.

So his lead was shortened. Whereupon he first bit all our friends, and then all of us. When my father saw the deep blue punctures in Pat's calf, he gave Peter, as a present, to a passing swagman. Together swaggie and Peter marched away from our house up the road. At the corner, by the vacant lot, Peter bit his new master — and, screaming at each other, the two vanished down the hill past the house where Billy Hughes lived.

That Christmas we drove up to Port Macquarie again, this time in a new Vauxhall. Sometimes, midst much grown-up excitement, both when my father drove and when my mother drove, we touched seventy-five miles an hour; but all the time, for Pat and myself, the trip was an interminable bore.

Just to get forty miles to Wiseman's Ferry, on the Hawkesbury River, was bad enough. But then, having at last crossed on the ferry, you had to drive to Gosford; and after Gosford to Newcastle; and from Newcastle to West Maitland; from West Maitland to Gloucester; from Gloucester almost to Taree; and from there, finally, to Port Macquarie. All Pat and I did was watch for hundreds upon hundreds of stone mileposts, Pat demanding tartly as we passed each one, "Well, are we nearly there *yet?*"

All the grown-ups did was talk about the Vauxhall; and gasp at the beauty of the Hawkesbury, the pastoral richness of the Hunter River Valley, and the wildness of the Bucket Mountains; and stop on the dusty road outside derelict wooden buildings called pubs, from which they would bring us soft drinks that made Pat sick; or pull up on sharp mountain bends and say to each other, "Look at that view." Views, I decided — like *Anthony Adverse* and *All Quiet on the Western Front* — were a grown-up bore.

Port Macquarie had not changed. The doctor's dog still swung on the tails of galloping and distraught cows; the blue pilot launch still bustled in and out across the bar; the church and the graves and the underground dungeons still reminded of different days.

The moment we arrived my father changed to khaki shorts and a shirt, and thereafter, at all times, was seen in nothing else. Once at dinner time in the boarding house, my mother protested, "Edward — you look like a tramp. Put a tie on." So he left the table and returned with three ties on. After that, most of the men in the boarding house came to dinner in bare feet, khaki shorts and a shirt, and when their wives nagged, retorted that if it was good enough for Mitt it was good enough for them — though only he used an old tie as a belt and fish hooks as fly buttons.

Much better dressed was Gar, who stayed at a hotel and always wore an elaborately swathed, swirling skirted, darkly floral, gauzy sort of gown of something called *voile,* and a big black hat and amber beads. We used to visit her every day and tell her how far we could swim now — at which she would fling her hands up in utter amazement and say, "You can't?" and give us the money to buy an ice cream each from the dago's when we insisted boastfully, "Yes we can."

She also used to nag my father about his money in the Bank.

"Mitt," she used to say, "have you taken your money out of the Bank yet?"

"Oh mater, for God's sake," he used to say, "not that again."

"Well," she used to reply, a bit huffily, "when that man Lang shuts down the Bank, and you lose all your savings, don't say I didn't warn you."

On the way to the boat-shed from my grandmother's hotel, my father invariably complained about his mother's "lunatic conviction that she knows *any*thing about economics."

"She means well," my mother would assure him.

The fishing was as engrossing as ever and was made more comfortable by the fact that my father had bought an outboard motor to attach to the back of the boat-shed's rowing boat. This saved not only energy but time — time which was spent in almost daily visits to Flinders' Beach to practise the growing cult of surfing.

A convoy of cars would drive the few miles from the boarding house to the beach and would park off the red dirt road under the shade of dusty pine trees. Crude, lantana-scented steps, cut into the crumbling wall that dropped forty feet from the roadside, led down to a small crescent of sand backed by grass and scrub. The men swam far out, seeking the big curling waves that would carry them shoulder-skiing back to the beach; the women breast-stroked more decorously; Pat went farthest out, clinging to my father's back. On the way, encountering fierce oncoming walls of foam, my father would dive forward, hard and deep, and some of the women would mutter, "He'll drown that child." But each time, as his black head surfaced, a small, sleek, blond head could be seen nestling between his right ear and shoulder: and they would swim on, happily.

I, in fact, was the one who nearly drowned. The men were playing cricket, with a tennis ball and a bat that one of the fathers had given to his son (and then used constantly himself, as fathers do), and the ball was hit over square leg — where I fielded — and into the sea.

It was no more than ten feet from dry sand, so I ran into the shallow water to retrieve it — and abruptly sank. I was in a deep gutter that ran parallel to the beach for about five yards and then swung out past the rocks: and the rip in this gutter flowed strong and fast away from Australia towards New Zealand.

With the tennis ball in one hand, I began swimming confidently enough towards the beach: and it was almost with detachment that I observed that I was proceeding backwards, fast.

The first to realize my danger was my mother, who started running hard down the beach. Still swimming, and still speeding out to sea, I watched those long legs striding. Always before, it had been across a tennis court, zestfully, to the accompaniment of a giggle of joy barely suppressed. Now — it distressed me — it was frantic and ter-rifyingly sacrificial. Looking at her face, as she plunged into the gutter and started swimming towards me, I realized that she was prepared to die. I had never seen a look like that before: and I cried the instant I saw it now. For both of us.

Then, in an explosion of decisive muscularity, the men acted. My father soared into the water, reached my mother, and, swimming with the rip, forced her to the rocks of the small headland; three of the uncles, having sprinted to the farthest rock of the headland, just as I was being dragged past it, linked hands, and the last of them, reaching far out, seized my left arm while the other two, by hauling him upright, yanked me out of the sea.

My mother, silent but purposeful, was on me in an instant, carry-ing me back over the rocks, across the sand, and up to the grass under the stunted trees. Suddenly I felt weak and shocked, glad to be towelled and dressed. My mother said nothing, drying and dressing me methodically. Pat watched, round-eyed. Then my father picked me up and carried me up the crude cliffside steps to the car, my mother and Pat behind us: and no one said anything. Unbidden and uncomplaining, Pat got into the back of the car, alone, as my mother took her seat in the front and held out her arms. I was handed to her — into her arms, onto her lap, my head against her breast — and, as my father started the car, reversing and then spinning onto the red dirt road, I heard liquid stirrings in the breast against my ear: but no one spoke. And I went to sleep.

When I woke it was dark, and I was in my verandah bed outside my parents' boarding-house room. My mother was sitting on the bed (changed now into a cotton dress, her brown hair brushed smooth and coiled in a plait round her head), and she held my hand. My father sat on Pat's bed, Pat huddled upright close against him.

"All right?" my mother asked, quietly but matter-of-factly.

"Yes," I told her.

"Good," she said and, bending over me, kissed me. Pat rushed across and kissed me too — on the eye — and my father, grinning wryly, tweaked my chin and put her back to bed. Then he and my mother stood arm in arm, looking at me for a moment.

"Now go to sleep, both of you," my mother ordered. "It's very late."

Together she and my father walked into their bedroom, and I twisted my head round to watch them.

They stopped, and quite abruptly my mother turned towards my father and dropped her head on his shoulder. He put his arms around her, patting her shoulder with one hand. For a moment they stood like that, still, except for the patting of his hand. Then he reached out and closed the door.

A familiar voice breathed across from the other verandah bed.

"Tone?"

"What?"

"I want to sleep with you." She didn't wait for answer but plodded across and clambered in beside me.

"Mummy said," she told me, "next time those silly buggers of men want to play cricket so close to the water, they can fetch their own bloody balls."

"Pat!"

"Well, *mummy* said it."

I had by now been at a preparatory school for a year, and Pat had started at kindergarten (where she had acquired friends and stopped cutting off clumps of hair and going walkabout. I think she must have done both because she was lonely; or because she needed attention). She became much more civilized at Mrs Ruthven's School for Infants.

I, at my preparatory school, on the other hand, became much less civilized. On the first day there I had been ordered to sing for some bigger boys and, for refusing, had been required to fight an opponent older, taller, and heavier than myself who split my lip and bred in me a powerful and undying dislike of compulsion.

To get to school each day I had to walk a mile. Which was half a mile beyond my cousins' house (they used to wait for me each morning) down a gentle slope, then up a short sharp rise, and then quite a long way to the right, until the road plunged down into a gully and laboured its way steeply up the other side. There, at the top of the hill, where housing and civilization had faded into straggling scrubland, stood the school — facing out over miles of wild crown land and virgin bush like a frontier fortress.

In front of this school were a tennis court, a dressing shed, and a playing field (whose surface was almost entirely shale). To the right, below the level of the school, was a swimming pool. Surrounding the playing field and the pool, as the terrain dropped sharply into a valley, was bush a million years old extending, blackish-green and deeply slashed, for miles in every direction. For the next four years all our activities were to be dominated by it.

The headmaster even used it as he taught us. Not for him the dreary desk: instead, he had us out on the playing field, marching up and down, towards the bush and away from it, rhythmically chanting multiplication tables, weights and measures, French and Latin verbs, and the dates of all the English monarchs, starting at "William the First, 1066 to 1087" and ending up with "George the Fifth, 1910 and still going strong."

Round and round we marched, chanting:

> *"Eleven eights are 88*
> *Eleven nines are 99*
> *Eleven tens are 110 . . ."*

or

> *"Sixteen ounces, one pound*
> *Fourteen pounds, one stone*
> *Two stone, one quarter*

Four quarters, one hundredweight
Twenty hundredweights, one ton" . . .

or

"Amo amas amat
Amamus amatis amant . . ."

Joyously, as we chanted, the headmaster, his black gown billowing, striding and intoning, switching from one part of our repertoire to another, would lead us to the very edge of the playing field and then straight off it — all of us stumping after him down its steep embankment of shale and onto the narrow bush track, marking time and shouting, *"Twelve inches, one foot; three feet, one yard,"* as we formed single file and then strode off again, along the track, under the gums and geebungs and banksias, *"Mensa, mensa, mensam,"* past the waratah and bottle brush, *"William the Fourth, 1830 to 1837; Queen Victoria, 1837 to 1901; Edward the Seventh, 1901 to 1910; George the Fifth, 1910 and still going strong,"* join the track that led up from the swimming pool, *"je suis tu es il est; nous sommes vous êtes ils sont,"* and back into the classroom, standing by our desks, marking time, till everyone had arrived, *"one rood, pole or perch."*

Learning with the Boss was sheer physical exhilaration. In winter time we chanted at the double, running round both the oval and our curriculum. And always, when we got back to our desks, there was a spelling bee or a mental arithmetic bee when, arbitrarily, the Boss would divide us into two teams, which stood facing each other, he in between them.

"How many feet in one furlong, twenty-one yards?" he would ask; and effortlessly the answer would come to us: "Seven hundred and twenty-three, sir." The test lay not in getting the answer right but in shouting it first.

"How many pounds in one ton, two hundredweight, three quarters?"

"Two thousand five hundred and forty-eight, sir."

"How many pence in eighteen and eleven?"

"Two hundred and twenty-seven, sir."

"Who reigned in 1099?"

"William the Second, sir."

"In 1353?"

"Edward the Third, sir."

"What's the Third Book of the Old Testament?"

"Leviticus, sir."

And so on, till our restless spirits and small tough bodies tired a little: then he would let us sit down — and teach us.

After school each day it was home with the cousins, Peter and Bill; either to their house or mine. Immediately on arrival, shoes and socks were shed, a peremptory shout of "Mum?" elicited the advice that the respective parent was either in or out, and our games began.

These had become considerably more sophisticated since the preceding Christmas (which had yielded all of us tennis racquets and Meccano sets, and me a camera and a miniature donkey engine as well), with the result that Jean had to pursue us less frequently with her riding crop and my mother had less occasion to lay about her with her open hand. Not even grown-ups could take exception to three small boys devotedly learning the rudiments of tennis on the cousins' court, or harnessing the power of a miniature donkey engine to a complicated Meccano system of pulleys and gantrys that lifted ever-increasing loads (until eventually the whole contraption collapsed under the strain — and we began again) up onto my back verandah from the garden twelve feet below.

Still less could they take exception to our making crystal wireless sets. Sharing the earphones from a head set, we would spend hours happily listening to static — which our minds translated instantly into the sounds of battlefields, racing cars, and ships at sea.

Not, of course, that these were our sole activities. The bush still fascinated us and, under its influence, we made endless bows and arrows, constantly experimenting with different materials and techniques in a vain search for the accuracy that had been both Robin Hood's and Deerfoot's.

The parents did not discourage us in this but simply ordered the girls to keep well out of our way. Inevitably Pat was the only casualty. Peter and Bill and I were shooting at a target fixed to the broad pink trunk of the gum tree in our back yard when my feckless sister, appearing from nowhere, wandered into the line of fire and caught my finest nail-headed arrow between the shoulders. She uttered not a sound as I plucked it out, not a sound as I took her to our flint-faced mother, and not a sound as iodine was poured into the wound.

"Serves you *right*," our mother told her. "You've been warned often enough." When the first aid was done we returned to the garden together; and as we walked Pat reached up to take my hand.

"I had to take you to mum," I excused myself. "If you don't put iodine on, you get lockjaw." She just held my hand and walked silently. "The nail was rusty," I elaborated. She just held my hand and walked silently. "Rusty nails are awful for lockjaw." Silence. "Pat!" — in desperation.

"What?" she inquired, halting and looking implacably up at me, knowing she had won.

"I'm sorry."

"Gimme a shoot of your bow'n arrow then," she demanded: and so, at last, triumphed in the diplomatic battle she had been waging for months.

Pat divided her free time equally between some little girls who lived down the road and were Christian Scientists, the mongrel puppy that had just been given to her for her fifth birthday, and myself: and to all of us she offered her unstinted affection.

Because her friends were Christian Scientists, Pat amiably attended a Christian Science Sunday school and greeted every wound which subsequently she incurred (and she was constantly bloody and wounded) with the phlegmatic assertion that God was Love and There was no Pain.

Because her puppy was a mongrel, she called it Tripe and lavished upon it all the grooming due to a champion spaniel, under the influence of which Tripe grew from a diminutive puppy into a big, broad-chested, quizzical-browed, and passionately friendly dog who, unlike Peter, had no enemies. Tradesmen, hawkers, beggars, burglars, relatives, honorary uncles and aunts, adults and children — indiscriminately he loved them all, and greeted all of them with a tongue like an anteater's. With one kiss, as he leaped with joy, Tripe used to lather your face from ear to ear; and although those who were not vehemently taken aback by this unabashed sentimentality were few and far between, Pat was not only not taken aback by it, she returned it, kiss for kiss, with relish.

Tripe's one vice was that he hated motorcars.

A car would approach: Tripe would career up the drive, effort-lessly hurdle the six-foot front gate, and crouch by the roadside. The car would pass: and Tripe would hurl himself into pursuit, snapping at the car's front tyre, screaming his hatred of inanimate things that moved, bluffing dog lover after dog lover (for fear of hurting him) into driving slower and slower (he screaming louder than ever then), until eventually — completely intimidated — his victim braked to a halt.

"Tripe!" one of my parents would bellow, and he would look around, delighted with himself, affectionate as always. "Come here."

Always then, although all this had happened fifty times before, he would come, eyes gleaming with innocent joy, stumpy tail vibrating with friendliness.

"Sit!"

He would sit.

"*Bad* dog."

Unrepentantly he would kiss the parental foot.

Then he would be walloped. Which, like Pat, he suffered silently, showing neither malice nor remorse. And no sooner was it done than he was out on the road again, chasing cars.

The time Pat spent with me (rather than with her Christian Scien-tists or her dog) she spent as partner in my balancing act, pillion passenger on my small bicycle, and model for my camera. I had been inspired to the balancing act by a travelling circus in Port Mac-quarie, and Pat and I spent hours on the front lawn trying to perfect the art. I used to lie on my back, extending my arms rigidly upwards, and instruct her, having placed her hands on mine, to stand on her head. She never hesitated. Just swung her legs upwards — and crashed to the ground when I dropped her.

So then, as I lay, I would tell her to put her hands on my raised knees, and from them to stand on her head: but my knees always buckled and still she would crash to the ground. It was typical of her chivalry towards me that she never either rebuked me (although, on her own, she could stand on her hands for hours) or disdained my frequent suggestions that we try again.

As a pillion rider on my bicycle (sitting astride a small rack, de-signed for parcels, behind my saddle) she was without fear but also without prudence. As often as not, as we hurtled down Nelson Road, she would dig both hands into my ribs and tickle me, which delighted her. But it also paralyzed me, which neither of us liked because then we fell off. The road was hard, its blue metal abrasive, and there are few sights more derisory than one's bicycle lying on its side, its wheels furiously spinning. Yet, bleeding and infuriated as I invariably was, I could never sufficiently overcome my devotion to the maniacal cause of it all to kill her.

Much safer than cycling with Pat was taking photographs of her — of which there were hundreds. Indeed, I never photographed anyone or anything else. To my eye, Pat was beautiful. So I would pose her, and look at her through the box camera's view finder, and see a vision of flaxen hair and blue eyes and pink skin and tiny white teeth under soft red lips that was the incarnation of sweetness and laughter and dotty determination; and I would photograph it. But when my film was developed, what confronted me always was a grey and distant little girl standing legs apart, hands behind her back and stomach out, looking unspeakably ordinary. So we would start again. I never lost my romantic vision of her: and I never captured what I saw.

Later I sought to create beauty in other ways. First by modelling clay — with which, a million times over, I attempted to create a butterfly. When I found that clay crumbled as soon as it began to dry, I remembered the technique used by the road builders as they laid their newfangled concrete roads and, using a skeleton of wire as reinforcement, pressed the wet clay into that: but still it crumbled: and still I created nothing.

For years I had this simple, lovely ambition — to mould with my fingers a lump of wet orange clay (from our back garden) into the shape of the tiny body and thin powdery wings of a butterfly. Then to let the clay bake in the sun until it became hard and strong and perfect. And finally, with my water colours, to paint it with the living colours of the bush. But all I ever got was dust.

The child's desire to create must be inextinguishable because my failures with both camera and clay deterred me not at all: I simply turned to other media.

In my head I heard glorious music — a mixture of the Chopin my mother played, the Negro spirituals on thick Edison discs reproduced by Gar's old phonograph, and the contemporary "Parlez Moi d'Amour" by Lucienne Boyer about which my father raved — so I sat at my mother's grand piano (a Steinway of satiny rosewood) and let my fingers wander over the keyboard as my mother's fingers so effortlessly wandered. But the glorious music in my head always vanished before I could translate it, and my fingers (forgetting at the last instant how to reproduce the fluid but precise touch of my mother's long fingers) always fumbled: and I played a thumping, discordant nonsense.

One ivory at a time, I could pick out a tune easily enough: but a tune as lacking in substance and colour as wet clay lacked the form and fragility of butterflies.

"Look, Tige," my mother said at last, "if you really want to play the piano, you'd better learn properly": and began teaching me.

I was desperately willing to learn: but not so slowly. I needed her kind of pianoforte at once. She laughed at that. "Well, you won't get it," she promised. "Till I married your father, I practised four or five hours a day to play like this. And I still practise."

It was true, she did. Scales and things called arpeggios and études, some of which had her eyes darting from the sheet music to her fingers and back to the music again, her jaw clenched tight, the way it was when she ran for a wide shot at tennis — only tighter.

"How long will it be before I can play music?" I demanded.

"A long time."

But I couldn't wait a long time! I needed to make something — a photograph that was Pat; a butterfly that was a butterfly; a tune that was music — then.

So I took up drawing and painting. But the only things I could draw at all satisfactorily were aeroplanes and sailing ships: and it was countless aeroplanes and sailing ships later before I understood that these were not what I needed. They were just something I did; not anything of which I was part. In them there was none of that red sheen one saw on young gum leaves when the sun hit them slantingly. None of those antipodean sunset clouds, black with the night to which they are about to give birth, yet laced all round with a thin border of pure, fiery gold. Nothing that I really knew. What I needed was to make something that transported me — like my canopy at

Bowral, like looking into slanted slabs of gold-flecked water, like
nearly drowning — but I could do it with neither pencil nor brush.

So I acquired thousands of silkworms and fed them mulberry
leaves and cosseted them in cardboard boxes until the first of them
began spinning themselves into their yellow cocoons. Then I unspun
the fine, fine thread and wound it onto old cotton spools from my
mother's sewing basket, feeling suddenly elated. With this pure silk
— golden-blond to the eye and exciting just to touch — I knew at
last that I could make something. A magical cloth, a canopy even.
Something.

But then Tripe ate all my silkworms — and the artist in me died.
From that day onwards, instead of trying again for myself, I let my
mother make my music, books feed my imagination, and movies become my magic.

One of the reasons movies meant magic was that I was hardly ever
allowed to go to them.

"Can I go to the pictures, mum?" I would ask, greatly daring,
about once a month.

"Ask your father," she would say.

"Can I go to the pictures, dad?" I would ask.

"*No*," he would tell me.

In case he should ever feel inclined to say yes, though, he decided
that I would now, at the age of ten, be paid threepence pocket money
a week. With this I was thereafter (as to such sybaritic pleasures as
sweets and the pictures) to be self-supporting: but I had to work
every morning to earn it.

On week-day mornings I had to go round the outside of the house,
examining every nook and cranny and garden and gutter, and tidy
away those bits of paper, and matches, and broken branches, and
dead flowers that are scattered each night by evil spirits who hate
anything immaculate; and on week-end mornings I had to clean up
after my father who was the messiest pruner, hedge-cutter, mower
of lawns, and fixer of mechanical defects ever to inflict himself upon
a dutiful son.

Nor was that all. My contract with my father contained (as one would expect in a contract drawn up by a brilliant lawyer) a number of penalty clauses that could wipe out my weekly earnings in a matter of seconds. Thus:

> If, when he came home from work at night, he could prove that our garden was in any way untidy, I was fined a penny.
> If, at the week-end, when he asked for a certain spanner, I handed him the wrong one, I was fined a penny.
> If, at any time, I said farve instead of five, I must go down to the back fence and say the word properly ten times, and forfeit a penny.
> Likewise for any other mispronounced vowel sound.
> If, at any time, I said something was "that big" or "*that* anything else" (instead of "as big as that") I was fined a penny.
> And if, at any time, I asked for a "lend" of something, rather than a "loan," I was fined threepence. (My father could not abide people who asked for a lend of anything.)

In consequence of all these provisos, I was usually well in debt by the time I completed my week's work and therefore financially incapable of going to the pictures unless Gar happened either to have visited us or to have had us to lunch at Edgecliff.

Of the two, I preferred her visits to us, because then I could wait for her on the corner by the vacant lot and, when she swung into our part of Tryon Road in her big Buick, try to race her the seventy-five yards to our front gate. I would run in my bare feet — and feel almost that I could fly. I was at that unique age where physical lightness and fleetness combine to give the illusion that one skims rather than runs; and I found a wild, sensual joy in it. At my fastest, I would spread out my arms and leap — at which instant, though I never wholly *expected* to take off and fly, I should never have been in the least surprised if I had.

Gar would pull up at our gate, Tripe snapping and screaming at her front tyres, and I would rush to her and she would say, "Darling — you ran *like the wind*. My *good*ness how fast you can run. *Just* like the wind." And I loved her, because only she appreciated that I felt like the wind when I ran.

Hysterical with joy at seeing her again, Tripe would leap up and kiss her across the face. "Aah," she would crow, in that voice which perpetual enthusiasm, bronchitis, sinus infection, and the wear and tear of age had made so fascinating; and would splutter and mop the kisses away. "No, you naughty dog. Down." So he would kiss Pat instead, who, devotedly, would kiss him back.

"Oh, Pat darling, *no!*" Gar once implored. "You'll catch terrible things doing that."

"What terrible things?"

"Terrible things like rabies and psittacosis and hydrophobia, darling. Now promise Gar you won't do it any more, because Gar would hate her beautiful little girl to catch hydrophobia."

Later that week I mentioned casually to my cousins that my grandmother had had rabies and psittacosis and hydrophobia.

"When?" Peter cross-examined suspiciously.

"When she was in the Far East," I told him — which finished that discussion since neither of us knew what the Far East was. On our maps, it was America: but Gar denied flatly that she had been to America since 1917.

Armed with Gar's money, I would approach my father and ask could I go to the pictures: and he would look up from his inevitable brief, his black Swan fountain pen poised from its underlining and annotating, and say no, children should be outside in the fresh air not sitting in stuffy picture shows, and anyway we had to learn the value of money which didn't just grow on trees, you know, specially since That Bugger Lang had closed the Bank.

Every Saturday thereafter I would explain that I had money of my own and ask again could I go to the pictures, until he said yes. Then Pat and I would go to the Lindfield Theatre to experience magic.

What was most marvellous to me was a blank screen being rendered suddenly animated and full of sound by nothing more substantial than a mote-filled wedge of light. But everything else was marvellous too. The insecticide smell of the place, its perpetual gloom, the rush for matinee seats, the ice cream at the interval, the sloping floor, the sense of losing oneself like a moth in the vast darkness, of being fascinated like a moth by that wedge of dusty light suspended on its side between the invisible tip-up seats and the invisible gilded dome. All of it was indescribably exciting — even Pat croaked, "Tone — I got to go," and I having to take her yet again. And to emerge from it, into the flat, prosaic glare of late-afternoon sunshine, was always to experience bitter disenchantment.

Such moments, though, were rare. Peter and Bill and I (like everyone else at our school) were given bicycles, and the time-wasting drudgery of walking vanished from our lives. We rode to school; we rode at school; we rode home after school; we rode far out into the bush; we rode to tennis lessons; we rode for the plain pleasure of riding.

At school itself we still clumped up and down the oval, chanting tables and dates and verbs and anything else the Boss wanted to pound painlessly into our fertile but slippery minds; but as well as the Boss, we now had two subordinate masters, each of whom was brilliant.

One of them, a dapper man who taught us English and French and copperplate writing, seemed old and faintly ridiculous; but, sensing this, he one day called a halt to our lesson and challenged the biggest boy at the school — who was twelve and had pubic hair — to a race over a hundred yards.

Out to the oval went he and the hairy boy, and all of us hairless ones with them. As he took off his jacket we arranged ourselves on both sides of the course, and he ordered the second biggest boy at school to give the starting signal, and the two smallest boys at school to hold a piece of string across the finishing line. Then, looking decidedly ridiculous in his long trousers and his highly polished tan shoes and his long shirt sleeves and his waistcoat with the watch chain across it, this old man knelt down, like sprinters do at the beginning of a race — only he was nearly bald and the hairy boy knelt beside him.

"Get ready," ordered the second biggest boy. "Get set . . . Go!" And off they dashed, the hairy boy leading by yards and all of us laughing and cheering. Well, jeering really. Jeering the old, balding, loping man in the shirt sleeves and waistcoat with the watch chain across it.

But in the last forty yards the old, balding man began to grin ferociously and, lengthening his stride, first caught up with and then flashed past his rival — whom he beat to the finishing line by yards.

"Well run, lad," he congratulated the hairy boy, shaking him by the hand: and respectfully we gave him back his jacket. Hardly panting at all, he put it on and ordered us to return to our desks: and we never again considered him ridiculous but referred to him invariably, with genuine admiration, as Streaker.

The other master was Mr Beatty — a much younger, fitter, and more fanatical man, whom we promptly dubbed Beatles.

Beatles coached us at cricket and rugby as if we were adult sportsmen; drilled us in military formations as if we were guardsmen; taught us entire operas by Gilbert and Sullivan as if we were ardent thespians; became our scoutmaster and cubmaster, initiating us into a troop lore of his own in which there was as much of the Australian bush and Kipling's Mowgli as there was of Baden-Powell; taught us semaphore and Morse, first aid and rifle drill, rope-splicing and wood-carving.

With the advent of Beatles into our children's life, the week-end ceased to be a time spent wholly with our parents: Saturday mornings were now devoted to competitive sport against other schools and tended to blur over into the afternoon, with me going to the cousins' place or them coming to mine.

Sunday, though, remained firmly parental and meant, nowadays, driving to Uncle Roy's place, where all the grown-ups played tennis and I hung around praying that, between sets or at afternoon tea time, someone would have a hit-up with me. Which no one ever did.

If the tennis was bad, I would climb the loquat trees at the top of Uncle Roy's chook yard and eat the firm yellow fruit. I did not like loquats, but I found eating them less boring than watching bad tennis.

At about three o'clock I would go into the kitchen, where Willy — who was Uncle Roy's wife but not an aunt — always made a sponge cake at this time on Sundays. After she had poured the mixture out of her big bowl into her buttered baking pan and slapped the pan into the oven, she would look at me, and I would ask, "Can I lick the dish, please, Willy?" and she would say, "If it doesn't spoil your tea." Then, assuring her it wouldn't spoil my tea, I would run my finger round and round the inside of the bowl, licking off dollop after dollop of delicious raw egg and flour and cocoa and sugar, until nothing remained but glazed pottery. It was a very exciting taste.

Once again, early in the afternoon, my father was brought home in the back of an uncle's motorcar and carried into his bedroom. Once again doctors came to him and he went to doctors (in Macquarie Street, where what my mother called "the specialists" worked — one of whom had taken out my adenoids and tonsils and another of whom, after a spectacular pre-anæsthesia battle, had performed an appendectomy on Pat) — but none of them could tell him why his head ached and why, occasionally, he collapsed in court.

Those were the days, though, when teeth were regarded as the root of all evil: so six of my father's excellent top teeth were torn out and replaced by a denture of finely wrought porcelain and gold, which he called "my bloody plate," and left out of his mouth as often as possible.

For this, my mother, at meal times, used occasionally to rebuke him. Then he would say, "Nag, nag, nag! Tige, get me my bloody plate," and I would go to the bathroom, where his denture lurked at the bottom of a glass of water, looking like something wrenched out of the jaws of a metallic and nightmare fish.

As well as extracting his splendid teeth ("in the trenches," he once told me, "we filled dental cavities with candle wax"), his doctors now prescribed a beverage called stout, which he loathed. It arrived in crates of a dozen, and he had to drink two bottles of it a day.

"Drink your stout, dear," my mother would say.

"I can't."

"Darling, you must."

"I hate the stuff."

One dinner time, greatly daring, I said, "Poor dad."

"No one," he assured me, "hates anything as much as I hate this muck."

"I hate tinned peaches almost as much," I comforted. "They're slimy and eating them makes me feel sick." Only the threat of a walloping made me eat them.

"Really?" he asked.

"Yes, dad."

"Liz," he shouted.

"What?" She was in the kitchen, talking to Ruth.

"No more tinned peaches for Tige. He hates them."

"He has done," my mother reminded him tartly, "ever since he was two."

"Well, I've only just found out," my father said complacently: at which my mother rolled her eyes upward in a way that would have earned Pat or myself an instantaneous bloody good hiding but got from my father only a cackle of laughter. It wasn't fair. Grown-ups never were fair.

Except once, when my father was still at home, sick, and ordered to stay in bed. Being bored, he kept shouting, "Liz — what the hell can I do?" until finally she shouted back, "Oh, for God's sake, Eddy, you're worse than the children: do whatever you want."

Instantly my father was out of bed, out of his pyjamas, into his khaki shirt and his khaki shorts with the rusty fish hooks instead of fly buttoms, and down to his workshop.

"Tige," he bellowed. I rushed to him, knowing that if he had to call twice my pocket money would be cut. "I'm going to make some new fly screens. Like to help?"

Although I hated all forms of carpentry (except my mother's), this was the first time my father had ever *asked* me to help him (instead of instructing me to), so I said yes, I would: at which Pat, who normally vanished for a long walkabout at the mere mention of household handiwork, became insanely jealous and insisted that she wanted to help too. By which my mother was rendered so suspicious that she decided to join us.

Which is how two such incompatible craftsmen as my parents, and two such ill-assorted assistants as their children, came to be working together on our back verandah, making fly screens for windows and doors.

It was a fine afternoon and for some time my mother and I, grinning conspiratorily as we remembered the sledgehammer, sawed the pieces of wood my father measured off, and Pat carried them back to him as he cut out squares of taut, shiny wire gauze.

The verandah floor was littered with the innumerable tools he required for even the simplest piece of woodwork, but the job proceeded smoothly until we reached the point where my father (wishing to sink the heads of the small nails in the wooden frames) asked me to hold the punch square on top of each head. Silently, then, I holding the punch, my father tapping it lightly each time, we proceeded from nail to nail.

And as we finished one screen, and my mother picked it up and carried it away, and my father moved to the next screen, Pat whispered in my ear, "Gimme."

"What?" I demanded.

"Punch," she said.

"No," I said and, ignoring her, squatted beside my father, ready to place the punch over the first of a new line of nail heads.

Instead there was a brief but shocking explosion in my head; and that, for the next few seconds, was all I knew about anything. I regained consciousness to hear my father asking sickly, "Have you got it out?" and my mother replying, "Yes."

"Is his head all right?"

"I think so."

I opened my eyes. I was lying on the verandah, my head in my mother's lap, my father squatting beside me.

"Don't move," my mother told me.

"My head," I complained, moving.

"I said, don't move," she repeated sternly, and then, to my father, "Where's Littly?"

"Littly," bellowed my father. "Come here."

She came and stood at my feet, looking down at me and both my parents with cold hostility, her hands locked behind her back, her stomach thrust farther out than ever.

"Say you're sorry to Tige," my father commanded.

"No," she refused, simply: and I gaped at the recklessness of her.

"Littly!" he thundered. "You've nearly murdered your brother."

"Don't frighten her," my mother murmured, frowning.

"As if anyone could." He sighed. "And you will now apologize to him."

"No," she said.

"Go to your room, I'll see you in a minute," my mother ordered in her quietest and most menacing tone.

Stolidly Pat turned on her heel and, without a word, left us.

"See if you can walk," my mother suggested.

I stood up, blood running down my cheek, and felt giddy, but said I could walk. I was led into the kitchen and there, with much hot water and disinfectant and bandages, treated for a head wound.

"What happened?" I asked. "And will I get lockjaw?"

"Your loving sister," my mother informed me, "stuck a chisel in your head! And no, you will not get lockjaw."

"Tetanus," muttered my father, which my mother ignored.

"But if you hadn't had a skull even thicker than your father's, you'd now be dead," she went on. "I had to *pull* the ruddy thing out. Embedded, it was. Edward, what are you going to do about Littly? We can't just belt her."

"Let's show her our wounded hero here. When she sees the bandage she'll feel sorry."

"If she didn't when there was all that blood around . . ."

"*Please*, Liz!"

"Oh, for heaven's sake. How you men ever lasted out a war I'll never know. Get her and we'll see."

"Littly!" roared my father. "Come here."

Defiantly she came; indifferently she surveyed each of us in turn.

"Now tell Tige you're sorry," my father bade her.

"No," she said — and returned to her room to await a bloody good hiding, watched all the way by all of us. As she shut her door I looked up at my mother, who had just turned to look at my father. For a moment they stared grimly; then, slightly, began to smile; then, silently, started shaking with mirth.

"Oh, darling," my mother apologized, "I'm sorry. It's awful of us to laugh when you're hurt, but . . ." My father was now falling about. "Edward!" she rebuked. "Edward, what about poor Tige?" He hooted at the thought of poor Tige. "Darling," she explained, "it's not that your father and I . . ." Then she hooted too and tears ran down her face, which made me hoot. "Tige," she gasped, "are you all right?" At which we all howled.

Suddenly Pat's door opened and, blue eyes blazing, she surveyed the three of us. "Silly buggers," she commented and closed the door again.

That was the last time she ever attacked me. It was the last time, even, that she demanded "Gimme or I scream." It was, in fact, the end of an era.

As his cell door swung open, the colonel looked up from his bed and was surprised to see the major — whose name he had at last discovered to be Lim Kuan Yew.

Between him and his neighbour, at ceiling height, there was a small square hole in the wall, a hole which housed the one bulb that lit both cells. Through this hole, each night, a garrulous Tamil, in crazily inflected English, hissed items of prison gossip.

"This Chinese officer," he had hissed the night before, "is a very terribly dangerous man. So it is imperatively necessary not to think that you can deceive him. Lim Kuan Yew knows almost everything about almost everyone, tuan: and when he wants to, he knows absolutely everything. So you must be most terribly careful of Lim Kuan Yew."

"Thank you," the colonel had whispered back. "I'll be careful."

"He has the memory of the proverbial elephant," the Tamil had further warned. "Did you know that his mother and father were killed during the Emergency?"

"Yes."

"It is said that this is what makes him so terribly dangerous. You must always remember this thing about Major Lim, my friends advise me."

"Thank you," the colonel had said again. "I'll remember."

And staring now at Lim, so unexpectedly arrived, he felt apprehension tightening his guts.

"Good morning, colonel," the major greeted.

"Good morning, Major Lim," the colonel replied, not moving from his bed: but the other man remained impassive, as if he had neither heard his name nor noticed the insolence of his prisoner's posture. Instead he looked slowly round the cell. Knowing his Asians, the colonel wondered how many of his possessions would survive this scrutiny.

"You seem comfortable," Lim observed.

"I've run out of toothpaste," the Australian demurred, hands clasped behind his neck. "That tube of shaving soap's just about had it too."

Since it was all going anyway, he might as well be insolent.

Lim picked up the colonel's one book and frowned as he looked at its title, then put it down on the bed again.

"Then we must get you some more toothpaste and shaving soap, mustn't we?" he remarked. "Did you bring volume six of Toynbee's *A Study of History* with you deliberately, or was it the only book you could find?"

"Deliberately."

"I thought you Westerners, if you carried just one book to war, always chose Virgil's *Aeneid* or *Winnie the Pooh* or something like that. Why Toynbee's *A Study of History?*"

"Experience has taught me that if one is to be allowed only one book to last a long time, it's best to take something almost unreadable. It took me twenty years to get through volumes one to five of Toynbee, so when I came away I reckoned volume six would last me out. I seem to have been right."

"You expect to be home within four years, colonel?"

"I think Toynbee will have killed me off long before then," the Australian countered easily.

Lim laughed. "I must congratulate you on your morale. Your seven colleagues are not in nearly such high spirits. Perhaps a visit from you would cheer them up?"

"Send me back any time you like."

"There's no need to send you back. They're here."

"No! And I'll be joining them?" The colonel was excited.

"Visiting them."

"When?"

Stepping back onto the gallery outside the cell, and standing aside from the door, the major motioned with his hand. "Why not now?" he suggested and, as his prisoner stood up swiftly from his bed, barked orders at the two soldiers accompanying him, and then strode off. Indicating that the colonel was to follow Lim, the two sentries let him pass, slammed his cell door, and stamped along behind him, their hobnailed boots clattering.

As he followed Lim down the metal spiral staircase and along bleak corridors and through heavy steel doors (unlocked by a guard as they approached and relocked after they had passed) the colonel reflected on the irony of a fate that had brought him back to this place.

It hadn't changed. Not in thirty years. Same old courtyards. No huts in them now, of course: but he could still visualize the huts — and the men.

For a moment he was twenty-three again. And optimistic, because he was only twenty-three. But then, drawing a deep, shuddering breath, he remembered that this was not 1944. Nevertheless, it was as if he had never left; and he ran his fingers along the white-washed walls, remembering that other time. Then it had been the Nips.

"Changi!" he gritted.

Lim swung round. "You said something, colonel?"

"No."

They entered what had been F courtyard, in 1945, and marched briskly towards the bottom wall, then turned right. There'd been a store room there, the colonel remembered. And a wireless set! Where the hell were they going? Farther on were only dark basement store rooms. Or had been, in 1945.

Halting at a low, heavy, wooden door, Lim nodded at the young soldier who guarded it. The soldier unlocked the door and swung it open, and Lim's two escorts stepped inside, into the darkness, carbines forward. There was a click, and lights blazed.

"After you," Lim invited mockingly, and the colonel, stooping, apprehensive, went through the door.

The windowless basement, now harsh with the glare of strong lights, was divided into two rows of wire-mesh cages. In each of which were at least four men. Filthy, emaciated, blinking, mad-eyed men. As if they had worked on the Thailand Railway. But that had been 1943. At the fifth cage, on the right, the escorting soldiers halted, and the colonel and the major halted too.

"Gentlemen," Lim advised his seven victims on the other side of the wire mesh, "Colonel Russell has come to pay his respects."

As they looked out at him the colonel at once realized that his only chance of being accepted by them was to join them. He turned to Lim . . .

"Hear you're collaborating," a voice said flatly, and he wheeled round to confront one of the seven, who now stood at the wire, talon fingers threaded bonily through the mesh.

"If you believe that, Tiny, you'll believe anything," he snarled —

grateful, though, that this was the one who had spoken to him. Six feet four inches tall, he was at least instantly identifiable.

"Yeah," Tiny agreed, "we'll believe anything."

"Put me in with them," the colonel demanded. But was certain that Lim would not. Prayed that Lim would not. And hated himself. And felt his bowels loosening lest Lim agree. And found himself thinking irrelevantly of Streaker. Why? Swift as bedbugs caught in sudden light, the shameful thoughts chased one another into the darker recesses of his mind. Christ. But someone was talking.

"Put him in here, Lim," Tiny promised coldly, "and we'll murder the bastard." He turned to face his sleek compatriot again. "The thing is," he pointed out, "we've talked about you often, you old bastard, and we've decided, rather than have you within a hundred yards of us, we'd cut your throat. In other words, we'd much rather you carried on licking their nasty little arses than have you here. Get it, you old bastard?"

Intently the colonel peered into Tiny's deep-socketed, bloodshot eyes.

"Got it," he murmured.

"They don't seem to like you," Lim observed.

"No," the colonel agreed and stared in turn into oddly expressionless eyes of each of his compatriots.

"Old bastard," each one said in turn.

"Bastards yourselves," the colonel replied and turned his back on them, so that they would not see his tears.

"Come," Lim ordered.

As they reached the door and Lim snapped off the light, a sardonic chorus rang out from the darkness. "Good-bye, you old bastard." And he heard them laughing as the door slammed to.

"You're starving them, aren't you?" he accused when eventually they took their seats on either side of Lim's desk.

"When Australia this year refused to sell China any more wheat, she sentenced hundreds of thousands of our people to starvation," Lim countered. "Our crops failed last year, in case you've forgotten."

"Your crops fail every year, so you should have learned by now not to alienate those who might send you wheat."

"Next year we'll take the wheat."

"The States and Britain won't stand for it. There'll be war."

"War?" Lim queried derisively. "When the present American President was elected by isolationists?"

"They'll fight for their investments," the colonel insisted.

"You said they'd fight to stop us landing in Irian. We've got a division there already. Not a murmur."

"And next, I suppose, you move into Papua-New Guinea?"

"Of course."

"New Guinea'll be to the Pacific what Czechoslovakia was to Europe thirty-seven years ago. Can't you see that?"

"Certainly. It will be handed to us on a plate. Just like Czechoslovakia was to Germany."

"Then you'll decide it's all too easy, and you'll land in Australia, and that's when World War Three will start."

"You honestly think, colonel, that America will dare enter *any* war against a major power with thirty million black hostiles in her midst?"

"Is that what you're banking on?"

"That's one of the things."

"You're mad."

"So you keep telling me. But let's drop the hypothetical future and discuss your literary efforts of the past week. Let me see: I have some notes here. Ah yes. Who was That Bugger Lang?"

"A labour politician who became Premier of New South Wales in 1930. Or thereabouts. My father and middle-class people like him regarded Mr Lang as a combination of Bolshevism personified and the Devil incarnate."

"And was he?"

"He was pretty far to the left."

"So, presumably, was the majority of the electorate?"

"I think it was a class and Irish-Catholic thing more than socialist principles that put Lang in power."

"I see. Now these books *Anthony Adverse* and *All Quiet on the Western Front* — I've never heard of them."

"*Anthony Adverse* was about fornication; *All Quiet on the Western Front* was about the futility of war."

"And these, as a child of nine, you were determined to read?"

"Because my father hid them."

"You had no scruples about spying on him to see *where* he hid them?"

"I didn't spy. I found them with that radar children have that guides them to parental hiding places. I just knew those two books were on top of my father's high wardrobe. So I got a chair and stood on its back and reached over: and there, on the dusty top, they were. Beside the long narrow box with the red ends."

"And what was in the long narrow box with the red ends?"

"Contraceptives."

"You knew that?"

"No. Only that they were grown-up."

"So you didn't talk about them?"

"I forgot about them."

"To change the subject a moment, colonel. Your sister — I find myself liking her very much."

"I found *my*self liking her very much."

"But was she really like that?"

"Well, she did all those things, and anything young is remarkable."

"We've all been young."

"Exactly. Even you would have been fascinating once."

"You find me dull now?"

"I find you . . . academic. And sad, trying to brainwash an old has-been like me."

"An old has-been or an old bastard?" Lim asked slyly.

The colonel decided to test his interrogator's sensitivity to the nuances of the language of Australians.

"Both, I suppose," he admitted with every appearance of gloom.

"You asked to see them. It was your own fault they abused you," Lim pointed out.

"They seemed to hate me," the colonel complained, probing.

"As I told you," Lim scolded, "you're alone now."

Looking down at his hands, the colonel reflected that this was true. Even though Lim had completely misinterpreted those toneless "old bastards," he was still alone. Tiny and the others had told him that his job was to keep out of their cage: but their goodwill did not alter the fact that they were doomed and that he was alone.

"We've advised your government we're holding your unloving friends," Lim told him abruptly.

"And me?"

"Colonel, how often do I have to tell you? You no longer exist — except on these." He tapped the ragged pile of soiled quarto and the neater stack of computer cards.

"Are you holding my friends as political prisoners?"

"As war criminals. We advised your government of that too."

"I can imagine the answer you got."

"It wasn't noticeably original. Canberra warned that if we executed them we would precipitate a Third World War. But why should you worry about seven fascists who hate you?"

"Executions always distress me."

"As a child, though, your games were an endless killing."

"I'm no longer a child."

"You're no longer anything," Lim emphasized. "This man Beatles — he was a fascist?"

"You mean because of his paramilitary games and so on?"

"Yes."

"He couldn't forget his years at the Front, and we were fascinated by them; that's all."

"Nonsense. You were only children."

"I had a book of photographs of the War when I was a child. I used to go back and back to the picture in it of a dead German. He was young and blond and good-looking, and I used to be absolutely obsessed with him — with curiosity about how he'd died, and how he could be young and good-looking when he was a Hun. All *our* dead, in the photographs, looked horrible. Something being done to death had done to them. So how did a Hun overcome this ugliness of being done to death? Shall I tell you something, Lim? That German kid lent a kind of beauty to slaughter. Know what I think? I think each generation of soldiers returning home from war breeds into its children this perverse doubt about whether there mightn't be a kind of terrible beauty in slaughter."

"Is that what Beatles did?"

"May have been. I mean, it was a time that bred this type, wasn't it? The day of the spell-binder who still had about him the stink of Flanders. The day of the leather overcoat. My father had one to drive in. His friends had them. Hitler had one. The Gestapo were soon to get 'em. In those days the world liked its youth poignant and doomed. It's how we grew up. Your lot are *still* poignant and doomed, aren't you?"

"Perhaps," said the major. "It's an emotional state I hadn't thought about. When you've finished writing about your childhood, you must do me a few pages on your later years of being poignant and doomed. They may help me."

"Help you what?"

"Understand you."

"What you want isn't something to help you understand *me*," the colonel argued, "it's something to convince you there's beauty in slaughter. You're fascinated by it too, aren't you? What started it for you, eh? Photographs in the *Straits Times* of dead Chinese bandits killed by British National Servicemen? Or was it a photograph of a young, blond, good-looking English boy killed in the jungle by Communist Chinese?"

"Our war is to liberate, not to kill," Lim announced loftily.

From the execution yard below shots rang out.

"Sounds like it," the colonel sneered.

Lim looked at the last page of pencilled writing. "Your sensible sister has just tried to murder you, which would have saved us all a lot of trouble. Go back to your cell, colonel, and carry on the absorbing story of your grossly over-privileged youth."

My father went back to work, engrossing himself in a marathon forgery case, endlessly studying his brief and peering through a magnifying glass at samples of writing; but by now I knew that something was wrong.

So many little things had changed.

For example, my parents (whose obedience to the rule "Not in front of the children" had always been implicit) had a corrosive argument in their bedroom, although Pat and I were in our verandah beds only ten feet away. I was terrified, not so much by the violence of their argument as by its quality, which was vitriolic. They seemed suddenly to hate each other.

Finally I pushed open their bedroom door and, as they swung round on me, begged, "Don't fight, please."

My mother said, "Oh *Tige*," and my father said, "Hell!" and I was not at all certain what either of them meant: but I stood my ground, irrelevantly aware that my mother was in her nightgown, long brown hair hanging down her back, and that my father had on only his pyjama jacket — beneath which the naked half of his body looked aggressively sturdy.

The value of those good manners about which he had in the past lectured me so vehemently then became apparent. Acknowledging my protest with a nod and a small smile, he said, "I'm sorry, son. Sorry, Liz."

"We didn't mean anything," my mother assured me.

"It sounded awful," I insisted.

"It must have," my father agreed. He took his pyjama pants from under the pillow on his side of the double bed and pulled them on. "I'm starving," he announced. "You talk to your mother, and I'll make us some tea and bread and butter."

The next change was that he gave up tennis and started playing golf and cricket. This might not have surprised me had I not discovered that he played golf rather badly and that he did not much enjoy either batting or fielding at cricket. Yet he had loved tennis.

On the golf course he was determined, and strong, and patient: yet there seemed a tenseness in him — of pain or preoccupation — that constantly distracted him, and worried me as I caddied for him.

At cricket it was even more apparent that all he sought was exercise. None of the team was an uncle of mine, and between them and him there was only a polite amiability. When he arrived he would exchange a few words with them and then sit with me until it was his turn to bat. At the crease he was competent and elegant, but invariably lost his wicket because of shots so improbably ill timed that his team-mates would mutter impatiently — until someone nudged and pointed at me, saying, "That's his boy." In the field, he ran hard and threw accurately, yet stood, without zest, looking sad.

All of this, though I cannot pretend that it made me anxious, had me wary. Of what, I did not know: but I *was* wary — waiting.

At the Chatswood Cricket Ground, one Saturday afternoon, I thought it had come — the unknown thing for which I was waiting. Next in the batting order, my father walked across to his Vauxhall and, climbing into the front seat, called me to him. When I reached him he had opened the front of his white flannel trousers and was adjusting something low on his belly.

"A box," he explained. "Know what for?"

"No."

"So's you don't get damaged here," and he rapped the light, reinforced codpiece sharply. "Very important. Understand?"

I shook my head from side to side.

"Well, I'll tell you on the way home," he promised. But he didn't. On the way home he said nothing — seemed unaware even that I was with him — and I, recognizing that black preoccupation that at other times made him slice his tee shots and misjudge his square cuts, thought it best not to remind him.

It was not till about the end of the season, on our way to the North Sydney Cricket Ground, that the unknown revealed itself. The match was on Number Two Oval, on a back street. We reached it a little early, and my father, looking at his watch, asked suddenly if I would like to see the house where I had been born. When I said I would, he started the car again and drove about two hundred yards down the road. Then, pulling up, he pointed.

"That's it," he said.

I was bitterly disappointed. The place where I had been born was a small, red-brick building totally inauspicious in spite of the brass plate on its front gate engraved with the words PRIVATE HOSPITAL. I gazed at the small red house for some minutes, resentfully trying to relate it in any way to myself. Failing, I turned to complain to my father. And it was then that the thing happened.

Slowly, his two hands gripping the top rim of the steering wheel so tightly that his forearms quivered, he lowered his head between them and, quite desperately, moaned.

It was some seconds before the horror in me gave way to a realization that he needed help. I reached out and touched his shoulder.

The muscle in it was knotted with tension. I touched his black hair, and was surprised by the toughness of it, and alarmed by the fact that he seemed not to feel my hand.

Remembering me at last, he lifted his head from the steering wheel and, turning slowly, looked at me. His face was white and damp and his green eyes were bloodshot and dazed. He closed his eyes and spoke slowly.

"Tige?"

"Yes."

"Promise something?"

"Yes."

"Don't tell anyone. Not even your mother."

I said, "No, dad," but he heard nothing. Instead he slumped slowly towards me: and I cowered swiftly away from him as he fell and lay sideways on the seat, breathing stertorously, his head just touching my knee.

After a while, though, I lost my fear of his unconsciousness and, overwhelmed instead by grief, put my hand back on his head, and, looking out at the dull red house where I had been born, wept.

I must have sat like that for half an hour before he stirred: and when he did so, I quickly and guiltily dried my eyes and took my hand off his head. He pushed himself upright and, pressing at his temples, collected his wits.

"You all right, son?"

"Are you?" I challenged. I had never challenged him before.

"I was tired," he lied categorically. "Understand?"

I nodded, and he started the car and reversed away from the house where I had been born to Number Two Oval, where his team was already batting.

"We thought you weren't coming," the captain greeted him and added that he had told the reserve that he would be playing in my father's place. "But I'll tell him you're here after all," he offered.

"No, no," my father refused. "He'll be more use to you anyway. Sorry I was late: I was showing Tony where he was born" — he pointed down the road — "and we got talking."

For the rest of the afternoon, lying on the grass, we watched cricket. At first I was afraid that my father was only biding his time, waiting for the right moment to extract from me a further promise of silence, but finally I realized that he had no intention of doing so, and then I relaxed. We barely moved and we hardly spoke. Once he asked, "Ice cream?" and, when I replied yes, please, wandered off and bought one for each of us.

Later he asked, "Piss?" and, when I said yes, led me to the dressing-room lavatories.

And towards the end of the game he asked, "Do you like cricket?" and, when I told him not much, sighed. "Neither do I."

"Why do you play it, well?"

"Don't say 'Why do you play it, well,' Tige."

"Sorry; well, why do you play it?"

"God knows."

"Why don't you play tennis any more?"

"Because I see two balls instead of one. Same with this bloody game. So from now on I think I'll stick to golf, where it doesn't matter to anyone else which ball you hit."

"Do you like golf?"

"Hate it," he assured me. "Golf, stout, my bloody plate, and Jack Lang — I hate 'em all. Tell you what, let's drive down to Miller's Point and see how they're getting on with the bridge."

So we left the cricket and drove about a mile to where the north pylon of what was to become the Harbour Bridge stood massively grey and expectant. From it a great arc of steel clawed out at the sky: and from the opposite side a second great arc clawed back towards us.

"They'll meet one day," my father explained, "and form an arch across the water."

"Will we really drive over the arch?" I asked.

"No," he said, laughing. "They'll suspend a roadway from the arch; and a railway line and a tram line on either side of the roadway; and on the outside, footpaths. When it's finished it's going to be a marvellous bridge. So who do you think's going to open it?"

"Gan?" I guessed.

He smiled. "The pater'd like that. No, not Gan. Jack Lang."

"Why?"

"Because he's the Premier of New South Wales, and whoever is Premier will open the bridge."

"Will he still be Premier when the bridge is opened?"

"As far as I can see" — my father sighed — "Jack Lang will be Premier for ever."

The following week I told my cousins that the only reason why my grandfather would not be opening the Sydney Harbour Bridge was that Jack Lang was going to be Premier for ever; but they didn't believe me. Ever since I had told them that babies came from their mother's belly, they hadn't believed a word I said.

Our house was an ugly house with only one redeeming feature: its floors were of rich red jarra. Everything else — proportions, materials, and design — was uncompromisingly tasteless. It had been designed to my father's specifications by one of the uncles, and in every inch of it one could see the influences of trench warfare. Both men had been concerned only with a house that was intact, waterproof, easily approached and easily maintained: and that is what they built. Now, believing that the quickest way to break a Depression was to spend money, my father decided to gild this unlovely lily with a second storey.

Three months later it was done, the second storey (consisting of two large bedrooms, with a bathroom between them, and a short wide hallway) achieving the remarkable feat of making the house, from the outside, look uglier than ever. We, however, were concerned not with æsthetics but with moving round, which all of us then did.

My parents moved upstairs, Pat moved to their room, Ruth moved to Pat's room, and I moved to Ruth's room. My old room — complete with my wardrobe, which was immovable — and the second upstairs room thus became available for any uncles who might visit us (which they usually did from New Guinea, where they all seemed to be involved in something called prospecting).

No sooner were we all installed in our new rooms than it was announced that my father must go on a long sea voyage for the sake of his health.

"The *sea?*" he screamed. "For the sake of my health? The sea will kill me. Don't these doctors know *any*thing? First it's all my bloody teeth out, then stout, now the sea! Haven't any of them ever *been* seasick? And it's not as if they don't *know* I'm the world's worst sailor — I *told* them."

But still everyone (the doctors, the uncles, Gar, Gan, and my mother) insisted that he must go on a long sea voyage and eventually he capitulated, on the two conditions that my mother accompany him ("to see I'm decently buried") and that he be allowed to choose his own moment of departure.

For weeks after that he became a fanatical student of meteorology, industriously checking back through decades of records on the behaviour of the Great Australian Bight and the Indian Ocean, seeking a period when, statistically, he should be able to travel what he called "this whole nightmare voyage" in conditions of tolerable calm.

"I shall most certainly be ill even then," he asserted. "But I might not die."

Eventually, on the basis of all the available data, he agreed on an autumn date of departure. As soon as she heard this my grandmother insisted that she must remain in Sydney that winter to be near the children. She would stay indoors: but if Ruth needed anything she would only have to telephone.

From that moment onwards my father so constantly studied weather maps, and so hilariously bemoaned his fate, that the subject of his long sea voyage became a joke. Thus it was only as I was preparing to go to school one morning, and as both my parents began anxiously urging, "Now you'll be a good boy, won't you?" that I realized they really were leaving us. It was a moment I found just as shocking as I had my kidnapping by Uncle Vere and Aunty Estelle from Port Macquarie to Inverell.

Being eleven, I preferred this time not to cry, as I had then; but knowing that I would cry, if I said good-bye, I left without a word. And then found that I was unable to drag myself away: so I hid in the downstairs lavatory and waited to be discovered — when *they* would have to say good-bye to me.

After a tedious half hour, during which no one came near me, I remembered that only the cousins and I ever used this downstairs lavatory. Even if I stayed there all day, my parents would still leave for Ceylon without saying good-bye to me. This prospect being intolerable, I returned inside the house and told my father, who was sitting glumly on the staircase in his khaki shirt and his shorts with the fish hooks, that I had come home because I had a toothache. Tactfully he did not cross-examine me.

"Your mother and I don't want to abandon you, you know," he told me ruefully. I said yes, I knew, and felt the tears come to my eyes.

"You'll be all right," he comforted. "Now go and say good-bye to your mother; she's a bit upset."

I went upstairs and kissed my mother good-bye, and then came halfway downstairs to my father again. I could not remember ever having kissed him before, or ever having wanted to, but I wanted to now; because abruptly the certainty hit me that I would never see this strong-legged, black-haired, green-eyed, disreputably dressed, strict but amusing man again.

So, mutely, I shook hands with him and fled.

In the ensuing two months, however, I felt the loss of my parents only once — that very afternoon when, having just arrived home from school, and dragged off my shoes and socks, I almost shouted "Mum?" But I remembered in time (gulping at the thought of a liner having already conveyed them, with awful indifference, out through the Heads to blue oblivion) and instead shouted "Ruth?"

"Hello," she said, smiling, coming out to my verandah bedroom — its walls were distempered pink — "I've made you a cake. Like a bit?"

Cakes being almost as rare and wicked as going to the pictures (because they ruined your appetite, gave you spots, and rotted your teeth), I was naturally suspicious.

"What sort?" I asked.

"Chocolate," she said, as if it were the most natural thing in the world. "That's your favourite, isn't it?"

It was not only my favourite, it was my idea of perfect sin. I could think of no more beautiful fate than utterly to destroy my appetite, my complexion, and all my teeth in an exquisite surfeit of chocolate-iced, chocolate-filled, chocolate cake.

"Is it iced?" I asked.

"Of course," she answered. "And filled. Told you — I made it for you."

And so began eight glorious weeks. Eight weeks in which I was never once corrected for an ill-chosen, misplaced, or badly pronounced word; in which I ate more between meals than I did at the luncheon or dinner table; in which, with Pat and Ruth, I saw every film currently showing in Sydney; in which I never went to bed at the statutory half-past seven, nor Pat at the statutory half-past six; in which the three of us swept round in taxis, paying courtly calls on Gar, her eye sockets looking more bruised and her voice sounding more croaky than ever, because of the winter and being constantly indoors; in which Ruth bought us such clothes as she thought becoming to children of our station; in which our house rocked with the kind of uninhibited nocturnal entertainments for which it had obviously longed all of its graceless life.

It was Ruth's entertaining that Pat and I found the most refreshing of her innovations. To ice creams, taxis, chocolate cake, picture shows, zoos, new clothes, and substantial increases in our pocket money we became quickly accustomed. I even became accustomed quite quickly to my new royal blue and maroon striped blazer (which, inexplicably, I told my cousins had been awarded to me for ballroom dancing): but we never quite grew accustomed to Ruth's parties.

For them the sliding doors that divided our dining-room from our sitting-room were pushed back, and all the movable dining-room furniture was bundled into the kitchen, and the Persian carpets (that Gar had brought back from the *Middle* East, which was even less comprehensible than the Far one) were rolled up and dumped in the spare room. What was left then was a room forty feet long with a dark red, gleaming hardwood floor, an even darker red and more sombrely gleaming grand piano, comfortable armchairs and sofas round the walls and, in the big hearth, a log fire blazing.

In this setting about forty people were entertained every Saturday night.

They were lovely people, dancing and singing and drinking lots of my father's accursed stout as well as the sherry and whisky he kept for visitors. Ruth received her guests at the foot of the staircase, dressed in one of my mother's evening gowns and wearing all the jewellery my mother had left behind rather than have it stolen in Ceylon by bloody rickshaw boys. Ruth was particularly partial to opals, which pleased me because my father had given my mother two superb opal rings before he realized that she regarded them as unlucky and never wore them. At last they were getting an airing.

Pat and I never really became friends with any of Ruth's lady guests, whose dresses and jewels, we perceived, had no quality at all, but with all of the men we were on terms of the closest intimacy. For one thing, we had known them all our lives: for another, they now revealed fascinating and hitherto undreamed-of social attributes.

Taffy, our milkman, for example, we had always known as a man with a marvellous pink complexion and very white, slightly crooked teeth — both of which, my mother had explained, were a by-product of his Englishness. When we had asked did he come from the same part of England as Anne (because her complexion and his were alike), my mother said no, he came from Wales and Anne came from Ireland, but complexions like that and teeth like that were English.

"Because the English don't have gold fillings in their front teeth like Australians do?" I asked, and my mother, bored with the subject, said, "Probably."

So Taffy had been unusual even when he only dipped his measure into the deep shining can and then poured the frothy milk into our white jug with the blue stripe round its rim: but at Ruth's parties Taffy became more than unusual, he became phenomenal.

His black hair glossy with a beautifully scented brilliantine, his beautiful pink neck encased in a stiff white collar, he sat on my mother's piano stool, swaying from side to side as she never did, looking wonderfully well dressed in his tight navy blue suit with the red tie and the rolled gold tie pin and the shiny patent leather shoes, and played for hours.

Not Chopin and Brahms and nocturnes and Sinding's "Rustle of Spring," as my mother did, but things like "Tea for Two" and "Knees Up Mother Brown" and "Tiptoe through the Tulips" and "Parlez Moi d'Amour" and "Frankie and Johnny Were Lovers" and "There's a Long Long Trail a-Winding." To which Ruth's guests sang and danced.

The baker, Fred, we had known all our lives too. Indeed it was his fault that I was called what I was. As a baby in my pram on the front lawn (where my mother had left me in the sun, on the principle that the glare would make me shut my eyes, and then I would go to sleep, thank God) I had been bawling my head off when he came to deliver bread. Handing my mother the loaf she had ordered, Fred had observed, "Good pair of lungs, that kid. Roars like a tiger." From which moment, I was never called anything else.

Fred was a tall, thin, badly put together man with Australian teeth and a sunburned neck with wrinkles on the back of it and a big bony Adam's apple; and my mother always said of him, "He's a nice lad, Fred, but no oil painting."

He once asked me did I like poetry and, when I said I didn't know, said he would tell me the most bloody lovely poem ever and, with great emotion recited:

> *Life is only froth and bubble,*
> *but two things stand like stone;*
> *Kindness in a-nother's trouble,*
> *courage in your own.*

By this I had been profoundly moved; and when I told it to my father, he had been too, staring at my mother with such emotion that she had bowed her head as she knitted and whispered to me, "Go out and play, Tige." Consequently, because it was not often I had managed to impress my parents, I liked Fred.

I had never dreamed, though, that he could sing; yet, at Ruth's parties, standing with one hand on the piano, Taffy accompanying him, he sang "Suvla Bay" and "The Rose of Tralee" in a manner that he himself plainly found heart-rending.

He had a very high voice ("Lovely tenner 'e is," the local taxi driver used to comment as Fred sang. "Never think it ter lookatim. Mora sorta barrertone likey looks, dunny?" My father would have been apoplectic at the way the taxi driver pronounced words), and as he sang in this very high voice his face used to go even redder than his wrinkled neck, and on his *best* notes, which were what he called "me vibrartoes," he used to stick his chin up in the air and strain at it, like Tripe howling, his lower lips and lower jaw and bony Adam's apple all quivering in time.

Then there was Ben, the gardener, who had been a groundsman at the Tennis Club until a heartless committee sacked him, because he was too old to work, and my father offered him a good wage to come and not work at our place. His silver head and bandy legs and brown hands with the darker brown blotches on them had thereafter become as much a part of our establishment as our two orange trees that never bore oranges but were vaguely decorative.

At Ruth's parties, though, Ben ceased being purely decorative.

Evoking female shrieks wherever he moved, he prompted the taxi driver to observe, "Look ut the ole ram. Marvlus, innit?" But most marvellous of all was Ben's talent with two dessert spoons, which he held together in one hand and from which, clacking them with the other hand against one of his bent, bandy knees, he produced a castanet-like accompaniment to Taffy's version of "Pack Up Your Troubles."

Midst all this revelry, the only time we gave a thought to our parents was when my mother's postcards arrived, saying that my father's carefully selected departure date had resulted only in their sailing into a gale; that this X was their cabin on the ship and this one their room at the Galleface Hotel.

But now Gar telephoned to say that she would be coming the following Friday to drive us in her American car to Circular Quay to meet the returning travellers as their ship docked, and at once Pat and I became tremendously excited. Ruth, on the other hand, fell into a profound gloom.

The moment my grandmother arrived (crowing at us and scolding Tripe and ignoring my grandfather, who felt that we must hurry) Pat and I reverted effortlessly to the ways of our austere past. Our recently acquired taste for high living was forgotten; bed times seemed suddenly proper, and correct pronunciations desirable. Seething, we were driven to the wharf where the ship would dock.

On the wharf itself we stood in a little huddled group watching the big ship inch towards us, my grandfather telling me the while a complicated story about the time, in 1889, when he had played rugby football for the New Zealand All Blacks and been kicked on the right temple, which was why he had lost most of the sight in his right eye and could not, from this distance, tell me where, on the ship's decks, my parents were standing. I could not imagine 1889. Nor could I see my parents — even though I had never been kicked on the forehead. Nervously I began to suspect that my father had died on the last leg of his voyage, and again felt desolate that I had failed to kiss him before he left.

And then, boring its way through a hundred shrill *coo-ees*, came an ear-splitting, larrikinish whistle.

"Mitt!" Gar at once croaked in her warm falsetto. "Darlings," to us who knew, "it's your father. There on the bridge, see?" And

there, beside the diminutive top half of the captain, was the diminutive top half of my father, semaphoring wildly with both his diminutive arms; and next to him, just as diminutive, peering intently
towards us, my mother.

Half an hour later we were together, in their cabin, all talking at
once.

"Have you been good kids?" my father demanded.

"Where'd you get that ghastly blazer?" my mother demanded.

"Yes, dad. Ruth brought it for me, mum," I said.

"*Bought*," my father corrected.

"Bought it for me," I repeated automatically.

"Ruth's been marvellous," Gar assured. "She's rung us every
other day and brought the children out to see us three or four
times . . ."

But Pat had had enough of small talk. Putting her arms lovingly
round my father's neck, she asked, "What presents have you got for
me?"

The best things among the gifts then displayed were a python's
skin, a faked parchment relic sold by the priests of the Temple of
Kandi, and a square sheet of raw latex. I was fascinated by all of
them: by their alien texture and the outlandish evocativeness of
them.

Pat, on the other hand, and I was relieved to see it, was unmoved
by the grey snakeskin, the yellow parchment, and the crepey latex,
her eyes having fastened with unwinking acquisitiveness on a gaudy
pile of saffron silks and fine silver bracelets. She was welcome to
them.

From the ship we drove to my grandparents' home in Edgecliff,
where my grandfather took me into his study and showed me a photograph, in sepia and yellowish-white, of three rows of men wearing
boots, socks, knickerbockers, jerseys, drooping moustaches, and
schoolboy caps with tassels.

"That's the All Blacks Team I was telling you about," he said.
"The 1888 team. And that's the 1889 team. And those" — pointing
at the wall above the ancient photographs — "are my caps."

Faded and fragile, their gold tassels tarnished, the caps looked as
out of place as human scalps or necklaces of sharks' teeth: but when
I looked from them to my grandfather, I saw that his face had on it

the expression that my father's and uncles' faces wore when they talked of the Somme and Passchendaele. So I assumed a countenance of rapt respect — at which I was very good with grown-ups — and thought about other things while my grandfather led me to further photographs of himself rowing for Australia and being a High Commissioner. It was all rather embarrassing and it only stopped when, on the second gong, we all trooped in to dinner — Uncle Jim and Uncle Henry as well. After soup, my grandfather carved and the maid carried our plates to us and then, creaking, held the dishes of vegetables at our elbows.

"You know my brother William died a year ago, Doris?" my grandmother reminded as she helped herself to peas.

"Yes," said my mother.

"Well" — complacently — "William left me five hundred pounds and I'm going to invest it in a gold mine."

Just for a second my grandfather paused in his carving; then, looking straight at my grandmother over the top of his pince-nez, pointing his carving knife at her for emphasis, he said, "I forbid it" — and I knew that this was the end of the gold mine. My grandfather had even more authority than my father, who had all the authority of God, and my grandfather had spoken. The entire family fell silent.

"But, David," my grandmother replied in her lightest and most *tink*ling croaky voice, "this is *my* money" — at which the silence became electric — "and I intend investing it in a gold mine."

Had he been a general, my grandfather, at that moment, would beyond doubt have had my grandmother summarily executed. As it was, he merely directed towards her, over his pince-nez and his high, flat Gladstonian cheekbones, a glance of withering distaste, and then instructed my father, "Tell your fool of a mother about old ladies and gold mines."

Never had I known such high drama. Compared with this battle — staged so grandly under the heavy gold and silver wheels, so publicly, like a royal birth, before an audience seated on high-backed, massive thrones of elaborately carved ebony — the brawl I had interrupted between my mother and father had been less even than a skirmish.

"Mater . . ." my father began patiently.

"Yes, dear," she answered, swinging to him, her heavily jewelled hands lying tranquilly on the lace tablecloth she had years ago brought back with her from Brussels.

"Mater, please don't interrupt, I want to explain to you . . ."

"But, Mitt darling, I don't *want* to be explained to. I just want to invest my five hundred pounds in this lovely gold mine I've heard about."

"Mum," my father said firmly, and the more familiar appellation penetrated her armour of tranquillity, "it's precisely because you've *heard* about it that I want to warn you. Women don't know about these things. Most of these so-called gold mines are just holes in the ground salted with nuggets by . . ."

"Salted, dear?"

"Artificially impregnated, mum."

"Good gracious!" Gar was quite shocked. "But surely that's illegal?"

"Of *course* it is" — with considerable impatience.

"I'm glad to hear it. Investors could easily be defrauded if that sort of thing went on."

"But, mum, it does go on."

"David," my grandmother demanded, "you must say something about this in the Upper House. Widows and pensioners could be deprived of their life's savings."

"Exactly," my father pronounced in his most biting forensic style. "Just as you will almost certainly be deprived of yours if you insist on ignoring the pater."

"But," my grandmother demurred in exasperation, "*This* gold mine is in New Guinea."

"What on earth has that to do with it?" my grandfather demanded.

"Henry prospected in New Guinea," she explained, nodding affectionately at her third son, who somehow looked as if he wished she hadn't.

"And is he now rich?" my grandfather inquired sarcastically — it being well known that Uncle Henry was poor. "On the contrary, he has so little that he lives here with us."

"And we love having you, darling," Gar crowed, reaching across me to put her warm, beringed hand over his; then added, "Anyway, I hardly think they'd bother, all the way up in the mountains of New Guinea. Among the cannibals."

"Woman," Gan snapped, "what on earth are you talking about?"

"Salting!" she retorted. "No, it's no use arguing. Henry was in New Guinea, I like the name of this mine, and it's my money — which I drew out of the Bank in *good* time before that man Lang closed it as I always said he would." The faces of all the men round the table blackened with a fury Gar appeared not to notice. "I shall telephone a stockbroker tomorrow. Mitt, you must give me the name of a good stockbroker."

"If it's gold shares you're after," my father retorted, "you can find your own broker."

"All right," she replied, lightly as ever, "I will. Now" — and she looked possessively round at her family — "let's talk about something else. Doris, dear, you *do* look well. It's lovely to have you both home. Children" — to us — "isn't it lovely to have mummy and daddy home?"

"Yes," we said, obediently: but the atmosphere had become sullen and no amount of mere grandfilial obedience could re-enliven it.

Nor was the atmosphere at home, the following morning, any better. Though our parents tried to make an event of this resumption of family life, they failed because they were both curiously preoccupied. In the middle of answers to our questions, or showing us something they had just unpacked, one or the other of them would prowl round the bedroom, opening cupboards and drawers, frowning. Finally, ignoring us, my mother said, "It's no good, Eddy. You'll have to go and see her"; and, muttering to himself, my father left us.

A few minutes later, having myself wandered disconsolately downstairs, I came upon him in the kitchen. He stood in the middle of the floor, looking stern but miserable, and in front of him, at the table, sat Ruth, sobbing.

My father noticed me. "Leave us," he snapped.

And then, as if I were no longer there, said quietly to Ruth, "All right, you're probably less to blame than I. Shall we try again?"

I fled upstairs to my mother.

"Ruth's crying," I reported.

"I'm not surprised," my mother observed grimly.

My father rejoined us.

"Well?" my mother asked.

"The lot's gone," my father told her.

"Six hundred pounds?" my mother expostulated.

"And your furs." He nodded. "And your jewellery."

"What are we going to do?"

"Give her another chance. We should never have put her in that position . . ."

"That was my fault," my mother insisted. "She seemed so marvellous with the children. And I thought she should have three or four hundred more than she could possibly need in case they had to have any awful operations or anything."

"Well, they haven't come to any harm, have they?"

My mother examined us. "Apart from that ghastly blazer of Tige's, no. You really think we should give her another chance?"

"Yes," he said, "I do."

Two weeks later I again came upon my father and Ruth in the kitchen, and again Ruth was sobbing.

"I'm sorry," he was telling her, "but you'll have to go. I won't bring any charges, but you'll have to go."

I rushed to my mother in the sitting-room. "Mum, dad says Ruth's got to go."

"Yes," she said, sighing.

"Why?"

"She took his wallet, Tige. She can't help it, poor lass, she's a ruddy kleptomaniac. But we just can't put up with it any more. So bring me that terrible blazer and we'll give it to the Salvation Army and try to forget her."

Thus Ruth left us; and Rob joined us.

"I've been reading what your Australian newspapers have reported about your family over the years," Major Lim revealed, casually pushing an untidy pile of photostated news items across the desk. "Your father's obituary, for example" — he tapped one.

"Where the devil did you get all these?"

"Party members searched the morgues of all your big papers — took photographs of anything relevant. Our embassy collected their contributions and the diplomatic pouch brought them here. On a

Qantas plane, ironically enough. Quite a simple operation, really."

"But with what purpose in mind, for God's sake?" The colonel sounded almost fretful: lately he had been sleeping heavily but waking exhausted.

"As a check. Against what you've written. And you'd be surprised how it does check. By the way, how do you feel?"

"Lousy."

"Well, I shouldn't worry about it. It's inevitable — but not, my medical staff assures me, deleterious."

"What're you talking about?"

"Drugs, my friend, drugs! I'm having them mixed with your food."

"Then I'll bloody well stop eating."

"Yes, you could do that. But if you did we'd force-feed you and drug you with a hypodermic. So be sensible. It's easier and more comfortable."

"What sort of drugs?"

"Perfectly harmless, I promise you. All they do is make you a little more receptive and a little less uncooperative."

"Uncooperative? When I've been writing like a bloody maniac?"

"Indeed," Lim placated, "indeed. And, really, we're very grateful to you. But now we've got to use what you've given us to make something out of you."

"I *am* something."

"No," Lim contradicted gently, sliding a fresh newspaper clipping towards his prisoner, "I'm afraid you're not."

A banner headline and a photograph cut carefully from the front page of the *Sydney Morning Herald* of June 2, 1975, lay on the desk.

"AUSTRALIAN COLONEL DEFECTS TO CHINESE," the older man read — and saw that the photograph was one of himself.

"Where's the rest?" he demanded, shaking the precisely cut clipping. "Where's the rest of the page?"

"In Sydney, I suppose," Lim replied. "In any event, we wouldn't have shown you any more than that. That's all that concerns you."

"It's a fake. You've forged it."

"It was cut out of yesterday's *Sydney Morning Herald* and you

know it," Lim replied patiently. "In fact, it's a report based on letters sent home last week by your seven colleagues. We allowed them
one letter each, after we'd notified your government they were to
stand trial. Six of the seven, when they wrote, mentioned you — not
very flatteringly, I'm afraid. And now nobody will want you but me.
Naturally this is distressing for you — that's why I've had you given
drugs — but you've just got to accept now that you've got nothing
and are nothing."

"Whatever it is you're trying to do to me depends on that, doesn't
it?" the colonel muttered. "On my being no one and having nothing?"

"Yes."

The elderly Australian fidgeted and then glanced irritably across
at Lim. "You've failed, well," he snapped. "I mean" — and he gig-
gled — "well, you've failed."

"Tell me," Lim invited.

"Get stuffed," his prisoner retorted.

"Then tell them about your grandmother's gold shares."

"She bought 'em at five shillings, and almost at once they went up
to fourteen pounds. Each! And in case you're not so hot on old-
fashioned currencies, that means her shares — her five hundred
pounds — went up by fifty-six hundred per cent. It was the beginning of her fortune."

"She was lucky, eh?"

"She was not: she was shrewd, and she was chivalrous."

"Chivalrous?"

"Till the day she died — which was the moment she no longer had
to endure her angina in order to protect her settlements from taxes
— she let all her men stay convinced she was an idiot and utterly
dependent on them. She had this marvellous gift for making you feel
important to her, interesting to her, cleverer than she was. She was
a marvellous woman."

"She's dead," Lim amended.

"She *was* dead," the colonel contradicted. "They all were, come to
that, except Pat: but you've brought 'em back to life. So I'm not
alone, and whaddyer propose doing about it?"

"Sending you back to your cell . . ."

"With plentyer paper?"

"With all the paper you can possibly want. To write. And kill them all off again!" Lim pressed the button on his desk. "I'll see you as usual," he promised easily, "in a week."

But as the colonel departed, a guard fore and aft, Lim frowned. Something was wrong. Somewhere in his prisoner there flickered a wholly unexpected ember of resistance. It wasn't defiance, nor was it his claim to have resuscitated the dead past; but it *was* something. He must proceed cautiously.

Cautiously, because his superiors wanted a defector from Australia to broadcast to the world. In the over-all Sino-Japanese strategy, this broadcast was a tactic of little significance. It was simply one of hundreds of small ruses that would simultaneously be practised. But it was the biggest task Lim had ever had assigned to him, and he was determined not to fail.

It was not just his vanity, however, which required that Russell should broadcast: it was also a report from Canberra, which, if it were true, could only mean that his first deception had failed.

Methodically he checked back on the complex weaving of his plot.

Here in Changi he was undermining the colonel's morale by confronting him with evidence of the hatred his fellow Australian prisoners bore him. The best evidence of this was the genuine *Sydney Morning Herald* report that Russell had defected.

He had told Russell that this report stemmed from letters written home a week ago by his seven compatriots. But the report had not stemmed from seven such letters (in fact he had not allowed any of them to write home) but from letters which his department had forged in the colonel's own handwriting and sent to his family and to the Australian press.

Inexplicably (so his embassy reported) these letters were now officially regarded as forgeries. In spite of the fact that the *Sydney Morning Herald*'s version of them had reached him that day, and that every other Australian paper had carried the same story, Australian Intelligence apparently suspected that Russell's letters were forged.

The possibility that he might ultimately fail to achieve the difficult task assigned to him made Lim anxious, but that he should be exposed, one-third of the way through that task, as a technical blunderer appalled him. Therefore Russell must broadcast, if only to prove to Australian Intelligence that the letters were not forgeries after all. Without such a broadcast, his masters' plans would still succeed, but his own reputation would be destroyed — and he was almost insanely jealous of his reputation.

After a moment's reflection Lim telephoned to another office and was shortly joined by the man whose task it had been to forge the letters the authenticity of which was now in dispute. Together, then, they compared photostats of the finished letters and sheets of the colonel's quarto manuscript: and detected in them no discrepancies — not even of style. Written with a ball-point pen, covered with Russell's fingerprints, they denounced Western Imperialism, decried the entire American way of life, and fervently embraced the cause of a socialist war of liberation. They contained warm messages of affection for the writer's family and country: but they irrevocably abandoned both. And every line and syllable of them had been lifted, with immense skill, from one or other of the colonel's own five manuscripts.

Lim asked only one question of his expert.

"Could it be *proved* that these letters were forgeries?" he demanded. "By examining fingerprints, handwriting, or anything else? Could it be *proved* beyond all doubt?"

"Never," the expert told him.

Dismissing the expert, Lim determined for the moment to forget his worries about the letters. Let the Australians question their authenticity: they could prove nothing. And soon the colonel himself, speaking live from Radio and Television Singapore, would remove every doubt. All Lim had to do was to persuade his prisoner to make the broadcast. Picking up his dossier, he read again the details of his plan.

Back in his cell, the colonel sat on his bed and fought the languor that assailed him, trying to assess the danger of it. He could recall and he could remember, he realized: but he could not — simply could not — anticipate or plan. The past was vivid, the future a wall of thick black glass. So it was the future that was dangerous.

"Must fight what they *will* do," he muttered, but then shook his head, trying to clear it, because he could not foresee what they would do.

He looked at the pen in his hand and at the neat stack of clean white paper.

"Lovely white paper," he murmured. "Hundreds of beautiful blank sheets of lovely white paper."

And then remembered (because it was past, and about the past his memory had a diamond-edged clarity) how lately he had become obsessed with the patterns and mechanics of writing. Yes, that was it. That, from the very beginning, had been the defence he had decided upon. Stupid to forget it. He must defend himself against the enemy with words. With the shape and arrangement of words.

He must write and then juggle his words, revising them, rearranging them, transposing and crossing them out. He must write and rewrite and rewrite, till his pages were a cat's-cradle of words that only he could unravel.

Then he could hide from Lim, deep inside the cat's-cradle.

He must transcribe the scored, patched, amended, emended, appended, elided, obsessively revised pages and send them to Lim cleanly copied — flushing the original pages, with their myriad corrections, down the squat-latrine in the corner of his cell. Misled by the tidy paragraphs and the unagitated hand, his enemy would detect in them none of the intricate gossamer strength of carefully woven words: he could hide from Lim, deep inside the woven words.

He could not plan — the drugs prevented that now — but he could remember and write and hide.

Rob instantly captured my imagination because she had looked after my father and his brothers when they were small, and had a vast repertoire of stories about them as children and my grandparents as young parents. Listening to her, I began faintly to understand the cycle of birth, childhood, marriage, children, old age, and death.

She herself had been the older of two daughters of a senior civil servant. Like my mother when she was a girl, the young Rob had gone to the best schools and had had hopes of becoming a concert pianist. The young Rob had even had *two* pianos — one for practice, one for family recitals.

But her father had fallen ill and on his death-bed had extracted a promise that, so long as her mother lived, Rob would neither leave her nor marry.

"And so, of course," Rob told us in her quiet, patient, reasonable voice, "I promised."

After five years her fiancé married someone else. By the time her mother died all the family money was gone. Confronted with the need to earn a living, Rob became assistant nanny to my father and his two brothers.

"Did they have to go to bed at half-past seven?" I demanded.

"At your age, yes," Rob told me.

"Did they have to work for their pocket money?"

"Yes."

"Did dad used to get belted?"

"Not 'did he used to get.' "

"Sorry, Rob. Used he to get belted?"

"Oh yes. They all did."

"Was Gar's voice all croaky and excited then?"

"No, your grandmother had a very pretty voice in those days. Your grandmother was a very beautiful woman."

"Gar was?"

"Yes. And she played wonderful tennis and golf."

"Gar did?"

"Better than your grandfather. In fact, she gave up tennis, I always thought, only because she did play it so much better than your grandfather."

"And golf?"

"Well, she could always play that with someone else." (I thought of my father playing golf because it didn't matter to his opponent how badly he played.) "It's only recently she gave up golf. Because of her angina."

"What's angina?"

"Angina pectoris. It causes your grandmother a lot of pain. Down her arm and across her chest."

All this I found fascinating.

"Will Gar die of angina?" I asked my father to prove to him how much I knew.

"Cold-blooded little brute," he observed and then, not answering my question, "I think you should go to a gymnasium."

"Why?"

"Because you're small for your age. And cold-blooded. You can learn to box."

"I don't want to learn to box."

"All the more reason why you should! Liz?"

"Yes?"

"We must find a gym for Tony and have him taught P.T. and boxing."

My mother came and looked at me thoughtfully. "He's all right," she objected. "A bit small for his age, perhaps. But he gets that from you . . ."

"More beef on him won't hurt."

"Oh, all right, if you say so," she agreed.

Which is why, once a week, this man used to hang me by my arms high up on a wall ladder, my back to the wall, and then get his head behind my shoulders and push outwards until my neck crunched and my arms creaked and my back broke in about five different places.

I hated him. All the other exercises I could do without effort: but for the wall ladder and the boxing I hated him.

"Hit me here, with your left," he would order, indicating his nose as we boxed. But as soon as I moved with my left, he would guard his nose with his right and hit mine with his left. Or my stomach. Or my chin. Always he made me throw the punches he wanted, and then — knowing that they were coming — brushed them aside and hit me instead.

"It's not fair," I protested.

"Well," he remarked, "you've got to learn, haven't you? Come on now, a left to my guts and a right to my chin. That's it" — blocking both and jabbing me twice on the mouth — "we don't want to grow up into a mother's boy, do we?"

"What's a mother's boy?"

"Someone — your right to my heart, Good!" — protecting his heart and practically destroying my solar plexus — "who's a softy."

I stopped boxing. "I'm *not* a softy."

"No," he agreed. "But for a kid your age you're far too polite."

The charge bothered me, so I took it to Rob, who disputed it stoutly. "You're just like your father was at your age," she comforted, "and now he's just like his father was then."

"Did you used to — used you to know mum?"

"I met your mother when she first came to your father's home to play tennis. She lived just up the road, you know."

"No. Where?"

"Oh," she and the Professor lived there after Louise, her mother, died. Of consumption, I think it was. Your mother played the piano beautifully . . ."

"As beautifully as you?"

"More beautifully. I hadn't played for fourteen years when I met your mother. Your father was nineteen then and anxious to go to the War, so he asked your mother to marry him and then he enlisted."

"Did they get married then?"

"No. It was five years before your father got back from the War and studying at the Inns of Court in London. They got married in 1920. And in 1921 you were born."

"What did you do after dad went to the War?"

"Oh, I stayed on a little longer, until your uncles went too. But then there was nothing for me to do, so I took another position."

There was something chilling and desolate in those words.

"Well, we're only little, Pat and me . . ." I comforted.

"Pat and I!"

". . . Pat and I, so you'll be here a long time, won't you?"

"I hope so," she said, smiling, "I've always felt at home with your family."

Rob taught me to understand a little of the continuity of family life; let me feel its texture, filled in all the family portraits. My father's display of paternal authority was based on his father's authority. Gan was spoiled by Gar: but Doc was lonely and shy without his Louise. I was like my father as a child: but Pat was like Gar as a young woman. I thought Rob wise and interesting, even though she was ancient.

She lived in my old room, and after a while I told her about building the wardrobe with my mother. She laughed, with that same cracked sound in her voice that Gar had (which, I decided, must be something to do with being old), and I warned her, "You mustn't tell dad though."

"Anthony!" She sounded quite shocked. "As if I would! If you only *knew* all the things your father told me that *his* father never got to hear about. All the scrapes he got into. Anthony, how could you *think* . . . ?"

"I'm sorry Rob," I said earnestly. "Really, I'm sorry" — and placated her. "I didn't know."

"It's one of the things I'm here for," she told me; and so became not only my confidante (as she had been my father's) but a source of much interesting material which subsequently could be used in conversation with my parents.

Thus: "How old was dad when you first knew him?" I asked my mother.

"Sixteen. I was asked to play tennis at his place on Saturdays."

"What was he like?"

"Like you. A bit bigger, but like you. A nice youth."

I had never heard my mother use the word youth before. Each of my friends she described either as a nice boy, a funny child, or a poisonous little brute.

"What's a youth?"

"Someone older than a boy and younger than a man."

"Did you decide to marry dad when he was a youth?"

"I suppose I did really."

"What was grandad like then?"

"Only ever saw him on the tennis court. He liked to win! Most men do though."

Somehow convinced by this that my mother preferred youths to men, I suddenly felt less dissatisfied than usual with the extreme slowness with which I was becoming a grown-up.

At school the influence of Beatles became predominant. With his lean legs and frame, his thin passionate face and lank, dark hair, he had a capacity for fanaticism that I had never before encountered. Occasionally, when he got angry, it was terrifying: but most of the time it was fascinating.

His technique remained the same — to take the enthusiasm and energy of children and channel them into pastimes and hobbies usually practised by adults. As eleven-year-olds he consistently matched us, at rugby and cricket, against teams senior to ourselves and, screaming from the sidelines, exhorted us to win.

"Tackle him low," he would scream as an adversary six inches taller and heavier than oneself thundered towards one. "LOW!"

"Fall on it," he would command as the ball was dribbled forward by a pack of brute enemy forwards perfectly prepared to hack one to death if one obeyed him. "Fall on it."

And, heroically, we tackled low and fell on it.

But if, during the day, on the playing field, I was heroic, at night, in my dreams, I became superhuman.

For one thing, I used habitually to broad-jump sixty-six feet!

Beatles had introduced us to broad-jumping, and I had at once recognized it as exactly that combination of running and leaping that intoxicated me whenever I raced Gar's Buick, my feet hardly touching the pavement. I loved the carefully measured run. I loved reaching my top speed and then hurling myself up and forward. I loved the flailing flight and the reluctant thudding down into a pit of sand. Awake, I longed to be able to jump twenty feet.

In my sleep, though, I would run hard and fast and take off: but as I began to fall I would draw up my legs . . . and cease to fall . . . and instead glide. Indeed, if I chose to tuck my knees right up under my chin, I so released myself from the tug of gravity that I actually climbed.

This procedure I could have repeated indefinitely (so that I could quite easily have jumped a hundred yards, or a mile and a quarter, had I wanted), but my father's constant admonition, "Tige, don't show off," used always to sound in my ear just as I sailed over the end of the twenty-five-foot sand pit and impose upon me a more modest effort. In mid-flight, therefore, I would line myself up with the adjacent cricket nets and aim to land by the far stumps. And so, exactly twenty-two yards from my take-off point, effortlessly, I would touch down — my cousins open-mouthed with astonishment.

I had another recurring but superhuman dream which was similar — but less inhibited. In that I would run down our side verandah, gather speed round the corner onto the back verandah, skim past the room that had been built for Ruth but now was mine, and,

at the top of the steep flight of wooden steps that led down to our
back yard — at the foot of which Peter, our first dog, had bitten all
the tradesmen — would dive forward, spreading my arms wide,
and fly.

It was perfectly easy and most stimulating: and my flights were
always swift and swooping, like a swallow's. First I swooped down
the staircase, then lifted sharply upwards (to clear the Barkers' seven-
foot paling fence), next swooped low over the Barkers' back lawn, up
over their other fence, down over the next lawn and up over the next
fence, up higher to clear the trees in the vacant lot on the corner,
and finally I landed gently, feet down, on Nelson Road, just in front
of Billy Hughes' place.

Naturally I never flew *into* Billy Hughes' place, because he had
been P.M. at the time of the Somme and Passchendaele, and I was
nothing if not a respectful child: but I flew as far as it, which nobody
else could do.

Of course Billy Hughes wasn't the only man I respected.

In order of priority, I respected my parents, Kingsford Smith,
Deerfoot, Jack Crawford, Uncle Al, and Beatles. My father said I
should respect Ellsworth Vines as much as Crawford.

"But he's American," I objected.

"You must learn impartiality," he told me sternly, but not knowing
what impartiality meant I did not bother.

One afternoon my father drove us all to The Gap — which people
jumped over to kill themselves on the jagged rocks below, at the
corner of the Pacific Ocean and Sydney Harbour — and when we got
there we all stood around looking at the ocean to our right and the
harbour to our left.

"What are we waiting for?" I demanded, looking with furtive opti-
mism for someone who might be about to jump over and kill himself.

"Amy Johnson," my father told me. "She'll fly over any minute
now."

And sure enough, just then, a tiny plane (no bigger than the one
that had plopped down beside the breakwater at Port Macquarie)
buzzed into sight — and all round the harbour's foreshores thousands
of voices cheered, and cars hooted their horns, and in the harbour
ferries blew their sirens; and the tiny green plane wobbled overhead
to land at Mascot.

"Fantastic," said my father. And even though she was English, I moved Amy Johnson onto my list of those I respected, placing her equal third with Kingsford Smith.

"Where they fly now," my father declared, "huge aeroplanes carrying twenty passengers will fly later." I thought him a bit mad on this occasion, but then he was grown-up and they were all a bit mad. Even Gar was mad about aeroplanes.

"Mitt," she said, "we must buy some shares in passenger planes."

"Your grandmother," Gan explained then, "has gone cuckoo about shares. With the world in economic ruin, she's buying shares in everything."

Whilst my grandmother was crazily buying shares in everything, anxiety about the world's state of economic ruin crept into our household for the first time. Not because we had become at all poor (successful barristers, it seemed, were rich, Depressions or no Depressions), but because others had become so desperately poor that curious political groups had mushroomed, and sober citizens like my father — he could afford to be sober — actually feared revolution.

Against the day of this disaster, he brought home sacks of flour and sugar and crates of tinned food, which he stacked against the wall of the kitchen; and iron bars, which he cut with a hacksaw into lengths that he could cement into every window frame in the house; and two rifles, with one of which he insisted that my mother practise on the back lawn after he had dragged her off to the police station to get a licence.

"Ruddy nonsense," she muttered. "Still, at least we'll die well fed!"

Darkly the uncles talked of the New Guard, anarchy, look-what's-happening-in-Germany, the unemployed, and That Bugger Lang. Irritably my mother lay on the back lawn each day and banged off ten rounds of .22 ammunition at empty IXL jam tins that I set up for her on the back fence. Usually she hit the tin, with a *whang* and a vicious little hole to prove it, but she remained uncharacteristically humourless about the exercise; and when I asked could I have a shot, and my father said yes, she snapped, "No, you may bloody well not." I supposed it was because I had no licence.

So my father made me a powerful catapult, a stone from which hit the IXL tins almost as savagely as a .22 bullet, and as I practised with it (not quite sure whether my enemies were to be the New Guard, the unemployed, Germans, anarchists, or Jack Lang) covetousness returned to my little sister's all-seeing, blue eye.

"Tone," she whined, "gimme a shot."

"No," I said. "You're too little" — and so implicit with crisis was the atmosphere that she hardly bothered to argue.

Tripe also sensed that all was not well and chased cars more hysterically than ever and ate the square of latex that my father had brought home for me from Ceylon, for which I would have thrashed him mercilessly had not my father said, "Good God, the poor brute'll die!" — so that Pat burst into tears and sat for hours with the poor brute's head clutched to her chest, wailing, "Don't die, Tripe. Please don't die."

"What's all that banging?" Gar asked as she arrived one Saturday and I met her at the front gate.

"Mum and dad shooting," I told her. "Because of the New Guard and all that."

Gar marched straight down to the back lawn and told my father not to be ridiculous, nothing was going to happen; and he told her to mind her own business, mater, because with all due respect she didn't know what she was talking about; and for the first time my mother looked faintly amused by her rifle as Gar stumped off up the back steps (that I, in my dreams, swooped down) and said to Rob, "I know I shouldn't say it, but Mitt's becoming impossible."

"He's worried for his home and his family," Rob explained. "And after all, what harm does it do?"

"Men," said my grandmother darkly, from which I concluded that she liked them no more than my mother did. "How long will that barrage last?"

"They'll be up any minute."

"Then I'll wait for them in the sitting-room where it's cooler. Tony" — and her hand with all the rings on it fell lightly on my head — "come and tell me what you've been doing at school."

Later, when my father joined her, I was sent away, so I went and found Rob.

"Why's dad worried for his home and family?" I asked.

"Well, he has lost one home already, hasn't he?"

"Has he?"

"At Cronulla, Tony."

"Oh yeah . . ."

"Not 'oh yeah,' Tony."

"Sorry, Rob. Oh yes. Rob, what happened at Cronulla?"

I had just been born she told me, and my father and mother were living in a cottage at Cronulla, on the coast, south of Sydney. One week-end, in their motor bike and sidecar, they took me up to Edgecliff, for the grandparents to see (I supposed I must have been beautiful and angelic then too), but when they got back with me, late at night, there was nothing left of their cottage but ashes.

"They lost everything," Rob said. "All their wedding presents, your mother's piano . . ."

"Isn't this her piano?" I asked, pointing through the kitchen door into the dining-room, where the grand piano sat in the corner.

"No, that's your grandmother's."

"Gar's?"

"No — your other grandmother's. The Professor's wife; your mother's mother, Louise."

"Oh," I said. I did not have the interest in dead relatives that grown-ups had. "What did mum and dad do then?"

"They drove back to Edgecliff and lived there, in your grandfather's big garage, until your father could start building another house."

"This one?"

"This one," she agreed: and at that the Lindfield house became more valuable to me. I looked at the sacks of flour and sugar and the crates of tinned food; I thought of Pat and Tripe; of my father saying, "Don't tell anyone. Not even your mother," and of my mother, her jaw clenched, playing intricate études on the rosewood Steinway that she had inherited from the dead Louise after the fire at Cronulla; and desperately I wanted to defend them all. But I knew neither how nor from what.

At various times in the past year we had driven to Miller's Point to witness dramatic events in the building of the bridge. We went there the day the two arcs, clawing out at each other from opposite pylons, met and were locked together in an arch. We went there the day the roadway suspended from the arch was finally completed. We especially went there the day that locomotives were drawn up, nose to tail, in a solid mass of dead-weight steel, from one side of the bridge to the other, to test it: and watched, terrified lest the whole thing crashed hundreds of feet down into the harbour because of some hidden flaw (though wouldn't it be *marvellous* if it did?).

But the biggest event of all in the saga of the Sydney Harbour Bridge — its opening — we did not attend.

"And see That Bugger Lang cut the ribbon?" my father snarled. "I'd cut my throat first."

Grown-ups in those days were always talking about cutting their throats first, or "cutting someone else's throat if he did" — and my mother even had a friend who had done it! Had stood in front of a mirror, with her husband's razor, and carefully cut her throat. I was horrified as I heard her telling my father about it. Shuddering, I had gone into the bathroom and, opening up my father's Bengal razor, had examined its oily and wicked blade. "I'll cut my throat first," grown-ups said. I knew I couldn't cut mine. And I would rather we missed seeing Jack Lang open the bridge than have my father cut his.

So, while most of Sydney lined the approach to the bridge, or watched from vantage points round the harbour, waiting for Premier Lang to arrive in state and declare our bridge open, my father and a friend played a round of golf on the deserted links at Killara. I was their caddy — and as usual my father played badly.

His opponent, on the other hand, was playing competently and needed only to win this fourteenth hole to go five up and settle the match. So, racing ahead of the two men, I found his ball on the edge of the fairway, moved it with my foot into an old divot hole, and then firmly, good and loyal son that I was, stood on it.

My father, unfortunately, did not take it that way. Already embittered by the knowledge that Jack Lang must at this very moment be opening the bridge, he glanced uphill as, striding briskly, he talked to his companion, and was horrified to catch me cheating. "Tig-ah!" he roared. "What the bloody hell do you think you're doing?" — and, scowling horribly, marched towards me.

Watching him come, and lamenting the fact that a man who couldn't see a ball three feet away sufficiently well to hit it could see one three hundred feet away so distinctly that now he was going to belt me for stamping on it, I resigned myself to the hiding of my life.

And for the only time in my life, by a miraculous intervention, was spared it: for across the links, shouting "Mitt, Mitt" and waving her arms, was running one of the aunts, whose home was nearby. She was dishevelled with excitement, running and shouting and waving her arms, and what she shouted was, "Lang didn't open the bridge! Lang didn't open the bridge! Lang didn't open the bridge!"

"Christ," said my father. "The New Guard always said they'd throw him into the harbour first. They must've done it." And ran towards the aunt.

Who flung her arms about him and whirled him round, chanting ecstatically, "He didn't open it! He didn't open it! Oh Mitt, isn't it marvellous?"

"What happened?" my father asked excitedly.

"De Groot opened it," my aunt said.

"De Groot?" My father had never heard of de Groot and sounded contemptuous, but to me it seemed exactly the sort of name the man who opened the bridge instead of Jack Lang should have had. A euphonious name. An adventurous name. When I grew up, I decided, I would call myself Anthony de Groot.

"It was on the wireless," the aunt explained. "Before Lang could do anything, this man de Groot, in uniform, broke through the police on his horse and galloped up the approach, waving a sword, everyone cheering, and slashed the ribbon. They had to tie it together later for Lang to cut with his scissors. So Lang didn't open the bridge; de Groot did. They've arrested him and put him in the Reception House. Isn't it marvellous?"

Abandoning golf for the day, we drove home, where all the talk was of de Groot's opening the bridge. The telephone rang incessantly. Mr and Mrs Barker hung over the back fence and my father asked them in for a drink. The Schmellings hung over the front fence and my mother asked them in for a drink. Almost without noticing it, as they sipped their sherries and whiskies, raising their glasses to de Groot, my father got through three bottles of stout. My pocket money was raised to sixpence a week. Tripe ate the fake parchment relic from the Buddhist Temple at Kandi.

"That dog," my mother said, sighing, "must have a stomach like a concrete mixer."

"Talking of which, Tige," my father murmured as he poured Mr Barker another whisky, "remind me to ask your mother to get some more of those double-strength cascaras." (It being well known that life at the Front had given my father a stomach like a concrete mixer. Nothing, it was said, short of a bomb, moved *his* insides.)

Eventually, tired of this adult obsession with Lang, Pat and I left it, she to visit her Christian Science friends, I to cycle to my cousins' home. There we played tennis — the version which caters for three players. Uncle Al was in the garden, digging, and occasionally watching us. Finally he said, "Serve deep and to the centre line against doubles players, Peter, and follow in faster to the net."

"Come and play with us," Peter suggested.

For a moment Uncle Al, the one-time Prince of Volleyers, hesitated. Then he said, "All right. Just for a few games."

Because he no longer owned a tennis racquet, he had to borrow one of ours, which meant that we still played cut throat, he against two of us, the third sitting out.

The next hour was fascinating. We were strong, agile children who had been daily banging tennis balls about for more than three years: he was a victim of war-time gassing who had played no tennis since 1914. Yet he walked onto the court and served balls so deep and well placed that the best we could do was hit them straight to him as, remorselessly, he strode towards the net. From both forehand and backhand, high and low, his flowing volleys drove us back, drove us wide, until finally he would put the ball away. We rarely won a point; we never won a game; and I never wanted it to stop.

It had to, of course, and when it did he said, "Thank you, boys," and went back to his digging, never to play with us again.

Enthused by this first example of great tennis, I began to nag and beg and whine to be allowed to see the championships played at Sydney's White City; and finally Gar persuaded my grandfather, who had four permanent seats, to let her take me whenever there was one to spare. At once Jack Crawford, with his long flannels and his sleeves buttoned at the wrist and his hair impeccably groomed, became my idol, and a Japanese player called Harada (who, leaping for high backhand volleys, always turned a complete circle in midair) my ideal. More fanatically than ever, we eleven-and-a-half-year-olds practised our tennis on every one of the afternoons not otherwise occupied by Beatles' scouting, bush lore, sport, and war games.

Every evening, though, at six I had to be home. Then, putting away my bicycle, I would swiftly circle the house, looking for any untidiness that could earn me a cut in my pocket money — dismally conscious of the fact that my father's talent for proving me inadequate constantly rendered me so blind that I could even fail to see sheets of newspaper. This chore done, I would wash, comb my hair, put on a tie and shoes and socks, and — until dinner at six-thirty — listen to the wireless.

My father disapproved as strongly of my listening to the wireless ("filling your head with drivel") as he did of my going to the pictures ("you should be out *doing* something") and reading too much ("you're becoming a bloody bookworm"); but since I only listened when I was clean and decently dressed for dinner, he found it difficult to find grounds for banning the habit. For the most part, therefore, I listened.

Which is how I came to be the bearer to the dinner table of tidings of electrifying impact.

As soon as the first words of the announcement were made I knew that I had a heroic role to play and that I must remember all of what was said. Squatting beside the radio (which lately had been moved to my parents' bedroom in a futile attempt to entertain my father when he was ill), I devoured every word — aware of this high adult drama — steeping myself in it. Then, when it had finished, I dashed downstairs to the dining-room, where my father had just taken his seat. (Was it a week-end, midday dinner? My recollection is that it was not dark. But it is not important.)

"Dad, dad," I shouted, taking the stairs two at a time.

"Don't jump downstairs and don't interrupt your mother," he snapped.

"But, dad . . ."

"Tiger!"

"It's important."

"Shut *up*." His expression was furious, my mother's astonished, and I knew that I had lost my audience, but I could not shut up.

"Jack Lang's been sacked!" I shouted — and had the satisfaction of seeing his face register incredulity, hope, suspicion, glee, and blankness in swift succession.

The blankness turned out, however, to be judicial rather than traumatic, which would have been more satisfying.

"Do you have any reason for saying this?" he asked coldly.

"Yes." I was indignant that he should doubt me, and he reacted to my indignation with a faint increase of warmth.

"What reason?"

"I heard it."

"Where?"

"On the wireless."

"What was said? Exactly. This is very important."

"I know. That's why I ran downstairs."

"Tige" — both imploringly and menacingly — "the exact words." But they were gone. "I can't remember," I told him sullenly.

"Hell's bells," he thundered, but my mother intervened swiftly.

"Try," she urged quietly. "You were sitting by the wireless. What did you hear?"

As suddenly as it had vanished, now it returned. Or enough of it to enable me to feel my part, hold my audience.

"There was a sort of shout," I told them. "The announcer shouted, 'Jack Lang's been sacked,' and then stopped and said something like, 'The Governor, Sir Philip Game, has dismissed the Premier and has exercised his . . . his . . .' "

"Prerogative," my father prompted.

"Yes, and then something about the constitution and procedure."

My father considered the law for a moment. "You know," he told my mother, "it could be done. It'd take guts — my God, it'd take guts; because if Lang's re-elected it's the end of Philip Game — but it could just be done. Unprecedented, of course, but it's feasible at law." The telephone rang, and suddenly my father was all smiles. "Guess what that'll be about!" He laughed and got up from the table. "Thank you for telling us," he said as he passed me and went into the hall.

"Yes," we heard him saying. "Yes, just this second. Tony told us. He heard it on the wireless."

I felt positively grown-up.

It was at this time that I had my last taste of paternal inflexibility. We were digging the front garden, he first with the spade, I following with the fork, and until I finished the whole of the front bed I could not go to the cousins' place to play tennis.

I hated gardening. Picks, mattocks, hoes, secateurs, forks, shovels, and spades were all totally displeasing to me. Not that I was lazy: I would mow lawns for hours and enjoy it — the pattern of it, the rhythm of it. But other horticultural implements, producing no patterns, lacking all rhythm, involving only grunting and shoving and heaving, I loathed.

Forking I particularly loathed because it spattered the narrow concrete path on the far side of the garden with dirt, and my father's declared method of removing such dirt was to sweep it back off the concrete and into the garden with the palm of his hand. In all of my eleven and a half years I had encountered no noise or sensation more repellent than that of dry dirt and concrete against the palm of my hand. Compared with this, the sound of chalk squeaking on a blackboard was mellifluous and sweet. Compared with this, the feeling of a toad under one's bare foot, or of unseen seaweed in the surf sliding shark-like along one's bare thigh, was caressing and tender. But my father enjoyed it, precisely as his father enjoyed it, and it never occurred to him that I, his dutiful son, would dare not to enjoy it too.

Thus irritated by the length of my task and bored by its plodding, grunting tedium, I progressed slowly along the bed. Lift fork high in right hand, lurch down, press deep with right bare foot, turn the soil, break up the clods, move left bare foot slightly — and repeat. Interminably.

Until the nauseating moment when — although I felt only the blow, not any pain — I uttered a short yelp and looked down at the purplish wound, on my left foot, from which protruded the farthest prong of the fork. As I watched, blood oozed up round the metal, trickled across my instep and into the garden, and I opened my mouth to scream.

But my father, leaping to my side, was too quick for me. "If you cry," he snarled, plucking the fork out of my foot, "I'll belt you."

Silently, therefore, I suffered him to lead me to the garden tap, turn it on hard, and push my foot under the rushing water until my wound, streaming blood, lost its dire, purplish, punctured look. Pat advised that God was Love and There was no Pain. Rob opened a window and passed something to my father.

"Foot out," he ordered. Obediently and trustingly I gave him my foot: over all of which, most treacherously, he poured iodine.

"Now," he said, holding my head against his chest as the tincture bit, "you can howl your head off."

Again my father collapsed, and this time was taken to the hospital where I had lost my adenoids and tonsils and Pat her appendix. The fact of his being in familiar surroundings diminshed our anxiety about him, and we soon accepted his absence there as naturally as we had his daily absences in chambers or in court.

At first we used to ask could we see him, but my mother always told us that he was tired and needed to rest and sent his love. After a while we began simply to ask her, when she arrived home for dinner each evening, "How's dad?" And she would say, "Sleeping mostly," or, "Better today," or, "He talked quite a lot and asked were you being good." We hardly missed him.

I missed my mother though. Every day when I got home I would shout "Mum?" I knew she was at the hospital but still I shouted it. And still I felt vaguely resentful when, instead of her voice calling back, "In here," Rob invariably appeared, saying, "She's with your father."

Once not even Rob answered.

"Mum?" I shouted, then "Mum?" again, and then "Rob?"

Not a sound.

I pictured myself deserted — or even orphaned — and wandered irritably, in my bare feet, into the kitchen. The door of Rob's room was open and just beyond it, standing with her back to me, sobbing, was Gar, with Rob's arms around her. Terrified lest they notice me, I tiptoed backwards out of sight and retired disconsolately to my room.

I could think of nothing to do. Normally I would have taken my racquet and a ball and practised volleying against the garage door:

but it seemed heartless to hit the ball, *ping* off the strings, *thump* off the door, *ping-thump, ping-thump,* endlessly, when Gar was crying.

I thought of taking the back wheel off my bike and adjusting the brake: but I had done it only the week before and I knew the brake was as good as it ever would be.

What to do?

I decided to cut my treasured snakeskin into strips and plait it into a belt which I could present, via my mother, to my father; and, feeling better at the prospect of something to do, rushed upstairs to my parents' bathroom to borrow my father's second cut-throat razor. He'd kill me if he caught me using it, particularly for slicing up the skin of an old dead python; but then, he wouldn't catch me, he wasn't home. Without a qualm I took the beautifully honed blade and ran downstairs again.

Now for the skin — in my bottom drawer with my cricket bat, my catapult, and the three once-used tennis balls Uncle Roy had given me. I opened the drawer.

No snakeskin.

Disbelief lasted several seconds, sick acknowledgement of the fact a few more, and black fury for hours. Tripe! Everything I loved, Tripe ate. And probably Pat fed it to him. I hated Pat and Tripe.

Petulantly I snatched my catapult out of the drawer, kicked the drawer shut ('Always leave things as you found them, Tige'—after picnics in the bush we even had to dig a hole in which to bury everything, including the ashes of the fire, and then, using a small leafy branch, smooth over the filled-in hole), and stumped down to the back yard, where I slammed stone after stone against the galvanized iron chimney of the incinerator. Clang they went — and I never gave my sobbing grandmother a thought: just chose a suitable stone, placed it in the leather, drew it back to my right eye (the fork held almost horizontally in my left hand, and at arm's length, as I sighted), then let it go. Slap went the rubber, whirr went the stone, and clang went the iron chimney.

"Gimme a go, Tone." It was Pat, and beside her, outrageously cordial, Tripe. As if they had never heard of snakeskins. Not to mention the parchment relic from Kandi, a whole sheet of raw latex, and about nine hundred silk worms. Ignoring them, I fired gibber after gibber at the incinerator chimney — and missed with all of them.

"Tone?"

"No."

"Why not?"

I refused to answer.

"Tone, why not?"

"Because."

Useless to say "Because you fed Tripe my snakeskin." She'd only cross her heart and spit her death and that'd be another argument lost. Sticking the catapult in the back pocket of my shorts and still ignoring her, I went down to the incinerator to collect all the gibbers, gooks, and goolies I'd fired at the chimney, stuffing them into my shirt pocket and the side pockets of my pants. Then I returned to my firing line — twenty yards from the chimney — and reached round for my catapult, prepared to resume my barrage.

No catapult.

But across the other side of the lawn was Pat, with a catapult, which she held with the fork firmly against her nose and the strong rubber thongs pulled as far away from her face as possible. She was, in short — with Tripe panting adoration as he squatted at her feet — about to shoot herself between the eyes. And fascinated by the laws of poetic justice, I let her do it.

As the small round stone, walnut-sized, whanged off her tough little skull, she turned upon me a look unbearably forlorn and reproachful and sank down on to her rump.

"You fired it the wrong way," I remonstrated, trying to excuse myself.

"I know."

"Does it hurt?" She had a wicked lump on her forehead.

"God is Love," she muttered. She had this marvellous gift, you see, even when she had just fed her dog your treasured snakeskin and stolen your catapult, of putting you in the wrong. I used to hate her for it.

Uncle Jim arrived from Edgecliff one week-end and said that as my father was ill he was going to act *in loco parentis*. I had no idea what this meant, but, being a doctor, he often used phrases I didn't understand, and at least this one sounded interesting, so I climbed into the rumble seat of his Ford (his new fiancée was with him in the front seat) and drove to Cronulla, where he had a cottage adjacent to the vacant lot upon which, twelve years earlier, my parents' first home had stood.

At the cottage were quite a few couples whom Uncle Jim organized, first into swimming, then eating, then playing rounders, and then cleaning up his garden. After that everyone just talked, and during the conversation a visiting English actress said how frightening it must be to swim in the Pacific with all those sharks.

Uncle Jim and this actress had already clashed twice: the first time when she refused to garden, saying, "But darling, no! It would ruin my hands"; and the second time when, being offered one of his cigarettes, she had reached forward, saying, "I don't mind if I do" — to which he, snapping his cigarette case shut, had snarled, "Well, I don't mind if you don't!"

Now he looked at her with frank distaste and asserted, "Rubbish. Sharks are cowards."

Affronted by his lack of chivalry, one of the men contradicted him.

"You don't know what you're talking about," Uncle Jim told him with a rudeness that made me wince, "and I'll prove it."

There and then, we were all required to leave the house and travel some distance to a concrete pool on the edge of a river. It was roofed over with corrugated iron and made secure against trespassers by a strong wire fence.

"That pool's full of sharks," Uncle Jim announced. "For the Aquarium or something. I'll swim two lengths of it."

Everyone protested, but he took no notice.

"Anyone at home?" he shouted, herding us all down to the edge of the wired-in pool. There was no answer. "Well," he decided, as if it were entirely reasonable, "I'll just have to break in." And, finding a loose section of wire, he wrenched it aside, squeezed through the gap, stood on the side of the pool, and dived in.

As he had said, the pool was full of sharks — grey nurses and tigers.

Deliberately he swam to the far end of the pool, turned, and swam back again. Then, standing shoulder deep, his hands on the concrete ledge, lethal shapes lying sullen all round him, he demanded, "Satisfied? Cowards, all of 'em!" — and hauled himself out of the water.

Whereas my father was dogmatic about words, Jack Lang, manners, and the law, Uncle Jim, I soon came to realize, was dogmatic about sharks, butterflies, orchids, mineralogy, medicine, and getting guests to clean up his garden. Both of them, though, were men of tremendous authority.

Back at his cottage, having ordered the girls to the galley, he himself went unashamedly to sleep, indicating first that the rest of us could do what we liked. So I did what I had wanted to do ever since I had arrived: I crawled through Uncle Jim's rank hedge and walked on to the vacant, scrubby plot that once, in my unaware infancy, had been my home.

Unlike the house where I had been born, the pull of this place was strong. There was about it a stillness that was haunted, that lured me farther in: until, halting, I noticed that there was a design in the long, rank grass, like a harp lying on its side. So I walked farther still, looking down, and there, embedded in the soil, paspalum growing tall all round it, was the rusted framework of a grand piano.

A little to the left, my foot felt something hard and smooth, and I knelt down and picked up a nugget, as big as a man's fist, of molten glass.

"They lost everything," I could hear Rob's voice telling me then. "All their wedding presents . . ."

I came very close to my mother and father in the time that followed, inching my way through the bracken and paspalum and scrub that had been their first home. I examined the molten shapelessness of wedding present after wedding present, wondering who had given it, what it had been. I re-created the geography of the house: here, because of the brass knobs, their bed; here, because of the lead pipes, their bathroom; there, around the piano, their sitting-room; there, where there was so much glass, the sideboard and the dining-room; and there, the kitchen.

I imagined the horror of driving home late at night, on a motor bike and in a sidecar, with a baby, to find your home razed, still smouldering, and nothing — absolutely nothing — left, so that you restarted your bike, turned it round, and left, empty-handed, never to return. Abruptly I made my way back through the long grass and the rank hedge to Uncle Jim and asked him when we were going home.

"Why?" he asked. "Bored?"

"No," I told him. "I want to find out how dad is."

So he took me home; where I discovered that my mother had spent all day at the hospital and, even though Rob had sent Pat to bed, was still there. It was unlike her not to come home in time to put Pat to bed and hear her Christian Science prayers.

Yet within seconds of her return she contrived as usual to still all my fears. We talked for a while and then she began playing the piano: not any of her usual pieces but a specially adapted score of *Madame Butterfly*. At half-past seven, as the clock struck, she smiled but did not, as usual, order, "Bed!" Instead, reaching out, she turned the page of her score and played on. It was twenty to eight before she finished, and when she did she sat for a moment, hands folded on her lap, back straight, staring at nothing, and then said, "Well!"

Not sure what she meant, what she wanted, I sensed that she was prepared to allow me to stay up even later but that there was nothing we could talk about.

"Play some more," I suggested.

She looked at the clock, and then at me, and then said, "Just one more before you go to bed. What would you like?"

"Schubert's 'Serenade,' " I told her, handing her the Schubert volume and noticing for the first time that it was inscribed Doris Bentley, her maiden name. She flicked the pages over, flattened them against the music stand, glanced briefly down the sheet, as if to see what it was all about, and then began to play.

For half of the "Serenade," which I had always found soothing, its single notes falling like drops of spring water into a still pool, I was content; but then I looked up from her fingers to my mother's face and saw that it was desperately taut — as if this piece, which usually she executed with ease, were infinitely complicated — so I looked away, in case she should catch me staring at her, and became aware that Schubert's "Serenade" was not soothing at all but desolate in the extreme. And when my mother, snapping the book shut, said, "Bed," I did not argue.

"What will you do?" I asked.

"Knit," she told me crisply. It seemed a dreary way of spending the evening.

School proceeded normally, even though the last term of the year was almost done and next year we would all be moving on to the secondary schools of our parents' choice. We gave not a thought to the fact that this meant the last we would see of the Boss and Streaker and Beatles. We were not grateful to them; we would not miss them; and we were too young to know how splendidly they had served us.

Streaker even alienated us a little by interrupting our reading of *A Midsummer Night's Dream* and inquiring, "If you found your house on fire, and you could save only one person in the family, who would it be?"

It was a fearful question which hurled us into a state of instant, harassed, and collective gloom. None of us wanted to answer quickly; each of us wanted to think; and Streaker let us have our way.

Distractedly I sought the solution, unable to believe, since a grown-up posed the problem, that there was none. Would I — should I — save my mother, or my father, or Pat?

My mother, I remembered, at Port Macquarie, had tried to save me. Pat, I remembered, had always been vulnerable — to poisons, and spiders, and arrows, and catapults. My father was strong and had saved my mother and carried Pat to the doctor: but the uncles, manœuvring him through the verandah door, had had to carry him.

I hated this dilemma.

"Well, Tony?" Streaker was asking, "whom would you save?"

"All of them," I asserted.

"Only one," he insisted gently.

"My sister," I said reluctantly, "because my father would save my mother."

In turn we answered, each of us saying "my sister" or "my mother" or "my father" or even, once, "my gran — she's old." And each time Streaker just smiled sadly, as if to say, "No — wrong!" and moved on to the next.

Until at last Fred (who was so stupid he had just pronounced "melancholy" melankerly) said stolidly, "I would save myself."

"That's right," Streaker confirmed — and we all looked at him and Fred aghast. "That's right. We would each of us save ourself."

But he was wrong: at that age we would first have saved another — even a grandmother who was old.

The night before Speech Day and its giving of prizes, I was tremendously excited: not because I was to be given any prizes — all of those had been won by a red-headed boy with glasses, called Ron — but because, when Speech Day ended, the holidays would begin, and I looked forward to fishing at Port Macquarie and to the new tennis racquet I had been promised for Christmas. It was to be an Alexander with a flat-topped head, like Jack Crawford's.

Once asleep, I dreamed — long dreams, at the end of each of which I would almost wake up, wondering how anything so detailed and protracted could possibly happen in a fraction of a second (as an expert in the newspaper had said it did), and then fall into another sleep and another dream. How could that rally I had with Jack Crawford — both of us using flat-topped racquets — which continued for more than a hundred shots, all on the backhand, his to mine, mine to his, his to mine, until my backhand developed the same glorious fluency as his — how could that have lasted only a fraction of a second?

Likewise the last dream of all, where I ran round our verandah and, as usual, became airborne as I swooped down the steep, back staircase and then hedge-hopped over all the neighbours' fences — how could that have lasted only a fraction of a second?

Especially when it ended so curiously. Usually I landed by lowering my legs and running lightly till I came to a standstill just outside Billy Hughes' place. On this occasion, though, I swooped back across all the neighbours' yards, over the Barkers' fence, and dropped down at full speed onto the last of our steep back steps, which jolted me considerably, so that I had to sit on the bottom step to recover. And there, standing in front of me, in white pyjamas with a white bandage round his head, was my father.

"Made a mess of that, didn't you?" he commented affably.

"Yes."

"Your mother wants to see you."

"All right." I got up to go to her.

"Tige?"

"Yes?"

"Look after her."

"Yes, dad."

And without another word, in his pyjamas, the bandage showing very white against his black hair, he walked away, up the side path to the high wooden front gate, opened it, closed it, and vanished.

Then I woke, with Rob gently shaking my shoulder.

"Morning, Rob."

"Good morning, Tony. Your mother wants to see you."

"I know."

"What?" She sounded almost afraid, or angry; and I felt foolish because I remembered then that I had only dreamed it.

"Sorry, Rob, I meant yes, I'll go."

"She's upstairs — in the spare bedroom."

I did not question the statement: I didn't even think about it. Grown-ups gave orders, children obeyed them. If Rob had said my mother wanted to see me up the back-garden gum tree, I wouldn't have questioned it: I would just have climbed the tree. So, sleepily, I went through the verandah door into the sitting-room, through the sitting-room (strange, the clock said six-thirty: usually we got up at seven), up the stairs and along the short hall, and knocked on the door of the spare room.

"Come in." My mother, her brown hair down over her shoulders, a pink, knitted bed jacket over her blue nightdress, sat in bed, propped up by four pillows. I had never seen her like this, not even when I was six and she had had mumps and we had poked our heads round her door to laugh with her at how awful she looked.

"Are you sick, mum?"

"No. Come here, Tige." I approached her, kissed her — around her eyes was black, like Gar's — and stood beside her.

"Up here," she said, patting the bed.

So I sat beside her, and she put her right arm round my shoulders, the angora wool of her bed jacket making my neck itch.

"Tige . . ." she started and then said nothing.

I did not look at her, nor she at me: whatever was coming, I knew that I was not meant to look at her.

"Poor little Tige," she whispered. To herself, not to me; so I pretended not to have heard. Then, taking a deep breath, she said carefully, "Darling, last night your father died. I know it's awful for you, and how much you'll — we'll all miss him, but just try to remember how gay and energetic he always was — and he wouldn't ever have been that again if he'd lived. He was very sick."

"Was that why we couldn't see him?"

"He didn't forget you, but this is bettei for *him,* son, do you understand?"

"Yes, mum," I said: but I did not understand. I felt that I had been robbed, and I wanted to cry. Not for my father's sake, for my own. I felt a passionate and overwhelming grief for me; and flung myself, howling, against my mother, revelling in the comfort of her arms round me and her tears on the back of my neck.

Almost at once the storm abated and I sat up, because the fluffy angora wool of her bed jacket tickled my nose.

"I'll need your help for a few days," she said.

"I'll look after you," I promised — but I was boasting, not comforting.

"Good boy. Now — will you ask Rob to send Pat up, please?"

"Yes, mum."

"Let Rob do it, dear."

"Yes, mum" — and I was out of the room and down the stairs.

"Mum says," I passed the message on to Rob, "will you send Pat up, please?"

"Of course," she answered quietly. "There's some milk there, and some bread and butter."

"Thank you, Rob."

As she left, padding out in her big sloppy slippers (she was the only one in the house who owned slippers) with that curious half-forward, half-sideways gait that elderly ladies assume, I sipped my milk and gulped down the slices of bread which no one but Rob could cut so thin and butter so thick.

When she came back I said to her importantly, "Dad's dead" — and then, in my windpipe, felt a frightening obstacle, like a brick, suddenly bruising and choking me, and heard a weird, shuddering, airless sob retching out of me. Three times it happened — not for me, for my father — before I composed myself.

"I'm sorry, dear," Rob consoled.

"Does Gar know?"

"Yes, she was at the hospital."

"She knew before, didn't she?" I accused. "That's why she was crying that day."

"What day?"

"The day she was in your room, and you had your arms round her."

"I didn't know you'd seen that. I suppose you heard too?"

"Yes," I lied. I knew how to get things out of Rob. She never told you anything you were not supposed to know: but if you knew it already, or she thought you did, she would discuss it endlessly, consolidating her role as confidante, enjoying the momentary illusion that she had dispelled her loneliness with conversation.

"Your poor grandmother came running in to me," Rob promptly related, "and flung herself into my arms and cried, 'Oh Rob, Rob — poor Mitt — my poor darling Mitt — death is written all over his face.' Of course I tried to comfort her, I said, 'Oh no, Lady Russell, no!' But she'd have none of it, Tony. She just kept on crying, 'I've seen him, Rob. It's on his face. Oh my darling Mitt. Why does it have to be Mitt?' "

"Where is she now?" I asked.

"She'll be here this afternoon. With Sir David and your Uncle Jim."

"Oh," I said. I could not think what we would all do.

"That reminds me, I'll need some things from the shops. Your mother isn't well enough to go to the village." (Lindfield's suburban shops were known as "the village.") "Do you think you could go for me?"

"I'll get some money from mum."

"No, no. Here." She produced her purse and extracted coins from it with maddening feminine deliberation. "Take this."

I cycled up to the shops and was positively put out, as I paid for flour and sugar, by the way the grocer made no comment on the fact that my father was dead.

Dead.

The brick-like word worked instantly, and I sobbed.

"What's wrong, Tony?" the grocer asked, coming round his counter and standing in front of me. "Hey! What's wrong, son?"

"My father," I said, gulping — pleased that it was so easy.

"What about your dad?"

"He's dead." I choked — and once again wept for myself.

"Oh no!" muttered the grocer. "Look — sit there, son. That's the boy. Sit there till you feel better. Would you like a drink? Of lemon syrup?"

"Yes, please" — wetly.

He bustled off.

Yet all the time I was thinking about the story my father had told my mother just before he went to hospital. It was about a grocer's assistant who was asked by a customer if he had any coffee sugar.

"No," he said, and the customer left.

"Don't ever do that again," the grocer rebuked his assistant. "If someone asks do we have coffee sugar, don't just say, 'no' — say, 'No, sir, but we do have castor sugar, brown sugar, loaf sugar, and icing sugar.' Always offer them something. Never let them leave empty-handed."

The next day a customer came in and asked, "Have you any toilet paper?"

"No, madam," the assistant replied, "but we do have carbon paper, emery paper, sandpaper and flypaper."

I had laughed uproariously when I heard my father tell this story, and he had looked round and demanded, "What are you doing there?"

So I had told it to Peter and Bill, and Peter had told it to Jean, who promptly chased the three of us round the garden with her riding crop, shouting, "Dirty little beasts!"

The grocer returned with the lemon syrup and his wife, and I let her pat my head while I drank the syrup; then left — and repeated the performance in the cake shop (where I was given two jam tarts) and the ironmonger's (where, to my chagrin — though what else I expected in an ironmonger's I can't recall — I was handed an enamel mug full of tepid water).

Back at home, Doc, my mother's father, had arrived. He was tall, with a ginger moustache and a pipe, which he kept alight with a succession of spluttering wax matches. Also, he drank whisky and was said to play good golf and marvellous billiards. Making no effort to talk to me, he merely grinned his slightly wolfish grin, said "Hello" cheerfully, struck one of his wax matches on the sole of his light tan boot, swept it to his pipe, which he sucked moistly, and then left me. Still sucking and tamping the bowl of his pipe, he plodded upstairs.

"Doris," I heard him call, "what can I do?"

"Stay here," she called back, "till this wretched business is over."

The wretched business began in earnest when my grandparents and Uncle Jim arrived. Both Gar and Uncle Jim behaved absolutely normally, not mentioning the thing that had brought them, but my grandfather called me to the end of the verandah, cleared his throat, and then pronounced, "Anthony, you have lost a wonderful father and I have lost a wonderful son. I hope you will always be as proud of him as I am." Then, a handkerchief to his eyes, he walked quickly away, leaving me on my own, astounded.

Because none of his words made sense. I hadn't lost a wonderful father, I had lost *my* father. Furthermore, other than Pat and myself, the only person who had any claim to my father was my mother. And I wasn't proud of him; I had simply been blindly possessive of him and dependent upon him and now he wasn't there. As my grandfather walked away from me, obviously sobbing, my only feeling for him was one of hostility.

Later we were all in the sitting-room.

"There'll be a service at the Shore chapel first," Uncle Jim told my mother, "if that's all right with you."

"Of course," she said. Shore had been my father's old school, the one I was going to next year.

"Will you come with us, dear?" Gar asked my mother. "In our car?"

"To the service?"

"Yes."

"No, thanks, mum." Sitting on the fender in front of the fireplace, my mother looked drained but composed. "I'm not going."

"But Doris . . ." my grandfather began.

"Of course not," Gar said. "After the last two months, day and night, you must be worn out."

"It's not that," my mother said. "I just don't like funerals. Neither did Edward. He always used to say, 'When I die, throw me into Limeburner's Creek, in my oldest pair of shorts, with a killick round my neck to sink me.' "

"I can just imagine," my Uncle Jim mused, "five hundred mourn-ers rowing up Limeburner's Creek to see Mitt, in his old shorts with a killick round his neck, thrown to the fish."

"Well," my mother responded wearily, "when I die, just toss me into the rubbish bin and tell the council to come and collect me. And if ever I get old and nasty," — she looked at me — "poison me!"

"What about . . . ?" Uncle Jim murmured, nodding towards me.

"Oh no," Gar said.

"He'll have to decide that," my mother declared. "Tige, do you want to go to the service for your father?"

I had never been in a place of worship since that fateful morning, eight years earlier, when I had been led out of Sunday school, but something now prompted me to decide upon a second visit to a house of God.

"All right," my mother agreed. "You can represent Pat and me." Deliberately she made it sound important: made me sound the man of the house. Then, just as deliberately, she turned to Uncle Jim and added, "But only to the Shore part."

Thus, the next day, I was driven with my grandparents to a small chapel with beautiful windows and banks of pews sloping down from the panelled walls to a white-marbled aisle in the middle. Every pew was packed. Every uncle and aunt I had ever known was there. Black, black, black — ties, veils, dresses, hats, armbands — all black. For my father. Scrubbed clean and brushed sleek by Rob, in my short-trousered suit with my socks neatly up to my knees and my shoes polished to a most unaccustomed brightness, I walked behind my grandparents, beside Uncle Jim, up the white marble aisle, between all the whispering, black-clad, sad-eyed, pitying uncles and aunts.

And, with a thrill of egotism, I knew that the whispers and sadness and pity were for me.

This, all over again, was Ruth begging her friend to admire the sleeping me; but Ruth multiplied by five hundred and deliciously intensified by grief. Quite deliberately — knowing that my hair was flaxen, my skin clear, my eyebrows black ("so marvellous," an aunt had once commented enviously, "that bleached hair with those brown eyes," and I had never forgotten it) — I looked as heroically, stoically bereft as any child could or ever had. And at the mere sight of me, I observed with undiluted gratification, most of the aunts sobbed aloud.

All the slow way up that aisle my progress was a triumph. But then, abruptly, my grandparents having turned into the left-hand pew nearest the choir stalls, my view of what, all the time, had lain in front of them and me was unblocked. Standing above a sea of wreaths, pointing itself at me, mute and menacing, starkly glossy and sinisterly geometric, was the coffin. Like a snake's head. I detested snakes.

The coffin horrified me. I could think of nothing else through all that followed. The organ played, the choir sang (serenely uninvolved), and the chaplain chanted (equally uninvolved): I heard them only vaguely. What concerned me was the snake's-head coffin. Pythons could swallow goats whole. My father was in there, swallowed. Uncle Victor, tears pouring down his face, stood up and addressed the congregation with all the affection that had made him my father's good friend and with all the eloquence that had made him a K.C.: but I heard not a word. In my struggles to obliterate the image of a snake, I had begun thinking of those small wooden containers in city stores which (with one's money and one's account stuffed inside them) were catapulted along a wire to a central cashier who took out one's money, stamped the bill, and sent back a few pence change. Perhaps Uncle Victor would attach my father's coffin to a wire and catapult it to some indifferent God who would eventually send it back with my father's khaki shorts as change.

Before any such thing could occur, however, I was walking down the aisle again — this time indifferent as to the impression I created — and climbing into a car, which took me home, where my mother and Pat were playing a card game that Pat always won.

"Come and help me," my mother pleaded as they began a fresh game.

I sat down with them and Pat beat us both.

I still don't know where they took my father.

Though I did not realize it, I was living out the last weeks of my childhood.

The strain of her long vigil took abrupt effect on my mother, and our doctor ordered her to bed. In her own room once again, she lay, day after day, doing nothing: just lay on her back, her long hair loose, her head turned away from the pillow that had been my father's, and did nothing. She didn't even shout "Shut up" when Pat and I argued.

Although Pat, at eight, had not seemed to grasp exactly what death meant either to her father or to herself, she had instantly perceived how it lacerated her mother: so she not only made her endless cups of tea and baked her a succession of disastrous cakes, but also borrowed for her and offered her the comfort of books on Christian Science.

Unable, with Pat's books, to order me, "Quick, throw these down the lavatory and pull the chain before Littly comes back," as she did with Pat's cakes, my mother began to read Mary Baker Eddy and the Bible.

In all my life I had only known her to go to church once, which was for the funeral of an uncle who had been killed when his plane crashed, and for whom my father had to deliver an oration. Now, though, she seemed to be stimulated by her Christian Science reading, possibly even converted. Certainly her mind recovered its liveliness and she began to be impatient of lying in bed.

Unfortunately, two weeks of unaccustomed inactivity had left her constipated, and this failure of the flesh she felt obliged, as a novitiate, to cure by Christian Science. After the most sincere but futile spiritual straining, however, she began to have doubts.

"Tige," she asked, "would you say constipation was mental or physical?"

"What's constipation?" I demanded.

"Not going to the lavatory every day."

"Aren't you?"

"No."

"Haven't you been today?"

"I haven't been for a week!"

"Mum!"

"Tige, don't mum me, just tell me whether you think it's mental or physical."

"When we don't go, you give us castor oil," I pointed out.

"You're no damn use," she muttered and returned to her literature.

I became very concerned for her, and the next morning, after I had kissed her, I asked, "Have you been yet?"

"No," she told me and resumed her reading.

I told Pat that mum hadn't been for eight days and I thought she should take castor oil.

"God is Love . . ." Pat began.

"But she isn't *going!*" I interrupted. "And if you don't go you die."

Pat remained fanatically unmoved.

The next morning I again asked my mother if she had been, and again, but this time not quite so offhandedly, she said no.

The next morning, as soon as I had kissed her, and before I could ask her anything, she said, "Tige, look in the medicine cabinet and see if there are any cascara pills."

I looked and there were.

"Bring me two," she ordered, "and a glass of water."

I was filling the glass with water when she shouted, "Make it four."

"The bottle says one," I advised.

"Then four should just about do it," she declared and, hurling them into her mouth, swilled them down.

Having forgotten completely that these were the double-strength cascaras made specially for my father whom the trenches had given a stomach like a concrete mixer.

In the ensuing days of volcanic scouring she had little inclination to read, and when at last her bowels found peace, leaving her limp and pale, she discovered that she had been purged of everything, including Christian Science.

"All I really mind," she confessed some time later, "is that it's put Littly off too. She's given it up because I was such a flop."

Privately I considered that Pat had stopped going to church not because she thought Christian Science had failed, but because she was now determined to spend her time looking after her mother; but I said nothing. Confronted either by my lapsed Christian Science

mother or my suspended Christian Science sister, I felt uncomfort-
ably comfortable in the knowledge that I had no faith to lose.

Life without a father involved many readjustments.

For one thing, my mother had to take a job because, as she explained, "Probate on your father's estate won't be granted for about
eighteen months."

"What's that mean?" I asked.

"That we've got very little money for eighteen months. After that
we'll have enough."

"What about dad's insurance?" (Rob had told me that Gar had
said thank God Mitt was heavily insured because Doris refused to
accept a penny from any of them.)

"The insurance company won't pay."

"Why not?"

"They say your father misled them about the seriousness of his
illness when he took out such a big policy."

"Did he?"

"I was with him when he discussed it with them, and when he had
his medical examination with their doctor: and both times he told
them he was certain he was dying."

"What *did* he die of?"

"He had a tumour — a huge sort of abscess — on the brain."

"What did the insurance doctor say when he examined him?"

"That there was nothing wrong."

"Well?"

"Well, I'd have to take the company to court to get anything out
of them: and all your father's clever friends tell me it'd cost me a
fortune to do that, and that I'd still lose. So I'll take a job instead.
But just you remember — don't you ever insure your life. Life insurance companies are liars and thieves."

We did not go to Port Macquarie that summer but hired a small
cottage at Dee Why. It was made of weather-board and fibro cement
and roofed with galvanized iron painted rust-red; and it consisted of
a front verandah, two side verandahs (each divided into two small
bedrooms), a dining-room (between the two side verandahs), a

kitchen, and a bathroom. The bedroom curtains were made of floral cotton bleached almost white by sun and salty air. The centrepiece of the dining-room was a massive table covered with a heavy green cloth with long green knotted tassels on it; and there was also in the corner an upright piano that made a noise like a sick harpsichord. On this my mother refused to play at all, and Pat and I played chopsticks. We thought both the piano and the cottage were lovely, and all our friends came to stay with us. Thus the bond with my cousins grew stronger — and the advent of adolescence more perceptible.

We twelve-year-old boys became vain and demanded grey swimming trunks, against which we looked more tanned even than we were.

We began plastering our hair with brilliantine.

We clamoured for long slacks with a wide waist-band, and when we played tennis at the week-end we wore white — our shorts impeccably ironed, our sandshoes immaculately cleaned.

We begged to be allowed to go to the pictures on Saturday nights because only kids went in the afternoon.

Our hero was a tall, superbly built life-saver, with not a brain in his head, who strode up and down the beach, through the hot, squeaky sand, with long effortless steps, and swam miles out to sea, through the roughest surf, with long effortless strokes; whose good nature was as vast as his teeth were flawless and whose looks were those of a film star. We called him Tarzan, and a smile from him was an accolade.

We allowed into our midst a number of girls. As many girls, exactly, in fact, as there were, at any given moment, boys; and we treated them exactly as if they were boys — except that we dressed and slept in different rooms, and took it in turn to have first use of the bathroom, and never asked them to pay for anything.

Accepting the fact that I was growing out of my childhood, my mother decided to teach me the economics of pleasure.

"From now on," she said, "I'll give you two shillings a week. Out of that you'll have to pay for your own pictures, tennis balls, tennis racquets, and sandshoes. All right?"

It sounded like affluence to me. "Can you afford it?" I asked.

"Can *you* afford it?" she parried.

"Ooh, yes," I declared greedily and settled for what she offered.

But a racquet cost seventy-five shillings — and a new one was needed each year — so, on the twenty-nine shillings that was the balance of my income, I did not, in the ensuing twelve months, live fast and loose.

I went to my new school and was greeted by my new masters, who said, "Ah, so you're Horse's son, are you?" because that was what they had called him when they had been at school with my father. I had never before heard him called Horse, but as soon as they said it I remembered the time he and my mother had argued, and I had seen him naked from the waist down, his brown legs so immensely strong. Horse was a good name for him. So I nodded and said, "Yes, sir"; and they said I must live up to his example. *And* to Sir David's. And even though I had no idea how twelve-year-olds lived up to the example of grown-ups (because whenever I had tried it it had earned me a belting) I said "Yes, sir."

This new school was nothing like the old one. There was no marching with the Boss, or sending Morse code across the gullies with Beatles, or having courtly discussions with Streaker. Instead, there were six hundred boys being systematically "educated." Confronted with the system, I accepted it: but I never enjoyed it.

At my old school, everyone had had individuality. Ron had had red hair and glasses and got top marks in everything. Fred had been stolid and stupid, pronouncing "melancholy" melankerly. Mike had had pubic hair. Eric had been mad, always pedalling his bicycle with the most furious energy, and once even riding into the back of a stationary baker's van and denting its metal door with his head. The two Wright brothers had been English and had had accents. Bowen had had a glass eye and kept prize bantams. Geoff had farted incessantly and been nicknamed Stinker. Peter had been the best diver, Bill the most stylish swimmer. Fraser had played perfect cricket shots. I had played rugby in bare feet. We had all had our idiosyncrasies and individualities.

But at this new school we were just parts of the system, units of the six hundred.

Not that we minded. On the contrary, we revelled in the anonymity of it, exactly as adults revel in the anonymity of a strange city — and sin doubly because of it. Anonymity made it easier to shirk work, less necessary to shine; anonymity concealed a multitude of sins, ranging from cheating (at divinity) to masturbation (in the lavatory); anonymity was painless. But anonymity is alien to children so our childhood days were ending. Ended for me, in fact, the afternoon the last of the rebels in my life was snuffed out.

Pat was on her way home from school when Tripe, as was his daily custom, met her at the corner by what had been the vacant lot (only now there was a house on it), and as they walked together, companionably and sedately, a car approached.

"Tripe!" Pat admonished, but he ignored her, running to the gutter and crouching low, tensing with the excitement of the hunt.

"TRIPE!" Pat commanded, but still he ignored her, just wagging his tail. And then, as the car passed him, hurled himself into shrieking, joyous pursuit.

Unfortunately this was a taxi driven by a man who hated dogs, a man whom Tripe had anyway discomfited too often in the past. So he waited till his tormentor was snapping at his front left wheel and then swerved sharply, left.

We heard Pat's screams and ran to her.

She had Tripe's head in her lap and he was dead: and now I knew what dead was. Part of the idyll was over.

"Colonel Russell, sir?" the Tamil hissed through the lighting aperture. "Colonel Russell?"

The colonel stood on his bed on tiptoe.

"Yes, Mr Sunderan. What is it?"

"It is about your request for informations from your friends in the basement."

"What'd they say?"

"I beg your pardon?"

"What did my friends say?"

"They say categorically that they have never written any letters to Australia since being imprisoned by the Chinese. And they are asking my contact to ask me" (Christ, the colonel groaned inwardly, why do these blokes always use ten words where one would do? Specially when each word sounds as if it's been uttered through a mouthful of glue) "so that I could repeat it verbatim to you, Colonel Russell — they are asking, 'How are you, you old bastard?' "

"Thanks, Mr Sunderan. Thank you very much."

"It is nothing. After all, we are both in the same kettle of fish. Will you be requiring to send your friends an answer?"

"No, it's too risky for you, Mr Sunderan."

"Risky? Who cares what we are risking? Please to tell me, how am I telling my friend who brings the food from the kitchen to tell his friend in the kitchen who will tell his friend who carries the food to the basement — how am I telling him to answer your friends?"

"Do you think they could just be told, 'She'll be jake?' "

"Certainly, colonel. May I ask, rather too boldly perhaps, this lady Jake . . . ?"

"No, no, 'She'll be jake' is an idiom. An Australian idiom my friends will understand without any risk of it getting your friends into trouble."

"Ah! Most wise, colonel. Yes, I understand. 'She'll be jake.' "

"Yes."

"Good night, colonel."

"Good night, Mr Sunderan. And thank you again."

Lying on his back in the darkness, Russell brooded on the news he had just received. It meant that Lim's story that his alleged defection had been culled from letters written by his colleagues was false.

But the cutting from the *Sydney Morning Herald* was real.

So Australia had some other "evidence" of his "defection."

He must try to discover what it was when next he talked with Lim. The guard had said that would be tomorrow.

"Are you telling me," Lim inquired, turning the last page of the colonel's manuscript face down on the back of the others, "that some of the idyll survived?"

"Of course."

"You use the word deliberately, do you?"

"What word?"

"Idyll."

"Yes."

"You must regret that it's gone."

"How often do I have to tell you?" the colonel muttered. "I regret nothing."

"When, finally, did it finish, this idyll?"

"The evening we heard on the wireless that Germany had invaded Poland. I remember I telephoned a friend as soon as the announcement was over — he was living in a boarding house and didn't have a wireless and when I told him he said, 'So it's ended at last.' Didn't seem anything else to say after that. We'd always known it would."

"Always?"

"When I was fourteen I heard a friend of Uncle Jim's ask my grandfather, 'Will there be a war, Sir David?' and he said, 'Of course.' Just like that. You see, he didn't really mind. He'd never been to one and would never have to go to one. Wars for him were things other men went to. But the next war was going to be the one *we'd* all die in. So we enjoyed the idyll while it lasted."

"Eat, drink, and be merry, you mean?"

"I mean nothing of the sort. What made our life idyllic was its intense discipline and respectability and conformity and pattern."

"Didn't your father's death break the pattern?"

"It seemed part of the pattern. He died, and that was the end of the beginning and the beginning of the middle. My mother and Rob and Pat and the cousins provided continuity to a background of a yo-yo craze, school, surfing, bed times, tennis, and splendid films. Musicals, with — let me think — yes, Grace Moore, Miliza Korjus, Jan Kiepura, Jeanette MacDonald, Ginger Rogers and Fred Astaire. Wonderful."

"Never heard of any of them."

"Pity. Very magical, they were, all of 'em."

"What happened to Rob?"

"She stayed with us till she retired."

"Why didn't you ever hit your boxing instructor where he wasn't expecting it?"

"He was a grown-up."

"Do you still have flying dreams and jumping dreams?"

"Precisely the opposite."

"Explain."

"Well, after the war . . ."

"Oh, by the way, where were you during World War Two?"

A slow smile spread across the colonel's face; then, like a small boy caught out in a carefully kept secret, he chuckled. "Here!" he admitted — and enjoyed hugely Lim's reaction. "So I've been through all this before and I know exactly how to cope."

"You were telling me about your dreams after World War Two," Lim reminded, and the smile faded from the colonel's face. "How were they precisely the opposite of your jumping and flying dreams?"

Wearily Russell sensed danger, but he could not avoid it. Irritably he told himself that he deserved shooting for admitting that he'd ever been in Changi jail before. From February 2, when he was captured, till today June 30, he had carefully concealed this fact: and now, out of sheer mischief, he'd blurted it out.

"Colonel!" Lim's voice was harsh.

"What?" Where the hell was he?

"Your dreams!"

"Oh . . . Well, after the war they always concerned me in some bloody awful situation — usually surrounded by thousands of murderous members of the Imperial Japanese Army — where nothing would work. If I was running, my legs wouldn't work. If I was fighting, my rifle wouldn't work. I missed with every shot, even at point-blank range, even though my life depended on it. I lunged so weakly with the bayonet it wouldn't go in; and struck so ineffectually with the butt that Nippon just brushed it aside. I'd sleep for hours in sheer terror — because dreams don't just last seconds: you know that, don't you?"

"I know that," Lim assured.

"It was so bad I got to dreading bed time."

"How long did this last?"

"Six, seven years. First four were the worst."

"And after seven years, no more dreams?"

"Plenty more. But . . . not regularly. And not just about the Japanese."

"What else?"

"Well, I'd lose my voice. Knowing that only a shout could stop whatever dire thing it was 'they' were about to do to me — or to someone else — at the crucial moment, my voice'd vanish and I'd strain and gasp, but the words'd just fizzle out into sort of frantic exhalations — until I couldn't utter a sound — and finally I'd become helpless and ridiculous."

"That was the crux of these dreams, was it? Becoming ridiculous?"

"Becoming ineffectual."

"I see. Now your grandfather, you wrote, accused your grandmother of buying shares in everything. What was the outcome of this lack of discrimination?"

"That she died richer than anyone else in the family!"

"She wasn't afraid, as your father was, of the possibility of civil war in Australia in 1932?"

"No."

"Why?"

"Because there wasn't going to be any."

"But it was happening elsewhere. Germany, for example."

"Of which my father and his like were acutely conscious. My grandmother, though, refused to accept that enough had occurred to goad Australians to strife. As it happened, she was right."

"Then did she believe that there would be no World War Two?"

"No."

"Did she say so?"

"No, but she didn't argue when my grandfather said there would."

"You didn't say your grandmother was present when this conversation about the likelihood of World War Two breaking out took place."

"That conversation was constantly taking place. The time she was present, my Uncle Henry brought it up."

"What happened?"

"He said 'Dad, I'm very intrigued by your views about another war.' And my grandfather said, 'Intrigued means conspired, so you can't be,' 'Interested then,' my Uncle Henry amended. 'I think you're wrong. Don't you, mum?' And she said, 'No, unfortunately I think your father's right. I only hope I'm dead before it happens.'"

"Was she?" Lim asked.

"Was she what?"

"Dead."

"Good heavens no. She couldn't die before it started because of the death duties that would have been due on all her settlements!

And after it started she couldn't die because she had to see her boys come home again."

"Did they all come home?"

"No."

"But you did?"

"Obviously. And the last thing she ever said to me was 'Tony darling, you must invest all your money in electronics. *They're* the gold mines of your generation.' Naturally I thought she was mad and did nothing of the kind. But when I found out how right she'd been, I at least got in on the manufacturing side. Did quite well too."

"Well enough for the government to call you up to help in its imperialist wars at least!"

"The government didn't call me up," the colonel corrected. "I volunteered. I volunteered for the Militia ten years ago when my son, aged twenty, was killed in Vietnam."

"You approved America's war in Vietnam?"

"No. I thought both the Vietnams and Cambodia and Laos should be given to China: but I saw no reason why China should also take Thailand, the whole Malay Archipelago, and Australia. I don't approve of Asian imperialism any more than you do of American imperialism."

"You say you liked Harada?"

"Harada? Oh, the tennis player? Yes. Marvellous."

"But he was Japanese."

"First, he was a tennis player." The colonel paused. "I only ever came to think of him as Japanese — in the yellow-peril sense that you imply — the following year. Or maybe it was two years later. No matter — it was when his partner Sato was returning to Japan (from Wimbledon I think: but again I'm not sure, and it doesn't matter). Sato had just been defeated, he was returning by ship, and because he'd been defeated he jumped overboard and was never seen again. It chilled me when I read that. That a man could kill himself because he'd lost a game. Ten years later, when I met his compatriots *en masse,* it chilled me even more. And you people are just as bad."

"Bad?"

"Frightening. Tell me, what's happening in the great world outside just now?"

"Well, we've sentenced all your colleagues to death. Their execu-

tions will take place, one at a time, beginning next week. But surprisingly neither Australia nor America has yet decided to go to war
with us on that account."

"You sound as if there were another account?"

"That's perceptive of you, colonel, and as a matter of fact there is.
Our armies will move into New Guinea in the middle of August."

"In six weeks?"

"That's right. It'll be our last territorial requirement — both as
territory that rightly belongs to Asia and as a colony that must be
liberated."

"Hitler said the same about Czechoslovakia."

"Colonel, be honest — do you honestly want to see a couple of
hundred million men slaughtered just for the sake of some of the
most wickedly mountainous country and murderously inclined sav-
ages in the world?"

"Do you?"

"Frankly, I don't mind. At least we Chinese can spare our half of
the two hundred million."

"Meantime, what's Russia doing?" the colonel asked.

"Worrying about Germany. That has been your mistake."

"It's been our mistake for thirty years."

"Perhaps. Now, you wrote that when you went round the garden,
looking for rubbish, to earn your pocket money, you were so 'intimidated' by your father that you wouldn't even see something as big as
a sheet of newspaper?"

"That's right."

"When did this start?"

"He sent me down to the garage once to get him his seven-eighths-
inch spanner. So I went down — all the spanners hung from leather
collars on the wall, all graded according to their size — and I looked,
and the seven-eighths-inch spanner wasn't there. So I went back and
told my father. Now my father, when he got irritated, used to breathe
out hard through his nose — like boxers do when they punch — and
that's what he did then. Then he said, 'Come with me,' so I went back
to the garage with him, quite happily, because I knew that spanner
wasn't there, but when we got into the garage, it was! And always,
after that, whenever he sent me for anything, I'd just stand in front

of it, knowing I wasn't going to find it, and not see it. It used to infuriate my father." As the major made notes, the colonel yawned.

"I'm sorry," Lim remarked, looking up. "I know this is tiring for you."

"Well, you're all over the place, aren't you? First this, then that. A man never knows whether he's coming or going. And whatever this dope is you're feeding me, it's got me silly as a wheel. Did you know I'm now spending about fourteen hours a day asleep?"

"I knew."

"Yet still I'm buggered."

"Emotional strain. You're lonely."

"Whose fault's that?"

"Mine."

"Was that Australian report that I'd defected your fault too?"

"No, colonel, that, as I told you, was your friends' fault. They denounced you."

"Don't believe you."

"Why not?" Lim sounded deadly.

"Because none of those men'd write that I'd defected. Not for my sake: they hate me. But if they were to write it they know you'd use it for propaganda, so they wouldn't."

"You credit them with too much subtlety."

"They didn't have to be subtle. We were warned about it: constantly. Before the Withdrawal. So how did you persuade Australia to believe I'd defected? Tape all my conversations with you and fake a broadcast?"

"You know that doesn't work any longer. Broadcasts have to be televised before they're believed nowadays."

"How did you fix it?"

"What?"

"The story that I'd defected. Forge letters from the other seven? No — couldn't be that. Australia wouldn't believe it from anyone but me. So maybe you forged one from me, eh? Was it from me?"

"You excite yourself unduly," Lim advised. "Calm down and tell me what happened to the Governor who sacked Jack Lang."

"He finished his term of office, then returned to London, where he became head of Scotland Yard."

"Colonel?"

"Yes?"

"If you'll broadcast on August fourteenth, I have been authorized to advise that the sentence of death passed on your seven friends will be commuted to sentences of imprisonment for ten years. I don't want you," — holding up his hand — "to give me your answer now. You must think about it. But while you are thinking about it, just take into consideration the fact that it's not only your seven colleagues you'll save, but quite possibly two hundred million or so youngsters as well. Or are you going to be like your grandfather? When those youngsters ask, is there going to be a war? are you just going to answer complacently, 'Of course.' You think about it. Maybe those youngsters have their idyll too."

Staring at the concrete ceiling of his cell, the colonel lay on his bed and wondered whether Lim would allow him to discuss with his compatriots the proposal that he broadcast. Not that he intended doing so: but he wanted them to learn that from him, not from the enemy.

Having thus decided that he would not under any circumstances broadcast, he proceeded to ask himself were there not perhaps some valid reasons why he should; and was irritated by his own equivocation.

But no, he told himself, it was not equivocation: it was preparation against all the possible arguments of others.

So what would they argue?

That by broadcasting he would save the lives of his friends — and possibly of millions of others as well. He didn't believe it. If the Chinese had decided that his friends should die, no mere broadcast would save them. If they had decided on making war in New Guinea, no mere broadcast would deter them.

Or they might argue that a broadcast from an insignificant colonel couldn't matter anyway. But it would. Not to those at whom it was aimed, but to the Chinese. *They* would regard it as a triumph. So they must be denied their triumph.

Or they might argue, if he refused to broadcast, that the repercussions would be nasty. Well, he'd have to put up with that as stoically as he could.

His eyes closed and a sick tiredness fell on him as he attempted to reason. He couldn't reason. He couldn't even think.

"I won't do it," he muttered, turning over on his side and curling up, "and that's final."

But then he remembered the *Herald*'s headline and found himself wide awake, his heart pounding at the shock of being labelled a defector.

He decided to review all that he believed to have happened since his capture on February 2.

He had been detached for questioning three days later.

He had been handed over to Major Lim after about two months, during which he had fainted at least twenty times.

He had attended and remained impervious to daily classes devoted to Marxist-Leninist dialectics and indoctrination.

He had written several hundred pages of manuscript full of facts, thoughts, dreams, and phony tails to his g's and y's.

He had been denounced in Australia as a defector — presumably because of a letter forged from his manuscript.

"Then why," he muttered, "hasn't anyone at home dropped to those awful squiggles?"

"Answer," he told himself. "They undoubtedly have."

"What's that mean then?"

"That they want to give the impression they've been hoodwinked."

"Why would they want that though?"

"Because," he anwered his own question, "that way they needn't kick up a stink. That way they can appease the Chinese and forget me."

And, turning, he buried his face in his pillow.

I was thirteen and I had taken the train, after school, from North Sydney across the bridge to Wynyard, and walked from Wynyard up George Street to King Street, where I caught a tram to the Edgecliff Post Office. Then I had walked about a third of a mile up Edgecliff Road to my grandparents' home. My grandfather was out on the pavement, in his oldest clothes, sweeping grass clippings (he had just mown the verge) off the cement pavement with the palm of his hand. It was a blazing hot afternoon and, as I approached, a middle-aged lady halted by my grey-headed, grey-moustached, high cheek-boned, nostril-flaring grandfather and demanded, "How old are you, my man?"

Flapping his hand at me from behind his disgraceful trousers, signalling me not to acknowledge him, my grandfather admitted that he was seventy-two.

"And they make you work in the middle of a heat wave like this?" she exploded. "Whose gardener are you?"

Mutely my grandfather indicated, with a grubby thumb, his own large home.

"How much do they pay you?" she demanded.

"Nothing," he confessed. "Just board and lodgings. It's because I'm so old, you see."

"But you've mowed this lawn beautifully," she protested. "It's disgraceful that you're paid nothing and made to work in heat like this. What's their name, the people you work for?"

"Russell," he told her. "Sir David and Lady Russell. They're hard people."

"I shall write to them," she promised. "Here" — she rummaged in her purse — "here's two shillings. Now go inside at once."

"Thank you, madam," he said in his usual courtly style, and she left.

"Well, young Tony," he then greeted me, as if nothing had happened, "what brings you here?" And without waiting for my answer tossed the coin at me. "Two shillings for you" — and made his way inside for the cup of tea that my grandmother had allowed to go cold for him on his dressing-table underneath the faded sepia photographs of the All Blacks in 1888 and 1889.

That night, after dinner, Uncle Jim said he was going to feed the possum that lived in the magnolia tree that grew as high as the two-storied house; so he and my grandfather and I walked out onto the dark second-storey porch.

"Here, possum," Uncle Jim called, peremptorily as always, and out of the rustling leaves, straight onto the waist-high wall of the porch, leaped a possum.

"Not there!" Uncle Jim rebuked it. "Here." Confidently the possum walked along the top of the wall to where his hand rested. Then, standing on its haunches, it took a firm grip on the half-peeled banana he offered and on the fingers between which he held it.

The possum ate briskly and appeared as ungrateful as Uncle Jim was unsentimental. When it had finished, it shook itself and leaped back into the magnolia tree. Uncle Jim turned to my grandfather.

"News looks bad, pater."

"Very bad," my grandfather agreed. "No one amasses armaments like Hitler's doing without eventually using them. The Germans will start a war in 1938 or 1939, before what they're beginning to build now becomes obsolescent. It's inevitable."

I looked at him, expecting compassion, because in 1938 or '39 I would be seventeen or eighteen — old enough to go to his inevitable war. But, as he surveyed me, he looked merely academic, and I did not enjoy the expression. For those who would weep and wail for me, and stand aghast at the selfless heroism of me, I was prepared to die a dozen valiant deaths in battle. Indeed, in my daydreams, I had frequently done so, enraptured by the perfection of my death scenes, which naturally I witnessed from beginning to end, including the best bit, after I was gone, when King George V, handing my mother a Victoria Cross, shed several tears: but for the academic, I was not prepared to risk so much as a scratch.

"So you're still writing?" Lim remarked as soon as the colonel was ushered into his office. Russell, taking his seat, did not bother to reply. Since Lim's sentries collected his carefully copied sheets of quarto each morning, the question was rhetorical. Indifferently he looked up at the slowly chopping fan, and beyond it at a gecko lizard clinging upside down to the ceiling. Funny, he thought, that the ubiquitous gecko never chose to visit prison cells. On second thoughts, not funny: sensible.

"I must admit," Lim continued, "I see little that's idyllic in this last lot. You didn't like school?"

"Whoever did? It was the hours after school that were marvellous."

"Were you clever at school?"

"I was moderately receptive of anything I was compelled to learn. Unfortunately compulsion and aptitude rarely coincide, so I was never brilliant at anything."

"I don't understand."

"I had an aptitude for German, but our German teacher was a woman. Nice woman, but unthinkable that she'd belt you. So I didn't learn much. She used to come into the classroom and we'd all stand — because she was a woman — and chorus, 'Good morning, madam.' And she'd nod and say, '*Setzen Sie sich.*' So we'd sit. And then the chaos would begin. A stock gag on rainy days, I remember, was to say to her very quickly and casually, 'Tickle your ass with a feather, madam?' and she'd rear up, as if you had, and snarl, '*What?*', and the culprit, all innocence, would say, 'I said, particularly nasty weather, madam.' No, I didn't learn much German."

"It doesn't say much for your capitalist system of education, does it? You loathed school as much as you loathed your grandfather."

"Absolute tosh. I loved my grandfather being Sir David; he often made me laugh, and he was always extremely kind. The only trouble between us was, I never could imagine 1888 and 1889. So I couldn't identify with the man he liked to remember. Now with my father and the uncles I could identify — because I could imagine 1914 and 1918. But *you* try feeling close to something in knickerbockers, a drooping moustache, and a tiny cap with a tassel on it."

"Didn't you ever feel close to him?"

"Not to the him he wanted. The him I felt close to was an old man who read a thriller every night before he went to bed; who hated motorcars and always walked the two miles or so into his city office, wearing an eyeshade. The grandfather I felt close to was the old boy who loved rice puddings and pretty girls and going to the pictures. That grandpappy I was mad about. But grandpappy the youthful international footballer and oarsman with the droopy moustache and the tassel on his cap was about as real to me as Fu Manchu. Sorry: unfortunate choice of words."

"Why did your grandfather hate cars? Was he so old-fashioned?"

"I was told he only ever drove once; onto the ferry at St George's River. Unfortunately, according to the legend, he also drove straight off the other end of it and into St George's River! After which he

neither drove nor willingly entered a car ever again. Actually, I suspect, the legend's a wicked lie; but it's rather nice, isn't it?"

"It's idiotic."

"So you won't be sending anyone in Australia a letter from me
saying I hated my grandfather because he couldn't drive?"

"Colonel, I've told you twice now, the only letters concerning you
that have gone to Australia were written by your colleagues here in
this jail."

"And I've told *you* twice, I don't believe you."

"What do you believe?"

"That you forged a letter from *me*. Well, it'll do you no good,
because ever since I started writing for you I've deliberately altered
all my g's and y's."

Lim's face remained expressionless, but his eyes glittered.

"Struck oil, have I?" Russell inquired amiably.

"Why are you telling me this?"

"To disconcert you: so what're you going to do about it? Can't
send another letter can you? Even if you could, you can't make me
give you samples of my usual handwriting. And even if you did
make me, you couldn't be sure you had."

"You seem to have forgotten the *Sydney Morning Herald* clipping."

"Do you honestly believe that forged letter of yours has taken in
the experts at home? That they wouldn't have compared it with past
letters I've written my wife or past reports I've written to Intelligence?"

"What reports?"

"On communications — which was my job in the army, as you
know. I never learned to type, so confidential stuff I always wrote by
hand. They'd have compared the letter you sent them with all of that
other stuff."

"Then why that headline and photograph in the *Herald?*"

"I'd have thought it was obvious."

"Not to me."

"Let me spell it out then," Russell said slowly and contemptuously, and prayed that it would be effective, because the last of his
energy and concentration was oozing out of him, along with the

sweat that drenched his khaki shirt. "That headline was to trick you. Officially inspired, it was, to make you think you'd got off with something that actually never worked at all. You've made a fool of yourself, Lim, don't you realize that?"

But Lim's self-assurance was not, Russell observed wearily, so easily to be destroyed.

"You're right about the letter being forged and supposedly coming from you," he admitted coolly. "But you're wrong when you claim your experts will detect that it's a forgery. They will suspect it: but they'll never be able to prove it. My expert promises that, and my expert forges currency notes that are better than currency. So your experts and I are now at deuce, to use a tennis metaphor that should please you. But it's my serve, and I'll win the game."

"What makes you think so?" Russell's voice sounded almost indifferent.

"You, relayed by Japanese satellite, are going to speak on television to Australia, New Zealand, Canada, and the United States, and explain to them how you've lost faith in the imperialist warmonger's cause. That will convince your people that your letter, for all its funny g's and y's, was genuine."

"Oh, Lim!"

"You think you won't broadcast?"

"I know I won't."

Lim pressed the button on his desk and, when a sentry appeared, addressed him briefly in Chinese. Then, rising from his chair and motioning Russell to do likewise, he said, "Come to this window with me."

Standing beside Lim, Russell felt tall, stooped, grizzled, and flabby; he also felt wary.

"Cigarette?" Lim offered. "Sorry — I forgot." And put the package back in his breast pocket, glancing, as he lit his own, at his prisoner, whose face, as usual, twitched.

Together they gazed out on an empty courtyard.

"What's all this about?" Russell demanded irritably.

"Patience, colonel."

The grass was green, the concrete paths gleaming white. Thirty years ago, Russell reflected, he had slept on a rice bag on that path, just there, and had worked building the aerodrome a mile away. The

Japanese had used it hardly at all then. No planes. In the past week hundreds of Japanese bombers had screamed low over the jail, heading for the aerodrome. Something was building up.

A squad of Chinese soldiers entered the courtyard and took up a position opposite Lim's window.

Two sentries dragged in an Indian, naked except for a loin cloth, and made him kneel, facing Lim's window, his head bent forward, his hands tied behind his back.

One of the squad marched six paces and halted behind the Indian, placing the mouth of the barrel of his carbine against the Indian's neck.

There was a long pause, whose silence was broken only by the chuff-chuff-chuff of the lazily revolving fan and the weird cry of the gecko on the ceiling. Then a shot rang out and the Indian pitched onto his face.

Lim drew hard on his cigarette and then, exhaling, indicated to Russell that he was to sit down.

"Rather like your bull," he commented. "Except, of course, that Mr Sunderan's corpse will yield no handle for a stock whip."

"Sunderan?"

"You never saw him, but occasionally you talked with him."

"What's he done to deserve that?"

"Comforted the enemy. Specifically, you!"

"I never even knew what he looked like," Russell mused. "How'd you get on to us?"

"I suspected you'd exchanged messages with your colleagues — your explanation of why you refused to believe they'd denounced you was too glib. Also, I'd had reports that you and Sunderan conversed after lights out. So I had Sunderan questioned, and after a while he confessed everything."

"And for that you execute him?"

"We would have executed him anyway. For being a Tamil."

"But you did it today to impress me?"

"Well, we know you don't like executions. You said so yourself."

"And you do?"

"Some I could enjoy very much. His" — taking a photograph out of his drawer and flicking it at the colonel — "I would love."

Russell examined the photograph.

"Guardsman Stogdale B. L., Right Flank, Second Battalion Scots Guards. Operation Lemon, 1949. He shot my mother and father."

"Not" — Russell flicked his thumb towards the window — "like that, I'm sure."

"Of course not. My mother and father served under Lew Kong Kim and had twice ambushed the Second Battalion's Right Flank that very day."

"Then what're you complaining about? They were fighting a war and they got killed. In addition to which, as you've already admitted, you can't even remember what they looked like. If you hate Guardsman Stogdale, it isn't because he shot your folks, it's because you hate all Europeans."

"All warmongers," Lim corrected.

"No," insisted Russell, "all Europeans."

"Maybe," Lim conceded. "But now you've seen what happened to Mr Sunderan, perhaps you'd like to change your mind?"

"I'm not broadcasting," the colonel stated flatly.

"Well" — Lim sighed — "only you can decide that. But at dawn, the day after tomorrow, unless you change your mind, the first of your seven war-criminal friends will be executed: with you as chief witness. And every alternate dawn thereafter there'll be another execution. Each one witnessed by you and directly attributable to you. I don't think you'll be able to stand it, colonel: so you'll let me know when you change your mind, won't you? Just shout for me from your cell. The sentry outside will be expecting it."

"I will not shout for him," Russell muttered, sitting on the edge of his bed, his head between his hands. "I will not shout."

But there were thirty-six hours during which his resolve must not weaken.

During which he must occupy himself as weeks ago he had planned: only now it seemed ridiculous. Never mind: he'd been in better mental condition then than now, and that was what he'd decided then, so that was what he'd do. At least it would be easier than reading Toynbee.

What to write about though? What'd Lim said? Not much that was idyllic in my last lot? Okay — that'd do for a start.

Lim, meantime, was equally preoccupied. Russell's admission about his handwriting had shaken him. Why then had Australia branded the colonel a defector? It worried him that he did not understand.

If Russell broadcast, of course, the letter would no longer matter: Australia would regard it as authentic after all, and the Americans would never forgive Australia for having produced a traitor.

But if Russell refused to broadcast, what then? Execute him? Face-saving but not profitable: and it was Lim's task to make political profit out of every prisoner assigned to him. Exchange him for a Chinese agent held in Australia? Not at all face-saving, and anyway the Australians didn't hold any Chinese agents.

No, if Russell refused to broadcast there would remain only one thing to do, and for that he must start planning now.

After gathering together all the manuscript pages Lim left his office in the jail and drove to another office in Singapore, where he explained what he wanted.

"How well must the piano be played?" the technician inquired.

"Very well."

"Can I use a recording?"

"Of course."

"She played as well as that?"

"I have no idea. But his recollection will be that she did, and anyway it is not his mother we are trying to re-create but the mood that his mother's playing induced."

"The tape will be ready by six o'clock tomorrow evening," the technician promised.

By the time we were fourteen the pattern of the second part of our youthful idyll was firmly established, in spite of the war in Abyssinia, the course of which my grandfather acknowledged with sombre satisfaction, saying, "I told you so, didn't I?" We were too young for this war, so we did not let it overshadow our lives. Our activities were those of a youthful tribe benevolently administered by despotic adults who now intruded less than they had.

"Don't be late for dinner," the parents commanded: and, by running, we were not late.

"Be home by half-past twelve," the parents commanded when we went to dances: and, by running, we were home at half-past twelve.

"Back at half-past eleven now, and not a minute later," they commanded when we went to the pictures: and we were in bed, asleep, by a quarter to twelve. Week nights we were in bed by nine.

The tribe expanded to include other fourteen-year-olds at school — and their sisters — and their sisters' friends at school. But only if their tennis was adequate. We had worked too hard — watering and rolling and marking the court, ironing our shorts, whitening our sandshoes, earning the money to buy the balls and racquets — to have our afternoon wrecked by one bad player. Thus to the cousins and myself was added first Hunter, then his sister Mick; then Murray and his sister, and her friend Dagmar, who was Czechoslovakian and beautiful and a powerful hitter of the ball; then Judy (who swam like a fish and played the piano) and Nyree (who was tiny and slight and left-handed) and each year perhaps three or four more. But not Simon who wore a cap: nor Cyril who was sloppy; nor Betty who had no backhand and always served doubles.

One afternoon when it was raining and tennis was impossible, I waited at Lindfield station till Pat's train brought her from the big school she now attended and we walked home together. Whenever there was no tennis I waited for Pat and we walked home together.

"Are you really going to learn the piano again?" she asked.

"Yes."

"You're silly," she told me. "It's awful. And you'll never be able to play like Judy anyway."

"It's a new system," I assured her. "You learn in a few months."

"I wonder how well Rob plays the piano?" she mused.

So when we got home, after changing into an old shirt and shorts and eating the bread and butter she had sliced for us, I asked Rob to play the piano.

"Oh," she said, "I couldn't. I haven't touched a note in — oh, it must be forty years.

"Well, try," I urged, dragging her to the piano and opening the keyboard lid. "Come on, Rob."

"I couldn't, Tony, really."

"Aw, Rob! *Please.*"

Reluctantly she sat on the stool, broad-beamed in her apron, stumpy-legged in the elasticated stockings she wore for her varicose veins. Tensely I waited for her to play — she who as a girl had had two pianos and was said to have played beautifully. She stared at the keyboard apprehensively; and I stared at her intently.

"No," she decided, "I couldn't."

"Please, Rob. For me. Just try. Please, Rob, just a little."

"Well," she agreed, nervous and flushed, "all right, I'll try."

After resting her hands flat on her knees a moment, she straightened her back, raised her wrists and allowed her fingertips to rest lightly on the ivory keys; then, smiling at me, she leaned slightly forward and began, quite effortlessly, to play.

It was one of the études my mother played, and her touch was very like my mother's. But even as I smiled back at her and she, nodding, turned mechanically to the keyboard, sudden bewilderment flooded her face, her fingers stiffened, the fluent arpeggios stumbled, and we found ourselves sharing a shocked, sick silence.

At first Rob stared at her hands, lying red and clumsy on the keyboard, as if they were some kind of loathsome toad; and then, snatching them back onto her aproned lap, flashing at me a glance of almost incredulous rebuke, she stood up stiffly and stumped off, into the kitchen, into her room, and slammed the door.

"Rob?" I called, fearful and pleading, begging her to realize that I had not known that grown-ups could be hurt by children. "Rob?" But she did not answer.

She left us shortly after that to live with her married sister on a pension and a small allowance from my mother, saying it was time she retired and Pat and I could always come and see her at her married sister's place, couldn't we? We promised, "Of course, Rob," and visited her about once every two months: but it was never the same. Each time we saw her — for tea, on the back verandah, in the afternoon sun — she looked a little less pink in the face and a little less broad in the beam. Each time it became a little more difficult to confide. Until finally, as she lay tiny and shrunken on a hospital bed, there was none of the old Rob left, nothing to say at all, and she died without any children to talk to because I hadn't thought before making her play the piano.

After that I was careful to listen whenever my grandfather talked about the memorable football matches of 1888 and 1889, and scrupulously careful not to question my grandmother about her one-time athleticism.

Not that my grandmother ever left time for questions anyway: with her it was all either answers or listening as she enthused about everything, from our latest feats to her latest voyage or my grandfather's latest cleverness.

"Darling," she said, "go into your grandfather's study and look at the marvellous picture he's done of his old home in England."

So I went into my grandfather's study and there was yet another picture by him of his old home. My grandfather drew pictures of his old home the way I had once drawn pictures of aeroplanes and sailing ships. Endlessly. Only this one looked peculiar.

"Well, young Tony," my grandfather asked. "What do you think of it?"

"Very nice," I lied.

"It's to be hung at an exhibition," he explained. "The idea is to paint a picture using unusual materials. I used mustard, cocoa, jelly crystals, and self-raising flour. Sir Thomas Beecham's going to open the exhibition and everything's for sale — proceeds to charity. Like to come? I'll introduce you to Sir Thomas. Great musician."

"Yes," I said, "I'd like to come, please."

A week later I trailed round a gallery exhibiting the curious works of Sydney's socialites. Compared with them, I decided, my aeroplanes and sailing ships had been masterpieces.

"There's Sir Thomas," my grandfather exclaimed. "Sir Thomas!"

Irritably the great conductor approached.

"Good afternoon, Sir David."

"Good afternoon, Sir Thomas. This is my grandson, Anthony. He's been clamouring to meet you."

We shook hands.

"That's my picture," my grandfather announced, tapping the frame. "I used mustard, jelly crystals, cocoa, and self-raising flour."

Bleakly Sir Thomas examined the mustard stone work, the green jelly-crystal lawns, the cocoa tree trunks, and the fleecy clouds of self-raising flour.

"Looks like it," he snapped — and strode off.

My grandfather looked kindly down at me. "Sir Thomas," he told me, "is not only a great musician, he's also an eminently honest and sensible critic of art! Let's go somewhere where I can buy you some nauseating concoction in ice cream. And while you're eating that, you can tell me what you want for Christmas."

At Christmas time, now, the entire tribe holidayed for eight weeks at Dee Why, most of it staying at the cousins' cottage or at ours, the girls sleeping on one side of the cottage, the boys on the other. We spent all day on the beach, and we boys learned not to question any girl who, inexplicably, might have announced that she wouldn't be surfing that day.

"Tony," my mother summoned me, very sharply, the first time it happened and I argued. I went to my mother's room.

"Yes, mum."

"Leave her alone."

"Why? Is she sick?"

"No. But at your age girls have to take things quietly for a few days each month. They're built differently, and work differently, from you horrors of boys, you know."

And since this, indisputably, was true, I left it at that and went surfing.

Of all the things that happened to us at this time, none was more marvellous than the overnight acquisition of the ability to surf. Not just to swim well, and survive the onslaught of heavy Pacific seas, and catch the occasional wave for some of its journey ashore: but to catch the right wave at the right moment and be swept by it, intoxicatingly, hundreds of yards, from deep water all the way up onto the damp sand.

One day we couldn't do it, the next we could — and the joy of catching "beachers" became ours. Line abreast, we would wait for the right wave — the full-bellied wave whose crest curls over and slides forward down its own flank just after it passes you.

Line abreast, as the sea began to swell and suck with the approach of this wave, we would turn and swim onto it as it hit us.

Swim fast with the head tucked hard down onto the chest and the legs well up: so that the wave got under and behind us. And drove us, arms underneath us, like a board, stiff like a board, down its flank, along with its crumbling crest, in front of its mounting foam.

After a few seconds our rigidly flexed, down-pointing bodies would be moving as fast as the wave itself, and our heads would be clear of the foam, and then we would lift our heads and, skiing on our shoulders and our stiff arms underneath us — skimming first the steep face of the wave and then the flat water in front of the wave — would plane deliriously along and along and along, watching the water and the legs flash past, until the last spurt of foam flung us onto the beach and, as it sucked backwards, left us high and dry.

By the following Christmas the wicked Italians had still not been curbed by the League of Nations, and back at Dee Why we wondered how Great Britian (of whose Empire we were a loyal part, one of her blessedly numerous patches of red on the world's map) could have failed to intimidate a race whom our parents called dagos and whose territories, on the map, were negligible.

A month later George V, who had been king all our lives, died, shocking us profoundly because we had never lost a king before and had always imagined him, like God, to be indestructible.

It was doubly disconcerting, therefore, to observe the comparative calm with which this shattering event was received by the grown-ups. Not that they were not moved: but they were not awe-struck as we were. Instead they talked of Victoria's funeral (which I had seen in the film *Cavalcade* — and not thought much of) and Edward VII's funeral, and of how the Prince of Wales had once, on his Australian tour, danced with a friend of my mother's called Eleanor. For months afterwards, they all said, Eleanor had been impossible. "Your father," my mother recalled, "used to curtsy every time he saw her." But then her fiancé had come storming down from his station, married her and dragged her off to the outback, where she had since had three children and lost all her looks, poor thing.

As I examined the photographs of our new king, I noticed a sadness in his young man's eyes: but I didn't think it was for Eleanor. I thought perhaps he was remembering the Front (my book of War photographs had several pictures of him at the Front. Indeed he was the only one in it who was as good-looking as the dead young German) or thinking about how he would cope, as king, with Hitler and the new war that had started in Spain; but I realized a little later, at the end of the year, when he had to abdicate, that actually it was Prime Minister Baldwin who made him look so gloomy.

"Interfering old devil," my mother said of Baldwin — and everyone seemed to agree with her, especially our new maid, a girl called
Ruby, who had six different photographs of the glamorous "boy"
king on her bedroom wall. Ruby was a smiling, round-eyed girl from
the country who had just joined the Salvation Army. She tended to
look straight at anyone asking her to do anything and then to giggle
and do nothing, but she was good-natured and obviously of irre-
proachable character.

"I'm sure that lass is not all there," my mother remarked, nevertheless.

And true enough, the abdication proved too much for Ruby. The
day it was announced she emerged from her bedroom, wearing only
her Army bonnet, and danced naked up and down the hall, singing
verse after verse of "Roll me over in the clover," which Pat and I had
never heard before, and kicking her tambourine. It was the end of
1936 — and she was the last maid we ever had.

"They're too ruddy hard to get and ruddy impossible to live with
when you get 'em," my mother declared. "From now on we'll do
without." And all over Australia the same decision was being made,
so that my grandmother's home, with its two maids from Lithuania,
became quite exceptional.

Unable to concentrate any longer — even to stay awake any longer
— Russell lay back on his bed. It was still quite early in the night,
and the first execution was due at dawn. Indifferently aware that he
was more heavily drugged than usual, he decided to sleep. Perhaps
they would forget to wake him at dawn. Perhaps he wouldn't have to
watch the execution. He had still not shouted for Major Lim. Within
a minute he was snoring.

About twenty minutes later, the door having been noisily unlocked, Lim entered the cell and looked down at his prisoner. Satisfied that the open-mouthed Australian was not feigning, he beckoned
inside the jail doctor — a very thin, balding Chinese, younger than
Lim, and even shorter. The doctor felt Russell's pulse, peeled back
Russell's right eyelid, and nodded his nervous approval.

Again Lim beckoned, and this time a guard carried in a large tape
recorder, to which was attached, by a long flex, a pair of headphones

set in foam rubber. Opening the tape recorder, Lim pressed a button and listened a moment at one of the earpieces: Pianoforte — Chopin. Not that he recognized it: but it was what he had ordered. Nodding, he eased the headset into place over Russell's skull and then, waving both sentry and doctor out ahead of him, left the cell, closing the door gently behind him.

Staring intently through the Judas hole, he was pleased to observe that the colonel's mouth had closed and his expression become serenely attentive. Knowing that Russell would continue to sleep and listen for more than an hour, and not wake till the dawn, he departed, satisfied.

Two hours later the jail doctor re-entered the cell and again, cursorily, examined the sleeping man. Then, removing the earphones, he switched off the tape recorder, closed its lid, ordered the guard to carry everything away, and himself followed.

Russell woke just before dawn, feeling strangely clear-headed and unapprehensive. Almost at once his cell door was opened and the guard indicated that he was to dress. With a weird feeling that all this had happened before, he slipped on his shirt and shorts and wooden clogs almost without thought; and when he found himself outside Lim's office door he realized that he had no recollection at all of having walked there. "I wonder," he asked himself, "if this is how it is for the condemned man as he walks to the gallows?" Then his escort opened the door and brusquely motioned him in.

In Lim's office the electric light shone bleakly, its sparkle killed by a faint luminescence from the sky outside. Lim, who was reading, did not look up when Russell entered; and since he occupied the only chair in the room, the Australian, after the briefest of hesitations, moved away from the desk and, standing at the window, looked into the courtyard below.

It was empty, its grass well tended and, in the revitalizing light of dawn, already perceptibly green.

Idly he remembered the courtyard as it had been. The young, skeletal men in it. All old now. Or dead. Mostly dead. Still, they'd outlasted Changi. Or had they? Changi was still here, and the same things exactly were going on in it.

"What are you thinking about?" Lim's voice, close to his ear, startled him.

"Nothing," he lied.

"Will you broadcast for us?"

"No."

"Then watch! Remember, though, you can stop what is going to happen at any moment. A nod will do — so long as it means you'll broadcast."

Russell said nothing. A squad of soldiers entered the courtyard and halted on the grass, facing the window.

"Cigarette?" Lim offered. Russell looked down at him contemptuously.

Lim shrugged and, with equal contempt, held his cigarette lighter in front of Russell's nose as he snapped it aflame.

"Look," he ordered: and Russell's gaze swung slowly back to the courtyard.

Where he saw his corporal, like a sheep about to be slaughtered, kneeling and leaning backwards, gripped between the knees of a Chinese soldier, his shaggy head pulled backwards by its hair, his throat arched tautly backwards with the pitiless pulling of his hair, and against his throat, by the distended windpipe, the point of a long knife. The knife was held in the Chinese soldier's right hand, whilst his left yanked back on the hair.

The corporal was humiliatingly trussed, Russell now noticed, and so placed that he knelt in profile to the window, his back pinned against his executioner's left leg by the right leg that straddled his chest, and his head dragged back over the left thigh so that his wide eyes stared up and rightwards into Russell's eyes.

The sky's grey was shot now with translucent greens and warmed with feathers of pink, and outside the jail walls a cock crowed; but on the lush grass of the courtyard there was only the tableau of five soldiers facing a sixth. Who held between his legs the tautened kneeling body of an emaciated man; who held at the arched throat of the emaciated kneeling man the point of a long, thin knife.

Desperately the corporal's eyes rolled even farther backwards until Russell could read in them their awful admission of abject fear: but Russell did not move. So the executioner pushed the point of his blade deliberately into the throat, beside the windpipe, then slit sideways through the windpipe and sawed slowly round to the left ear and then back to the right. Finally, as the trunk convulsed and the blood spouted, he gave the shaggy head a last contemptuous yank and broke the neck. Then, stepping swiftly backwards, away from the spouting blood, holding the slaughtered, kneeling, blood-spouting body fastidiously away from him by its almost severed and disarticulated head, the executioner, looking up at the window, released his grip and allowed his victim to sag leftwards onto the red, glistening grass.

The five soldiers came to attention and turned right and, after the executioner had joined them, marched out of the courtyard, closing behind them the wire-mesh door that led into a wire-mesh corridor. Stamping loudly on the concrete, they marched away, leaving the corporal's trussed and pallid carcass grotesquely alone in the middle of the dawn-lit courtyard, at the edge of a wide segment of red, glistening grass.

Russell turned towards Lim, eyes glassy; and Lim, who had been watching him curiously, ignoring the courtyard entirely, now led him away from the window to the office door, where he looked into his prisoner's eyes and said, "Colonel?"

But Russell did not answer.

"Colonel," Lim said more sharply.

But Russell still did not answer.

Lim slapped his face. "Colonel," he snapped.

"Bastard!" Russell told him.

"Now will you broadcast?"

"Now I hate you Chinks enough never to broadcast."

"We shall see," Lim murmured. "You have six friends left — and you'll witness the killing of the next of them forty-eight hours from now."

"Why like that?" Russell snarled, coming suddenly to life. "Why kill him like that?"

"To persuade *you*. Everything, colonel, is to persuade you. And it wasn't we, you know, who decided how he should die. The sheep, at Inverell, remember? Before the bull? With the others it's going to be the same."

"Like sheep?"

"Not like sheep. But in ways you've indicated will most appal you. Your friends, too, of course. But for them it's soon over. You're the

one who matters. And it'll never be over for you. Will you be able to
live with seven particularly hideous executions, all of whose ingen-
ious subtleties were dreamed up by yourself, do you think? Or would
you rather broadcast?"

"I will not broadcast," Russell vowed — and was led back to his
cell, where, flinging himself onto his bed, he went promptly to sleep.

Waking to the clatter of the arrival of morning rations, he sat up
and swung his legs over the edge of his bed. For a moment fear
churned in his bowels; then, quite deliberately, he quelled it. The
seven would die, he told himself indifferently, and he would die. For
him and for each of them there would be seconds of terror and pain
such as they had never imagined; but then release. Irrevocable release. The only kind of release for which they could ever hope in this
captivity.

Seconds of terror and pain, he reflected. Seconds aren't long. Not
as long as the hours women endure in childbirth. And the pain no
worse than my grandmother endured, repeatedly, with her angina.
Not even as much as my mother endured with the week of coronaries
that killed her. Women, of course, are better at pain. Still, men can
stand it — for a few seconds. And death's nothing to worry about.
Compared with this lot, in fact, death sounds lovely.

The thing was that he must not think of this lot. Till he was gasp-
ing his last in the courtyard he'd first known thirty years ago, he
must fight the present by concentrating on the past. Until he was
dead, his past was in jeopardy.

"It's all I've got," he shouted. The Judas hole flashed open. "It's
all any of us has got," he told the eye at the Judas hole earnestly. "A
past. And you're not mucking up mine."

When soon the guard shoved food into the cell and a mug of milkless tea, he ate the food and drank the tea and then, taking up his
pen, started to write.

We moved from the house in Tryon Road to another house by the
sixteenth hole of Killara Golf Course. This house was more than a
mile from the station, in the opposite direction from the old one; and
as Pat and I, after school, walked to it for the first time, we felt

desolate. To turn right out of Lindfield station, instead of left, was to abandon the environment of our childhood and to enter a new one that we might not like.

A mile was a long way to us because of the time. To walk a mile took about twelve minutes: and twelve minutes occupied only by walking were interminable. We took the fact that grown-ups never understood this as further proof of the axiom that they themselves had never been young; and when they added insult to injury by themselves never walking the mile, always finding excuses for taking the car, we muttered mutinously about one law for us and another for them.

Pat, though, had never been one just to mutter.

"Tige," my mother one day asked me, "how does Littly get home so early when you're not with her?"

Like lightning my mind processed the question. My mother was alleging either that when Pat walked home with me I delayed her for some purpose that was probably forbidden: or that when Pat walked home without me someone was giving her a lift, which was emphatically forbidden.

"What do you mean?" I asked, summoning to my sister's defence all of my considerable resources of obtuseness.

"You know perfectly well what I mean," my mother — never patient of obtuseness — retorted.

"No, I don't."

"Yes, you do."

"I mean I don't know why."

"Why what?" she asked crossly, irritated that I had contrived to confuse her.

"What you said," I replied, sounding as injured as I dared. I was fifteen, but she could still deliver a powerful clip to the ear when she felt like it.

For a long moment she glared at me as if she felt like it, and I gave her back my injured look, and it was touch and go, but then she said, "You're quite right. I had no right to ask you to tell on Littly."

I was not falling for that one. "There's nothing to tell, mum," I vowed, taking my leave of her.

"Where are you going?" she demanded suspiciously.

"To hit a ball against the wall," I replied, giving her my innocent look this time. Every afternoon at home I took a racquet and a ball and banged it for an hour or so against the wall, which my mother knew.

"All right," she said. "But don't say anything to Pat."

"No, mum." And rushed outside to do precisely that.

"I run," Pat explained blandly.

"All the way?" I sneered.

"Yes," she snapped and walked off. Being loyal to sisters is a waste of time.

So the following day I told Peter and Bill I couldn't play tennis with them, and then, instead of waiting at the station till Pat's train arrived, hid behind the public telephone box and let her walk past me.

Whereupon I followed her.

Halfway home she waved to the baker sitting high on his cart behind a brown horse with wildly rolling eyes. He reined the horse to a halt, Pat climbed up beside him, and the horse trotted off — Pat and the baker in animated conversation behind it.

"You'd better not let mum know you're getting lifts from the baker," I accused when I arrived home five minutes later than she.

"You'd better not let mum know you only polish your shoes on the side that's seen," she retaliated. "You aren't always standing with your feet together, you know."

Arguing with sisters is also a waste of time.

Some weeks later, though, my mother having discovered the hideous truth and forbidden Pat ever to travel on the baker's cart again, I was quite touched that my sister stoutly defended me against the charge, made by one of her friends, that I had told on her.

"He did *not*," Pat shouted. "Tone never tells."

"He never does anything else either," the friend observed ambiguously and nastily.

"I know," Pat agreed. "But he never tells."

The following week I again found Pat, halfway home, waiting by the roadside.

"What're you doing?" I demanded accusingly.

"Waiting for the milkman," she told me coldly. "Mummy only said I couldn't get lifts from the baker."

As I grew older, discipline became more irksome. My mother may have been glad to do without hired domestic help, but I — suddenly an unhired domestic help — was not. Endlessly I seemed to hear the maternal voice demanding, "Tige, have you made your bed?" or "Haven't you children started the washing up yet?" or "Tony, how often do I have to tell you *not* to hang your clothes up on the floor?"

It was on the last issue that I determined to make my stand. I had learned to sleep so stealthily that, to re-make my bed in the morning, I had only to smooth the counterpane over neatly burrowed sheets and blankets; when I washed up I simply shovelled everything out of the sink and demanded that Pat not only dry it but wipe it clean; but hanging up clothes took hours of the time I could least spare — which was when I changed immediately after I got home from school — so I adhered stubbornly to my practise of sloughing off everything where I stood.

After about three weeks of acrimonious dispute I was delighted — if surprised — to discover that my mother had capitulated. Every week-day afternoon thereafter I shed my school clothes on the floor; each morning I picked up what I needed and left whatever was dirty where it was; over the week-end I shed and donned and shed repeatedly; and on Monday morning I left the floor strewn with tennis shoes and socks and shorts, with swimming trunks and handkerchiefs and ties, with slacks and underpants and shirts and jock straps. But every night, when I went to bed, my room had been tidied. Smugly I rejoiced in victory.

On a Saturday morning, three weeks later, however, I found my wardrobe empty of slacks, tennis clothes, linen, ties, and even jock straps: and I had an important tennis party that afternoon at the house of a new friend called John, whose sisters were said to be potential champions.

"Mum," I shouted, irritated by her carelessness. "Where's my tennis things?"

"With all the rest of your clothes, I suppose," she shouted back.

"Well, where are *they?*"

"Where you left them."

"But I left them . . ."

"Exactly," she finished nastily.

"What do you mean?" Suddenly I felt sick.

"I mean," she advised coldly, "that they're still on the floor."

Which they were. All of them, from weeks back, under the bed in a tangled and noisome heap that was grey with dust and fluff and even, I suspected, fungus.

"Aw *mum!*" I snarled.

"What?" she inquired coolly, standing now in my bedroom door and smiling at me as wolfishly as her father ever had.

"*Look* at my things," I demanded.

"Um," she observed. "Filthy."

"Well, how'd they get under the bed?" I was almost in tears.

"I swept them there each morning. I thought that must be what you wanted when you went on not putting them away."

"But I haven't got anything clean to wear to John's this afternoon."

"Better wash some now then, hadn't you?"

"But they'll never dry in time."

"Then you'll just have to iron them dry," she instructed — and left me hating her passionately.

I continued to hate her passionately through several steamy hours of ironing, and I only forgot to hate her after I had hit two smashes into the stomach of a girl who had obviously disliked me as much as I disliked her the moment we were introduced. But I hung up and folded away religiously after that.

Russell awoke, feeling ill, to find Lim at the foot of his bed. "What time is it?" he demanded.

Just after eight. I'm afraid you've missed your dinner, but I thought you'd probably prefer the extra sleep. I gave orders you weren't to be wakened. How do you feel?"

"Sick."

"How so?"

"I dunno. My brain feels bilious."

"Not very medical."

"I'm not a doctor."

"You've written quite a lot today," Lim remarked, and Russell's eyes flickered to the locker beside his bed, looking for his quarto pages. "I had it all brought down to my office first thing this afternoon while you were asleep," Lim explained. "Very interesting."

"You flatter me."

"But a trifle callous, surely? I mean, such pretty stuff after the events of this morning."

"This morning was your idea, not mine."

"No, colonel, quite the contrary. As will be the events of the morning after tomorrow. Unless of course . . ."

"Save your breath."

"Well, think about it anyway. Your very tall colleague is the individual concerned, in case you're interested." There was a knock on the cell door. "Ah, some tea for you, and a little rice."

"Both liberally laced with dope, no doubt," Russell observed.

"No doubt at all," Lim agreed. "But only to help you sleep, I promise you."

"I hadn't imagined," the Australian sneered, "you were feeding me pep pills."

"Then I'll wish you happy dreams and leave you."

"Go to hell," Russell told him sourly and began drinking his milkless, sugarless, and largely tealess tea.

An hour later Lim and the doctor failed to wake him as they walked noisily into his cell. He merely sighed like a child, rolled over on to his side, and slept more deeply than ever.

"How's he taking it?" asked Lim. In a jail full of Indians, Malays, and Eurasians, English was the *lingua franca;* and it was in English that he and his colleague now conversed.

"Very well. He's fit for his age." The doctor had studied in London and his English was more clipped than Lim's, but always nervous.

They left the cell, made their way along the gallery, and descended the spiral staircase.

"What about the executions?" Lim unlocked a heavy door and allowed the doctor through, then followed and pulled the door to behind him. Side by side they walked a second whitewashed corridor.

"He'll take them because subconsciously it will make him feel safer," the doctor stated. "Then he'll hate himself doubly and crack!"

"Is that a certainty?"

"No," the doctor admitted. "But it's a strong possibility."

Lim unlocked another door and allowed the doctor to pass into the jail courtyard. A brilliant moon sent their shadows scuttling squatly ahead of them as they marched across the open square of pallid concrete towards the passageway that led under the tower to the main gate. Neither man spoke until they were midway through this passage; then Lim, whose office was on the first floor of the tower, halted.

"I hope you're right," he said grimly and watched the balding doctor walk jerkily to the main gate, where a sentry, opening a small portcullis, allowed him to pass out of sight.

As if to confirm his sudden doubts, it was reported to him next morning that Russell, after some initial grogginess when he awoke, had begun writing with zest and had even, twice, been heard to laugh.

Another year's schooling ended, and I discovered, with very mixed feelings, that my grandfather was going to present the prizes at Speech Day.

He duly arrived and treated the headmaster with such flagrant *lèse majesté* that I hid as he approached, hoping to avoid the reprisals that would inevitably be visited upon anyone even associated with him, still less related to him; but his one good eye detected me and he promptly sought me out.

"Hello, young Tony," he greeted. "I trust you've won no prizes?"

"No," I mumbled.

"Speak up," the headmaster snapped.

"*No!*" I shouted.

"Excellent," my grandfather congratulated. "I disapprove strongly of small boys who win prizes." And then, to the headmaster, "Don't you?"

"Not entirely," he replied, with a smile that can only be described as bleak. "But your grandson obviously does." And, bestowing upon me the sort of glance I imagined Bloody Jeffreys must habitually have directed at the dock, he took my grandfather by the arm and led him firmly away.

But my grandfather was unrepentant. As if, already, he had not sufficiently blighted the remaining year I must spend at this school, he proceeded now to make a rollickingly anarchic speech that convulsed the parents, puzzled the student body, and terrified me.

"In conclusion," he said, "I offer you boys only one piece of advice. Mathematics is a low form of animal cunning, and I urge you, all of you, to have nothing to do with it."

Then he sat down, looking well pleased with the thunderous applause of the grown-ups, and smiled his most amiable smile at the headmaster: who, as he well knew, taught and loved mathematics.

That long Christmas vacation, the tribe surfed and began to treat girls rather less as if they were boys. A few of us were already leaving school to go into business, and the rest, after a year in sixth form, were destined to scatter to various faculties of the university. Our days together were numbered.

We should have known it, of course, because a band of Evangelists invaded Dee Why and repeatedly advised us that, the end being nigh, we should prepare to meet our doom. But we believed that our circle, being charmed, was invulnerable, so we carried on surfing and taking it in turn with the girls to have first use of the bathroom and feeling vaguely perplexed that Benito Mussolini and General Franco and Herr Hitler didn't want to do the same.

My mother and Aunty Ock, we knew, were more worried than we by what was going on in Europe, because they used to change the subject when they realized we were listening; but not even they seemed inclined to prepare to meet their doom.

"Here comes that mad female again," my mother hissed one day after lunch, as we sat in the dining-room whose windows opened out onto the front verandah. "Tell her I'm out" — and flung herself onto the floor beneath the window.

The female evangelist stumped up onto the verandah, leaned on the window sill, and demanded, "Gentleman of the house in?"

"No," I said.

"Lady of the house in, well?"

Furiously the lady of the house, lying full length two feet under the nose of the lady of the evangelists, shook her head.

"No," I said — at which some of the tribe became hysterical and fled to the back lawn.

"What's wrong with them then?" inquired the lady evangelist.

"I don't know."

"Youse comin' to our meeting?"

"No, thank you."

"Why not?"

"I'm Church of England."

"C. of E.!" she exclaimed in disgust. "Dead as doornails" — causing my mother to roll over onto her back with delight, which I did not find helpful.

"What're you then?" the lady evangelist asked Judy (the one who swam like a fish and played the piano).

"Presbyterian," Judy told her.

"Worse than the C.'s of E." she was told. "Youse kids'd better all come to our meeting. Otherwise yer doomed. Orl right?"

"Yes," I said.

"You'll tell the lady of the house I've bin, won't yer?"

"Yes," I said.

"C. of E.," she muttered to herself as she turned away. "Dead as doornails." She stumped down the steps and across the buffalo-grass lawn to the front gate, and there, shaking her fist at us, shouted, "Dead as bloody doornails, I tell yer! You make sure you come to our meeting."

Back at school, the headmaster, surveying me grimly, inquired, "Do you share your distinguished grandfather's views on mathematics, Russell? — and when, despairingly, I replied, "Yes sir," surprised me by not clouting me.

Later, during the lunch hour, I found myself in the company of a friend who had become obsessed with pornography. Not that he wanted himself to read it (he was a lazy youth): he wanted merely to be presented with succinct and salacious résumés of it. And I, compliant as ever, felt obliged to satisfy him.

There were, however, difficulties, chief of which was the fact that I had no idea where one obtained dirty books. Admittedly, down near the North Sydney Post Office, there was a shop that sold little blue books called *What Every Young Boy Should Know* and *What Every Young Girl Should Know,* but we had all long since discovered that we knew it: so what was I to do?

Suddenly inspired, I remembered *All Quiet on the Western Front* and *Anthony Adverse,* and found them that afternoon, no longer hidden, in the bookcase between *Edward, My Son* and a volume of essays by Professor Murdoch. Their spines had faded, there was dust on the edges of the pages, and they smelled musty and dead: but I opened them eagerly.

For the rest of the afternoon I researched conscientiously, mining for pornography; and next day, casually, at lunch time, I remarked, "Read a couple of dirty books yesterday."

"Honest?"

"Yeah."

"What'd they say? Tell us."

"In one of 'em a German bloke said, "How'd the cow shit get on the roof?""

"No! Did it really say *shit?*"

"Yep."

"Gee! What about the other one?"

"Well, there was this man and this girl and they lay down together and he put his hand inside her blouse . . ."

"Did it say that?"

"Yeah. And they kissed and then waves broke over them."

"Were they on a boat?"

"Must've been." We fell momentarily silent at such an undirty dénouement.

"Why don't you try and find some books about Germans making girls do it? You know, like they did the Belgians."

So each lunch time after that I had to make up dirty bits about Germans making Belgian girls do it, which, because I knew nothing about it, became so exhausting that eventually I started spending my lunch hour with another friend called Dougie, who sat beside me in French and was interested not in pornography but in aeroplanes. I didn't know anything about aeroplanes either, but at least I didn't have to make up daily anecdotes about flying.

At home one day my mother said, very sharply, "Don't hit Pat there, Tige," and when I asked, "Why?" replied tersely, "Because I said so."

This meant I could no longer punch my sister in the chest when she tickled me. Which she did, without mercy, whenever she wanted me to do anything.

"Well, where can I hit her?" I demanded, because one can hardly punch one's sister on the nose or in the stomach.

"Nowhere."

"It's not fair," I later protested to Pat, though I knew I was wasting my time; she, where fighting was concerned, being about as fair as Al Capone.

" 'Tis."

" 'Tis not."

"Twice as many isses as you say is nots and no back answers."

"Why shouldn't I hit your chest?"

"Because now it's my bosom," she explained loftily — and made me abruptly aware of all the time I had *not* shared with her in the past three years. Yet what could I have done? She hated tennis.

Nevertheless, I then and there resolved to be nicer to her and felt again that passionate protectiveness towards her which once — long ago — I had known whenever I heard the wild, abandoned crying of crows in the steep gullies beyond our first home.

But quite soon after that she tickled me again, until I almost expired with helpless exhaustion, so I decided to kill her instead.

The year 1937 should have been a traumatic one. The Führer rampaged and created his Hitler Youth; refugees from Austria and Germany began to arrive, miraculously acquiring blocks of flats (almost, it seemed, as they disembarked) in all the best parts of Sydney; the Sino-Japanese War broke out; and those of us who had not left school already now sat for the examination which would make us eligible for further education at the university in 1938. But, in spite of everything, we remained innocently serene.

Hitler, we felt confident, would be restrained by Britain (which our parents, quite properly, called Home).

We had done too much gardening ourselves to be impressed by the fanatically borne shovels in Hitler's flaxen-haired and frozen-faced youth.

Those distraught and lamentably few representatives of Europe's Jewry who now sought sanctuary among us we dismissed simply, not knowing what we did, as reffos — just as we dismissed all our Italian and Greek café proprietors as dagos.

We were incapable of regarding a war between, on the one side, the inventors of market gardens and, on the other, the manufacturers of shoddy toys, as in any way an omen of the yellow peril to come.

And finally, we were too well disciplined not to learn enough to pass our examinations even though the process of learning seemed rather to insulate us against the chill of current events than to make us aware of them.

Fabius Cunctator seemed more real to me then than Benito Mussolini. Madam's German lessons seemed more German to me then than Hitler's Third Reich. To construe Cicero was always less of an effort to me then than to feel really involved with a Europe festering and psychopathic. We were youthful, healthy, naïve, and clear-eyed: and we were as comfortable with what we knew of contemporary Europe as we would have been in the company of a syphilitic covered in weeping yaws.

So it was Wimbledon that obsessed us. And Donald Budge's backhand. And Alice Marble's serve. And the invincibility of Bulldog Drummond. And the virtuosity of a boy called Menuhin who performed at the Sydney Town Hall. And Grace Moore's *One Night of Love*. And the records of Gigli and Björling. And the sprinting of Jesse Owen. And the madness of Mischa Auer. And Count von Luckner arriving in Sydney on his yacht and tearing up telephone directories with his bare hands to convince us that he was a good bloke and not one of Hitler's spies. In which he failed because someone made public the fact that tearing up telephone directories is a knack, not a feat of strength, with the result that everyone started doing it to prove that von Luckner was a bloody fake and probably a spy as well, and for months it was impossible anywhere in Australia to find a telephone directory that was intact.

"Of course he's a spy," said Uncle Jim fuming. "They should lock him up."

"At a reception last night I saw him bend a penny between his thumb and forefinger," my grandfather remonstrated. "He's strong all right."

So Uncle Jim took a party aboard his motor cruiser and sailed up along the coast to the mouth of the Hawkesbury River, and from there inland to Refuge Bay, and all the way the men in the party discussed the vital information von Luckner could have transmitted back to Adolf Hitler as he covered the same course, which mystified me because we passed only beaches and cliffs. But once we had dropped anchor in Refuge Bay, each of the men tried — and failed — to bend a penny between his thumb and forefinger, so then they decided that the German Count must, after all, have been a good bloke and could not, therefore, have been a spy.

At that, as if relieved of a great anxiety, they all became tremendously light-hearted and threw one another off the cruiser into the water and swam ashore. To pump ship, they said; which sounded exciting to me, so I swam after them. But when we got ashore I found that pumping ship meant merely going behind a rock and having a piss, which not only disappointed me but puzzled me at first, because I couldn't help wondering why they hadn't just pumped ship in the water as I had. As I watched them, however, I realized that this mass pumping of ships was, in fact, a ritual: and I remembered that in the past, at picnics, on long drives into the country to see boring "views," at Flinders' Beach as they changed into their "togs," and after they had been fishing, the men had invariably congregated somewhere, to the accompaniment of much ribaldry, to pump ship. It was, I decided charitably, probably a relic of the Somme and Passchendaele.

At that moment, though, my reveries on ritual relics of the War were interrupted by a great clamour of exclamations like "Jesus!" . . . "Who died?" . . . "Someone's rotten" . . . and "Who cut that one?": and as ten adult males indulged in schoolboy excitement over a fart, I reflected cynically that, with grown-ups, it's all right so long as it doesn't make a noise.

"I thought," Lim advised casually, "I'd drop in before you went to sleep."

Looking up from his pillow, hands clasped behind his head, Russell replied, "You could've saved yourself the trouble."

"I could have, but I didn't, because I can't bring myself to believe that a Church of England colonel will refuse to save a fellow Christian from death by needless execution."

"Actually, I'm an agnostic colonel."

"You wrote today that you were C. of E."

"You've forgotten my Jesus song at Sunday school."

"Will you save him?"

"You know I can't."

"I know you won't."

"Same thing."

"It seems an Australian trait."

"What does?"

"Ruthlessness. Even here" — he waved the colonel's output of that day — "you dismiss Hitler's victims simply as reffos."

"We dismissed 'em simply as 'bloody reffos,' if you must know. A sort of last, lurid affirmation of our Britishness. After the war, of course, we called them New Australians. Naturally, we still *meant* bloody reffos, but we said New Australians. In the end, though, we quite took to the idea and began to mean what we said. Funny how things change."

"But not enough for any of *us* to become New Australians?"

"Why would any of you want to become Australians of any kind? Thought we were nothing but imperialist warmongers to you?"

"True! Tell me, do you people still regard us simply as a race of market gardeners?"

"Not entirely."

"What do you regard us as a race of?"

"Bastards!" Russell retorted and then, smiling ruefully, rebuked, "You're losing your grip, son. Let yourself right in for that, didn't you?" He yawned prodigiously.

"Tired?" Lim inquired.

"Bored," Russell told him, fighting to keep awake, to keep caring enough to be rude. "By the way, what's the date?"

"The fifteenth of July."

"*March, July, October, May,/The Ides fall on the fifteenth day,*" the Australian recited; and, when Lim looked completely blank, murmured, "Put that in your computer and check it."

"My computer," Lim murmured, displaying one of its buff cards, "is more interested in why you obliged your school friend with excerpts from pornography."

"Told you. I was essentially a compliant youth." He moved his hands from behind his head and folded them across his chest.

"To the point of degrading yourself with obscene literature?"

"Come off it! Anyway, I couldn't even find any, let alone degrade myself with it."

"At fifteen and sixteen one would expect you to have progressed beyond mere reading."

"We were Australian fifteen- and sixteen-year-olds, Lim, not Asians. Unlike you lot, we hadn't been brought up from the age of eight to wander round with a cigarette in the corner of the mouth, hissing, 'You want my sister? Velly nice. Velly clean . . .' "

"That'll do!" Lim gritted his teeth.

". . . so we matured later," Russell finished blandly. "Which made us extremely randy."

"Why did you trouble yourself with this friend if it was so exhausting each day to invent pornography?"

"I only invented very clean pornography," Russell demurred. "Sort of unconsummated rapes."

"Why did you do it?"

"I liked him."

"You were attracted to him?"

"As one is at that age."

"So you pandered to him?"

"It was all we had in common — this sort of nebulous randiness. Not about the girls we *knew*, of course."

"Why not?"

"It was universally accepted you'd do it with a girl you knew only after you'd married her; and, frankly, we did not, at that time, feel like marriage."

"It's strange, actually, that you make so little mention of sex in these notes of yours."

"Difficult stuff to describe" — Russell yawned — "specially when it's only masturbation."

"If I say sex and childhood to you, what do you think of?"

"A kid I knew when I was five. From up the road. Came rushing along one day and said he'd seen his big brother's thing all stiff."

"Yes?"

"Well, I didn't believe him. After he'd gone, though, I stood alone on the middle of the front lawn and took mine out and watched it. Eventually my mother saw me from her bedroom window and

shouted, 'What're you doing, Tige?' So I told her: I said I was waiting for it to get stiff. But she said, 'Ooh, I shouldn't bother about
that. Come in here and I'll cut your fingernails.' So I put it away and
went in to her and forgot the subject for years." Russell blinked
heavily. "Kids're funny." And before Lim could reply, was asleep.

Once again, Russell observed how dawn's curious luminescence
killed the brilliance of the light bulb in Lim's office; how detached
from the rancorous affairs of men seemed the upside-down gecko;
how sluggishly the fan on the ceiling chopped through air that was
already humid; how fresh the grass looked in the empty courtyard
below.

Once again Lim stood beside him at the window and, with an
elaborate flick on his Ronson, lit a cigarette.

The soldiers marched into the courtyard, carrying between them
three lengths of iron piping, a pulley, a coil of rope, a larger coil of
green plastic garden hose, and an empty oil drum. As if they had
rehearsed what now they were to do, they set about lashing the three
lengths of pipe together at one end, and suspending from that junc-
tion the pulley. Then, having threaded the rope through the pulley,
they stood the pipes on end and splayed them out to form a tripod, in
the apex of which was suspended the pulley, from which, limply,
hung one end of rope.

Then the officer whose nickname was Tiny was escorted into the
courtyard and brought to a halt underneath the pulley. His arms
were tightly bound behind his back.

Perfunctorily the nearest of his escorts put a leg behind him and
pushed, so that he fell to the ground; efficiently his second escort,
dragging more rope through the pulley, put a clove hitch round his
ankles; and briskly the two escorts together hoisted him, feet fore-
most, aloft.

As his pinioned body slowly revolved, the empty oil drum was
placed underneath his head, the nozzle of the green plastic hose was
thrust inside it, and a tap was turned on. After a few splutters, water
began thrumming hollowly into the drum, shallowly splashing. At
the same time the mummy-shaped victim was lowered until his head
and chest were inside the drum.

The water continued to splash shallowly — but the hollow thrumming ceased.

Then the splashing stopped, changing to the clean, continuous note of water jetting into water.

Occasionally the head-down dummy body convulsed on the end of its rope and began again its slow revolving; but mostly it was still, conserving its strength.

The clean, continuous note grew higher as jetting water met rising water, until the bubbling surface of the water rising inside the drum became visible to the man who watched from Lim's window.

For a few seconds, as nozzle and rising surface met, there was a gurgling battle of wills; but the nozzle was soon submerged, and after that the water began to deepen soundlessly.

All that could be heard in the courtyard, then, was the panting of the man whose head and chest were inside the drum, and a small, sharp splash when the water first touched his hair and he jerked his trunk upwards, away from it.

His stomach muscles being unable to support him in this new posture, however, he soon fell limply back, so that his hair floated round his head as a halo and swirled gently as he revolved.

When the water rose into his eyes, he again arched forward and upward: and again, inevitably, sagged backwards and down. Straight down.

When the water reached his nostrils, he arched and fell back, arched and fell back, arched and fell back, his whole body writhing and convulsing: but soon only his head moved, reaching up, like a flower stretching to the sun: until finally the bubbles came.

Russell was shocked that there were so many bubbles. And relieved when the last big one, wobbling upwards like an inflated plastic bag, signified that it was over.

He turned away from the window.

"Colonel," he dimly heard himself addressed. "Colonel!"

"Yes" — vaguely.

"You can go back to your cell now. I'll call on you later."

The year I went to the university our tribe disintegrated, its various members swept helplessly into the clutches of new friends at work and new romances in suburbs hopelessly distant from Lindfield. But still we failed to realize what was happening.

I, in fact, was too busy not working at the university to realize anything. Being at the university, I discovered, was like being at school, except that one sat beside pretty girls, was not compelled to learn, and was *trusted* to attend lectures — which was fatal.

Only the Professor of Latin ever called a roll: so at Latin lectures the minority present would answer to the names of the majority absent with such flagrance that once he looked up and declaimed, "I have just called forty-three names and forty of them have been answered; yet I can see only eleven of you here. I shall therefore call the roll again."

Which he did. And on that occasion all forty-three names were answered; so he opened his Livy in disgust and began to construe mournfully.

"Are you brilliant or lazy?" one of the girls asked me, puzzled by my failure to take notes during a lecture on T. E. Lawrence.

"Neither. It just doesn't seem relevant."

"What doesn't to what?"

"Any of what we're doing to what's happening," I told her, and for the first time admitted to myself that Hitler and Mussolini had become the ultimate realities in our lives.

"If there's a war, will you go?" she asked.

"No," I said. "I couldn't kill." But I knew that I lied — that I would go and could kill. The knowledge depressed me.

And when war did at last break out, we all volunteered to go to it.

Inherently afraid of the sea, and impatient of delay, I rejected both the Navy and the Air Force and decided to join the Army.

"If that's what you feel you ought to do," my mother accepted, smiling tautly.

"We must get you commissioned," my grandfather advised.

"Why?" I inquired.

He looked at me magisterially over his half-moon pince-nez, nostrils flaring wider than ever, and demanded, "Don't you want to be an officer?"

"I don't even," I assured him, "want to be a private."

"Now that, young Tony," he observed, "is ridiculous. So come and I'll take you to lunch."

As we walked up Castlereagh Street he talked tactfully, not about the war but about tennis. Striding briskly, walking-stick emphatically tapping, green eyeshade eccentrically askew over the eye that had not been kicked in 1889, he discussed the difference between the service actions of Ellsworth Vines and Jack Crawford; then, on the corner of Martin Place and Pitt Street, he halted and, throwing up imaginary tennis balls and swinging lustily with his walking-stick, illustrated his point.

Elaborately derisive, the lunch-hour mob swirled around him, but he ignored them and continued to throw tennis balls above his head and to clout them in the manner of Ellsworth Vines and Jack Crawford alternately. He knew passers-by were laughing at him; but it was to his grandson he was talking, not to them. And now at last, like everyone else, I could admire him.

"Oh, darling," croaked my grandmother when she heard that I was about to enlist, "how proud your father would have been of you." It was a thought that had not occurred to me.

"Good boy," said Uncle Jim, putting his arm round my shoulder with an unaccustomed lack of reticence.

"See you in North Africa," said Uncle Henry, whose battalion, in which he was a captain, was about to embark.

"I wish you didn't have to go," muttered Pat, holding my hand tightly, reminding me of when she had been little, making me wish I'd given her everything she had ever asked for and never punched her in the chest.

"You take care of yourself," my mother instructed, looking fierce. "And come home soon."

They were all admirably composed and brave: but *I* knew what I was losing. So after I had left them, when I was alone, I cried.

"You cried?" Lim looked both curious and contemptuous.

"Why shouldn't I have cried?" Russell retorted sullenly. The morning's brutal drowning had shocked him even more than the savage murder, two days earlier, of his corporal; and the ritual lectures on the theory of Marxism-Leninism, even though he ignored them, he now found exhausting. He loathed the lectures. Loathed sitting cross-legged on the concrete floor among an audience of Malays and Tamils due for liquidation, yet compelled each day to listen to the dogma which required their killing. He was sick of cynicism and liquidations and executions and everything Chinese.

As if sensing his mood, Lim asked, "Would you persist so honourably in your refusal to broadcast if we said that you were to die next, rather than one of your compatriots?"

"Try me," the Australian snarled — and hoped that the terror in him was not evident. Feeling his hands (which rested on the bed on either side of his thighs, as he sat facing Lim) begin to tremble, he pushed them under his legs.

"We may do that," Lim threatened. "But you still haven't told me why you cried. You were a man."

"I was a boy."

"At nineteen?"

"In those days, in Australia, nineteen was a boy."

"We have soldiers of fifteen."

"More's the pity."

"You say your tribe was scattered. Tell me about it."

"Well, one of the cousins, Peter, joined the Air Force. Got all sorts of gongs. The other cousin, Bill, was in New Guinea. Army. So was Hunter. Dougie was killed over Germany. Uncle Henry was blown up in Tobruk. Dagmar, who'd gone back to Czechoslovakia in '38, was put in a concentration camp. John — the one whose sisters were red hot at tennis —was executed by the Japanese. Poor Johnny. Jim . . ."

"Your uncle again?"

"Another Jim."

"You didn't mention any other Jim."

"Well, I do now. Knew him all my life. Good bloke. Mad on radios, so he ended up running one of those hair-raising watching and listening posts on some Nip-occupied island or other. Radioing back what he saw."

"Like you were before you took refuge at Bukit Langkap?"

"*We* were entitled to observe and maintain contact until the last day of the Withdrawal: Jim was on active service in enemy territory."

"They caught him, of course?"

"They did not. Though one of them," — Russell laughed at the
recollection of it —"did blunder onto him in the end."

"So?"

"So they both fled! Jim straight to his radio, from which he sent
the ambiguous but resourceful message: *'Have been overrun by Japanese!'* " Russell laughed again. "As he later said, 'Japanese' could
have meant any number, from one to a million. He just left it to
Australia to draw its own conclusions. And what Australia concluded
was that Jim and his boys had been overrun by at least a battalion:
so they radioed back that a submarine would pick 'em up that night,
which it did."

"That all?"

"That all what?"

"Of the tribe?"

"Good God, no. Don died in Thailand, on the Railway. So did
Peter . . ."

"Your Air Force cousin?"

"No, you dim-wit, another Peter."

"Whom again you haven't mentioned?"

"That's right. Like I didn't Malcolm, or David, or Hughie, or
Doolie, or another David, or . . ."

"Did they all die?"

"No."

"Of your immediate circle, how many died?"

"*Our* lives were charmed: of us, only Johnny."

"Or perhaps, like you, rather than fight, they all surrendered?"

"No — I was the only really dedicated coward of our lot."

"Dedicated to cowardice as you were, did you ever think you'd
crack up as a prisoner of war?"

"Never." Russell's voice was crisp.

"Still," Lim suggested, "the Japanese were only trying to kill you,
weren't they?"

"Whereas you?" Russell prompted.

"I told you. Weeks ago."

"Tell me again, well."

"*We* are going to break you."

"Gonna take you a hell of a long time, isn't it?"

"On the contrary, we're ahead of schedule."

"Prove it. Gimme an example — any example you like — of how I'm breaking."

"A minute ago, like the child you once were, you said, 'Tell me again, well.' "

"I did not."

"I'm afraid you did. What a ridiculous language yours is, by the way. 'I'm afraid you did,' I say, and what I really mean is, 'I'm delighted you did.' But to continue, and it's very significant, you've reverted to these childish speech patterns on at least four other occasions that I can remember without even consulting my notes."

"I bloody well have not."

"But again I'm afraid that you have, colonel."

"I have not either," Russell bellowed — and stared aghast as the infantile "either" echoed in his brain.

"Have you neither?" Lim jeered.

"Well, what do you expect? I'm exhausted," the Australian protested — and again was appalled, because in his own voice he heard distinctly the beginnings of a childish whine.

"You are not exhausted; you are merely reacting to our drugs and so on by becoming, as expected, increasingly literal and juvenile in your attitudes."

"Feeding me monkey glands, are you?" It was a drowsy attempt at mockery.

"Not exactly."

"What good's my becoming literal and juvenile doing you?"

"In itself, no good at all; but as a classic symptom of something else, it's very gratifying indeed."

"And what's this something else?"

"I'm afraid that's our business."

Russell's eyes closed and he swayed as he sat on the edge of his bed: so, placing a hand on his shoulder, Lim pushed him gently sideways.

"Lie down, colonel," he murmured.

Russell toppled onto his side, his legs hanging over the edge of the bed.

For some seconds Lim examined the drawn face and the moist, greying hair that lay thinly over the left temple. A vulnerable temple; and visible in it, throbbing vulnerably, a pulse; and behind that, inside the fragile skull, a vulnerable brain. Lim hated all men whose colour reminded him of Guardsman Stogdale, but Russell reminded him of a sick child. So he lifted the sleeping man's legs onto the bed and quietly left him. Sighing almost petulantly, lips moving slightly, Russell slept on.

The following morning he washed and shaved wearily, observing with a twinge of self-pity that even cleaning his teeth had become an effort; and after breakfast, lying on his bed, he decided that he could no more be bothered writing than he could struggle with the prose of Mr Toynbee.

For a moment he frowned, dimly aware that there had been a reason why he had written every other day; but then he sighed and told himself again that he couldn't be bothered. Turning on to his side, he drew his legs up, so that his knees were close to his chest, and closed his eyes.

Almost at once, it seemed, Lim arrived and sat on a chair handed in to him by the guard.

"What's wrong, colonel?"

"I'm not well."

"Nonsense, you're perfectly well. A little tired perhaps . . ."

"I . . . am . . . not . . . well!" Russell shouted, raising himself up on one elbow.

"You're nervous. Naturally, you're nervous."

"I'm ill." He fell flat on his back again and closed his eyes.

"But you mustn't let yourself go. You must write."

"No."

"I said, you must write."

"And I said, no. Anyway, I can't. I'm too tired and I can't think. I can't make my mind go any farther forward than it has. I can think backwards — whole wodges of stuff when I was a kid — like the time Pat hit me on the head with a chisel . . ."

"You've written that already."

"I *know*" — peevishly. "But that's the sort of thing I think of. The only sort of, I mean. Whole wodges of it — and then I realize all I'm doing is remembering off by heart what I've already written. And it's bloody tiring, so I'm not doing any more."

"But I need to know more."

"Too bad. Anyway, there isn't much more."

"No? Maybe it would help you if, just this once — just this once, mind you — I let you talk about your life since you were twenty. Yes? Come on now. Regale me with your life since the war."

As he met Lim's eye, Russell hauled himself resignedly into a sitting posture, legs along the mattress, back supported by the bed's iron frame. His eyes were bloodshot, and his face — except for a red patch where he had lain on it — sallow.

"When the war ended," he said wearily, "I was twenty-four. A bit mad and twenty-four. By thirty-five I'd stopped being mad — well, anyway, I'd settled down enough with a wife and kids and this new job to give the impression I was sane — and after that I just got a bit older and more successful and less flexible each year. Gave up tennis, took up golf. Got spectacles for reading. Went through a girlie period, with this small flat at Kings Cross and kidding myself the two lasses I took to it — once each — liked *me* rather than the good time I showed 'em. Then I got mad with the remorse and took the wife on a trip round the world. Thought I was in love with a Frenchwoman in Cannes — Françoise, her name was, about thirty; lovely — until the wife got herself picked up by one of the boys, gigolos, on the beach; whereupon I fell smartly out of love with the Frenchwoman and whipped the wife off to Claridges in London, and to lots of theatres and rich dinners, till we got used to being companionable again. You companionable with your wife? No, I imagine not. In '65 our boy was killed. And since then we've just pottered. Growing gladioli. Buying the odd painting. Reading biographies. Forgetting at last to talk about the war. Having a drink together before dinner. Cutting out bread and potatoes. The occasional couple in for a game of bridge. Difficulty hearing — but hating noise. Funerals. Suddenly lots of funerals. That's all."

"Sure? You won't get another chance. It's like your mother and the stick. You go back to this particular stage of your life now, or not at all."

"Well . . . each new car got heavier and safer. Stopped going to films much or watching T.V. at all. Gave up smoking twice. Decided *not* to get another dog. Sold the tennis court to a speculator who put a hideous little blocklet of flatlets on it. Bought the wife a mink — at last! Saw some of my contemporaries' sons hitting thirty and getting that soft look successful men's boys do get when they follow dad into the business. Suppose I was only jealous: my boy'd always be only twenty. Golf handicap began to go up. Rotary began to be a bore."

"And your military career?"

"I told you. After our boy was killed I joined the Militia. When you people overran Thailand in '73 . . ."

"Thailand asked for a Chinese presence to defend her against imperialist aggression," Lim interrupted.

"Put it how you like," Russell accepted indifferently, "but after it, when Malaysia asked for a Western presence to defend her against Communist aggression, I decided to help. With the result I was sent practically everywhere but Malaya. Until this year. And the rest you know."

"Yes, the rest I know . . ." Lim paused. "Tell me, what are your views now on broadcasting?"

"The same."

"In spite of this morning? And the other five mornings to come?"

"Yes."

"We haven't shaken you at all?"

"Can't get much nastier, can it?"

"Than what?"

"Slow drowning and throat cutting."

"Colonel," Lim warned with a kind of gentle insistence, "you've only just begun."

"Whaddya mean, I've only . . . ?"

"You killed them."

"Ah, for crying out loud."

"Oh yes. And I don't just mean that you were responsible for their deaths."

"What else?"

"As I told you after the execution of your corporal — you devised the method of his execution. Of today's too."

"You're crazy. I never said a word."

"You've written tens of thousands of words."

"About executions?" Russell sneered.

"About, among other things, what has appalled you during your life. And since it's our aim to appal you rather than simply to kill your friends, we're naturally relying on you for inspiration."

"Then you'll have to repeat yourselves quite a bit, won't you? Because killing the sheep and the time I nearly got drowned are the only things I wrote about that really hit me."

"The only things you mention specifically, yes," Lim agreed. "You'd be surprised, though, at the heap of guilts and fears our computer has turned up from under your apparently innocuous slabs of prose. And from comparing your five manuscripts — their omissions and glossings over. No, for what we need, you've got in you more than enough revolting methods of killing; and I guarantee you won't be able to stomach the later ones, even if you've found the first two easy."

"Easy?" Russell exploded. "Christ!"

"Then why not stop them? One word from you . . ."

"May save them and me, but it won't stop you people from walking into Papua."

"So?"

"So you're not walking in under the convenient cover of a slanging match between the States and Australia about the possibility of *all* Australians being as treacherous and pusillanimous as Colonel Anthony Russell, which is what you want, isn't it?"

"Naturally."

"Then you'll just have to carry on with your executions, and I'll just have to stick them out, or go mad, 'cause you're not getting it."

Rising from his chair, Lim shrugged and, stepping to the door, rapped on it with his knuckles. It was unlocked and opened immediately. As he left, he indicated to the guard that the chair should remain. Russell gazed at the locked door and the empty chair and then covered his face with both hands.

"Jesus," he whispered, half praying, half anguished, "what'd I write? What're they going to do?"

As he thought about it, the next morning, he decided that it must be to sexual guilts and fears that Lim had alluded. With psychoanalysts it always was sexual guilts and fears. So what had he written — or omitted, or glossed over — that was by implication sexual?

Nothing.

No, that was stupid. Just saying "nothing" was stupid. What could it have been?

Well the head-shrinkers always started with the parental thing.

The row!

Clearly, then, as if someone were reading them to him, he heard his own words: . . . "but I stood my ground, irrelevantly aware that my mother was in her nightgown, long brown hair hanging down her back; and that my father had on only his pyjama jacket — beneath which the naked half of his body looked aggressively sturdy."

Aggressively sturdy. Surely they hadn't thought he'd meant . . . ? No; ridiculous. Still, an odd choice of words. Freudian? That bloody computer'd certainly think so. But even if it did, what could they make of it that they could use in an execution?

Unless . . .

Slowly raising his head, he sat so still that he became aware of his stillness: of the cell's stillness. Terrified to move, lest he communicate with "them" the sudden frightful possibility that had come to him, he remained utterly still. No, he told himself; don't think about it. Think about something else. Like what? Like anything. Pat. Like Pat trying to balance on his knees. Ah, yes. Like the trapeze artist in gold lamé tights high in the apex of the tent at Port Macquarie. Pat had looked up — everyone was looking up, all eyes focused on the dizzily high up figure in gold lamé — and had whispered, "Daddy?"

"Shush," he admonished as the drums began their deathly roll. He thought she wanted to go to the lavatory. At this sort of moment Pat always did want to go to the lavatory.

"But daddy!"

"Look at him, Littly." The drums began to thunder, and her mother and brother pretended not to know that Pat wanted to go to the lavatory.

"I am looking, daddy," she protested. "Daddy, is *he* God?"

That had been their last Christmas at Port Macquarie, Russell reflected. His father had died the following year. Funny about that dream — seeing him with the bandage round his head, and his saying, "Look after her." Had it been a visitation? Or merely a sleeping boy's subconscious reaction to the exhausted return, late at night, of a mother whose husband had just died? Doubtless she'd come in and kissed him as he slept. Crying probably. And Rob, too, Rob probably whispering, "You must get some sleep, Mrs Russell." Yes, probably he'd heard it all as he almost woke up, and added it all up in his subconscious, and got the right answer in a dream.

But he hadn't got the right answer. He hadn't known his father was dead until his mother told him.

"Poor little Tige," he heard her say again, and a lump came into his throat and childish tears to his old man's eyes. "Darling, last night your father died. I know it's awful for you, and how much you'll — we'll all miss him . . ." Russell sobbed aloud and wondered why she'd said "you'll," so that she'd had to change it to "we'll all?" Wasn't she sorry dad was dead too? It's all right for her. Her father's still alive.

Actually, though, he isn't, Russell at once admitted; and remembered the old man lying mutinous in a hospital bed.

"How's the army treating you?" the old man had asked.

"Fine thanks, Doc. How're the doctors treating you?"

"Bloody awful. Won't let me drink. Here" — opening a drawer and producing a few pound notes — "be a good lad: nick out and get me bottle of whisky."

"Doc . . ."

"Tony, I want a drink." The matron had said he was dying. Not painfully — just dying. "I don't mind snuffing it, if I must, but not of boredom. Scotch is a great reliever of boredom."

"I'll go and get it now," the youthful Gunner Russell at once agreed.

"If you run — you *can* run in those boots, can you? Good — if you run, you might just get back before the end of visiting hours."

In his hot uniform and heavy boots, Gunner Russell ran: and returned just in time.

"Here's the change."

"Keep it. No use to me. Never talked much, you and I, have we?"

"No."

"My fault. Always liked you and Pat, though." He poured himself a stiff shot, tossed it back, and wiped his damp moustache with the back of his hand. "That's better. Dotty — your mother — had a bad time while your father was ill. Men shouldn't be slow dying." He poured himself another whisky. "Here's to you."

A bell rang.

"I'll come again," Gunner Russell promised, shaking the old man's hand.

"Won't be necessary," the patient replied and stuffed the flat whisky bottle well under his mattress: where it was found, empty, next morning, when they carried his body out of the room.

"Dotty — your mother — had a bad time while your father was ill." He repeated the words to himself, assessing them in the light of what he now knew of death from malignant tumours. No wonder his mother had said "you'll" and had to change it to "we'll all."

After Aunty Ock telephoned his regiment and asked that he be advised of his grandfather's death, he had been granted three hours' compassionate leave to console his mother, who was on her way to the hospital to make arrangements. But when he got there, an hour and a quarter later, she had left.

"Which way did she go?" he asked, knowing that it would take another hour and a quarter to get back to camp. That left only thirty minutes to find and comfort her.

"I don't know, dear," the matron admitted, looking distressed.

Boots clumping, he ran out of the hospital, down to William Street, and then, illogically, down towards Woolloomooloo. Had he thought about it, he would have known that Woolloomooloo was the last place to look for his mother. But he did not think: he just ran fast and with certainty down the hill. A minute later he saw her. She turned and waited for him.

"Hello, mum."

"Hello, Tige."

"I'm sorry" — steering her back up the hill.

"At least he had one last good drink." Her smile was wan.

"I got it for him yesterday. He asked me to."

"Well, if you hadn't, I probably would've."

"Mum, I've only got another twenty minutes. Come and have some tea with me."

"Let's go in here," she agreed, pointing to a Greek café with a sign on the window proclaiming, "Your Gallant Allies." Only Italians were dagos now.

They sat at a small not very clean table and drank strong sweet tea from chipped cups. His mother liked her tea weak and sugarless.

"Mum?"

"Yes."

"It's a bad time to tell you, but I'll be home this week-end on final leave."

"'Stop worrying about me," she ordered, opening her purse.

"No," he protested. "I asked you." For the first time in his nineteen years he was earning money. Five shillings a day. "Five-bob-a-day butchers," a Labour M.P. at Canberra had dubbed him and his fellow volunteers. Later, all the volunteers went overseas to fight, and the Labour M.P. became a member of the War Cabinet. Russell didn't care about being called a five-bob-a-day butcher, however; he was just glad that for once he could be host to his mother.

"I'm paying," he insisted. "I asked you."

"So you did," she said, closing her purse and accepting his hospitality. "Thank you."

As he paid the small bill she waited for him out on the pavement. Then they walked together back to William Street and caught a tram. At George Street they got out.

"You all right?" he asked.

"Of course. Quick, there's your tram for Central." They kissed.

"Bye, mum."

"Bye, darling."

Why, he wondered, had no words been invented to describe what one meant when one wanted to offer comfort? Same with sex. Why no words for that marvellous moment at the end? Tahitians, before the missionaries got at them, used to do it publicly. If they felt like it, they just lay down and did it: and people either watched and offered advice, or stepped over them and left them to it.

I bet Tahitians had words to describe the end, he thought. *And* I bet the missionaries banned them.

The sex-mad Inverell girl said if you did it to yourself your spine dried up and you turned into a hunchback.

"Do what?" he asked and, when she told him, protested, "But I haven't."

"It's all right if someone else does it for you, but," she qualified. "Shall I do it for you?"

"No," he cried and fled, because he knew that the sex-mad girl would say anything to get her way, and he had no desire to be turned into a hunchback for her sake.

Maybe that was why grown-ups were always urging him to keep his back straight.

"Shoulders back, Tige," his mother was always saying.

"Sit up straight," his father was constantly exhorting.

"Oh, *what* a beautiful straight back," Gar was in the habit of crowing. When what they really meant was, don't do it to yourself or your back will grow crooked and humped.

Well, he hadn't. Then. And later he'd forgotten all about becoming a hunchback — although he had inclined to the theory that it stunted your growth. Like smoking.

Lim entered his cell, a cigarette between his lips.

"Stunts your growth," Russell cautioned.

"I beg your pardon?"

"Granted" — a pert but witless retort fashionable in his youth, which threw him now into a fit of giggles.

"What are you talking about?" Lim inquired, sitting down, facing the Australian, who sat on the edge of his bed.

"Smoking. Stunts your growth. So does the other."

"What other?"

"If you don't know, why should I stop your back getting hunched?"

Eyebrows raised, Lim wrote deliberately in his notebook.

"What you writing?" Russell demanded.

"That you're alert but incoherent."

"Gonna rush off and consult your computer?"

"No, the doctor."

"Am I sick?"

"Do you feel sick?"

"Only of you."

"Then you're not sick." Lim rose from his chair to leave.

"No," exclaimed Russell. "Don't go."

Lim smiled. "I must," he said and held out his packet of Chester-fields. "Cigarette?"

"Thanks." Russell took one and Lim lit it for him.

"If you want me," Lim said casually, "just tell the guard."

Lim and the doctor agreed that Russell having said "No, don't go" was a significant step forward in their campaign. His unthinking ac-ceptance of a cigarette was also encouraging.

"He probably feels ill now he's smoked it," the doctor observed, "because I should imagine he's lost his tolerance of nicotine, but that's all to the good — he'll sleep."

"This tendency to incoherence doesn't matter?" Lim asked.

"On the contrary," the doctor replied. "It had to come."

Meanwhile Russell sat cross-legged at his morning dialectics class and wondered why he had been so frightened of the sex-mad girl.

Well, not frightened, exactly, but afraid of offending her. As he had been with Beth, who had wanted to suck his sweets and then put them back in his mouth. Why not just punch them both in the chest? Neither of them had bosoms. Kissing Helen, square on, like a budgerigar, though, was beaut. Like singing. Quietly he began to sing.

> *"All the birds of the air*
> *fell a'sighing and a'sobbing . . ."*

The lecturer on Marxism-Leninism stopped talking, and the Malay sitting beside Russell nudged him.

> *"When they heard of the death*
> *of poor Cock Robbing . . ."*

"Silence!" shouted the lecturer.

> *"When they* HEARD *. . ."*

"SILENCE."

> *"Of*
> *the* DEATH *. . ."*

"Tuan!" the Malay next to Russell, who looked heartbroken, implored. "Tuan."

"*O . . . of*

poor

Cock

ROBBING."

Suddenly Russell found himself being man-handled out of the class by two flint-faced guards. He was astonished to find that his own face was wet with tears.

"Hey," he protested, "what's wrong?"

Not answering, they marched him roughly to Lim's office and, in aggrieved Chinese monosyllables, reported his offence.

"Why did you sing during your indoctrination class?" Lim demanded.

"What the hell are you talking about?"

"Go to your cell and sleep," Lim instructed and ordered the guards accordingly.

"Now you're talking," Russell acknowledged ungraciously and was led away.

"Watch him closely tomorrow morning," the doctor advised. "He should crack soon."

Russell stood at the office window, staring fixedly down, and Lim, brown eyes narrowed, cigarette burning unheeded close to the olive skin of his boy's fingers, watched him intently. As the fan chop-chopped, strands of fine grey hair rose and fell softly on the back of the Australian's head. His forehead was creased with tension, and a vein in his temple swelled and flattened rhythmically.

For minutes he stood like this. Lim dropped the butt of his cigarette on the floor and, as he lit another, saw Russell's lips compress and his nostrils distend and his left eyebrow jerk up into a sharp circumflex of revulsion.

Now, as the pulse in Russell's temple changed its leisurely ebb and flow to a swift flick-flick-flick, and the pupils of his eyes dilated, every muscle in his face — round his lips and nostrils and eyes, in his cheeks and on his forehead — seemed to go into spasm.

And then, his respiration having become rapid and stertorous, he uttered a series of shuddering moans and turned away from what he saw.

Lim led him to the doorway.

"Now," he whispered, gripping the Australian's arm tightly and shaking it, "now do you believe me?"

Barely comprehending, Russell looked down at him.

"How did you know?" he whispered.

"How did we know what?"

"What I'd been thinking." Russell pointed at the window.

"We know everything, colonel."

"Oh Christ."

"Christ won't help you," Lim assured. "God won't help you. No one will help you. You're alone."

Each phrase rang like a further peal in an intolerable knell of despair.

Yet, incredibly, the tautness and desolation in Russell's face suddenly dissolved. "Thank you for reminding me," he murmured. "Hate's what I need, not help. Long as I can hate your guts, Lim, I'm no use to you."

"*He*" — Lim jerked a contemptuous thumb at the window — "will be relieved to know that."

"He, being dead," Russell retorted, "will never know pain or misery again, so he doesn't care. I care *for* him, because I'm selfish, but he doesn't care about me or anything else."

"You're very philosophic."

"I learned that truth when I cried after my father died: because it was sad for me. That's what bereavement means."

"I wonder if you'd be so philosophic about your own death?"

"If it was painless."

"And if it was not?"

"If the pain was brief."

"And if it was long?"

"How long?"

"Hours."

"In the context of a lifetime, hours isn't long."

"Weeks then."

"I wouldn't believe it could last weeks. Every minute I'd be sure it'd stop the next minute."

"A day then?"

"If I knew it was going to last a day, I'd die of fright in seconds."

"Could you endure" — pointing to the window — "seconds of that?"

"Edward the Second did, way back, because of his lover Gaveston. *He* did, this morning, because of me. So I suppose I could, sometime, because of you."

It was as he was marched back to his cell that Russell remembered how originally (when was it? it seemed years ago) he had planned to resist Lim and his computer. How could he have forgotten? And how long had it been since he wrote anything? He must start again, right away.

Five minutes later a telephone rang in Lim's bungalow outside the jail, and Lim, just returning from his dawn rendezvous with Russell, hoping for an hour's sleep, ran irritably through his small garden to answer it.

"Yes?"

"The Australian prisoner is writing again," a guard's voice advised.

"Okay."

Lim hung up. But it was not okay. He telephoned the doctor, who answered sleepily.

"Russell's writing again."

"Are you sure?"

"Would I be wasting my time ringing you if I wasn't? What's it mean?"

"I don't know," the doctor muttered cautiously. "It depends what he's writing."

"I thought you said he was close to cracking."

"He was."

"Was?"

"Is."

"Then why is he writing?"

"It depends what he's writing," the doctor insisted.

Lim snarled something curt and obscene in Chinese and again hung up.

The morning I finally parted from my family to go to war wasn't the first time since my childhood that I'd cried.

The first time was the Sunday evening after we had moved to our new home by the golf course.

I had borrowed Uncle Roy's tennis court for the Sunday afternoon and had invited the cousins and Mick and Hunter and Dagmar (with whose beauty and forehand volley I was besotted) to play on it. All Sunday morning I had spent mowing and rolling the grass and marking the shaven surface with impeccable lines. I had saved my pocket money for months to buy three new balls and cream buns and soft drinks and a chocolate cake. Loyally Pat had helped me, emptying the catcher of its sweet-smelling cuttings, holding one end of the string along which I so carefully wheeled the marker, keeping the ants off the cakes and the sun off the soft drinks. Together we finished working just in time for me to shower, change, and greet my guests.

The tennis that afternoon was good. It was not often we could play on grass (the cousins' court was gravel), and it was very rare for us to have a ball boy; but Pat, determined to make my party a success, fetched and threw tirelessly.

At twenty-five past six, reluctantly compelled at last to admit that we could no longer see, we stopped playing and rolled up the net and thanked Uncle Roy and walked to St Leonard's station, where we caught a train back to Lindfield.

Up the station steps we swarmed and through the ticket barrier; but Pat, who was only ten and exhausted from ball-boying, and laden down with the basketful of empty soft-drink bottles she insisted on carrying, lagged a little, so I stood at the barrier and waited for her.

And when, a few seconds later, she caught me up, we were alone. The other five had rushed leftwards off the station, chattering and laughing.

Incredulous and despairing, I watched my uncaring friends vanish: and tensely Pat watched me.

"They forgot we don't go that way any longer," she explained.

"They didn't even say good-bye," I muttered, horrified to feel tears in my eyes. From which Pat at once averted her gaze.

"They're so used to us going with them, that's why. It was a beaut tennis party, Tone. They all enjoyed it, really they did."

"Then why didn't they say anything?"

"They'll feel awful when they notice you aren't with them."

"I worked all morning and spent all my money," I raged — not even thinking about how Pat had worked too, and been rewarded by being allowed to collect all the balls we hit over the fence and carry the basketful of bottles we had emptied.

"They should've said something," Pat agreed, switching tactics cleverly. "The pigs."

"Dagmar's all right," I interceded on behalf of Czech beauty and volleying perfection.

"She's a pig," Pat averred stoutly. "They're all pigs."

"Dagmar isn't."

"Why didn't she thank you then?"

"She doesn't know we've moved."

"She does so."

"Shut up."

"I will *not* shut up. She should have said something to you and she didn't. She's a dirty pig."

So I punched her on the chest.

Momentarily her blue eyes glittered, but then compassion overruled rage.

"Come on," she urged, plucking gently at the sleeve of my white, cable-stitch sweater (we all wore white cable-stitch sweaters). "Let's go home."

"Home," I jeered, making it sound like Devil's Island.

"They'll ring as soon as we get home," Pat promised. "Even Dagmar will."

Which, of course, they did, all of them, apologizing and thanking profusely and saying it had been a beaut afternoon and how about coming to the pictures tonight; they'd shout me because I'd paid for the balls and the cakes and the bottles of soft drinks. So I gulped my dinner and rushed off to the Lindfield picture show, leaving Pat to wash up on her own. I never did thank her for carrying away the grass cuttings and helping with the marking and acting as ball boy and so loyally averting her gaze when I cried, because those things were due to me: but I did feel guilty about leaving her to wash up on her own instead of taking her with me to the pictures.

"You've decided to be a good boy and start writing again, I see," Lim observed from beside his bed.

Russell looked up and, detecting a faint air of uneasiness, in spite of the other's crisp accent and even crisper khakis, felt absurdly elated.

"Decided to be a bad boy and start writing again," he corrected.

"Nonsense, you know I've always wanted you to write."

"You deliberately drove me to the point where I couldn't write another word," Russell contradicted.

"Show me what you've written."

"You can read, learn, and inwardly digest it," Russell agreed, handing over the few sheets of paper, "while I sit through yet another of your bloke's futile attempts at converting me to the lunacies of Uncle Mao."

"Today," Lim murmured, beginning to read, "you will be excused that."

"Hoobloodyray! Why?"

"Yesterday you started singing during the indoctrination period and my colleague didn't like it. If you were to return today he would lose face, because the rest of the class would see that you hadn't been punished. And we can't have that, can we?"

"I can, but you can't. Looks like that's the last of Mao's crap for me then, doesn't it?"

"No. Tomorrow there will be a fresh class for you to join."

"You mean to say, knowing you're going to machine-gun the lot of 'em tonight . . ."

"This afternoon actually."

". . . you'll still ear bash 'em with indoctrination muck all morning?"

"It keeps them quiet," Lim explained, then tapped the paper. "This is a touching little tale."

"I'm a touching little author."

"But selfish."

"Then or now?"

"To your sister then; to your colleagues now."

"What'll happen to you," Russell inquired, almost with insolence, "when your bosses find out there ain't gonna be no broadcast?"

"My bosses wouldn't like that at all," Lim admitted smoothly. "Which is why there *is* going to be a broadcast. What happened to Dagmar?"

"Eh?"

"Dagmar. You told me she went back to Czechoslovakia in 1938 and was imprisoned by the Nazis. What happened to her?"

"She survived her concentration camp, but after we'd all sent letters saying, 'Marvellous. How are you? What can we send you?' she wrote back and said not to write any more please, it'd only get her into trouble. That's the blessings of communism for you."

"So you blame us for your loss of contact with Dagmar?"

"Well, I don't blame President Kennedy."

"Seen your cousins lately?"

"Haven't seen them since the war."

"And the rest of the 'tribe,' as you call it?"

"Hardly at all."

"And I suppose it's the Communists who're to blame for that too?"

"No, the war was to blame for that."

"But it was not the war that was to blame for Dagmar?"

"If it wanted to, the tribe could reunite tomorrow."

"Doesn't it want to?"

"The war split us up. We parted youngsters; came back six years later old men. If we'd reunited, we'd have seen what old men we'd become and it'd have destroyed our belief that we'd ever been young — or that the war had been *about* anything. We'd all have liked to see Dagmar again though. Seeing her out of a concentration camp would've proved we'd won something. But when she wrote and said no more letters please, we realized we'd either never won anything or, if we had, that we'd just lost it again. It'd all been for nothing;

was more than likely all going to start again. Bloody discouraging."

"Are you still discouraged?"

"Yep. I reckon we're going to do a Munich on you lot when you walk into Papua-New Guinea; and then you lot're going to do a Poland on us when you walk into Australia."

"Happily the General Assembly of the United Nations doesn't reflect your views. It held an emergency meeting yesterday and almost unanimously accepted an Afro-Asian resolution condemning Australia's administration of Papua-New Guinea as neo-colonialism and recommending an Indonesian administration instead."

"What was the vote?"

"Only Australia and Portugal voted against it."

"Britain?"

"Abstained."

"The U.S.?"

"Supported the resolution."

"And if Indonesia gets the trusteeship of Papua from the Security Council, she'll naturally ask for immediate Chinese aid?"

"Naturally," Lim murmured.

"Then what in God's name are you doing wasting your time on small fry like me and . . . ?"

"Wars," Lim explained, "are lost by generals and won by small fry. You and your friends must do your bit."

"On *your* side?" Russell scoffed.

"On the side of the world's small fry," Lim amended; but seemed unsurprised when his prisoner responded only with a snort of contempt. "Time I left you to think things over."

Now Russell laughed with genuine amusement.

"What's the joke?" Lim inquired.

"I was thinking of Pat."

"Why?"

"Your saying you'd leave me to think things over. Reminded me of Pat left locked in our room to think over how to spell 'Tony.' Ah dear. Happy days."

"But beyond recall," Lim suggested.

"No," Russell demurred. "Thanks to you. Never realized how lucky I'd been, until now."

"Had been. Past tense," Lim pointed out.

"I'm enjoying it at this very moment," the Australian disputed. "Present tense. I'm grateful to you. . . ."

"He says," Lim reported irritably, "he's grateful to me. What are we going to do?"

"My role is purely medical," the doctor insisted. "There's nothing I can do about his emotional attitudes."

"You're a psychoanalyst."

"Not even psychoanalysts can prescribe anti-gratitude pills!"

"Don't make jokes, doctor. There's very little time."

"Then increase the pressure. Make the executions worse."

"I watched him this morning," Lim objected. "I don't think we can."

"You misunderstand me," the doctor elaborated hurriedly, anxiously. "I mean, make them worse in terms of quantity. So far he has stood up to three separate executions on three separate mornings, yes?"

"Yes."

"Then next time make him watch four executions, one after the other, in one morning. You can be reasonably sure he will not be able to take four."

"Reasonably sure isn't enough," Lim objected.

"Plenty of blood will make it absolutely sure. You have been stupid to forget that what he really hates is blood. Make him see lots of blood for a long time: then your Australian will break."

After my father died, my mother stopped playing the piano. She didn't just play less, she stopped playing altogether, as if she had lost her pleasure in it: and I missed her playing.

I missed it so much that soon after we moved to our house by the golf links I decided to take lessons myself, from a man in town who guaranteed to teach me in three months how to bash out any popular tune. And in a way he did. From a stumbling repertoire of major and minor chords, I learned to lend a wary left-handed rhythm to the laborious course of a melody line that my right hand plotted in octaves relieved by an occasional recklessly diminished seventh.

It did not sound remotely like the songs Judy played, still less like anything my mother played, yet it was almost a year before I admitted defeat and resorted instead to Wilhelm Backhaus' records on the gramophone — whilst the deserted rosewood Steinway brooded silently in the corner. In winter time, indeed, as its dark flank reflected the glow of flickering logs in the fireplace, it used to look almost sullenly abandoned; and sometimes, as I sat reading beside Pat on the sofa, I would glance across at my mother, to see if she had sensed her piano's aura of rejection; but she never looked up. She just read her book and knitted, totally absorbed.

Yet she was invariably aware when the clock's hands reached nine.

"Bed, Tige," she would say then, implacably. I was fifteen and it wasn't fair — not in the winter time when it got too dark for tennis at six o'clock. After so short a time on the court, one needed *hours* of reading in front of the log fire to complete the day's quota of pleasure: but instead one got, "Bring some more wood in, will you please, dear?" and "Go on, you two, get the washing up done," and "You done your homework?" and "Hold this skein while I wind it, please," and finally, just as one had begun to escape into the richer world of Sapper and Dornford Yates, "Bed time, Tige." Always, as I left the sitting-room, I used to feel as flushed and sullen as the Steinway: but my mother never noticed that either. Never even cared that every winter's night, at nine o'clock, I hated her.

That was the year I first met Johnny. Well, got to know him. He had been at the school for three years, but I only noticed him that year when I discovered that he played elegant tennis.

"No" he disputed, "it's my sisters who're elegant. You should have a game with them."

"When?" I demanded crudely. Which is how I came to be invited to their place on the Saturday I discovered all my clothes, for three weeks back, swept under my bed.

And on various subsequent Saturdays, infrequent but memorable, until we went our separate ways to the war.

David, who was the youngest, was the first to go to the war. Without a word, he vanished down to Rushcutter's Bay and joined the Navy and, almost before we knew it, departed for the Mediterranean, an alien figure already in his bell bottoms and tiddly ribbons, staggering under the weight of a massive kit bag that reeked of tar.

Meantime Billy Hughes, looking shrunken and ancient, emerged from his house in Lindfield to make fiery recruiting speeches in Martin Place. As Australia's war-time Prime Minister from 1915 to 1918, the theory was, he would appeal irresistibly to the martial instincts of young Australians in 1940: but it did not work out that way. Little deaf old Billy, aided and abetted by brass bands, merely embarrassed us. I waited for weeks till neither he nor the brass bands were performing before volunteering for the Army, and I suspect that my cousins and the rest of the tribe did the same: but I don't know, because now each one made his own decision, chose his own time, and then — to an ingratiating staff — presented himself for recruitment at a hut in the middle of Martin Place a few yards from what used to be an underground gentlemen's lavatory.

Later, about to go home on pre-embarkation leave, I called into Prouds, the jewellers, to buy my mother and my girl-friend gold brooches enamelled with my regimental colours. The shop was full of soldiers buying gold brooches enamelled with their regimental colours. I found myself standing at the counter beside Peter, my cousin, who was in the Air Force.

"Do they sell gold brooches with Air Force colours on 'em too?" I demanded.

"No," he said. "I'm buying a watch."

So he bought his watch and I bought my brooches and then we adjourned to a milk bar where we bought each other chocolate malteds for the last time.

After that, he trained in Canada, and flew fighters in England, and was shot down into the sea by the Japanese, but managed to get into his inflatable dinghy and be picked up by Air Sea Rescue. I've seen him only once since we sat in the milk bar and looked at the watch he had bought for the girl he eventually married — but that does not mean that he is not inextricably a part of my life.

Like all the others I haven't seen since I grew up during the war.

Is it always an aspect of growing up that one sheds the companions of one's youth? And of growing old that one remembers them again?

Johnny was typical of them, and of us, and of all that I remember.

On his embarkation leave he got a little drunk and confessed to his sister, "I don't want to go."

Nevertheless he went: to Rhodesia, to complete his flying training. But one day, after he had landed, he collapsed — and was compelled at last to admit that every time he flew he was airsick, to the point almost of unconsciousness.

Naturally he was grounded; equally naturally he transferred away from his new desk Air Force job into Australia's new Armoured Division, which, as everyone was aware, was imminently due to depart for the battlefields of North Africa.

But time passed, and passed, and the Armoured Division was despatched neither to North Africa nor anywhere else, so Johnny had his wisdom teeth pulled out, which cured him of airsickness, and transferred out of the Armoured Division to become an observer, flying over the mountains of New Guinea, "liaising" between Americans and Australians. On about his fiftieth mission he was shot down, captured by the Japanese, and executed.

Johnny and Dagmar: they had their own tribes and neither was a senior member of ours. Yet ours couldn't survive the years and the events that had taken them from us.

It all stopped — the idyll — with Billy Hughes making bad speeches in Martin Place, and boys buying gold brooches in Prouds, and women knitting khaki balaclavas instead of white cable-stitch sweaters: but what matters is that it lasted nineteen years and hasn't yet been forgotten.

"And now," Lim instructed mildly from his chair by Russell's bed, "write it all again."

Russell jerked upright. "Write all what again?"

"It! All of it. The story of your early life."

"I can't." Russell's face crumpled. "It'll take me months."

"Of course," Lim agreed. "But we're not short of time, you and I. And you're not doing anything else. I mean, it's weeks since you last read any Toynbee."

"He's inbloodycomprehensible," Russell muttered. "Give me Joyce's *Ulysses* or *Finnegans Wake* any day."

"No — I'll give you Russell's Russell."

"I couldn't face it," the Australian begged. "Honest, Lim, I couldn't face it. I never even understood how Lawrence managed to rewrite *Seven Pillars* so often. Matter of fact, in the end I decided he hadn't — that it was just another line he was shooting. But in any case, please — I can't do it again."

"Perhaps you'd rather we pulled out half your fingernails — those on your left hand, since you'll need the other to write with — to persuade you?"

"But you need me — to broadcast."

"You can broadcast perfectly well without the nails of your left hand. You can even broadcast without the nails of both feet."

Russell began to cry — not noisily, or violently, but despairingly.

"Oh come, colonel," Lim chided. "It's not much to ask of you. Just take a sheet of paper and write down: *'The first thing I remember is biting my mother's thumb . . .'* "

"No!"

". . . or *'Lying swaddled in a shawl as a baby with the smell of tennis balls and grass in my nostrils . . .'* "

"NO!"

"And you needn't be so fussy this time."

"Fussy?" Warily Russell brushed the tears from his eyes and blinked at his interrogator.

"You needn't correct and revise and rewrite this time," Lim explained. "Just bash it off and send it to us."

"You knew about that?"

"Your cell's bugged for sound, and any time we wanted to we could look at you on closed-circuit television. We did and do so regularly."

Russell's eyes darted round the white blankness of his cell walls.

"So that's how you knew about Mr Sunderan talking to me?" he accused, attempting to divert Lim's attention while he searched for hidden microphones and cameras.

"Yes. And you'll find nothing," Lim assured him. "Better men than you have tried. Now look — why not just accept that you're helpless in the hands of experts who're going to get from you what they want? I mean, you're not so far from our point of view even now."

"I couldn't be farther." For the first time Russell's voice had some strength in it.

"Not really. Take your views on the two Vietnams. They should have been given back to China, you said."

"Only because it's my belief no equatorial country is capable of running itself. If I had my way, I'd assign every country on the equator to the permanent custody of an imperial power. That what you want me to write?"

"Not exactly."

"I wouldn't mind writing that." Russell was struggling to recapture the initiative. "Yeah, I'll write about that."

"You will not write about that!" Lim shouted.

"Then you better get me *Finnegans Wake*."

"That's enough!" Lim was clearly rattled. "Now I'll tell you what you're going to do . . ."

"I *can't* write it all again. I've said everything."

"You haven't said a tenth of it."

"Tell me some of the other nine-tenths."

"In twenty years you never once mentioned the weather."

"I told you about an earthquake!"

"So, apart from one earth tremor, you grew up in a climate that was perpetually sunny, did you?"

"No, winter it got colder. We used to wear sweaters even. And in the summer it got hotter and we didn't. Sometimes, in fact, it got bloody hot and then we just panted, and bush fires started, and everyone prayed for the southerly to start blowing and the rain to come. Sometimes it just got steamy, like it is here; then a storm'd come. There was a terrific storm in 1932 — Easter 1932. Mum and dad were out; Pat and I were sleeping on the verandah; Rob was in her room; and all hell broke loose. Thunder, lightning, tiles crashing off the roof, branches crashing off the gum tree, wind screaming, rain lashing — it really was something. Pat hopped into bed with me — and this screeching cyclone tore at the house, well, at all of Sydney really, for hours. To give you an idea what it was like — there's a shelf of rock at the foot of the cliff at Bondi. The morning after that storm there was a rock on that shelf that hadn't been there the night before. It's a solid cube, about the size of a large bedroom, and it was hurled up off the floor of the ocean and deposited on the shelf by that storm. She can be a violent old country, Australia."

"And you were trying to convince me," Lim rebuked, "that you'd

said everything. What about your grandmother's Lithuanian servants? Did they die in solitary penury like your Rob?"

"Rob didn't die in solitary penury; and my grandmother's servants, as you insist on calling them, in your quaint feudal way, having
both married clever young men, are now as comfortably off as I am.
Or, rather, was."

"Yes," Lim agreed. "I think 'was' is more apt. Now, what you're
going to do is this. You're to rest this morning; and this afternoon
you can get into the writing groove again by getting down on paper
your impression of how the first three of your seven colleagues were
executed. Tonight I'll have you given something to make you sleep
really well. Tomorrow morning, at dawn, you'll come down to my
office for the fourth of these ordeals you've inflicted on yourself, and
then you'll come back here and, except for your hours of indoctrination, write all day about how once you were young. And you'll go on
writing, if necessary, for ever — till you dread half-truths and lies
even more than blank sheets of paper. Or, conversely, you can put
an end to it all by agreeing to broadcast."

Without a word Russell reached over to the top of his bedside
locker, picked up some paper and a ball-point pen, and began writing.

"He said," Lim recounted to the doctor, "surely we wouldn't pull out
his fingernails, because we needed him to broadcast. Do you think by
that he meant he'd begun to accept the idea of broadcasting, or that
he didn't believe we'd dare televise a man with maimed hands?"

"I can't answer that. I didn't hear his voice," the doctor equivo-
cated.

"Well, hazard a guess."

"Guesses are unscientific."

"Then be unscientific."

"I would guess he's begun to accept that in the end he'll broadcast."

"He cried when I told him to start writing again."

"Yes," the doctor said, nodding sadly, "it's a pity time is so short.
There's nothing, in the long run, breaks them like writing."

"Make quite sure Russell's condition tomorrow morning is one of
implicit acceptance," Lim ordered.

"Yes, comrade major," the doctor acknowledged. He sounded aggrieved.

Tensely Russell stood by the window that looked down from Lim's office into the courtyard, waiting for the soldiers to come in; waiting for it to begin.

Lim rose from behind his desk and walked slowly across to the window. His open-necked shirt and his shorts were crisply laundered; his knee-length socks were as neat as his shoes were glossy; his black hair, though thick, had been carefully combed; his smooth skin looked fresh and cool; and he smelled, Russell noticed, of toilet soap.

Lim examined his prisoner clinically. The grey hair raggedly long; the recently middle-aged features sagging with misery and exhaustion — and a touch of petulance; the lined, carelessly shaven cheeks patchy with grizzled stubble; the puffy, yellowish pouches under each eye; the bloodshot eyes themselves; the lips white-rimmed with dried spittle; the wrinkled turkey neck and throat; the crumpled shirt; the baggy shorts; the bare, hairy legs; the hands febrile, twitching, unclasping and reclasping; the smell of sweat.

For an instant Russell's eyes flickered down to meet Lim's, then jerked away, back to the empty courtyard. Deliberately Lim felt for a cigarette in the pack that protruded slightly from his shirt pocket, but his eyes never left Russell's face. Slowly he lifted the cigarette to his mouth and, placing it between his lips, reached into the pocket of his shorts for his lighter. Almost contemptuously, then, he flicked it to life under Russell's nose.

Irritably aware that this had become a ritual mockery, Russell simultaneously became aware that the ritual squad of executioners had at last made their entrance: and with them, their victim.

"How have you decided this one shall die?" Lim asked.

"If I'd decided, I'd at least let the poor bugger have clothes on," Russell retorted. "Why do it to him naked? Isn't agony enough for you? You got to be perverted as well as sadistic?"

All the time he spoke he stared unwaveringly down into the courtyard: and unwaveringly Lim stared at him.

"I suppose that's the same whipping triangle?" Russell muttered, after a silence that had lasted perhaps a minute.

"The same as what?"

"As the Nips used."

"Probably."

"Better tell your dim-witted soldiery they've tied Barney on back to front then. Or are you going to have him whipped across the guts?"

Lim ignored the question, watching Russell: who suddenly stiffened and turned pale, eyes wide, lips turned down and twitching.

"What's the matter, colonel?"

"Animals! Look at 'em. Christ, look at 'em! Yanking bits out of him. *Ergh!*"

"What bits?"

"As if I'd know . . . all that blood . . . as if I can tell." He clapped his hands to his ears. "Don't," he whimpered. "Don't. Just die!"

"He'll not die yet," Lim contradicted. He pulled Russell's hands down. "And you must listen."

"I feel sick."

"Of course."

"I'm gonna faint."

"If you faint we'll punish you."

"Jesus, look at that blood. Where's it all coming from? Why doesn't he die? Guts hanging out like that, why doesn't he die?"

"Because you can still stand him living."

"Kill him!" Russell bellowed down at the courtyard. "Stick your knife in . . . Oh God, I can't stand it . . . That's it, that's it. Go on, go *on*, man . . . Ahh." And after that long, sobbing exhalation he let his head fall to his chest.

"Is he dead?" Lim asked flatly.

"Yes."

"Will you broadcast?"

"No."

"Then watch your next friend die the same way, only more slowly."

"No." It was a whimper.

"Colonel Russell," Lim warned soberly, "either you watch your next friend die or you die in his place."

"Like that?"

"Of course."

And slowly the Australian lifted his head until he was staring into the courtyard.

"Watch," Lim ordered. "Watch it all again."

"But it's Corporal Edwards," Russell quavered. "He's only twenty."

Lim remained silent.

And Russell went on talking, the words beginning to run into one another as minute succeeded minute, becoming a babbled thesaurus of terror and torment, and dissolving finally into a gibbered plea for the *coup de grâce.*

"Now will you broadcast?" Lim asked.

"No . . ." Russell was sobbing. "No . . ."

"Then watch again."

And Russell watched. And quavered; and lamented; and babbled; and gibbered — until it was over. But when Lim, looking anxious now, asked him to broadcast, he shrieked, "NO!!"

"In that case, will you watch another one or go down there yourself?"

"I'll watch. Because" — venomously — "there's only one left. Gary's the last. After Gary there's nothing you can do."

"You are the last," Lim corrected. "And we can do frightful things to you. But watch your Gary. This will be the worst."

Obediently the Australian watched — and croaked a ghastly commentary, as he saw his naked compatriot lashed to the triangle, face upwards, abdomen taut, legs wide apart.

But then his face — all flaccid, tear-stained, stubble-smeared terror — hardened perceptibly and his voice lost its accent of despair. Lifting his head till his jaw line was taut, glaring out of the window, he muttered, "So you didn't forget the bull" — and turned slowly to face his interrogator.

"*Watch,*" Lim snapped.

But Russell merely shook his head — because he had at last decided to kill Lim, and to kill anyone who might rush in to help Lim;

and to kill anyone who might rush in to help the first one who had rushed in; and to go on killing till he himself was killed.

"I'm gonna kill you," he shouted, putting his hands round Lim's throat.

-But realized despairingly that the words he had thought to shout had been barely audible, that his hands were almost powerless.

"I'm gonna," he tried to roar, but the glottal stuck in his throat and seemed impossible to expel. Carefully he took a deep breath. "I'm . . . unna," he gasped, "k . . . I . . . y . . . uhh" — and found his fingers sliding off Lim's throat, like butter down the side of a hot saucepan.

He could not shout. He could not kill. Nothing worked.

Nothing worked.

That meant something. From way back, a million years back, and deep down, deep under the detritus of everything hateful that had ever happened to him, that meant something.

Nothing worked.

What's it mean?

Think.

Can't think.

Make yourself think.

Nightmares.

Where nothing worked.

He was having a nightmare. Must make an effort: wake up. Someone talking. Lim.

"Come at once," Lim was saying. "Something's wrong."

Nothing's wrong. Only a nightmare.

(Why was he walking? Being led by the arm? Ah, of course — sleep-walking.)

Make an effort. Wake up!

(Sitting now. Tired. Sleep.)

No. WAKE UP. Stop the nightmare.

With a tremendous effort he lifted his head and opened his eyes. Lim sat facing him across his desk.

"You're lucky," Russell mumbled. "I was dreaming I was going to kill you — only nothing'd work."

"I see," said Lim, lighting another cigarette, putting it vaguely aside on an ash-tray, sounding strangely uncertain. "Well, you rest there. You're overwrought."

But Russell, frowning and absorbed, had started peering intently at the office window. Next, equally intently, he peered at Lim. And finally, rising very deliberately, he walked to the window and looked into the courtyard.

Which was empty, its grass, in dawn's innocent light, fresh and green.

Dourly the Australian returned to the desk and, taking insolent possession of Lim's cigarette, sat down. "So," he said, leaning back, drawing on the cigarette and exhaling violently upwards at the motionless gecko, "I haven't really seen anyone killed! How'd you do it?"

Behind him the door was flung open and the doctor rushed in.

"Get out," Lim snarled. "You're too late."

Eyes flickering from Lim to Russell, from Russell to Lim, and back again, the doctor seemed incapable of movement.

"OUT," Lim shouted.

Timidly the doctor departed.

"How'd you do it?" Russell asked again.

"You were hypnotized at night," Lim indifferently revealed. "As you slept. We put earphones on your head and hypnotized you. Each night before an execution was due we simply told you that when you stood by that window, and I lit my cigarette lighter, you'd see one of your friends put to death by whatever means seemed nastiest to you. The rest we left to you. You did it revoltingly well."

"You made me do it revoltingly well when you hypnotized me."

"Not possible: not unless the things you were to see were acceptable to you anyway."

"By which you mean?"

"That everything you thought you saw, whether *you* dreamed it up or *we* suggested it to you, was in fact perfectly acceptable to you. You were willing for all of it to happen."

For a moment the Australian seemed lost in thought, ill at ease; then he smiled. "All of what?" he inquired blandly.

"Throat cuttings, drownings, skewering with a red hot . . . ."

"I don't know what you're talking about," Russell interrupted.

"You'll deny it?"

"There's nothing to deny. Nothing's happened."

"You *thought* a lot of things had happened."

"*You're* telling *me* what I thought?" Russell sneered.

"Yes."

"And you think you can blackmail me with these thoughts *you* say I've had?"

"Yes."

"And you honestly think anyone'll take *your* word for what I might have thought?"

"Yes."

"Even when I deny it?"

"Even then."

"Why? It's purely academic, of course, because I still don't know what you're talking about: but why would they believe you if I deny what you say?"

"Because you'll also confirm what I say."

"Yeah, and I can just see me doing it. 'He's right,' I'll say. 'Everything he says about me is right. He's a good bloke and I'm a flaming monster, so believe him, not me.' "

Opening a drawer, Lim extracted a handful of photostats and tossed them across the desk.

"Those are what your fellow countrymen will believe," he asserted, and Russell found himself looking at reproductions of his own long and graphic accounts of three executions.

"The third," Lim suggested, "must be the one you regret most. I imagine your army psychiatrists will have a field day with that one. Or will you find today's four even more embarrassing?"

"There's nothing here about today," the colonel countered, "and these're all forgeries — like those letters you sent."

Lim opened a second drawer and pressed a button, *clack*. A fast whirring sound, rising to a whine, resulted; at which the gecko scuttled irritably to the farthest corner of the ceiling and the colonel's eyes narrowed with apprehension. Again Lim pressed a button, *clack*, and the whirring whine died. Then he pressed another button. *Clack*.

"Listen," he ordered.

"How have you decided this one shall die?" Russell heard Lim's voice inquiring — and then heard his own voice, deeper than he had expected, replying, "If I'd decided, I'd at least let the poor bugger have clothes on. Why do it to him naked? Isn't agony enough for you? You got to be perverted as well as sadistic?"

Lim turned off the recorder. "A good question that," he remarked. "Condemns you out of your own mouth. No — don't say anything yet. Let's hear some more. Some of your later observations."

Again there came that sharp clack, and the whirring whine; and again the gecko — peevishly — scuttled. A second clack, and the tape stopped winding forward. A third, and once more Russell heard his own voice.

"Jesus, look at that blood. Where's it all coming from? Why doesn't he die? Guts hanging out like that, why doesn't he die?"

"Because you can still stand him living," Lim's voice commented cruelly.

"Kill him," Russell's voice shouted, so harshly that the diaphragm of the loudspeaker vibrated and blurred the sound (but not the words). "Stick your knife in . . . Oh God, I can't stand it . . ." His voice was full of anguish — for himself. "That's it." He sounded excited and approving. "That's it" — encouraging as well as exhorting. "Go on, go on, man." And then, as if uttering a long sob of despair and relief, "Ahh."

Lim switched off the machine and looked up at Russell. "Every word uttered by you in here and in your cell, ever since you came to this jail, has been recorded," he told the Australian. "The tapes we've got of you, plus what you've written, could prove you guilty of almost any crime of selfishness anyone wanted to level against you. Particularly the crimes, as you yourself so admirably put it in this tape, of sadism and perversion."

"Yes," Russell agreed, "I suppose they could. So what're you going to do about it?"

"That depends on you."

"If I broadcast you won't send 'em home?"

"Unless you broadcast I will show your seven colleagues — who, by the way, we're repatriating the day after tomorrow as a gesture of our goodwill towards Australia — I will show your colleagues your essays on how you chose that the first three of them should die; and I shall play back to them this recording of your commentary on the — if you don't mind my saying so — obscene deaths you prescribed for what you thought the remaining four of them. Do you understand me so far?"

"Perfectly," Russell replied, and Lim was surprised at the steadiness of his voice.

"Your colleagues, of course, will not be greatly enamoured of you in consequence, and their reports on you, when they get home that same day — we're flying them: by Qantas, which we think is a nice touch — their reports on you probably won't be glowing. Just in case they decide not to put in adverse reports on you, though, we're making arrangements for a world-wide release, through Reuters and so on, of the relevant portions of your autobiographical notes, your three essays on how to execute compatriots, and a transcript of this tape. In this way we'll ensure that the peculiar significance of such recorded remarks of yours as, 'So you didn't forget the bull,' are properly appreciated by what will no doubt be the largest audience any colonel in history, not excluding Nasser, has ever attracted.

"In short, using only your own words, we will bring it about that you are ostracized by the whole of the Western World — and then we'll send you home."

"Why don't you just crucify me?" Russell asked quietly.

"If we wanted to dispose of you, I'm sure we could do better, with you as technical adviser, than mere crucifixion. But we don't."

"Not even after I've broadcast — assuming that I do?"

"Colonel, what sort of impression do you think it'd make on world opinion if, the minute you'd broadcast for us, we killed you?"

Russell looked slightly shaken at this. He had always believed that his captors intended executing all their Australian prisoners, whether he broadcast or not. Uncertainly he asked, "What happens to me if I do broadcast?"

"You'll live here in luxury. A bungalow, servants, a car, a generous income, pleasant company . . ."

"Female?"

"Of course. And only the most discreet supervision."

"The alternative?"

"A life of total ostracism commencing August the fourteenth."

"Why the fourteenth?"

"The scandal of your return will distract attention from our infiltration next day of Papua-New Guinea — and alienate American sympathy. Americans are just as prudish about other people's moral shortcomings as Australians. Your kind of moral shortcomings they'll loathe."

"One thing," Russell said, "you haven't anticipated."

"Yes?"

"None of this stuff you're going to release makes sense, *except* in the context of my being hypnotized."

"That's right." Lim seemed unperturbed.

"What's the use of releasing it then? Who's going to take any notice of my description of Lofty being drowned when Lofty's hale and hearty and been home for days? People'll only think I've gone mad, been seeing things: which won't worry me at all."

"Ah, now I see what you're getting at. You think we won't release the fact that you functioned under hypnosis? But we shall, colonel. We shall be completely frank. 'We chose Colonel Russell,' we shall explain, 'because he was obviously the one of the eight terrorists we'd captured with the least moral fibre. We told him that if he refused to work with us . . .' "

"By broadcasting?"

"Exactly. But please don't interrupt . . . 'if he refused to work with us, we would kill his colleagues. Needless to say' — (we shall hasten to add at this point) — 'we never had any intention of killing these seven men even though they were guilty of war crimes, because killing is not our way: but we did intend to compel Colonel Russell to make a plea for world peace. So we told him that he must either broadcast or forfeit his colleagues' lives. But imagine our horror when we discovered that he was perfectly prepared to accept their sacrifice to save himself.

" 'Imagine also our dilemma.

" 'We desired only to preserve peace and to repatriate these seven war criminals as an earnest of our desire; but Colonel Russell preferred world war and executions.

" 'So we decided, all right, let him see some of his executions; perhaps then he'll change his mind, because what decent man wouldn't? And we hypnotized him; and, under hypnosis, we said to him, "Tomorrow, at dawn, one of your friends will be put to death. You must choose which one. And you must choose how he will die."

" 'What took place,' we shall conclude, 'is evidenced by these photostats and by these taped recordings — which we are releasing because we feel that the peace-loving peoples of the capitalist world are entitled to learn by what sick and decadent minds they are led into imperialist wars.' "

His dissertation ended, Lim sat back in his chair and looked questioningly at Russell: who, apparently absorbed in an examination of his own fingernails, seemed to be waiting for more. But Lim, declined the bait.

"Very plausible," Russell commented finally. "Except how'd you know, on the day it was done, before I'd said or written a word, that I thought my corporal had had his throat cut?"

"Just between ourselves," Lim confessed, "we did rather *prime* your fertile imagination by suggesting to you that the first one be done that way. And of course Mr Sunderan's execution, which was the real thing, I assure you, did rather set the scene for you. But we shan't ever admit it. And you performed so well afterwards, I honestly think no one'd believe us if we did."

"You're probably right," Russell agreed. "Well, what happens now?"

"You have till tomorrow night to decide whether, on August the fourteenth, you will broadcast — or return to Australia."

"Fair enough." Russell stood up. "Can I go now?"

Lim pressed the button that called in the guards.

"You can go," he said.

They met the following night in Russell's cell. As he entered, Lim noticed in the Australian's recumbent posture an air of relaxed calm. He decided to waste no time.

"Well?" he asked.

"Nothing doing," Russell told him.

"You've considered the consequences of that decision? What your people will think of you?"

"I told you long ago: I am what I am. And even if that's something much nastier than I had thought, I still accept me. Streaker prepared me for that over forty years ago."

"In that case, your written and spoken accounts of their executions will go to your colleagues tonight."

"Let them."

"And the full story will be released on the fourteenth."

"So be it."

Lim rose from his chair and knocked on the cell door.

"We'll not meet again," he advised as the door opened.

"What'll happen to you," Russell asked, "now that you've failed?"

"I haven't failed," Lim told him coldly — but slammed the door as he departed.

Confronted by three senior officers the following afternoon, he felt less than confident. They were, respectively, a general from Staff Headquarters, an Intelligence colonel, and a Japanese liaison officer: and Lim had been summoned to explain to them his handling of the Russell case. They sat, impassive as tortoises, facing him from behind a long, unadorned trestle table. Bare-headed, Lim stood to attention before them. Beside him was a small table on which were visible numerous documents, a pile of buff-coloured cards, a tape recorder, and dozens of reels (each marked with a date and a title) of tape.

Lim began by explaining that, of the eight men captured at Bukit Langkap, his computer had selected, as potentially the most cooperative, Colonel Anthony Russell. Respectfully he handed to the most senior of his three inquisitors the buff cards that corroborated this statement; and gratefully he observed how all three nodded as they read what was printed on the cards — as if they saw in the computer's assessments a wisdom to match their own. Lim began to feel easier.

Instructed to continue, he said that his orders were to extract, before August 1, from the computer-selected prisoner a promise to broadcast on August 14. But because the computer had itself declared (and here he passed across several more cards) that no such promise could with certainty be expected before mid-October, he had from the beginning borne in mind the need for an alternative exploitation of his prisoner's personality.

Noticing that his superiors had begun to scowl, he hastened to detail the methods he had nevertheless employed to break Russell's resistance to the idea of broadcasting. He showed them photostats of the letters he had had forged and sent to Australia. He showed them the *Sydney Morning Herald* clipping proclaiming Russell's defection.

He told them how the seven Australians had rejected Russell utterly, reviling him and laughing contemptuously at him.

He told them how, from the beginning, Russell was subjected to the latest hypnotic drugs.

"But in spite of drugs and interrogation, in spite of his friends' insults and his own country's indictment of him as a traitor, he did not succumb," Lim explained.

So the pressures on him had been increased; and at the same time the ground work for an alternative exploitation of his propaganda potential had been laid.

At this point Lim suggested that perhaps his superiors should read for themselves the extent to which the prisoner had been demoralized whilst under the influence of hypnosis; and he passed each of them photostated copies of Russell's descriptions of the first three "executions."

Ten minutes later, when they looked up from their reading, Lim switched on his tape recorder, and they listened to Russell's account of the supposed disembowelling of his four remaining compatriots.

"In spite of these illusions, and his belief that he could have saved his comrades from the fates he had seen them suffer, he still did not break. Nor did he break when it was revealed to him that, though none of these killings had happened, all of them — precisely because he *had* 'seen' them — must have been perfectly acceptable to him. And, finally, he did not break when I threatened him with publication of the barbarities he had invented and found acceptable for his friends."

"Was he never close to breaking?" the Intelligence colonel asked.

"Often, comrade colonel. But always we needed more time. He always managed to recover."

"There is no possibility that he will broadcast?"

"None."

"Then what is your alternative plan?" snapped the general.

"To send him home, comrade general!"

"And how will that serve our purpose?" The question was icy.

"He will arrive home fit and well. He will fly home first class, his VIP departure having been televised and relayed to Australia at our expense. By the time he lands in Sydney, three hours later, he should be regarded as potentially the worst security risk his country has ever known. Nothing he says will be believed. He will tell of our plans to move into Papua–New Guinea and no one will believe him. And America will be alienated from Australia because so high-ranking a communications officer has defected to our side. By returning to Australia and denouncing us, Colonel Russell will help our cause even more than he would by broadcasting his support of us.

"And what will be done with him between now and then?"

"He must be put on a special European diet, given a new uniform, be allowed to swim and sunbathe, given a daily massage, a good haircut . . ."

"Excellent," the Intelligence colonel interrupted.

"I will personally escort the Australian to his plane the day he flies home," the general promised. "Colonal Russell must be seen to have been a welcome guest in Communist Southeast Asia."

Two weeks later every television station in Australia featured the "live," satellite-relayed transmission of Colonel Anthony Russell's departure from Singapore Airport; and everyone in Australia who could watched it.

There was considerable sympathy for the colonel. Not only had hand-writing experts recently branded as almost-certain forgeries the letters on the basis of which, earlier on, he had been accused of defecting to the enemy, but his seven fellow prisoners, home almost a fortnight now, had revealed that, according to jail rumour, he had steadfastly refused to broadcast enemy propaganda, in spite of being threatened with death.

Even more endearing was another rumour brought back by the seven that Colonel Russell, compelled to attend indoctrination lectures, had disrupted them utterly with a noisy rendition of his favourite hymn.

As commentators waited in their various studios for the satellite relay to begin, they seized upon this agreeable morsel and questioned whichever relative or friend of the returning colonel they had been able to locate.

No, the seven admitted, they did not know which hymn; they only knew that some Malays, on their way to be shot, had shouted to them that the colonel had infuriated their dialectics instructor by singing a rousing hymn.

No, Mrs Russell said, she had no idea what her husband's favourite hymn was; he never went to church.

No, Colonel Russell's sister, Patricia, said, she didn't know what her brother's favourite hymn was; but she wasn't surprised it had upset his Chinese captors, her brother had a terrible voice.

No, said the colonel's cousin, successful businessman Peter Johnson (DFC, DSO, and Bar), the only thing he remembered Tony singing was "Oh, Rose Marie": and that had been at kindergarten, where he had had a girl friend called Beth with whom he always shared his sweets.

No, Mrs Russell further advised, *her* name was not Beth.

Thus, sympathetic and well briefed, most of Australia settled down to watch Colonel Russell walk across Singapore Airport's tarmac to the newest of Qantas's airliners. He was escorted, a Chinese commentator with an American accent reported, by General Chin Peng, whose People's Army had liberated Thailand only seven months ago, and Singapore's Foreign Minister, Mr Stephen Lung.

The camera focussed on the general and the foreign minister alternately as they walked on either side of Russell, and both were seen to be smiling cordially — which perplexed not a few Australian viewers.

Then a guard of honour was seen. As the colonel passed them, they presented arms. And watching Australians began to fidget.

At the foot of the metal steps that led into the first-class section of the enormous plane, a Chinese civilian stepped forward and seized Russell's hand in both his own. At once the picture changed from long-shot to close-up, showing the Chinese civilian's face and the back of Russell's head. Smiling and gesticulating, the civilian for several minutes directed at Russell what were clearly the warmest of felicitations and then, looking embarrassed, stepped aside and waved the Australian up the steps. As the general and the foreign minister followed him, the commentator observed that the civilian who had just spoken to Colonel Russell was none other than the celebrated international pianist Li Tu-hsiu, who was on his way home to Peking after a successful tour of Eastern Europe.

Seconds later the general and the foreign minister (their farewells, according to the commentator, concluded) ran down the metal staircase, which then was towed away. At once the huge plane lumbered to the remotest corner of the airport, turned, hesitated, lunged suddenly down the runway, seemed for more than a minute determined not to be separated from mother earth, and then, shrieking, arrowed its way aloft. And all over Australia television sets were switched off: but no one seemed anxious to discuss what had just been seen.

An hour later a Yugoslav migrant who worked in the despatch department of Brisbane's *Courier Mail* remarked casually that he wondered whether Russell had talked in Chinese or Russian to the pianist Li Tu-hsiu. His work mates were unanimously of the opinion that Russell would speak neither language: Australians didn't.

"He must have spoken Russian or Chinese," the Yugoslav insisted. "Li Tu-hsiu speak only Russian and Chinese. I hear him last year in Beograd. Bloody beautiful. But big newspaper story how this Li Tu-hsiu lonely as he speak only Russian and Chinese."

Again all the Australian drivers and despatchers argued that Russell wouldn't have talked Russian or Chinese.

"He must!" the Yugoslav insisted. "I seen him talking with this Li. Youse seen him too."

Bored, one of the drivers decided to go for a beer. At the bar he found himself standing beside a junior reporter.

"I'll have a schooner," he told the junior reporter. "Been arguing. Given me a thirst."

"What about?" the reporter asked. "A schooner for me mate, Shirl."

The driver told him: whereupon, not waiting for the round owed him, the reporter returned to his office and spoke to a sub-editor, who approached the editor.

"Front page," the editor ordered and then telephoned a superintendent of police. Who telephoned a Special Branch colleague in Sydney.

"Yes, we know," Sydney replied, sounding displeased. "One of the secretaries at the American Embassy spotted it; and a music student in Melbourne; and a teacher in Adelaide. We'll be having a word with Mr Russell as soon as he gets into Mascot."

In the remaining hour before the Qantas plane landed, officialdom moved fast. An Intelligence officer who could lip read Russian was rushed to a TV studio in Melbourne and shown a videotape of Li Tu-hsiu talking to Russell. The pianist, he reported by telephone to an emergency meeting in Sydney of Security and Intelligence experts, had spoken Russian throughout.

Clinically and objectively the meeting discussed the disagreeable implications of this report. Then a brigadier, who acted as chairman, summed up.

"Russell," he said, "is either being framed and innocent, or he's been lying to us and is guilty: not just of recent defection but of possible long-term espionage as well." He gazed round the table, looking for any expression of dissent: but there were no dissenters.

In support of the hypothesis that he has been and is a traitor are the following facts:

"As a student in 1939 he declared himself a pacifist.

"As a prisoner of war from 1942 to 1945, and subsequently, he consistently derided the entire officer class and is known to have said that, if ever there were another war, the powers that be would either have to make him a general or shoot him.

"In 1967, rather surprisingly, he joined the Militia — having lately become something of a tycoon *and* an expert in electronics.

"In 1973, even more surprisingly, he joined the Regular Army with the express desire that he be sent to Malaya, even though his memories of that country must have been most unhappy.

"In February 1975 he was captured, offering no resistance, at Bukit Langkap.

"A few months later, letters, apparently from him, were received here in Australia. In them he — if it was he — renounced Australia and threw in his lot with Peking.

"In spite of reports that he has been ill treated and threatened with death, we have just seen that he is fit and obviously popular with his captors.

"He was one of eight captured. The other seven, when repatriated only two weeks ago, were ill and emaciated. And when they left Singapore they were shoved into the plane — economy class — dirty and unkempt, by a Chinese major called Lim, who wouldn't let even our High Commissioner speak to them.

"Russell, on the other hand, gets a red-carpet job at the airport.

"And is seen in animated conversation with a man who is speaking Russian, even though our security clearance on him indicates that he *admits* to no foreign languages at all.

"So much for the prosecution.

"Now for the defence:

"Who wasn't a pacifist in 1939?

"Why shouldn't he have been derisive about the running of the war he fought in? It was a complete balls-up.

"He joined the Militia because his son was killed in Vietnam.

"He became a regular because he had a special skill to offer and we needed it in the division we sent to Malaya.

"*Unless* he had an accomplice in the computer section, who so programmed the machine that the rendezvous message it sent was what he and Russell wanted, and not just another mistake like it's always bloody making, it was not his fault he was captured at Bukit Langkap. And we've uncovered no such accomplice.

"There wasn't much point him resisting capture. He and others were outnumbered a hundred to one; and anyway they were still entitled to be in Malaya, the time limit imposed by the Malayan Government having not then expired. In those circumstances, one goes quietly and waits for the High Commissioner to procure one's release. Unfortunately, neither we nor the High Commissioner ever heard about Russell and Co for weeks, so they weren't released.

"The letters apparently written home by him after his capture, though they are covered with his fingerprints, could well be forgeries. Apart from the improbable distribution of the fingerprints, there are calligraphic details that don't match his normal handwriting.

"Similarly, whilst one of the most damning bits of evidence against him is the conversation he appeared to conduct with that pianist, we must remember that our attention was drawn to it by, among three others, a migrant from Yugoslavia. Admittedly we've nothing on this migrant — but the fact that he's a Yugoslav could be taken to support the theory that his apparently casual revelation about the pianist was Party-inspired.

"Certainly the music student's a Party member. Point is, can a nineteen-year-old student, fourth-generation Australian, be seriously suspected of so important a ploy?

"As to the U.S. Embassy secretary — he should be clean enough, but funnier things have happened. He, by the way, claims that the C.I.A.'s latest advice is that Russell has spoken Russian for years and had an affair in Cannes some years ago with a woman called Françoise Sainson, a known Russian agent.

"As to the fourth caller, we can't find anyone teaching in Adelaide, or in South Australia, of the name given.

"In other words, it *is* just conceivable that all four callers are Communist agents acting under orders, to make it quadruply sure we fall for a very subtle job of framing.

"Which could also mean that everything to do with Russell's imprisonment, his appearance at his departure a few hours ago, and the circumstances surrounding his departure may have been stage managed for the sole purpose of making us suspicious of him and the Americans suspicious of us.

"Now, it would be a disaster if the Chinese, simply by keeping Russell well fed and his mates starved, could sow in our minds the suspicion that he is a traitor — if in fact he isn't one.

"And it's going to be dead easy for them, once they've implanted this suspicion in our minds — and we've got to face it, they have — to nourish it with clever touches.

"So remember how the departure was covered. We saw Russell being smiled at and back-slapped: but we never saw *his* face at those moments. Those TV cameras were masterfully handled. When the guard of honour presented arms, we saw them, not him. For all we know, he could've been spitting.

"Same thing when this pianist bloke talked to him. Sure he talked Russian to Russell; but Russell may not have said a word to him. May not even have understood a word.

"So what it all adds up to is this. Do we believe this thing is a Chinese manœuver to throw us and the Yanks at each other's throats — and reports from Port Moresby are that the Chinks are likely to walk in at any moment, so they could well be trying to pull off just such a stunt — or do we believe Russell's been spying for the Commies for years, is now no use to them, so is being sent home to rattle us?

"If it's the latter, we've got to arrest him.

"If it's the former, we've got to give him the returning hero treatment.

"Well, we've got twenty minutes before he lands. It's decisions I want now, not discussion, so I'm simply going to ask each of you in turn to say either 'arrest him' or 'hero treatment.' Is that understood?"

Eleven men nodded.

"All right, gentlemen" — the brigadier sighed, pointing to the man beside him — "starting from here, your verdicts."

And nine of them said, "Arrest him."

Thanking them, the brigadier left the conference room and walked quickly to his office, where he telephoned Canberra.

"Prime Minister," he announced, "it's my opinion, and the majority opinion of my colleagues, that Russell should be put on ice."

"If it's any comfort to you," the Prime Minister replied, "the cabinet's opinion is the same. Are your people waiting at Mascot?"

"Two lots of my people are waiting at Mascot," the brigadier advised. "One with a brass band and banners saying WELCOME HOME. The other ready to cordon off the plane and whisk him away."

"Well, dismiss the band and the banner wavers," the Prime Minister instructed, "and keep me fully briefed. You and the Minister for External Affairs are *ad idem* on the details of Russell's detention, are you?"

"Completely, sir."

"Let's hope Washington'll buy it, then. Good-bye."

Even before the plane began its approach, Mascot had been cleared of spectators and control tower's dialogue with the plane's flight deck was such that, on a night when there were no flying problems, the captain was seen by his co-pilot to be sweating; and heard to mutter, "They can't be serious."

Nevertheless he buzzed for the chief steward, who appeared at once. "That Pakistani student kid," the captain said. "Take the Health boys straight to him as soon as we land."

"Why?" the steward asked.

"He's a smallpox contact."

"Aw, no."

"You heard me."

"That means quarantine for the lot of us."

"Sharp, isn't he?" the captain asked his co-pilot.

"As a tack," the co-pilot confirmed.

"Back to your patients," the captain ordered. "We're putting her down."

As the plane rolled to a halt and the shriek of its engines subsided, three health officials strolled toward it, casual in slacks and short-sleeved shirts, impassively officious.

The steep metal staircases were rolled into position and the doors of the aircraft opened. Slowly the health officials climbed the stairs and entered the plane and were led to the Pakistani student. After a brief examination of his passport and vaccination certification they adjourned to the flight deck. A few seconds later the captain made an announcement.

"Ladies and gentlemen," he said, "I'm sorry to have to tell you that, through no fault of yours, or the company's, we are all smallpox contacts. This means we will all be transferred immediately to the quarantine establishment on North Head. All your baggage will go with you. There will be no Customs formalities for the moment. And obviously no opportunity for you to see any relatives or friends who may be waiting here to meet you. Qantas Airlines wish to assure you that anything they can do to help you will be done, and you will be able to telephone your families and friends, and our Public Relations people, as soon as we're settled in at Quarantine. Now, if you'd just remain seated, there'll be transport here almost at once. Thank you ladies and gentlemen — and once again, I'm very sorry. For all of us."

A babble of protests, lamentations, and recriminations rang through the plane; but, impassive as ever, the health officers herded the three hundred and fifteen passengers and crew out of the plane and into a succession of military Hovercraft, each of which, the instant it was full, wafted off across the tarmac, onto the waters of Botany Bay, out briefly to a lazily rolling Pacific, in through the Heads and up over a recently built approach from the harbourside beach to a settlement of empty white huts.

Into one of which Colonel Russell, who had been lifted from Mascot by helicopter, was led, alone.

"Good evening, colonel," he was greeted as soon as he stepped inside.

"Good evening, sir," he replied, saluting the stranger on whose shoulder tabs were the badges of a brigadier.

"My name is Jackson," the brigadier introduced himself, "and this is Captain Campbell. I'm afraid we must ask you some questions."

Half sick with apprehension and half perplexed, Russell waited for the unpleasantness that must come. And yet, what could they do? So his imagination had played tricks that revealed him as selfish, sadistic, and even obscene: there was no law, civil or military, that made nasty imaginings punishable.

So this Brigadier Jackson and his offsider Campbell thought him contemptible because they'd read Lim's bloody photostats and listened to Lim's bloody tape recordings: there was no law that entitled brigadiers and captains to carpet the contemptible.

Come to that, he didn't care much for the look of them either. The brigadier was an obvious piss-pot — you didn't get veins on your nose like that living on milk — and the captain was a tight-lipped, beady-eyed, unmistakable wowser.

Yet clearly they thought they were onto something, because the wowser — what was his name? Campbell — was busy spreading about the table a pile of documents you couldn't jump over, and the piss-pot was sitting at the head of the table looking like God.

"Sit down, Colonel Russell," the brigadier invited, taking off his cap and setting it carefully by his right hand. He had a crop of thick white hair, cut *en brosse*, and a red furrow across his forehead where his cap had been.

Russell sat. "Before we start," he said, "I'd like to ring my wife."

"Later," Jackson told him. "We've explained to her there'll be some delay."

"What do you mean by 'some delay?' "

"You've been in Communist hands for six and a half months, colonel. There must be a lot you can tell us. And a lot you mustn't tell anyone else. Naturally we've got to get all that cleared up before you go home, where every radio and TV station in Sydney, and all of Australia's papers, will have reporters waiting to get at you."

"Yes, I suppose so," said Russell, who had not thought of this.

"Cigarette?" Jackson offered.

"Thank you." He leaned forward to the brigadier's lighter.

"Well, I think we'd better get on with it. Proceed, Captain Campbell."

Campbell coughed, looked up from his papers, and stared at Russell with eyes of that curious brown which always has in it an ill-tempered tinge of orange.

"Colonel Russell," he asked, "what languages do you speak?"

"None fluently."

"What languages do you speak unfluently?" Campbell's voice was as humourless as his face and as irascible as his eyes. Definitely a wowser, Russell told himself and answered, "French, German, Italian, Malay, and a few words of Japanese. A hangover from my p.o.w. days."

"I see. Er . . . look at this letter, would you, please?"

Russell examined the last letter he had written to his wife before his capture.

"Did you write that letter?"

"Yes."

"Did you write this letter?"

Russell glanced briefly at Lim's forgery.

"No."

"It's in your handwriting."

"I don't write my g's or y's like that."

"It has your fingerprints on it."

"It's on paper like the stuff I had in my cell. I suppose they took the top blank page off the pile when I was out being questioned or something."

"So you admit that the fingerprints are yours?"

"They could be. So what?"

"Leave the questions to us, please," the brigadier instructed.

"If the fingerprints are yours, why shouldn't the writing be yours also?"

"Because of the g's and y's."

"But why would anyone make so fundamental an error on an otherwise perfect forgery?"

"Because whenever I wrote for them, I used to put squiggled tails on my g's and y's."

"Then why shouldn't *these* g's and y's be yours?"

"Because they're not."

"But you have written g's and y's like these?"

"Only while I was in Singapore."

"This was written while you were in Singapore."

"Look, what're you trying to prove?"

"We're not trying to prove anything," Jackson intervened, rubbing his bibulous nose. "We're simply trying to get things straight. Carry on, captain."

"You say you wrote for the Chinese," Campbell resumed. "What did you write?"

Russell told him.

And was asked again. Differently: but again.

And once more was challenged about the possible authenticity of Lim's forgery.

Round and round the questions went, always on these two subjects. Only on these two subjects. Campbell, with the maddening persistence of a blowfly, took no notice of Russell's anger and returned constantly to the same points. It was four hours before the questioning stopped and Russell was left alone to sleep.

And when his interrogators departed, the one door leading out of his room was locked and an armed sentry appeared outside the one window, which was double glazed, bolted, and barred.

Meantime Washington had contacted its ambassador at Canberra. Washington, he advised the Minister for External Affairs, wanted to know why Russell had ever been allowed to hold down any job in communications. Washington also desired details of every signal relating to U.S. Top Secret matters to which Russell had had access since 1973.

Frantically signals clerks searched for back files that were lost. Furiously the signals officers finally responsible threatened to throw the book at everyone subordinate to them if the files were not found forthwith. Sourly civil servants pestered the military for quick results. Grimly the cabinet discussed how best to gloss over whatever those results might be.

And at dawn, on August the fifteenth, Port Moresby reported that, overnight, five large forces of Chinese troops, and one of Japanese, had crossed from Irian into Papua-New Guinea. Already at least half of the territory's scattered European tea planters, miners, missionaries, and officials had been murdered; and Indonesia was claiming that a People's rebellion against imperialist colonialism had erupted.

The door of Russell's hut was unlocked and a young soldier entered.

"Private Konrads, sir," he introduced himself, standing to attention. "I'm your batman, sir," and offered a cup of tea.

"All right. Thank you."

"Shower cubicle and toilet here, sir," Konrads advised, opening the door to what Russell had already discovered to be just that. "I'll bring you your breakfast in half an hour; and the brigadier says please could you be ready for futher debriefing at 08.30 hours?"

"Debriefing, they call it, do they?" Russell sounded bitter. "All right. Tell the brigadier I'll try to be here."

Konrads smiled. "Anything you want, sir, just ask." But he locked the door behind him.

Russell took a shower and shaved. There was no window in the shower cubicle. Konrads brought him his breakfast and later removed the plates and cutlery, the cup and saucer. Exactly at eight-thirty Captain Campbell arrived.

The morning was spent examining in detail everything that Russell remembered writing for Major Lim. Everything, that is, except his descriptions of the three executions he had "witnessed." About them he said, and intended saying, nothing.

The afternoon was spent examining in detail everything he remembered of his indoctrination lectures, and his attitude to the dialectics of Marxism-Leninism.

"Look, Campbell," he snarled finally, "I am not a Communist.

These dialectics you keep talking about don't mean a thing to me, if only because they're sheer jabberwocky. Not even Toynbee and Joyce addle me like your bloody dialectics."

"No one was talking about Toynbee and Joyce, colonel," Campbell rebuked.

"Weren't we?" Russell frowned. "Oh no. That was a joke between me and Lim."

"So you two joked."

"Ah, for Christ's sake," Russell said — and was allowed to go to bed.

But the following morning Campbell confronted him as dourly as ever, producing, as well as his usual pile of documents, a small stack of buff-coloured cards.

"Computer?" Russell asked wearily.

"Yes. Now yesterday you stated, and I quote, 'Lim kept on saying if I didn't broadcast for them on August the fourteenth he'd have the other seven executed one by one and he'd make me watch.' "

"You got total recall or something?" Russell demanded.

"Why do you ask that?"

"You didn't take down anything I said yesterday, or the night before: how come you remember it verbatim?"

"Everything you say is recorded," Campbell explained, "and processed overnight."

"Got closed-circuit TV on me too?"

"So Private Konrads' been talking, has he?" Campbell's voice was raspy. "Well, by the time I've finished with him . . ."

"It wasn't Konrads," Russell replied dejectedly. "It was the same in Changi, that's all."

"You didn't tell me that."

"I forgot," Russell lied, sick with himself for having brought to Campbell's notice something that he had deliberately suppressed.

"I'm sorry, colonel, but you couldn't have forgotten it, because I carefully asked you questions designed to prompt a recollection of it if you'd ever been aware of it. So why did you conceal from me your awareness of the fact that you were at all times watched and taped?"

"I didn't conceal it from you. And I don't remember any questions of yours that prompted me to recall it."

"Interesting," Campbell commented.

"What is?"

"That lie. All your lies are interesting, but this one is especially interesting. We'll discuss it at length later. Any idea why you should have been singled out in Changi? I mean you, rather than any of the others."

"No."

"Perhaps Lim thought you were the weakest?"

"Perhaps."

"Or sympathetic?"

"Don't be ridiculous."

"What did Li Tu-hsiu say to you at Singapore Airport?"

"Who's Li whatever-you-said?"

"A pianist. He spoke to you at the foot of the aircraft steps."

"Oh, him. I don't know."

Campbell assumed an expression of polite disbelief.

"I don't know, I tell you," Russell reiterated.

"No idea what he was talking about?"

"None."

"What language did he seem to be talking?"

"Swahili, you silly bastard."

"I see. Now why, when I gave you so many chances to mention that you'd had everything you said in Changi taped, and everything you did watched on closed-circuit TV, why did you refrain from telling me about it?"

"Granting that you ever did ask these questions — which I don't — what's it matter anyway?"

"It matters because, if your cell wasn't bugged, the presumption must be that you weren't really a prisoner: that you were one of them, and your being kept in a cell was part only of what, on your return here, would become your cover story."

"Well, now I've told you it *was* bugged."

"But very late in this piece, as if you'd just remembered you *should* have told me about it much earlier."

"I deliberately didn't tell you."

"Why?"

"I didn't want you to know some of what they taped."

"You were ashamed of some of it?"

Russell thought a moment. "No, but I couldn't see any sense volunteering the kind of information that'd let people like you look down their long wowserish noses at me."

"I see. Well, perhaps now you'd better volunteer it."

"It began with Lim's threat that he'd have one of the others executed in front of me every other day, as he d executed Mr Sunderan," Russell related flatly. "It ended up with me hypnotized and thinking I'd seen all seven of them killed."

"How did they die?" Campbell asked.

Russell hesitated. "Nastily," he admitted finally.

"So you *are* ashamed?"

"I've told you, no. I told Lim no too."

"You appreciate, do you," Campbell inquired contemptuously, "that they couldn't hypnotize you into seeing anything you weren't in the circumstances prepared to accept?"

"It was explained to me," Russell replied. "You know, the second I looked at you, I knew you were a wowser."

"Tell me," Campbell ordered, ignoring the jibe, "how they died."

"All right," Russell decided — and told him.

"Fascinating," Campbell murmured when it was done. "Quite fascinating. Though whether your story is genuine and a criterion by which morally to judge you, or a fake and an indication of the thoroughness with which the Chinese have rehearsed you, is something we still have to determine. We'll continue after lunch."

"What about my wife?"

"What about her?"

"I still want to telephone her."

"Not yet."

"A letter then?"

"Out of the question."

"Look, you can't do this to me . . ."

"Under emergency regulations passed by the federal government last night, we can do what we like to you."

"I'll shout. There are more than three hundred people off that plane quartered here — I'll howl the place down till they start demanding explanations."

Campbell tapped the wall with his swagger stick. "Sound-proof. Windows too — double glazed. In case a quarantined person goes psycho."

"You honestly think . . . I mean, does the government honestly think I'm a spy?"

"It honestly thinks there's a strong likelihood that you are."

"But my boy was killed in Vietnam."

"Plenty of parents, here and in the States, blame the government rather than the enemy for that."

"You're seriously suggesting," Russell asked, "that ten years ago, when my boy was killed, I blamed Menzies, decided to get my revenge, joined the Militia . . . ?"

". . . and worked your way up to a key job in military communications so that you could pass information on to the enemy?" Campbell finished. "Yes, we're seriously suggesting it."

"How do I disprove it?"

"By cooperating."

"All right, I'll cooperate."

"What did Li Tu-hsiu say to you at Singapore Airport?"

"I told you, I don't know."

"How long have you spoken Russian?"

"I've never spoken Russian."

"Not as well as you understand it, no: but you speak it all right."

"I speak no Russian."

"What sort of a man is Major Lim?"

"He did his job."

"Efficiently?"

"Very."

"But you were too clever for him?"

"Time was too short for him."

"If he'd had longer you would have collaborated?"

"In the time he had I did not collaborate."

"I have endless time, colonel."

"For you, captain, that won't be enough."

"Why?"

"I dislike you. Makes me immune to your persistence."

"But you didn't dislike Major Lim?"

"Felt rather sorry for him, actually."

"And were your sympathies personal or political?"

"Quasi-paternal."

"Even though people like him killed your son?"

"People like us killed his parents."

"So quite paternally you loved him?"

"My *sorrow* for him, I said, was quasi-paternal. I had had so much, I realized, that he never had."

"So you never hated him?"

"I often hated him. As often I've hated my mother, my father, my sister, my wife, and my son."

"He seems to have made quite an impression."

"Reminded me of my dead young German."

"What?"

"Poignant and doomed."

"Which dead young German?"

"Like the Prince of Wales. Before Baldwin got at him."

"Stick to the point, colonel. We don't have all day."

"You said your time was endless."

"But not my patience."

"And when that expires?"

"There are tougher methods."

"I'll faint. I'll become, in fact," he recited, grinning, "a tiny foetus, back in the womb, insulated against external brutality by a sea of swooning helplessness."

Campbell wrote fast, biting his lip; and then, looking up, glared suspiciously. "Where'd you read that?"

"In jail."

"Who wrote it?"

"A wiser man than you."

"Private Konrads!" Konrads appeared instantly, and Campbell handed him a slip of paper. "I want to know who wrote that," he ordered. "Author and name of book." Konrads left them.

"Our computer'll provide the answer in a matter of minutes."

"You want to bet?"

"I don't bet, colonel. We haven't fed only case histories into our computer, you know. Every single book of captivity memoirs has gone in as well. You'd be surprised what solitary confinement does for people's literary styles."

"Like hanging," murmured Russell.

"Pardon?"

"It concentrates the mind."

"Then concentrate yours on Major Lim, who apparently struck a quasi-paternal chord in your heart simply because he reminded you of an anonymous dead young German."

"Be glad to."

"Who is this dead young German?"

"No idea."

"Colonel Russell, hasn't it yet occurred to you that you're in big trouble?"

"I'm sorry, captain, but that I cannot accept."

There was a knock on the door.

"Come in," bellowed Campbell.

Konrads entered. "Author and work unknown, sir," he reported handing back the slip of paper and leaving at once.

Russell began to laugh.

"Who wrote this?" Campbell demanded, waving the slip of paper.

"Oh, captain," Russell rebuked, half mocking, half incredulous.

"Answer me!"

Russell began to giggle helplessly.

Briefly Campbell surveyed the man whom he, his computer, his superiors, and his government alike suspected of treason: and it offended him to observe that the man looked happy.

"Why, all of a sudden, are you happy?" he asked.

"Because suddenly I see what's happening," Russell replied. "Dear God, the stupid games we mortals play."

"You'll forgive me if I *don't* see what's happening?"

"Oh, absolutely."

"And you won't mind explaining?"

"Not in the least." Russell sounded positively jovial.

"Good," Campbell commented, pulling from his briefcase first a ream of paper and then a handful of ball-point pens, which clattered as he dropped them on the table. "Good," he repeated, watching Russell's face stiffen into lines of acute apprehension.

Campbell pointed at the paper and the pens. "Take all the time you need," he said. "Start with the first thing you remember. And write me the story of your life."